The Vain Conversation

STORY RIVER BOOKS

Pat Conroy, Editor at Large

THE
VAIN CONVERSATION
A NOVEL

ANTHONY GROOMS

FOREWORD BY
CLARENCE MAJOR

AFTERWORD BY
T. GERONIMO JOHNSON

The University of South Carolina Press

Published by the University of South Carolina Press
Columbia, South Carolina 29208

www.sc.edu/uscpress

Manufactured in the United States of America

27 26 25 24 23 22 21 20 19 18
10 9 8 7 6 5 4 3 2 1

ISBN: 978-1-61117-882-1 (hardcover)
ISBN: 978-61117-883-8 (ebook)

This book was printed on recycled paper
with 30 percent postconsumer waste content.

Dedicated to the memory of Alberta Grooms Ford,
beloved family storyteller, and to George and Mae Murray Dorsey,
Roger and Dorothy Malcolm, and Clinton Adams

Forasmuch as ye know that ye were not redeemed with corruptible things, as silver and gold, from your vain conversation received by tradition from your fathers.

The First Epistle of Peter, 1:18

Injustice is relatively easy to bear; what stings is justice.

H.L. Mencken,
Prejudices (1922)

But what has our 230-year national experience been but a dialogue about race?

David Mamet,
"We Can't Stop Talking about Race in America" (2009)

Also by Anthony Grooms

Bombingham: A Novel
Trouble No More: Stories
Ice Poems

FOREWORD

Willa Cather in *Death Comes for The Archbishop* was able to create imaginary conversations and actions that gave her main character (based on Father Jean Marie Latour) and story depth and motivation, metaphors and textures, a sense of fullness and believability, that may not have been accessible to her had she written the book as a biography restricted to facts and speculation.

Truman Capote's decision to write *In Cold Blood* as a "non-fiction novel" gave him a similar freedom to create a fictional *truth* out of facts that may have, by their very strict nature, placed limitations on Capote's ability to tell a fully rounded story complete with details that facts alone could never render.

The same can be said of other books based on real events or real people, such as Leo Tolstoy's *War and Peace*, about the Russian aristocracy as it was in 1812; and his *Anna Karenina*, whose protagonist was based on Anna Pirogova, a young woman who attempted suicide; Richard Wright's novel, *Native Son*, based on an article he saw in a newspaper; *Schindler's List* by Thomas Keneally, about the life of Oskar Schindler during World War II; Agatha Christie's book, *Murder on The Orient Express*, and *Psycho* by Robert Bloch.

Anthony Grooms' novel *The Vain Conversation* is based on reported news stories of a murder of four people. Grooms granted himself the same kind of fictive freedom Cather and Capote and the others mentioned above assumed. It gave him the chance to create his own "truth" and fictional reality.

Grooms' novel is set in the 1940s, before, during and after the war. The reader is brought into the lives of the boy, Lonnie Henson; his father Wayne Henson; the dog Toby; Lonnie's mother Aileen Henson; Aileen's Aunty Grace; Wayne's "colored" friend Betrand Johnson; Mrs. Crookshank, owner of the diner and a reporter; Luellen, Betrand's wife and his mother

Milledge; Beah, the cook at Mrs. Crookshank's diner; her lover Jimmy Lee; and Vernon Venable, Jimmy Lee's employer; Sheriff Cook, and a variety of other characters. As characters they have the ring of truth because what they experience sounds familiar to us; we recognize the validity of their lives. We see them come to life.

But what were the facts? Some of the main facts of the case: the murder of the four sharecroppers took place in rural Walton County, Georgia, on July 25, 1946. The victims—shot sixty times—were two couples: Roger Malcolm and his wife Dorothy Malcolm and George W. Dorsey and his wife Mae Murray Dorsey. It's a *fact* that four people were murdered on that day.

Both couples were African-American; and despite an FBI reward offer of $12,500 for information leading to their capture, the murderers were never identified and brought to justice. Mae Murray Dorsey was pregnant at the time, and her body was found with the fetus cut out.

Time magazine, August 5, 1946, reported that Loy Harrison, the employer of some of the victims, reportedly saw the killings. He is quoted: "A big man who was dressed mighty proud in a double-breasted brown suit was giving the orders. He pointed to Roger Malcolm and said, 'We want that nigger.' Then he pointed to George Dorsey, my nigger, and said, 'We want you too, Charlie.' I said, 'His name ain't Charlie, he's George.' Someone said 'Keep your damned big mouth shut. This ain't your party.'"
This is Grooms' imaginary fictional account:

"The crowd was coming toward them, about fifteen men. Two of them were Cook's deputies...

"'There are women in the car,' Bertrand said. 'A pregnant woman.'

"All was lost now. All the dream of whatever God had created for them, lost.

"He wondered at that moment why it was that he had been born and survived war, only to meet his fate, here, in his home country.

"A car was pulling up behind them... Oh, God, let her get away. Let her run!... Cook, pointing to Jimmy Lee, was rushing past Jacks..."

Readers looking for the facts will turn to the historical record. Readers who want the experience of an imaginative version with depth and nuance and fully developed characters to carry the story will find satisfaction in Anthony Grooms' novel. It is a fine novel, beautifully written.

He explores the subject for all it is worth. And the novel exists independently of the set of facts regarding the mass murder that inspired it. The reader need not know anything about the actual murders because this is a work of art—a work of art that earns its rightful place (to borrow words from William Faulkner's Nobel "Banquet Speech") as "something that did not exist before."

It is a novel I will never forget. Its lessons are deep. Those who turn to this book will come away with a greater understanding of human nature. This book should also be seen as a true testament to what Georgia and the Deep South generally were like before and during the 1940s.

Clarence Major

ACKNOWLEDGMENTS

I am grateful to family and friends, ancestors and descendants, whose love and guidance have formed a great circle of spirit that encourages me to embrace the adventure that is life. Especially I am grateful to my wife, Pamela B. Jackson and our son, Ben, for all you do to make my life busy, full of laughter and wonder.

I am especially grateful to William Wright, poet and editor, for his encouragement and advocacy; to J.D. Scott, photographer, for his artistry and generosity; and, to Pam Durban, novelist and teacher, for her insight and support. Also, I am grateful to Clarence Major, T. Geronimo Johnson, Joe Taylor, Gray Stewart, Tayari Jones, Jonathan Haupt, and Dianne and Ernest Baines for their advice and support of my vision.

"Bye and Bye" is a traditional folk spiritual. "Tobacco is a Dirty Weed" was written by Graham Lee Hemminger, and was first published in *The Penn State Froth* in November, 1915.

PART ONE
RIVER OF JOY

ONE

Blackberries. Blackberries. The boy's head was filling up with blackberries. He had moved slowly, deeper and deeper, into the bramble, until he was surrounded by it. The tangle of vines arched above and around him so that it seemed he had entered a cave of brambles. *A gift from God,* the boy thought. Light dappled through the vines. The thicket swayed gently in the breeze and the fine thorns scratched against him. He didn't care. He was in the world of blackberries.

He knew how to step through the bramble to avoid a serious scratching, and how to share the bramble with a black snake or a ringed king snake. Thrashes and chickadees and sometimes a more brilliant bird like a yellow finch might land on a vine, bowing it and then springing to another. Only the ticks bothered him. They hid in the brittlegrass and broomsedge that edged the thicket. He rolled his pants to his knees, and let them crawl up his naked calves until he could see them and pick them off.

He left his pail at the edge of the patch and with his cup in front of him balanced on one leg and leaned over the briars to the nests of plump berries. They were so fat that three of them filled his palm—and the season was just beginning. In spite of his eating one for every three he kept, the pail was filling, nearly a gallon, and he had only been picking half an hour.

A shadow passed over and he looked up to see a turkey vulture. He liked them. They were like kites, the way they sailed on a breeze. Once, not far away, on Christmas Hill, he had followed a vulture back to its nest in the abandoned house on the adjacent ridge. It was an old settler's house, his father had told him. It was a two-story wooden house with a rusty weather vane in the shape of an eagle on top. The vulture had flown into one of the upstairs windows, so the boy went into the house, climbed the dry rotted stairs to the second floor. Loose plaster crumbled under his feet and he thought the creaking floors must be paper-thin. In the second room of four he came upon the nest. The stench stupefied him. Before he got his bearings in the guano-splattered room, a bald, red-faced and completely white-feathered chick, the size of a small chicken, rushed at him. It spewed vomit at him, so unnerving him that he took three steps at a time, tumbling more than running down the stairs. The chick was the ugliest thing he had ever seen, and yet it would grow into such a graceful and beautiful bird to look at in the air.

At the end of the memory, he heard a rambling and puffing coming up the hill on the wooded side of the bramble. Once before he had heard this sound and a small black bear had run out of the woods. But there was something else, some popping and snapping of twigs. He heard a ripping of leaves and saw leaves floating down from high in the trees. Somebody was shooting. He squatted down in the briars. It got quiet for a moment, then he heard men's voices and another shot, a snap from a little gun. It remained quiet for a few moments, and the boy crawled out of the patch and sneaked along the crest. Then he saw who the men were and he felt relieved. They were Sheriff Cook and some other men. Two of the men were dragging something. He stood up, thinking maybe they had shot a bear. But it would have been a bear with a flowered dress on.

The seasons went through a cycle and the boy just stood, getting a year older in a few minutes. His heart knocked against ribs. He did not realize that the moment, as prodigious and capricious as it seemed, was as deeply rooted and prickly as the blackberry vines. It was also a moment that jinxed him. The men were dragging a colored woman. She was dead.

He sneaked from tree to tree, staying just below the ridgeline. Soon he could see cars on the road, where the road dipped down to the old iron bridge and crossed the Appalachee River. They dragged the woman below the road, down the slope, to the shoal. It was hard for the boy to see from where he was, so he climbed down the hill to the level of the road and went along the bushes until he saw where the men had dragged the woman.

A grist mill had been there, just at the little cataract that spilled to the east of the bridge, but the mill had long since burned and where it stood was now a sandy beach with a scattering of cord grass and saplings. The water was not deep here. It gurgled around rust-colored boulders and pooled just before it made its leap over the falls.

From his position on the hill above the bridge, the boy recognized several of the dozen or so cars parked along the side of the road. There were Sheriff Cook's battered police car—an old Ford, Mr. Venable's black Nash Ambassador, and Mr. Jack's new Buick wagon with its wooden doors and its hood the color of dried blood. The men rolled the woman's body down the embankment, and it came to rest in the weeds just out of the boy's sight. At the bottom of the embankment, partly blocked by the roadbed, he saw movement, and he realized that there was a crowd. Then he saw the barrel of a gun, and his heart thumped. There was killing going on, he thought, and he had better go home. But his legs would not carry him. He watched while Mr. Jacks and Sherriff Cook slid down the embankment where they had rolled the body. Above the rush of the falls, he could hear shouting and then he was shocked to hear another gun shot, a heavy gun, a shotgun. Now he moved closer, sliding on his rump down the hill to the level of the roadbed. Cautiously, he surveyed the road, and tried watching and listening for an approaching car. Except for the sound of the falls, all was quiet. Taking in a deep breath, he leapt into the road, kicking up loose gravel as he ran with his head down, crossed the road and hid in the bush just at the top of the embankment.

Then he saw clearly the crowd of people, about forty, he thought. And as his racing mind settled, he saw who they were, though he did not know them all by name. They were men he had seen in Venable's feed store, local farm people. There was the clerk from Mason's Five and Ten, located on Main Street in the town of Bethany. He recognized the heavy-set deacon from First Baptist Church, a man his mother said was a cousin of his father's. Indeed, the man had come to their house several times just after his father died. Three women stood in a group slightly apart from the men. They seemed to have been chatting and laughing as if they were on the church yard. Two young men dragged the body of the woman by her feet. The flowered dress had come up over her head and her fat thighs and underpants were exposed. The boy knew one of the young men as a carpenter's apprentice, a baseball player who had just graduated from the high school that spring and one whose athletic body he admired. Seeing the young man put the boy at ease and he thought he might reveal himself, walk down to the shoal and see what the killing was about. It was clear that a colored woman had been killed, and he wondered if she were a gangster of some kind. He had heard that gangsters still roamed the back roads, robbing banks in small

5

towns like Bethany. But he had never heard of any colored gangsters, and the dead woman *was* colored. He moved closer to the crowd, crouching, still not ready to reveal himself. About halfway down, he was near enough to get the attention of the young man, who had stepped to the rear of the crowd as the other men gathered around the body. But before the young man's name could form on the boy's lips, he saw, lying beside the woman's body, the bodies of other people. He swallowed air. Peering through the legs of the men, he counted four bodies on the ground. Only one of them was dead.

At first he thought that one of the living ones was a white man, and then, with a sudden recognition, he let out a shout. He knew them. He knew what was happening to them. He knew them all.

It seemed to him that he might have blanked out and slowly, his face tingling, his senses returned. He remembered to breathe, then hyperventilated. He shook his head to clear it and one by one focused on the people on the ground. He rubbed his eyes. Yes. There they were, unmistakably.

The man he thought was white was Jimmy Lee, who had come by his house not a week ago to buy his sister's old baby crib. The woman next to him, her belly big with child, was Jimmy's girlfriend. Next to the girlfriend, was Bertrand. He looked again, squinting his eyes as if doing so would sharpen his vision. It was not Bertrand, and he looked away from the squat, thick man attempting to rise only to be kicked down by a booted foot.

He looked across the river, sparkling with the afternoon sunlight. Shadows seemed to swim in the riffles. On the other shore was a stand of sycamores with massive trunks. The deep woods behind the trees were getting dark and the sycamores' white bark shone brightly. When the boy looked again at the bodies, he saw first the dead woman, her dress still pulled over her torso. It was Luellen, Bertrand's uppity wife.

In his superhero comic books, a muscled man in costume would throw himself into the crowd, karate chopping and kicking at the villains until they ran. Then, with no more than a nod to the victims, he would sprint away, leaving them stunned, grateful.

The white men kicked and spat on the colored people as they, except the dead woman, tried to stand or gesture. One of the white women looked in his direction. He could see her crow's feet crinkle and her eyes dart around like beads. He felt like the wind had blown right through him. When the woman turned away, he felt his pants grow warm and he realized he was pissing on himself.

6

Suddenly there was a shot, different it seemed, from the others. He looked back to the crowd and saw the light-skinned man fall. It was as if he were falling from the sky. The boy hadn't seen the man get to his feet, but only fall. The white men tussled above the body, pushing one another in and out of the circle in order to kick or club at the body. Then someone cleared them away. It was Sheriff Cook. He pushed the men back, making a circle around the dead man, as if to give him space. It was silent for a moment and then there was a cacophony of firing and the body seemed to wallow across the ground. One of the white women threw up her hands and turned away, the other two, laughing, held on to her.

More people arrived, sliding down the bank, slick now from their tramping. Two men brought down a chest of beers, and when they were noticed, people left the circle around the body to buy beer. Someone shot again, followed by a volley.

The boy did not look. He was trying to find a way to climb the bank without being seen. Darkness was settling in the woods, and he could see the patches of the sky over the crown of the hill. He started on his hands and knees, crawling and then scrambling through the leaf litter with the musk of the humus filling his nose and mouth. He slipped and lay flat until he had regained his senses. He could hear hooting and shouting from the crowd below and he sensed that no one was looking at him. Quickly he found a tree trunk wide enough to hide him. He was only halfway up to the road. He could see the crowd still, a tight circle of men next to the river, the three women still standing to one side. There were children, too, at least two boys. He thought he might know them. Probably he went to school with them, but then he focused on the top of the hill where the sky was pale blue, almost white in contrast with the gloom of the woods.

He reached the top of the hill and squatted again. All seemed quiet; the crowd was out of sight, behind him. Before him, and a little below him lay the road. On one side, it went up, cutting through the hill and curving out of view, the gravel looking nearly as white as the sky. On the other side, it went down to the bridge. He gazed at the top of the hill for a moment, calculating the shortest and safest path home. He would continue uphill, he knew, crossing the roadbed, and going back to the bramble where he would find the old spring path. Another volley of gunfire made little pops and one gun boomed. He knew it was Bertrand, and a scene flashed through his mind as clearly as if he were witnessing it. "Bertrand," he said. He was

7

unaware that he shivered until he looked at his hands in front of him and clasped them in his armpits. Tighter and tighter he drew into a ball, trying to control the shaking. When he could stop shaking, he would run uphill and cross the road just where it curved. Releasing a heavy breath , he stood, started to run, and stopped again, nearly throwing himself to the ground.

A yellow dog stood in the middle of the road. It was mud-spattered and lean, and it crouched with its tail between its legs when it saw him. "Toby," he said aloud. Then he ran toward the dog, forgetting for the moment about the killings. It was Toby, his dog from long ago, he thought. The dog cowered, flattened itself into the road as he approached, and then with a growl, it shot past him running up the hill. He staggered a few steps, not sure now which direction to go. Then he heard the coarse sound of a car grinding down the gravel road on the other side of the bridge. It would have been someone coming from the direction of Bethany, he thought. He was tempted to look to see if it would be someone who could rescue Bertrand. But soon there was hooting and gunfire, and the boy clenched his fists, swallowed hard. He took several steady breaths, began to climb the embankment toward the field where he had left the blackberries. The sun was gone and the light was swooning towards blue-black. Stars were beginning to flicker in the sky above the road. From higher ground, he could see the bridge and in the failing light make out people, boys mostly, watching. They climbed the diagonals or sat on the roadbed and swung their legs over the side of the bridge. Two boys had climbed high into the truss and swung like monkeys from the struts. He knew some of the boys from school and felt now it would be okay to join them. That way, he told himself, he could see what was going on, and he would be with a group and no one would bother him.

He started down the embankment, losing sight of the boys. As he landed beside the roadbed, the lights of a car shone on him. His muscles tensed and he went up on his toes, ready to dive for the bush. But he didn't move. Though poised to spring, flexed so tightly they ached, his muscles failed him. The car approached, slowed as it went by. It was Mr. Jacks' Buick wagon, now appearing purple in the dim light. Mr. Jacks was alone in the car, and as he drove by he peered out at the boy. Their eyes met momentarily, and the vacant, black look in Jacks' face—nearly the look of a snake, the boy thought—sent a shiver through him. After the car passed, he ran.

When he was at the top of the hill, he thought he was far enough away that he no longer had to run. Now, the gurgling of the river, echoing

8

up the ravine, and the rustling of the breeze through the woods predominated, though when he listened he could hear occasional shouting and laughing from the bridge. He walked blindly at first, until he realized he was following the path through leaf litter where the woman's body had been dragged. He followed it until he came to the place where she had been shot. He did not recognize the place, until his foot slipped in the bloody leaves and roused a swarm of flies. Now, he began to run, crazily, not caring the direction. Branches cut across his face. He stubbed his toes on stones. He tripped, got up, kept running downhill, and he thought he was nearing the road. He heard the groan of a car, and knew to be safe he had to get away from the road.

Suddenly, he ran into a wall of vines. His legs tangled in the vines and when he tried to draw them back, they tangled even more. He tore at the leafy strands, but the vines seemed alive, wrangling and writhing and entrapping his body the more he fought to get through them. Finally, he gave up and let his body fall forward. He breathed heavily and slowly became aware of a faint floral odor, like a sour lilac. Kudzu. He was trapped in a drapery of kudzu vines that hung from trees over the road. Once again, he struggled to free himself, but exhausted he resigned himself to hang, like an insect in a web. "Oh, Bertrand!" he said over and over. "Why Bertrand?"

TWO

In the spring of the year before—the last year of the war, 1945—Lonnie's great Aunty had come from Savannah to live with him and his mother. His father had been in the army for nearly three years, first at Fort McClellan, Alabama, and then in Africa, Italy, and Germany. The war had consumed everything—meat, milk, sugar—and Lonnie's eight-year-old imagination. He saw the war pictures in the newspapers and newsreels when they went to the movie house, but in his mind he saw gigantic dirigibles shooting ray guns down on people fleeing through crowded city streets and robotic goons in hand-to-hand combat with muscular GIs and comic book supermen. "You too young to worry about war," his mother would tell him, but he wasn't worried. He only wanted to know where his daddy was and when his daddy was coming home. "He'll be back right soon, right soon indeed, but I can't say when, though. He's got to kill some bad men," his mother said. "Like Tom Mix and Superman."

Great Aunty wasn't so hopeful. "Only the good Lord knows what's true," she would say. She chewed tobacco and used a blue pee pot for a spittoon. Lonnie's job was to empty it, as well as all of the chamber pots. He also had to bring in wood for the stoves and to take care of Toby, his daddy's dog. "War," Aunty said, "is a'bomination in the eyes of the Lord. Lord said 'Love your enemies, as yourself.'"

"But what you go' do, Aunty, if they attack you? Whole country can't turn the other cheek. We turn the other cheek, you go' be learning to speak German, if they don't kill you . . ." Lonnie's mother said. She turned to him. "God on our side, so don't fret none 'bout your daddy. He'll be home, come next year. Lord willing."

These exchanges were frequent and Aunty never pushed, always allowing the boy's mother the last say for soon, his mother left also. She went to Marietta, just outside of Atlanta, to work in an airplane factory. It was only two hours away by train, and she came home once every month or so. When she was gone, the old woman reigned, even though some days her arthritic hips prevented her from getting out of bed.

One Sunday at suppertime, they sat at the kitchen table eating cabbage and bread and a rare serving of pork. Toby sat just outside the screen porch door on the stoop with his bowl of scraps. He was a yellow mutt, old as Methuselah, still trim and able to trample through the woods.

"I tell you this now because you're going to have to learn it," Aunty declared, her finger pointing toward the ceiling, "and your momma ain't about to tell you. God's truth is a hard truth, little boy. Hard, but you learn it and you learn to live with it."

He didn't understand her talk, coming as it did in her wheezy, phlegmy voice, directed at the air around him as much as at him. She told him that she had been born during a war, The War Between the States. She, of course, could remember none of it, but she did remember the limbless men in her family who had survived it, their stories of carnage. She said they talked of battlefields where, for as far as they could see, from one horizon to the next, lay bodies and parts of bodies, and a man couldn't take two steps without stepping on a body. "And I had always wondered why men would do such a thing to one another and why God would allow it. Does God care that a man puts a bullet through another man and widows his wife and orphans his children? Don't think that He does?"

Lonnie picked the pork out of his cabbage. He liked both cabbage and meat, but he didn't like them together. He found a piece of boiled bacon and slipped it into his mouth. The fat was smooth on his tongue, and the cabbage flavor made it sweet and he found it hard to chew.

"But war still didn't have much of a meaning to me. Of course I have never been a soldier. Thank God I didn't live when there was war in this country, and praise God it won't come here today. But in '82 I lost my beau to war with the Indians out in Dakota. Ralph Hughes was his name. Handsomest boy there ever was, at least was to me. Straight, thick black hair and black eyes. And tall and lean as a stick. A black Irishman." She closed her eyes and Lonnie stopped chewing the bacon and looked at the old woman's quivering wrinkled cheeks. When she opened her eyes, she seemed not to see him. "I always did like a man with pretty hands—and we had plans." Now, she regarded Lonnie. Her finger wagged. "Plans. You would've grown up in the West, young man, if I'd had my druthers. We both would have been Westerners. Pioneers! There was nothing for us poor folks here in Georgia." She paused and looked down to her lap, wrung her hands. "That was long ago." Slowly, she rose from the table and removed the dishes to a wash pan on the stove. After she had cleaned the kitchen, they sat on the back stoop, Toby beside them and, as if the cleaning had been just a mere pause in her story, she resumed: "I should have made a family for myself, a good one. But I always bore a hard feeling for the Indians. Luckily you don't see too many of them around in Georgia anymore, but when I see one, it makes ice come up on my skin and I go cold to the bone, too, just thinking about Ralph and thinking about what all, not just Ralph, but everything—the life that was taken from me. Somebody should pay for it. I still think that. The Bible does say, 'Love your enemies,' and funny thing is, I don't even think of Indians as my enemy. I mean, I don't feel at war with them. I just get cold and I want them to pay for what they did to Ralph—"

"What did they do to him?" Lonnie interrupted. She looked up at him, as if surprised that he was there. "Oh, why child, they *killed* him! Just twenty-three years old, but they killed him."

"He was a cowboy."

"He was a soldier. In the cavalry. A horseman." Toby yawned wide and wagged his tail against the boy's leg. "I ought to forgive. Lord knows the Indians have suffered in this country 'til you hardly see one. Even if you go out West, you'd hardly see one. I need to forgive, for the Bible tells me this." She stroked the boy's shoulders. He felt her wrinkled hand against his neck and he wondered about how old she must be. "But son, how can we redeem ourselves so that He might redeem us? We live in the way of sin from which none is free. We all travel that road, the same as our forebears." Her voice trailed off and for a long moment she was quiet. "He makes it so hard."

"Maybe it's supposed to be hard."

"Live long enough, you'll know for sure."

Had he understood them, her words might have seemed prophetic to the boy.

The next morning, while bringing water up from the spring hole, the boy heard a car braking and sliding in the loose gravel on the road. He put down the bucket and ran to the front of the house, and there he saw a tall man standing over Toby and wiping his brow. Toby lay in the road, breathing heavily, but otherwise still. Even from the distance of a few yards, Lonnie saw Toby's pupils were fully opened, the expression in his eyes blank.

"Why did you kill my dog, Mister?" Lonnie asked. Suddenly, he was overwhelmed. Toby was leaving. His daddy had left. His ma was gone. And, now, Toby. He didn't know what to say, so he repeated himself. Then his words became garbled, he sat in the middle of the road and bellowed.

"Fuck," The man said and wiped his palm across his mouth. He looked at the boy and back to the dog and then to the weathered house.

Toby whimpered and now began to drag himself into the ditch. His hind legs had been crushed. Blood squirted from his chest. When he'd eased his quivering frame in the low grass of the ditch, he lay still except for an occasional wag of his tail.

"Why did you hit my dog, Mister? " Lonnie followed the dog. "Why did you?"

"It was an accident, son."

"Why did you, Mister? Why did you hit Toby?" Lonnie kneeled to the dog, reached out for him but did not touch him. He wanted to hold him, to draw him into his lap as he had done many times, but he felt that to touch the animal would break him.

"I hate to see an animal suffer," Lonnie heard the man say. "God, I hate to see it. But accidents happen." The man was quiet for a moment, and then he called to Lonnie, "Look."

Lonnie looked to see the man fingering though his wallet. "Look, I'll bring you some money. Now, just hush up, and I'll make it right for you."

Until then, Lonnie hadn't realized that he was crying. Shaking, he stood, stamped his feet. "You didn't have to hit him. You didn't have to kill him." Behind the man, Lonnie saw Aunty coming across the yard, hobbling on a cane. Her long dress and apron brushed against the white heads of plantain and set them bobbing on their stalks in a trail behind her. She carried a shotgun in her free hand. When Lonnie saw the gun, he stamped again and ran to Aunty, pulling at her dress. "No, Aunty, please. No."

"Shut up," Aunty said. But he bellowed and she propped the gun against her hip, and with her free hand slapped him in the face. "Children ain't got no obedience these days," she said to the man, who seemed surprised by her sudden violence.

"Well," the man said, "He . . . He lost his dog."

"Every old dog has got to go sometime, Mister," the woman said and held out the gun to the man. "Least you can do is to let him not suffer so."

"I hate to see an animal suffer," the man said, but did not move until Aunty pushed him with the stock of the gun.

Lonnie turned his face into Aunty's apron, but smelling its sourness, he turned again to look at the man and Toby. Aunty held him by the shoulder. "You run along back inside," she said, but did not loosen her grip. "Ok, then. Watch. It won't hurt you to see. He's a poor dog, but in a minute, he will be at peace. That's is what a life is, just a roiling and a scuffling until at last God sees fit to bring you to your rest."

The man lifted the shotgun to his shoulder and sighted down the barrel. He swayed a bit. Lonnie looked at Toby, now lying quietly in the ditch, his rib cage rising and falling rapidly. He looked at Aunty, her lips set firmly in a web of wrinkles, her eyes, black, glossy. He pulled away from her, and came to where the man stood. He breathed through his mouth. Snot ran down his nose. The man lowered the gun. "I'll buy you another one," he told the boy. I'll buy you any kind you want. I got a boy about your age. I'll buy you whatever you want."

Lonnie tried to stop the quivering in his cheeks. "Do it then. Kill him, then, won't you?"

Again the man lifted and lowered the gun. "You reckon the boy ought to see this?"

Aunty snorted. "Boy will see worse if he lucky enough to live long." Then she directed Lonnie to go back to the house and when Lonnie didn't move, she said, "You can throw him over there in the woods. Let him feed the buzzards." She pointed across the road to a drapery of dust-covered kudzu and poison ivy. "And leave my gun on the front porch." She turned and began to hobble back to the house.

Once again the man put the gun to his shoulder. "God," he said, "why doesn't he just hurry up and die?" The dog's chest kept swelling and falling rapidly. "I hate to see the thing suffer. I'll make it up to you, son. Nothing like a boy and his dog. It's American like apple pie. "

One blast from the gun and Toby's breathing stopped. In spite of his swaying and trembling, the man's aim had been true and the shot had torn into the dog's head. Of what Lonnie could see of the dog's eyes, they seemed dull, and he imagined that Toby's soul had stepped outside of his body and was floating up into the air towards heaven.

Then he turned to the man who was handing him the gun. "Well, now, that's better," the man said and looked around. "Look here." He breathed heavily. "I'll bring you some money. How about that? I got to get down to the bank, but I'll bring you some money." The man lit a cigarette and threw the still flaming match to the roadbed. "Who lives here, anyway? Who's your daddy, boy?"

Lonnie told him.

"Wayne Henson?" The man looked at the boy. "I reckon I can see that. This where he lives. Your daddy's a good man. Good worker. I reckon he'll be home soon."

"He's in the war."

"Like I said, he'll be home soon."

The boy was puzzled, and then he lost his breath in anticipation.

The man took a long drag on his cigarette. "Like I said boy, the war is over."

"Over . . . ?"

"You goddamn hillbillies got a radio? The war's been over—three, four weeks. Your daddy probably half way home by now. But listen, I'm going to make it up to you about this dog, you hear? I'm going to bring you some money."

Lonnie didn't care about money, but he nodded in agreement. The man got into the car and drove away, leaving the boy standing beside the road.

Aunty didn't believe the war had ended and when the boy insisted on the veracity of the stranger, she moved a chair to the stoop to await the arrival of the mailman. Toby's corpse still lay in the ditch and the faint smell of the kill came to them in whiffs. The old woman cursed the stranger for not following her instructions, and, anticipating a rank smell, instructed the boy to pull the dog out of the ditch and further into the woods across the road from the house.

The dog was not heavy and the corpse slid along easily on the leaf mulch. The boy gripped the dog's front paws, and let the claws dig into his palms, but he could not look at the dog. When he was out of sight of the house, he let go, started to walk away, but turned back. His stomach tightened and he opened his mouth to bellow, but only a crackle came out of his throat. Then he thought he must bury the dog and looked around for something to dig with. Finding nothing, he raked leaves over the body with his hands, until Toby was buried under a knee-deep mound of leaves and twigs. He had no sooner finished, when he heard the approach of a car, and ran to the road to see the mailman's car, already stopped at the mailbox and Aunty speaking to the man. By the time, he got across the road the car was pulling away. He tried to read Aunty's face, but her stern look gave him no clue.

"Is it true?" he whispered.

She looked down at him, and without a sign of pleasure in the news, said, "Yes."

Lonnie sighed. It was a long sigh that came up from behind his navel. "Aunty, it is over?"

"Yes, it is over." Slowly, she started back to the house. "Don't mean your daddy will be back, though. Don't mean nothing until you see him in the front door. Many a men go off and you don't hear from them ever again. Don't know if they're dead or alive."

"He'll be back."

The old woman looked at the boy and grunted. "Go wash your hands."

Three days passed and the boy's anticipation grew. He busied himself: straightened the parlor, dusted his parent's room, swept the front stoop, and fiddled around in the kitchen until the old woman threw him out. Then three more days passed. His eagerness failing and growing into anxiety such that he flagged down the mailman to ask again if the war had indeed ended. Securing the answer, he asked if soldiers had returned. The man knew of some soldiers who had returned, but knew nothing of Wayne.

Then one afternoon, when the heavy humidity and heat forced them to find shade in the back yard, Lonnie thought he heard a car pull off the road and into the driveway on the other side of the house. Lethargy held him fast to the grass on which he lay. He raised his head and saw the old woman, slumped down in her chair, her head lolling across her shoulder. A car door slammed. Lonnie sat up. He soon realized someone was in the yard, and he walked around to the front of the house. He saw a man with his back to him, bent over talking to the driver of the car. A duffel bag sat beside the man's leg. He wore a uniform. He stood, still with his back to Lonnie, and the boy, knowing the man his father, started walking toward him, saying nothing, his arms open, tears in his eyes and a smile so wide it cracked the skin on his lips. He reached the man just as the man turned. "Daddy," he said softly, and embraced his father.

THREE

The next day passed quietly as Wayne settled into his home. Lonnie helped him unpack the duffel bag, which contained an Eisenhower jacket, a few khaki shirts and pants, underwear, dress shoes, a bottle of French perfume for Aileen, and a Colt M1911 service pistol. The gun was angular and sleek, unlike the bulky revolvers the boy had seen in Western movies. "Is it a spy's gun?" he asked. His father laughed and allowed him to hold it. It was heavy, Lonnie thought. Then Wayne put the gun into the bureau drawer and locked it. Later that day, they walked around the place—to the dilapidated pig pen, the chicken coop with its roof fallen in, the fallow garden. At first the boy peppered his father with questions about the war, but the man's responses were aphoristic, curt, or silent altogether, so the boy settled on his presence. They buried Toby. The buzzards had picked him down to skin and bones. Wayne dug the grave. They pushed the skeleton into it with their feet and covered it.

"He was too good to lay out for buzzards," Wayne said.

"Daddy, I tried," the boy said, looking up at his father's face. The man seemed about to cry. After a moment, he put his hand on Lonnie's head and rested it there.

The old woman greeted Wayne as if he had only run into town and back. She cooked for him, and the three ate in silence. Now and again Aunty would remark, "I didn't think you'd be coming back. Thought sure they'd killed you."

Three days after he had returned, a tall, slender woman, Mrs. Crookshank, came to the door with a large purse and a box camera in hand. She was known as the widowed proprietress of Maribelle's Diner, but that day she came as a reporter for the *Talmaedge Tattler* which was publishing a special article on the men coming home from the war.

"May I come in?" Mrs. Crookshank pulled open the screen door before Wayne could answer, and he led her to the parlor, a neatly furnished, dark room just off of the house's common room. The woman seated herself at one end of the sofa, took a school composition notebook and pen out of her purse, and snapped it shut. "Now," she said, adjusting her cat-eyed glasses, "Give me your full name and the names of your parents."

Wayne told her.

"And your wife is?"

"Aileen," he said.

"And this young man?" she turned and smiled at Lonnie who was standing in the doorway. "I take it, he is your boy."

Wayne nodded.

"Are you happy to have your daddy back?" the woman asked Lonnie. Despite the woman's officious manner, Lonnie thought the question silly, and he stared at her. "But of course you are. May I say, 'You betcha?'"

"Uh?"

"In the article, I'll say you said, 'You betcha.'"

"Okay."

Mrs. Crookshank winked at Lonnie and turned to his father. "Now, Mr. Henson, what do you want to tell the good people of Talmaedge County about your homecoming?"

Wayne moved restlessly in his chair, pushing himself into the cushions. He rubbed his hands together as if warming them, then folded his arms across his chest and tucked his hands into his arm pits. "Well—" he started and cleared his throat. "Well, I am glad to be back home. I just got back. It's good to be back." He stopped speaking and his face reddened.

Lonnie thought that his father would cry and he fidgeted, first wanting to go to him, and then afraid to embarrass the man. "We're going to raise pigs again!" the boy blurted. "Now that Daddy is back, we're going to raise pigs and plant a big garden. And Daddy said we might get some chickens and a cow, too."

"Oh, that's lovely," Mrs. Crookshank said. "Our farms have been so lacking during this war. Now that our men are back, we can—"

"There's a lot of work to do," Wayne said. "And this time, now—now things are going to be different than before the war. I am going to have some things I always wanted. Ain't fixin' to be working for nobody else but me from now on."

"You want to go into business—"

"I'm tired of this sharecropping. It ain't worth it for a poor man. Just work yourself to death for the likes of—and the war, too—when you have been there and you come back here, you don't want things to be the same. You understand, lady? Things ain't the same."

Mrs. Crookshank busied herself taking notes. No longer smiling, she avoided eye contact with Wayne. Then, almost absently, she said, "I suppose you saw a lot of things over there, Mr. Henson. A lot of ugly things."

Wayne looked not at her but at his hands in his lap, then at Lonnie. "Not so much what I saw, as what I did."

There was a moment of stillness and then Mrs. Crookshank snapped open her purse, put the pen and notebook away, and picked up the camera. "I am sure the readers would be interested in a picture, Mr. Henson. Perhaps we can get you and your son . . . and the lady of the house?"

"She's at work," Lonnie said.

"Oh, what a shame. That would be such a nice picture, too. Tell you what, when your momma is not working, maybe one Saturday you all come on by Maribelle's Diner and have a meal on the house. We'd just love to do something for our service men and their families. Just love to."

Two weeks more passed before the boy's mother came home. Just as her husband had done, she arrived in the afternoon, having taken the noon train from Atlanta and a hired car from the station. Lonnie saw her from the corner of the house and started to run toward her as she dragged her suitcases across the lawn. But then he saw his father, coming from the front door, walking in hurried strides. She let go of the suitcases and stood with her arms beside her. Just before he reached her, she covered her face, and, as he embraced her, she fell into him. Lonnie heard her sob loudly and then breathlessly call out his father's name. He watched them embrace for such a long time that he began to perspire from standing in the sun. Then, thinking the reunion had gone on long enough, he joined them. Still in his father's embrace, his mother put her hand around the back of his neck and drew his face against her warm body. "Daddy's home," she said to him, and began to sob again.

Aunty cooked a big, plain supper that night. She made cornbread and sweet tea. The family sat around the table, quiet at first. Slowly they began to tell stories. Lonnie told of Toby's death. His mother told about the airplane factory and the women she had met there. She said that after she learned that the war was over, she decided to work as long as she could before the returning men replaced her. She had not thought to hurry home, thinking that Wayne would not arrive for many months. Wayne talked mostly about his trip home. He said it had slipped his mind until he had seen Aileen, but he had stopped over in New York City. The big city had made him nervous. Even with a map, he never knew which way to go on the streets. Luckily, he befriended a colored man, a GI from Detroit, and his friend had helped him see the sights. Lonnie was excited that his father had seen New York City and asked about the landmarks, the Statue of Liberty and the Empire State Building. Yes, his father told him, he had seen those things, but he hadn't gone up in them. He'd wanted to save what money he had. And besides, it wasn't much fun to see those things without his family.

With army pay and Aileen's savings, the family had a bit of money for once. They repaired the pig pen and the coop, bought a shoat and a few hens, and planted a fall garden. They also purchased a second-hand car, a 1939 Ford Tudor Deluxe. It was a fancy car, more than what they needed, Aileen argued, but Wayne liked the car. It ran eighty-five horsepower on a V-8 engine and the upholstery was like new. It had been driven by a judge from Greene County and his widow was willing to let it go for just two hundred dollars. When she found out that Wayne was a veteran, she knocked twenty dollars off of the price.

Fall set in. Yellow sweet gum, russet oaks and the occasional flame-red maple dressed the woods. The days shortened considerably. Still the Indian summer persisted. One day, when the family was sitting to supper, the kitchen door open to the warm evening, Aileen announced, "I have a little surprise. A baby sister or brother for you, Lonnie." She patted Lonnie on the head. He took comfort in her soft fingers in his hair, and longed for her caress the moment she took it away. The idea of a baby was abstract to him, distant, and he fidgeted, resisted the impulse to crawl into his mother's lap.

"What are you so proud of, suh?" Aunty abruptly turned to Wayne. "You look like the cat that swallowed the canary. You reckon a baby's got to eat?"

Wayne looked at Aileen, amusement on his face. "I reckon. I reckon we'd feed the little feller."

Aunty chewed quietly for a while and spat gristle into her palm. "Then I reckon it's time to make *my* 'nouncement. Been thinking this a while, and now just as good a time as any.

"I just come to look after the boy while you were away. So now, now I will go on back to Savannah where I belong."

"But you belong here, Aunty Grace," Aileen argued. "You can stay as long as you want."

"Don't matter what I want. Matters what the Lord wants. Lord says it time for me to go and leave you to your family. Lord blessed you real good, Aileen. You got your husband back. You got a boy and a baby on the way." She laughed dryly and coughed. "You ain't got no use for an old woman like me. My day gone, anyway. This is a new day, now."

"Now, Aunty, this is just as much your day as anybody's—"

"Aileen, use your common sense," Aunty said. "You are home. Wayne is home. Now it is time for me to go back home. Savannah is my home. Isn't that right, Wayne?"

Wayne chewed quietly. The supper was cabbage and beef and a side of sliced ripe tomatoes, the season's last. "We sure appreciated having you," Wayne said at last, "and you are welcomed any time."

The next Saturday morning, Aunty presented herself at the front of the house wearing a black dress, a black shawl, and a black brimmed hat made of straw. She had two suit cases. Aileen made her a box lunch, and without much fanfare, Wayne drove her and the family to the train depot. Shortly after noon, she boarded the train with the help of a colored porter. Aileen waved goodbye furiously, but Aunty only nodded curtly through the train window.

Back in the car, Aileen patted at her tears with a handkerchief. "I hate to see her go. She's the last of my family." In fact, Alieen had other family, various cousins whom she rarely saw.

Wayne said nothing and Lonnie felt sad only because his mother was sad. He thought he might miss Aunty. On the other hand, just seeing her packed and standing by the car seemed to have lifted a darkness from the house.

"But she had to go," Wayne broke the quiet inside the car with a soft declaration. "There was just too much happiness in our house for her."

"What's that supposed to mean?" Aileen asked.

"We are happy. We are going to have a baby. We are going to do all right, and well—I hate to say it, Aileen, but Grace is hung up in the past.

Whatever you do, you mustn't let something hang you up. That old woman has been stuck for the past seventy-five years. Either it's her daddy in the War Between the States or her beau in the Indian War." He paused and slowed the car. "You've got to move on. That's what we're doing. We *are* moving on."

Lonnie leaned over the seat back, pondering his father's words. He didn't understand them, but was afraid to ask their meaning. His mother said nothing, and then Wayne changed the tone brightly, patting Aileen on the hand, "I know! That lady—Mrs. Crookshank—promised us a meal." Wayne looked over the seat back at Lonnie for confirmation. "Why don't we go by her place and have a fancy lunch?"

Maribelle's Diner was located on the main street, just down from the bank, the courthouse, the jail, the general store and the Baptist and Methodist churches that formed the town square. The train depot was located next to the Feed and Seed, down the hill from the square and next to the river.

Half of Maribelle's dozen or so tables were taken. The family sat at one of three booths at the front of the restaurant, next to the windows that looked out onto Main Street. Floral curtains framed the windows. At the back of the restaurant, serviced by a separate entrance and separated from the larger dining room by a railing, was a dining room with one large table. "When did Maribelle's start serving colored?" Aileen wondered aloud. "I know this isn't the nicest place, but I didn't think they served colored here."

Wayne took menus from between the salt and pepper shakers and handed one to his wife. "Colored got to eat too."

"But they don't have to eat here," his wife whispered, and then noted that Maribelle was known for its cakes.

"They won't bother you, sitting in the back."

"You have to look at them."

Wayne put down the menu sheet and looked out of the window. "No you don't."

A man in a fedora entered. Lonnie looked up and dropped his fork. It was the man who had run over Toby. "Leave your fork on the table," his mother chastised. The man passed by their table, not waiting to be seated. Lonnie looked down, hoping the man would not recognize him. Then the waitress came to take their order.

"Is the owner here?" Wayne asked. "Mrs. Crookshank." The waitress said yes, but that she was busy. "I'm a veteran. She said I should stop in for a free meal."

"I'll tell her," the waitress said with a nod, and stood with her pencil and pad ready. They ordered fried chicken. Then Lonnie's attention turned again to the man who had killed Toby. He sat at a table in the middle of the room and rested one foot on the railing of the chair next to him. He had already been served a Coca-Cola and was smoking a cigarette. The fedora lay on the table in front of him.

Lonnie tapped his mother on the elbow. "That's the man," he said and pointed.

"Quit your pointing," Aileen said. "I taught you better."

"What man?" Wayne asked.

Lonnie pointed again. "The man that killed Toby."

"Lord," his mother said and looked about nervously. "Oh, Lord."

"He said he was going to give me some money."

"That figures," Wayne said with a sigh. The man was Vernon Venable, the owner of Thousand Acres, the plantation that Wayne had share cropped for. "Son," he said a little louder than he needed for Lonnie to hear. "You can't depend on everything you hear from people. Not everybody tells the truth, and some people will say anything to get what they want—"

"Hush up," Aileen whispered. She put her hand on top of Wayne's.

"The boy's got to learn, some people aren't worth—"

"We don't need trouble, Wayne."

Just then Mr. Venable scooted his chair, pushing it away from the table. He looked in their direction, right at them, it seemed to Lonnie, and beckoned his hand. Lonnie gasped, looked at his father, whose face went pale and tense. But then he realized the man was waving to someone on the street. In a moment, Sheriff Cook came in, and Mr. Venable shouted "hey" to him, and the sheriff, a short stout man, danced between the chairs, his leather gun belt squeaking every time he twisted his hips. In a moment, Mrs. Crookshank came out. She brought the sheriff a soda, patted Mr. Venable on the back, and laughed loudly about something the family didn't hear. Then she scanned the restaurant, and saw the Hensons. She patted Mr. Venable again, and smoothing her apron, came to their table.

"It is so good to see you again," she said to Wayne with a little nod of her head. She tussled Lonnie's hair, and extended her hand to Aileen. "I know I must have met you before, this being Bethany and all, but it has been a while, Mrs. Henson." Aileen nodded. "Y'all ain't got your drinks yet?" Mrs. Crookshank waved to the waitress, and told her to bring drinks.

She cleared her throat and clapped her hands to get the attention of the diners. "Yoo-whoo, patrons! Patrons of Maribelle's Diner! We have a very special person with us today. This is Private First Class Wayne Henson, not long home from fighting Nazis in Germany." She turned to Wayne whose face had reddened. "Private Henson, we are so proud to have you back and we thank you, and we thank God for your service."

"Amen!" a voice said from the back of the restaurant. It came from a dark-skinned man and it resonated in a baritone. Lonnie thought the man must have been one of the colored preachers. The man said nothing else, but it seemed that his voice, interjected into the silence following Mrs. Crookshank's speech, was an affront to the diners. They turned to look at him, some scowling, and then they turned back to look at Wayne, whose strained smile embarrassed Lonnie.

"Here, here!" Mrs. Crookshank said, and then the diners offered up words of gratitude and praise and were soon back to their lunches.

The waitress brought their sodas, and a moment later, their lunches. The plates were heaping with food, and the waitress made a point of saying it was on the house. "How nice," Aileen said. She smiled broadly and looked across the table at her husband. Then suddenly she pulled Lonnie next to her and kissed his cheek. "This is so nice, everything." Lonnie thought both of his parents would cry, but then his mother handed him a bottle of catsup.

The food was good. Lonnie kicked his feet as he tasted it, everything in turn and then a sip of grape Nehi. His father, who had been taking big forkfuls of food, put down his fork and stood up.

"Keep your seat. Keep your seat." Venable was approaching the table. Lonnie stopped chewing and his stomach seemed to flip.

"Mr. Venable, sir," Wayne said.

"I told you to keep your seat," Venable said. Venable was just over six feet tall, only a little taller than Wayne, but his lean features with a beaked nose, high forehead and slicked-back curls made him seem much bigger than Wayne. "Welcome back, soldier." Venable made a playful salute to Wayne, then nodded at Aileen and winked. "Whenever you are ready," Venable put his hand on Wayne's shoulder, "you come on by the feed store to talk to me about cropping."

"I don't know, Mr. Venable, I've been thinking—"

"Come talk to me." He nodded to Sheriff Cook and left.

One Saturday morning, a few weeks after Aunty had left, Wayne, wearing his Ike woolen army field jacket, took Lonnie hunting. They went down the spring path, toward Christmas Hill, an old homestead reclaimed by woods. They passed several fields, occasionally let to sharecroppers by Venable or Jacks, the big landowners. Since the war these fields had fallen fallow, but rabbits still foraged in the grasses along the border with the woods and in the blackberry bramble on the northern foot of the hill. Wayne carried the shotgun, the one that had killed Toby. It was a 12-gauge Winchester 21, good for hunting squirrels, turkeys, grouse and quail, as well as rabbits. On the path they spoke quietly, the boy asking about the gun and hunting. The boy wanted to go deer hunting, but Wayne snorted, told him that deer hunting was for rich men who could afford blinds, who had the time to sit around all day drinking liquor. They had pigs anyway, and didn't really need the venison. When they left the path, Wayne insisted on silence. They walked slowly, stopping frequently to listen and to scan the trees for squirrels and the underbrush for birds or rabbits.

They startled a covey of grouse, rare for the area. Lonnie cringed, nearly shouted as the birds exploded into flight and alarmed gobbling. Wayne aimed but did not manage to fire a round. He raised a finger to his mouth and pointed to Lonnie to walk in the direction where the covey had flown. Slowly, they made their way. When Lonnie snapped a twig under his shoe, Wayne froze in his tracks and indicated for the boy to stop. After a minute, they heard birdsong from the treetops and continued slowly through the underbrush, stepping quietly, bent low to camouflage themselves. Lonnie began to feel as if he were in a story about hunting in which a boy and his father hunted for a magic bird. He pretended they were Creek or Cherokee, and he became more aware of the woods' sweet leaf-rot, the curly blue lichen on the tree trunks, the red winterberries, half hidden in the litter. He wanted to smile, except that his father looked so intent, his jaw twitching. They tracked the birds for thirty minutes, hearing them in the distance occasionally, but eventually losing them.

Coming to a jut of rock that overlooked a small creek, Wayne sat, broke open the gun for safety, and took turkey and cranberry jelly sandwiches from his pocket. "Hunters got to eat, even if we don't catch anything." He handed a sandwich to Lonnie, who found a seat on a corner of the rock and leaned his back into his father's side. They hadn't finished their sandwiches when they heard the boom of a shotgun and what sounded like applause, the flapping wings of the grouse. Lonnie felt Wayne's body jump and tense, and he turned in alarm to see what was wrong with his father. The shot came again, closer, and again Wayne tensed, his face pale.

"Pa?"

"It's all right," Wayne said breathlessly. He was no longer sitting on the rock, but squatting above it as if ready to dive to the ground. "Just another hunter." He laughed nervously and put his hand on Lonnie's shoulder. Then he stood, snapped the Winchester shut, and wiped sweat from his forehead. His sandwich lay on the ground, broken open so its contents were dirtied. Again, Wayne laughed. He kicked at the sandwich. "Go ahead and finish up, lest we let that bastard get all of our birds." Then another blast came, this time just on the other side of the ridge above their heads. Wayne pushed Lonnie to the ground, threw himself beside the boy, and aimed the gun in the direction of the blast. Again they heard the explosive flapping and guttural bird call.

Without standing, Wayne called out. "Whoo-whoo. Hey now, we are down here. Hey now, whoo-whoo." A man presented himself at the top of the ridge. Like Wayne, he wore an Ike jacket. He was the colored man from the restaurant. He broke down his shotgun, and came down the hill and stopped a few feet from them. Looking up at him, Lonnie thought the man looked very tall and in the shadows, very black. Nervously, he looked at Wayne, but was confused by the expression he saw on his father's face, trembling and blushed. Lonnie looked at the colored man. He, too, seemed confused, his forehead furrowed. Then Wayne raised his hand slowly and saluted the stranger.

The stranger shook his head. "No sir. You're not supposed to—"

"I will." Wayne's voice was hoarse.

"I'm just a corporal—"

"I *will*."

In the distance something frightened the covey and the sudden clapping of its wings cut through the woods. The men looked at one another, Wayne holding his salute. Then the colored man straightened his shoulders and saluted in return, holding the salute stiffly. Soon both men seemed on the verge of tears. The boy took his father's free hand, the shotgun seesawing in the crook of his elbow, and tugged. Only then did the two men relax.

"You were there, too?" Wayne asked.

"Yes sir. Third Army."

"Yes. Third Army." Wayne named his battalion.

"761 Tank Battalion," the stranger replied. His voice resonated a little.

"Excuse me, sir." Wayne nodded and held out his hand. He said his name.

"I know who you are," the man said, shaking hands. "I saw you at Maribelle's a few weeks back. Bertrand Johnson."

Wayne said he knew the family. "Nice folks. I am sorry I didn't know who you were in the restaurant. If I had've, I would've said something, cause it's important that we stick together." Bertrand kicked a little at the leaf litter. "I mean, we have been through something folks around here don't know nothing about. You can't talk to them about it. They don't know what you talking about, lest they been there. You ever have the feeling you want to talk about it, but you can't find no one to talk to. Can't find the words to talk to them about it so they will know."

Bertrand answered slowly, his voice losing its resonance. "Yes sir, I know what you mean."

"Good." Wayne nodded, looked off to his right. "I live over yonder, off of the state road, on the road that cuts down through some of Venable's fields."

"I know where you live. I grew up right over the hill a bit."

"Oh yeah?"

"Yeah. Been seeing you around since you were about five or six, I reckon, though, I didn't know your name until I read about you in the paper."

"Oh yeah?

"Yeah."

They faced each other squarely, and Lonnie thought they might be getting ready to fight. "Well, then," his father said. "How about you come by the house and we can talk about what we did over there."

Bertrand sighed deeply. "But, you know, folks around here don't like mixing."

"Mixing? I don't give a damn what folks like." His father rubbed his hand across his brow. "And, hell, Corporal, I ain't planning to *mix* with you. I just want to talk to you." He wiped his mouth. "Don't you think, Bertrand, that after all we have done, after all . . . that we two *soldiers* have done, we can mix if we want to? God damn it, things have got to change in Talmaedge. We just can't go on the way we used to after the rest of the world has turned upside down."

Bertrand seemed to think, shifting his weight, then he smiled, broadly, and nodded. "Amen, Mr. Henson."

Wayne's shoulders relaxed and he smiled. "Name's Wayne, Bertrand." He pointed to Lonnie and introduced him.

"Did you kill anything?" Lonnie asked.

"Lonnie!" His father startled him. Then he put his hand on the boy's shoulder, "Oh, he means *birds*. Did you hit any birds?"

Bertrand said he had two, and they walked to the ridge top to look at them. Bertrand gave one of them to Lonnie, and in parting the two men agreed that they would meet again on the next Saturday and hunt.

But on the next Saturday, the family rose long before dawn, packed the Ford and started the eight-hour drive to Savannah. That week the mail man had brought a telegram from a cousin. Aunty had passed.

After the funeral, they went to the water front on East River Street. Lonnie had never been in a big city, much less a port city, with its oily river full of the traffic of seal-skin gray naval ships—destroyers and cruisers. He stood by the riverbank and waved to the sailors. On one ship, two sailors, their white caps glowing in the sun, leaned on a railing. They waved back. Suddenly, Lonnie thought he wanted to be a sailor and to go upon the water to far away countries. Seeing the sailors cheered him up, especially after the somber funeral, little of which he remembered, except for Aunty's placid face, her shrunken frame in the same black dress she had worn to the station and her hands folded across her stomach holding a silk lily.

Constantly wakes lapped against the pilings, and from the distance came a knocking of a pile driver. Military men, both soldiers and sailors, roamed the streets. They smoked, laughed and more than once whistled at Aileen in spite of Wayne's presence. From alleyways came heavy whiffs of dead fish, stale beer and dank cellars. Lonnie could have walked up and down the slippery cobbled street all afternoon, but his mother insisted they leave the waterfront and they shopped Bay Street without buying anything, until they came upon a store that sold furniture. Aileen spotted a baby's crib, painted white with pink and blue scrolls along the headboard. She kissed Wayne in public when he bought it for her.

FOUR

"I missed you last Saturday." Bertrand stood on the back porch stair of the Henson house. The morning was warm and foggy and a light rain fell through the mist. Wayne opened the door and invited Bertrand from the stoop into the screened-in porch. Lonnie stood behind him.

"Well, I don't reckon I will," Bertrand said. "I only dropped by because you said we might go hunting, and I missed you last Saturday."

"Step on in, Corporal."

"No sir, "I see that I'm disturbing you now. I shouldn't have come by so early. But I missed—"

"We've been up for hours," Wayne said. "I have just this minute come in from feeding my pigs and pulled my shoes off. I didn't think you would be out hunting with the weather."

"I just thought it would clear—"

"Now come on in, soldier."

Bertrand nodded, smiled, and stepped onto the porch. Wayne stepped back, giving Bertrand room, inviting him into the kitchen. Again Bertrand hesitated and asked if he should take off his boots.

"We don't stand on ceremony," Wayne said. "You make yourself comfortable."

Quickly Bertrand leaned his gun on the wall, took off the boots, and spoke to Lonnie, calling him "young squire."

"What's that?" the boy asked.

"You haven't heard of the Knights of the Round Table, King Arthur, and all that?"

"I have, but what is a squire?"

"A young knight. A young hero." Bertrand winked at Lonnie.

"I ain't no hero."

Bertrand reached out as to pat the boy's head, but drew his hand back. "Well, not yet you aren't, but I suspect one day you will be."

"Aileen," Wayne called, as he led Bertrand through the house to the parlor. "Aileen, we got company." Wayne waved Bertrand to the sofa and sat in the chair across from him. He crossed his legs at the ankle, wiggling his socked toes. "Go tell your momma we have company," he told Lonnie.

Lonnie left the two men, each staring at the other and smiling. Neither said anything. The child rushed through the house and found his mother in the bedroom in the back of the house where they had set up the crib.

"What company?"

"Bertrand."

Aileen looked puzzled a moment and then an expression of recognition came to her. "He's in the house? Where is he?"

"He's in the good room."

"Your daddy let him in the good room?"

Lonnie ran back to the door of the parlor, not wanting to miss what the men were talking about. He found them still staring, smiling, making small talk, seemingly comfortable in each other's presence. Aileen followed and stood behind Lonnie. Wayne introduced her to Bertrand. Bertrand stood. Aileen nodded.

"He's the one who gave us the bird we ate the other Sunday."

"I thank you," Aileen said, neutrally. "It was right nice of you." She turned to go, but Wayne stopped her, asking her to bring coffee.

"No sir," said Bertrand. "I didn't intend to come in. I think I'll be heading on, anyway. I doubt the weather will clear."

"I don't think it will," said Aileen. She started away again, but stopped to call Lonnie to come with her. In the kitchen she measured the coffee into the pot, dipped in water from the water bucket, stoked the stove and set the pot on to boil. Her movements were stiff and she talked in a hush. "I don't see what's so important that he got to bring him in the house, into the good room."

"They are soldiers. They saluted and everything."

"That don't make it right. I met colored people, too, over at the factory and I'd bring them home too, if there was cause. But to sit him up in the front room and to tell me to make coffee. He must think he's Ole King Cole or someone." When the pot began percolating, she sent Lonnie to find out what Bertrand took in his coffee.

The men were no longer smiling. Wayne sat with both feet on the floor. Bertrand leaned forward. They generated such intensity that Lonnie did not want to interrupt, lest he break the charm that had settled in the room. His father was talking about hedgerows and cold, and from what he could make out, the story seemed to include a fairytale landscape of dark walls of vegetation that rose up around the road so that the soldiers seemed boxed into a rat's maze. He understood something of his father's feeling, for he had gone deep into corn fields with the tassels waving above his head and stalks surrounding him for as far as he could see. If he tried running the lancet leaves would whip him, but to stand still was to suffocate in the sweet, milky perfume of the corn and gnat swarms. But his father spoke of cold, of ice and mud, and of men with numb fingers and blackened toes.

"I didn't know what you took so I put some sugar and milk in it." Aileen handed a cup of coffee to Bertrand, who rose quickly and accepted it with both hands. She handed the other cup to Wayne who took it and set it down on the coffee table. Wayne started his story again, but Aileen interrupted to ask if he needed anything else from her. Then she tugged Lonnie on the ear, indicating that he should follow her.

They sat for most of an hour in the back bedroom, while Aileen sewed ruffles on a skirt for the crib and Lonnie thumbed through a Superman comic book, one he had read several times. He wondered what the men talked about, but it was useless to strain since he couldn't hear them. Finally, he heard Bertrand leaving and he started to the door, but his mother sharply told him to sit. Presently, Wayne came and stood silently at the entrance to the back bedroom. Aileen did not look up from sewing. "Did you have a nice little visit?"

Wayne rubbed his index finger and thumb across his eyes and pinched the brow of his nose. He sighed deeply. "I wouldn't call it nice."

"It looked pretty nice to me," Aileen said. "The two of you sitting there with your coffee cups and your shoes off—" She looked at her husband. "Who told him to take off his shoes, anyway? We don't know how clean—"

"He's clean. And he is my friend."

Aileen poked her needle into a pin cushion and set it and the cloth inside the crib. She smoothed her dress. "Wayne, listen to me, honey. I know you've had a hard time. I myself cannot even imagine what it must be like to go over there to a war. But I did listen to the radio and read the newspapers up in Marietta. I heard. I know it was rough. But you are back now. Over there is over. Now, we have got to make a life here in Talmaedge County, and that means we live by the way of life in Talmaedge County. I don't have to tell you what that is. When I came here from Savannah to be with you, I adapted myself to Talmaedge County—but not even in Savannah would we have had a colored man sitting up in the good room. Nowhere, least nowhere I've been have I seen that."

"Maybe you ain't been nowhere."

Aileen stood, faced her husband and braced herself with one foot. "I've been around enough to know that you're heading for trouble. We don't need trouble. We got a boy to raise and baby on the way and that little bit of money you brought from the army won't last."

Wayne's body stiffened and his fist balled and relaxed. "I got plans—"

"Plans? Come spring you'll be asking Venable for a share to crop. Is that your plan? And let me tell you that Venable won't be giving a share with anybody he thinks is a—" she leaned toward him and whispered— "a nigger-lover."

In a quick motion, Wayne drew back his fist and held it as if to strike her. Then he slammed his fist into the open door, rattling the clothes hangers on the coat peg. He drew in a breath deeply. "I'll be a nigger-lover then. What's it to you? What's it to Venable? Bertrand is . . . Bertrand is a respectable man. He's a school teacher. He's a church man. He's a soldier. He fought Nazis . . . He. . . ." Wayne covered his face and breathed heavily into his hands.

Aileen had stepped back, close to Lonnie. Her voice was less shrill. "That might be so, but Wayne, it still don't make him equal." She pushed Lonnie in front of her and slowly made her way past Wayne. When she was beside him, she said, "I know you're right. I'm just saying don't get into trouble." Then, she put a hand on Wayne's shoulder, while keeping the other on Lonnie. "It'll be all right, honey. I know it will."

Bertrand visited two weeks later. It was a Friday afternoon, after school. The weather was clear, the sun low in the sky. The air was becoming chilly. The men met by the Henson wood shed, a large plank and tar paper lean-to that sat under an old black walnut tree. The men pushed logs upright to make seats for themselves, rolling the nuts underfoot, peeling off the dry husks. In front of the shed was a large oak log, a makeshift chopping block. To one side of it were piles of the stony shells and peeled husks. Inside, the shed smelled faintly sour of the rows of neatly stacked fire wood, mostly oak. Outside lay a pile of logs to be sawn and split.

Bertrand looked around admiringly. "My daddy always said a man with firewood is a rich man."

Lonnie agreed. After all, he thought, without firewood people would be cold and couldn't cook their food. But his father chuckled at the adage. "It'll take a hell of a lot more than wood to make me rich." Wayne settled on a log and took a pint of whiskey from inside his Ike jacket. "How about a little fire to go with your wood?" He uncapped the bottle and offered it to Bertrand, who waved it away. "Come on, Bert. A taste—a little toast to the old times, to all the men who didn't make it back."

Bertrand took the bottle and hesitantly sipped. He winced. "I'm just not used to it!" They laughed.

"Run up to the house and bring a glass of water for Bertrand," Wayne said to Lonnie. "Go on now." Lonnie dashed to the house, hating to miss even a word of the men's conversation. When he returned with the water, his father was constructing a small teepee of kindling for a camp fire. Lonnie gave the water to Bertrand, and rolled a log into position next to his father. Soon pine smoke frilled around them as the fire blazed. Lonnie smiled, rubbed his hands together and leaned over the fire. Bertrand gulped down half of the water and carefully splashed liquor in what remained. Wayne took back the bottle, clanked it on Bertrand's glass and both men drank. Then he turned to Lonnie and told him to go away. The boy protested, and went back to the house, but rather than going inside, he circled the yard and sneaked to the rear of the shed. He could not see the men, but could hear them with little effort.

For a moment he watched a cross spider wind its web around a moth. This spider was brown and harmless, unlike the black widows which populated the woodpile. He lay against the lean-to, looking above the tree line at the first stars piercing the sky. There were a crescent moon and two bright stars, one which he knew to be the evening star. The pine smoke wafted to him and he breathed deeply, filling his lungs with its sweetness and the autumn air. He closed his eyes and listened to the quiet voices of the men. His father was speaking and Bertrand was grunting in agreement. They were making a song of it, a little bit of speaking in Wayne's hushed voice and Bertrand's resonant grunt. The fire popped and wheezed. Lonnie imagined the world of his father's words, the cobblestone streets of a town and gunfire all around. A heavy acrid smoke caused him to hack up and spit out black phlegm. His eyes burned from smoke and sweat, and the man next to him shouted for him to pursue. To where, he wasn't sure. He followed the man in front of him. There was a blast and a rain of glass and stone shards and splinters of wood. He went on, firing at fleeting shadows that whisked around corners or heads that suddenly appeared in windows. The GI in front of him stopped beside a shop's doorway. The door hung by one hinge, and on a signal, the GI kicked the door down, and the two of them entered, carbines ready with bayonets. In the dim light, mottled by passing clouds of smoke, he could see that it had once been a dress shop. Now the mannequins posed naked, and their glassy stares caused his heart to thump in his ears. He thought of them as once being alive. He moved carefully through the store, aware now that a third GI, a guy from Mississippi, was covering him. He heard a sound coming from the behind a large counter, slowly moved toward it, avoiding the Gaba Girl, posed with an arm raised to her head. Suddenly there was a scrambling, like a large rat clawing on wood, and he turned to fire at it. It was a Jerry, getting to his feet, his hands raised above his head. The Jerry was yelling something, pleadingly, but he couldn't make it out. It was almost like English, but butchered somehow. He stood just a minute, looking at the Jerry, as much surprised by the sudden surrender as anything. The Jerry was young, and as Wayne's eyes adjusted he could see that he was probably not yet twenty. His face was sooty with not a single wrinkle, his eyes round with fear. He gasped as he breathed. He saw the boy was beginning to tremble as if he were cold but he, himself, felt nothing. There was another blast. The storefront window shattered. He jabbed the bayonet. He felt it crack through the boy's solar plexus and slide until it hit something hard inside the body. The boy shook, screamed. He grasped the barrel of the carbine and tried to push it out of himself. Quickly his efforts grew weak and he fell hard on his knees. Still he held the carbine, and looked up. Wayne looked back at him, and he felt nothing for him at that moment. He pulled out the bayonet with a *thwack* and the young man fell forward, his head landing at Wayne's feet. Someone fired behind him, and Wayne turned and continued through the building, firing and moving carefully.

The men stopped talking for a while and Lonnie opened his eyes to see more stars in the sky. His mother called to say that supper was ready. No one answered. She called again, and then Bertrand answered, "Coming!"

Lonnie sat up just then, wondering what had happened to his father, and then he heard a loud, grievous sigh. It sounded like an animal. He moved quietly around to the front of the shed. In the flicker of the yellow light from the camp fire, he saw the men embracing, his father on his knees with his head against Bertrand's shoulder. Bertrand looked at Lonnie. Lonnie couldn't discern the look. He felt that the colored man was violating a trust, taking advantage of his father's friendship. At that moment, he hated the man.

His mother called again, and this time Lonnie answered, but no one moved.

Supper was beans, turnips, fried meat, and cornbread, but no one ate. The three of them sat for more than twenty minutes without talking, staring at plates that glowed golden in the kerosene's lamplight. Occasionally, Aileen shoved food around with her fork, but neither Lonnie nor Wayne pretended to be hungry. Finally, Aileen told Lonnie to go and do his homework. He moved slowly from his chair, but she rose impatiently, took the plates off of the table and scrapped the food back into the pots.

In the everyday room, next to the kitchen, Lonnie sat at the table to figure long division problems. Though the work was not hard to him, he couldn't concentrate, and so he figured and re-figured the same problem. He remembered the colored man's eyes, usually big, were slits, and his mouth had drawn down at the edges. The man had looked directly at him when he had come around the corner of the shed, and then he looked away and skyward, as if he were tolerating a bad smell. Meanwhile his father, was grasping at the man's clothes, and pressing his head against the man's shoulder as he sobbed. The sobs were deep as if his father lost his breath between each one. He had wanted to push the man away, and yet he couldn't move to save his father. All he could do was to answer when his mother had called in order to interrupt the colored man from answering.

Now he heard his mother moving about in the kitchen, seemingly making unnecessary noise clanking the spoons in the pots and slamming the door to the ice box. Then she cleared her throat and spoke his father's name. His father answered softly, and she spoke to him so quietly that Lonnie could not hear. He put down the pencil and looked toward the kitchen. Because his mother had pulled the door shut, he could only see a sliver of lamplight coming from the room. Quietly, he moved, sitting in

36

a square chair between the kitchen door and the stair. As he listened, he looked at the flame in the kerosene lamp on the table next to his arithmetic book. The flame was a steady, little golden spear emanating from its tip the slightest bit of a vapor. It cast the soft shadow of the table onto the floor, and of a china cabinet against the curtain that framed the arch to the parlor. He could see a portrait of his father's mother in a large oval frame on the wall. The picture, half in shadow, looked only a little like his father. She was plump, rustic, and even in the portrait her eyes appeared to sparkle. He had never known her, or any of his grandparents, all having died before he was born. His mother's people in Savannah were all cousins, none to whom she was close. His father's people in Talmaedge seemed to have all died out or moved West to Kansas and Nebraska, except for a cousin who had married well, to a woman in the county establishment. Otherwise, his had been a family without much land, poor laborers on other white men's farms, serving as overseers or tradesmen until the Civil War, when they sought their fortune as infantrymen.

"What is it? Tell me, please." He heard his mother say. "You told him, but you can't tell me? I'm your wife, Wayne. I love you no matter what." He heard his father gasp and shift in his chair. Then in a cracking voice, his father said, "I killed a boy. He was giving up. I killed that boy, no older than . . . my own boy."

Lonnie felt cold and his stomach knotted as he imagined the boy's face again, the sooty face coming out of the shadows, the big eyes and slack mouth. "But you didn't mean to do it," Aileen said. "Whatever you did. It was wartime. You did what you had to. It was your job. And don't think for a moment that he wouldn't have done it to you."

"I don't think he would have."

"Never mind that. It wasn't your fault." He heard the rustle of their clothes and something dropped from the table. "I just thank God it wasn't the other way around. What would I do without you?" His mother was crying now and Lonnie, too, felt his nose close up. "God. Thank God for His mercy."

He heard his father stand, and he moved to the edge of his seat, preparing to return to his homework. "Yes," Wayne said. "God has had mercy. For some reason—so, understand this, Aileen, I've got to do something to make this right. Understand it's not the shooting of a German soldier. I don't know how many German soldiers I might have killed, but it is that one *boy*. That is the one God made me see and I *killed* him, so it must be made right."

"But how can you make it right?" His mother's voice was harder now. "What can you do?"

"Something, goddamnit. Something to make up for it."

"But what? You don't know his family. You don't speak their language. No way in the world to find them. Best thing is just to let it go. Go on with our lives here. You get some of that GI Bill money they're talking about and learn a trade or something. We don't have to stay here. We can go up to Atlanta or back to Savannah. We got a chance in this world, Wayne. Don't let something like this drag you down, honey."

Lonnie stood and sniffled. The prospect of living in Savannah, on the big, oily smelling river was exciting to him.

"I don't know. Do you think that will be enough?"

"Yes. Yes, yes. It'll be enough. It's not like you planned to kill that boy. You didn't start the war. They did. They should be making it up to us." She was quiet for a minute and Lonnie realized his parents were kissing. "Thank God, you are alive. Thank God, we can go on."

The coming weeks brought excited joy to the household as Wayne scoured the advertisements in the Atlanta newspapers for a trade school. He invited Bertrand into the house to help him look. Aileen was not happy to see the colored man sitting in the lamp light at the table in the everyday room. She told Wayne that she didn't know which was worse, having a colored man in the house in the daytime or in the nighttime, as people driving by would see his car parked in the yard. But she eventually acquiesced. She made little sense out of the forms, so it was good to have the school teacher there, she said.

Among the notices for carpentry, plumbing and crop dusting schools was one for agricultural techniques. Wayne tore this one from the page and carried it in his pocket for a day, until Bertrand advised that in order to put such skills to good use, he would have to buy a farm, not just a few acres, and certainly nothing akin to Thousand Acres, Mr. Venable's plantation, or Woodbine, Mr. Jack's plantation, but at least a hundred acres. Otherwise, the only work he would get would be for Venable or Jacks or someone like them. Together, they settled on a school for rural electrification. That job would keep him in the country, possibly even in Talmaedge County, since most homes in Talmaedge had no electricity. "It'll be good to bring power to the people," Bertrand said. Bertrand helped Wayne compose a letter of interest, and when the application for the school came, he helped Wayne to fill it out. The plan was to move to Atlanta for at least little while. The "Servicemen's Readjustment Act," the GI Bill, would pay living expenses for the family and for Wayne to study at the trade school, and Aileen said that she could find a job in one of the textile mills. The prospect of the move filled the house with excitement. Lonnie asked incessantly of his mother about the big city, but she had little to tell him. She had worked at the airplane plant in Marietta, a town fifteen miles from the city. Except for the air force base, it was nearly as rural as Bethany. Marietta did have a nice little square, a bit bigger than Bethany's, and it had a movie palace. She had enjoyed watching the movies on her days off.

On the evening that Wayne finished the application, he poured a bourbon and water for Bertrand and himself and opened a RC Cola for Lonnie. They sat in the everyday room, around the table and Wayne allowed Lonnie to pick up the neatly addressed envelope and examine it in the lamp light. The envelope, yellow from age, had a stamp depicting the Marines raising the American flag on Iwo Jima. It amazed Lonnie that in that envelope was the promise of their future.

"It's as good as done," Bertrand assured Wayne. "They'll take you, no doubt—they have to according to Uncle Sam. And then you will be set. You can go anywhere in the world with that skill, anywhere where they need electricity. And you will be getting good pay and helping people all at the same time."

Wayne admitted that he was nervous about it, but Bertrand waved him off. "Well, I am not an educated man like you are," Wayne said.

"Where do you think I started from?" Bertrand asked. "A lot of it's just common sense and good luck. This young squire," he nodded to Lonnie, "he'll have the luck now. Once you get up a bit, see. Once your daddy gets going a bit, then it's so much easier for the children to get a leg up in life. That's why I came back to Talmaedge—well, because of my mother—but also to help the poor children whose parents don't have anybody to help them. I figure I can teach them a little something, at least what I learned."

Wayne sipped from his glass and sighed. "This is a modern age, now, Bertrand. You ought to be teaching *all* the children, not just the colored ones."

"That's good of you to say," Bertrand said slowly and looked down.

"How would you like that," Wayne said to Lonnie, "to have Mr. Bertrand as your teacher?"

Lonnie gasped. His face burned. "Maybe," he said softly, but the idea of the round-faced colored man as his teacher dumbfounded him. The other children would tease him if they knew a colored man taught him, and if they found out that this teacher was his father's friend, the teasing would doubtlessly turn to bullying. But then he thought it all akin to a fairytale, something impossible, a fable for his father's imagination.

"Well, you needn't worry about it," Bertrand said and patted Lonnie's shoulder. I don't teach your grade anyway." They all laughed uncomfortably. Bertrand quickly finished his drink and announced that it was time for him to leave.

"But I am serious," Wayne said. "And I want my son to know that I am." He was looking at Bertrand as he spoke. "We have fought the most terrible war there has ever been. I hope it is the last war anybody will ever have to fight. And why shouldn't it be? Look a-here, white and colored together—we fought it, and so many people. They are saying *millions* of people died. " He leaned forward and grasped Bertrand's arm. "They are saying that maybe *ten million* people died, by the time they're finished counting. I go crazy thinking about it. It's like somebody's taking a hammer to my head, and yet, I was there, and you were there to see it."

"Yes," Bertrand said meekly. "I saw the Jewish camps. One of them."

"So, what are we going to do, then? Are we keeping on in the old ways?" He turned to Lonnie and pulled him close. "No, son, we're fixin' to change things. I ain't a fool to think that it's going to happen overnight, but it's got to start somewhere."

Bertrand nodded. "I hear you, Brother Wayne."

Just then, Aileen entered. She had been lying down, complaining of a backache. Lonnie looked at her stricken face. "What's the matter, Momma?"

"Nothing," she said curtly and motioned to her husband. He followed her to the back bedroom, and in a minute returned in a rush. "We need to run over to see Doctor Talmaedge," he announced. "Something is wrong with the baby."

Bertrand stood abruptly, but Wayne asked him to sit with Lonnie while they were gone. Wayne had grabbed the car keys and his and Aileen's coats, and rushed to the back of the house before Bertrand answered.

Losing the baby was an abstraction to Lonnie. His mother had barely begun to show, and, except for the crib, there was very little evidence that a baby was on the way. On the night his mother went to the doctor, he had waited very late sitting in lamplight with the colored man. At first the man had tried to comfort him, though neither knew what the problem was. Then the man had tried to carry on small talk with him, asking him questions about school and telling him about American history, the subject that the man had studied in college. When Lonnie ventured to ask questions about the war, like his father, the man went vague or silent. After a while, he began to fall asleep and the man suggested he go to bed. He would not. He did not want to leave the man in the house while he slept. The man worried aloud that his wife would be wondering where he was, and Lonnie suggested that he go home; but, the man dutifully sat, at times dozing, at times seemingly deep in thought.

He was relieved when his parents returned, his father helping his mother to the bedroom. Wayne spoke quietly with Bertand and sent him on his way. Then he sat and drew Lonnie into his arms. "Your ma's going to be all right," he said, his mouth against the boy's ear. "These problems happen to women, but the doctor said that she can have another baby." Lonnie leaned his head on his father's shoulder. The Ike jacket scratched his cheek pleasantly and he soon fell asleep. In the morning, his mother told him that the baby would have been a girl and that she would have named her Eliza, after her own mother.

FIVE

Just as Bertrand had said, a letter of acceptance for the trade school came in a few weeks. It was a wonderful Christmas present, Wayne announced. The classes began in March, so the family had some time to plan. Bertrand, who knew Atlanta better than any of them, suggested that Wayne move ahead of the family and find a place for them to live. He could room at the white YMCA on Luckie Street, not far from the school, and use the trolley to get around. That way he could leave the car for Aileen and when he had found a place for them, Aileen could drive over to Atlanta. Aileen didn't know how to drive, a fact that seemed to surprise the colored man, since he said his own wife was a good driver. Wayne said that he would teach her, and Lonnie thought it was a fine plan since he could sit in the back seat and learn to drive, too.

Christmas Eve day turned cold and blustery, though the sky was clear except for a few high clouds. With numb fingers, Wayne and Lonnie chopped down a small pine that grew at the edge of one of Venable's fields and affixed it to a wooden stand. Aileen helped them decorate it with glass bulbs, tinsel, and a star. On the holiday morning, Lonnie found that all the gifts under the tree were for him: two pair of dungarees, two flannel shirts, a pair of shoes, two comic books, a slinky, and a Captain Marvel set of flying heroes—Captain Marvel, Mary Marvel and Captain Marvel Junior. They were like paper dolls, only they flew like paper airplanes. It was a bonanza, he thought, so many toys, when the last year he had only gotten new clothes and oranges. He was outside, risking losing one of the flying toys to the wind, when Bertrand's car pulled into the yard. With Bertrand was a doleful-faced woman whom Lonnie assumed was his wife. The woman sat in the car while Bertrand got out, leaned in again and brought out a cake wrapped in waxed paper. Bertrand called "Merry Christmas!" to Lonnie and went to the door. Wayne answered the door, received the cake with loud appreciation, and called to Aileen. He invited Bertrand to come in, but Bertrand indicated the woman. Again, Wayne called to Aileen. He went to the car, still holding the cake, and greeted the woman. As far as Lonnie could see, the woman remained stiff and polite. Wayne called Lonnie to the car to present himself and to thank the woman for the cake she had made for them. On closer inspection Lonnie saw that the woman, dark and smooth skinned, had a pleasant look about her, but there was something peculiar, too. Some quality in the way that she spoke—crisply, properly, and aloofly—scared him. She seemed refined, but sad. Bertrand, on the other hand, seemed as jolly as Santa. After a few minutes of chatting, Bertrand got into the car and drove off.

"Now that wife, Luellen," Wayne said later, as he told Aileen about the meeting, "she is a strange bird. Wouldn't you say so, Lonnie?"

Lonnie agreed, though he couldn't say in what way the woman was strange. "She was like a mean teacher," he said.

His parents laughed. "I don't know how mean she is," Wayne said, "but she *is* a teacher over at the Normal School. Both of them."

For supper they had oyster stew, Wayne having caught the fishmonger in town and remembering that Aileen, being from Savannah, liked oysters. There was a turkey, too, not a large bird, but more than the three of them could eat in a week. "This is a special dinner," Aileen announced, "our last Christmas in this house for a while, maybe forever." Wayne offered a grace. Not a religious man, he nonetheless thanked God for his family, for their safety, and for the bright future ahead of them. He nearly came to tears. At the end of the meal, they ate the strange woman's pound cake. It was delicious.

One morning in late January, Lonnie woke to find the landscape glazed with ice. Overnight, frozen rain coated and bowed tree branches. The road in front of the house looked like a frozen river, and his heart leapt, for he knew there would be no school that day. He dressed in the cold room and went down to the kitchen, warmed by the stove, where Aileen was already cooking.

"Good morning, Mr. Sleepyhead."

"Morning."

Aileen gave him a hug. "Busses won't run today. I don't see much of anything running."

"Where's Papa?"

"He went out early with the gun. I told him there ain't no critters out in this weather. But he went anyway, probably just as much for the walk as anything."

Lonnie was disappointed that his father hadn't taken him. He ate his breakfast and went outside to do his chores. The world was transformed to platinum and crystalline grotesquery. He pushed against the porch screen and a pane of ice shattered and tinkled to the ground. The wood shed seemed more a cave, with stalactites hanging over the neatly stacked cords of wood. When he swung open well house's doors, ice cracked, then exploded in a shower, and as the bucket chain rattled through the pulley, chunks of ice dislodged and splashed into the echoing well. By lunchtime, Wayne had not returned and Aileen wondered aloud about his whereabouts. Perhaps he had met with Bertrand and they had become caught up in war talk. He hadn't had breakfast, she reasoned, so he would soon come home for lunch.

The afternoon wore on, and Wayne did not return. Aileen went several times to the porch, yelling toward the woods for him. Then she debated with herself as whether or not to send Lonnie to find him. "Go just to the edge of the woods," she instructed, "and call him." Then she mumbled, "No need you traipsing in the woods in this weather. Hunters, too."

Lonnie had been at the woods' edge many times, but today, in the muted light of freezing rain, the trees looked foreboding. To cross from the bright, ice-covered field with its tortured shapes into the dark woods with its ice canopy was to cross a spectral frontier. He called for his father, listening as his voice echoed down the creek valley. His mother had told him to call and return, but he braved a few steps into the woods. Above him the branches, bent with ice, made a metallic net, a vision that frightened and thrilled him. He imagined for a moment that he might be Captain Marvel Junior.

His father would be Captain Marvel, and even though Mary Marvel was Captain Marvel's sister, not his wife, his mother would have to be Mary. The path into the woods leveled for a while, then sloped down toward the creek, and then up again, running on the hillside parallel to the creek. He decided that he would go to just where the hill sloped, and as he did so, he saw where his father's boots must have cracked the frozen leaf litter, and he followed on. At places the path was slippery and he slipped several times, never falling, but intensifying his effort to tread the slippery ground. Soon he was on the level path again, under a grove of big-leaf pines that stood between the deciduous trees and one of Venable's fields. He saw his father's tracks again and followed. Now he thought how surprised his father might be to have him appear along beside him. Behind him there was a loud yawning and then a crash like cymbals, as a branch broke and fell through the canopy. The forest seemed alive, sentient—despite the absence of the squirrels and birds, the trees and undergrowth, though bare, seemed quickened, shimmering like quicksilver.

The path wound back into the deciduous woods. Again he climbed through the ravine above the creek until he came to the creek's end, now an old spring, so long unused it had once more transformed into a marshy place in the nook of the hills. The path snaked around it, and he continued, looking for signs of his father. Soon he came to the foot of Christmas Hill, where there was said to be the haunted homestead. Here the skeletal remains of a blackberry bramble resembled a tangle of new fence wire. He thought better of going further, remembering that his mother had said only to go to the woods' edge. Perhaps now his father had returned anyway, he thought, and might be looking for him. He went back down the path, and as he reached the last hill before home he heard the car horn blowing in long urgent blares. He rushed along, slipping and catching himself. His bare hands went deep into the frozen hummus and he got up with his hands blackened and burning with cold. The horn continued to blow. He moved faster. Out of the woods, he saw his mother standing by the car, the driver's door open. His heart stopped. She ordered him into the car and made several agitated attempts to start the car before it cranked. Lonnie's asked her where they were going and what was the matter. She said nothing. She found the reverse gear and released the clutch, sending the car spinning on the ice, then lurching until she had backed it into the road.

"Where are we going?" Lonnie screamed. He felt himself losing his breath and tears coming.

"To town," Aileen screamed back at him. "Now let me drive."

She found the first drive gear, and again spinning on the ice, the car jerked forward. They went along slowly, the engine revving for the second gear, and with some effort she placed the gear and the car jerked forward again. She never gained enough speed to shift to third. She steered through the middle of the road, following in tracks already laid.

Again, Lonnie questioned her, and again she admonished him just to let her drive. On the level, straight part of the road, she steered well, but turning the curves she seized the wheel and grimaced, while the car fishtailed. She managed going up the shallow grades, but coming down she simultaneously pushed the brake and the accelerator causing the car's engine to sputter and the wheels to spin and whine. Slowly, erratically, they made their way along the frozen road past the ice-laden fields and forests. Aileen turned onto the main road without braking, causing the car to slide and then straighten. The main road, to Lonnie's relief, had less ice. Here she accelerated and shifted into the third gear with ease, but now the car seemed to be going too fast, the boy thought. He gripped the arm rest. The muscles in his mother's jaw formed hard knots.

"Is there something the matter with Daddy?"

Aileen did not answer, seemingly absorbed with steering. They were ascending a rise, and Lonnie noted that the speedometer read thirty-five miles. He recognized where they were, though the thicket seemed disguised by the ice. At the top of the hill would be a long, steep slope toward the river and the old iron bridge. He warned his mother, but she did not seem to hear. "We are at the river," he said again. Even on dry days, cars seem to swoop down the hill with too much speed. At fast speeds, aiming for the bridge was a bit too much like aiming for the eye of a needle. From the crest, he saw the narrow bridge and the river, slate and frothy at the riffles, thirty feet below it. Aileen saw it too, and began to apply the brakes, but the car fishtailed, and she slammed the brakes causing them to lock and the car to slide. Aileen raised her hips from the seat and stood on the brake, but the car kept sliding, first head on, then sideways, and then head on again. She twisted the steering wheel wildly and Lonnie braced himself against the dash. The car continued to slide, picking up speed as it slid, crookedly, now, toward one of the diagonal beams of the truss. It might hit the beam on Lonnie's side, and teeter over the bank into the river. Just as Lonnie imagined the worst, the car grounded itself into the ditch and stopped with a jerk that sent him tumbling onto the dashboard and against the windshield.

Neither he nor his mother said anything for a moment, and then, she, still gripping the steering wheel asked if he were all right. He pushed himself down from the dashboard and said he was fine, though he felt as if someone had hit him hard in the front of the shoulder. "Jesus, sweet *Jesus*," his mother screamed. "Why have you forsaken me?" Then she laid her head against the steering wheel and began to sob. Though he tried, Lonnie could not console her.

Nearly an hour passed before they heard a jangling over the sound of an engine downshifting. It was an old Chevy pickup with chains on the tires. The truck stopped beside the car and an elderly colored man got out. He asked if they were all right and waited to hear what they wanted him to do. Aileen said they needed to go to Bethany Clinic. Lonnie's stomach clenched. He knew then that something bad had happened to his father. Maybe shot.

On the way, the old man handling his truck skillfully on the icy hill, Aileen explained rapidly that Sheriff Cook had come by her house to tell her that her husband had had an accident and had been taken to the clinic. The Sheriff had other business and could not give her a ride into town, so she had tried to drive herself. The man nodded and said he was sorry to hear about her husband. His hair was gray with a yellow tint and a matted ring where his cap fit. He talked about the weather and about having been prepared for it, with chains for his tires, and bricks to weigh down the back of the truck. No other word about Wayne was mentioned until they got to the clinic. But Lonnie's mind was busy with what might have happened. He reasoned that they wouldn't be rushing to the clinic if his father were dead.

Aileen tried to pay the colored man. He would not accept her money and he wished her good luck.

SIX

The boy enjoyed the woods, just as his father had, and now that his father was dead, the woods in spring reminded him of the walks he had taken with the big man. He loved the dogwoods, particularly, to see them from the roads or to stand on a ridge and look through the dark trunks and fissured branches and witness the white flowers. They looked like angels.

Wayne had taught him the names of trees and shrubs and told him stories about their uses. How sassafras made a tea that cured a stomachache, and how white pine sap cured a bad cough. The dogwood, too, was more than just something to look at. Its bark, made into a tea, could cure a fever, and a peeled twig made a good toothbrush. Wayne knew these things, he said, because he had Indian blood—the blood of the Creeks ran in his veins, bringing with it the potent knowledge of plants and animals and the love for the land. They were white men, Wayne had insisted, but beneath their white skins pulsed the pure blood of America. So the two of them were more than father and son, they were blood brothers, brothers of the spirit. On some days, Lonnie imagined that the spirits of his blood brother, Wayne, and his faithful mutt, Toby, accompanied him through the woods; when a bush seemed to quiver and no wind blew, or when he discovered a new dogwood, nearly fully mature, where he hadn't noticed one before—when these miracles happened—he told himself they were his father's gifts. To his mind, Wayne was the miraculous facilitator even of Bertrand coming weekly to their place to help his mother, coming to talk with him and to tell him stories. Lonnie loved the wild azaleas, too, with their thin, sprawling branches and blossoms the color of pigs' nipples—and the ghost gray trunks of white oaks with their soft, pink and green leaves. The leaves held the surprising color of the sea foam the time he had seen it near Savannah when they had driven to Aunty's funeral. Spring in Georgia was a miracle. Perhaps a miracle wherever it occurred, but since he had only seen Georgia and, for that matter, Talmaedge County, he only knew spring in his own backyard. Only here could the dead rise.

Bertrand came often that spring, usually walking the path, and by the time Lonnie or his mother saw him, it was as though he materialized, a spirit, by the woodpile or by the porch door with one of his wife's cakes in hand, asking Aileen what chores he might help her with. Though Lonnie and Aileen managed with much of the daily work such as feeding the animals, Bertrand was helpful with the harder tasks: splitting logs for firewood, plowing and disking the garden, repairing the pig pens and chicken coop. At first Aileen tried to pay him, but he refused, saying that Wayne had been his friend and a fellow soldier. It was his Christian duty.

On one such occasion Aileen had jangled a palm full of coins out of the screen door right in front of his nose. "Now, I can't have you working here for nothing. People will say I am taking advantage of you, Bertrand. Please, I never want them to say a thing like that." Bertrand considered, gestured as if to accept the coins—but when she jangled them again, he shook his head.

"Whyn't you give little Lonnie a treat. Call it my treat, if you will. Like I said, I don't mind the little chores at all. You know, Mrs. Henson, Wayne was a good man, a unique man, and I feel I owe him just this much."

"He *was* good." Aileen withdrew inside the screen door, fisting the coins and shoving her hand into her apron pocket. "I appreciate it. I do." She sniffed and withdrew into the house.

Lonnie studied the colored man for a minute. Compared to his father, Bertrand was short and round. He had thick shoulders, a thick waist, and squat legs, yet he exuded a heroic quality, a confidence not unlike the quality Lonnie ascribed to Captain Marvel and Superman. Bertrand had traveled to places beyond Talmaedge County, places like Atlanta and London. He had even been to Africa, in the war, but all he would say of it was that he hadn't seen any jungles where he had been. It had amazed Lonnie that there were places in Africa without jungle, but Bertrand had patiently described the Sahara desert, the great savannahs, the big cities. When schoolboys challenged Lonnie about it, Bertrand had given him a picture postcard with a map of Africa, and showed him where the deserts and jungles were. He had taken the card to school, and the boys had taken it from him, called him a nigger-lover, and torn it up. They said his father had been a nigger-lover too, and crazy enough to blow off his own head.

Lonnie walked with Bertrand across the yard to the edge of the woods. In spite of his squat body, the man had a graceful gait and the boy found it hard to keep up. "Mightn't you go on back to your momma?" Bertrand said, as he crossed from the yard into the woods.

Lonnie's stomach tightened, but he followed on. Bertrand stopped, faced him, and waited.

"I got a question to ask you."

Bertrand smiled and nodded.

"Them boys I told you about? Ronnie Davis and all. They ..." Suddenly the boy's throat closed and he hated himself for crying. "They said Daddy killed himself." Saying the words brought on a rush of tears and stomach cramp. The man sighed heavily and put his hand on the boy's shoulder. The thick hands steadied him, held him upright, and suddenly the boy couldn't resist embracing the man and burying his wet face against Bertrand's shirt. "Why do they say that?" He sobbed. He hadn't even cried like this at the clinic, when they arrived to find his father gone.

The man patted his back and stroked the back of his head. "You just cry, if you need to. But God knows your daddy slipped. Everybody knows your daddy slipped."

He slipped, of course, the boy thought. That was what Sheriff Cook had said, and what Doctor Talmaedge had said, too. But the boys, with their faces in ugly sneers, said he had blown off this head. He had turned funny. He was shell shocked. He was a nutcase from the war.

"No," the colored man was saying, "Your daddy was a good man. A kind man. A man with his eyes on the future. That's who your daddy was. He was a great man."

On his next visit, Bertrand asked Aileen if his cousin, Beah Thompson, could buy the baby crib. She could pay five dollars for it and having it would be a big help to her. The cousin was the daughter of the man who had given them a ride when they wrecked the car. Aileen said that the crib had cost fifteen dollars, and that she would think about it. Later she told Lonnie that they needed the money. She had already sold the Ford to Wayne's cousin. The car had sat on the side of the road, just where she had wrecked it, for two weeks, when the cousin offered her fifty dollars for it. "Why I let him jew me down, I don't know," she complained. She was considering selling a couple of acres of land, but worried that they only had four and would get so little for it, might as well keep it. Or maybe, she speculated, they should sell everything, the house included, and move to Atlanta. At least there she could find work. But she couldn't part with the crib. She wasn't ready for that.

The next day, Maribelle Crookshank stopped by. Rather than come in, she stood by the front stoop chatting for about ten minutes. She, too, asked that Aileen sell the crib to Beah. Beah cooked at her restaurant and made the best fried chicken in the world, Maribelle said. "She's a good girl, but has gotten herself in trouble with a lowlife scoundrel named Jimmy Lee." She clucked her tongue and looked off into the distance when she said the name. "But what can we do? We try to help them. Don't we, Aileen? As God is my witness, we do try."

Neither Beah nor Aileen said much when Beah and Jimmy Lee came for the crib. Aileen told Lonnie to lead Jimmy Lee around through the kitchen door and to the back bedroom. She stood on the front stoop, side by side with Beah, both women looking in the distance, commenting on the obvious, the insignificant.

Two things impressed the boy: It was the first time he had ever seen a pregnant woman, other than his mother, up close. Beah's belly wasn't very big, he thought, but she had a nice shape, as though a moon was waxing in her. At that moment, he thought it would be fun to be a doctor just to see how that baby would get out.

It was also the first time he saw Jimmy Lee, not that it made much difference at the time. He was just another yellow colored man—but, the boy liked him. Jimmy Lee had a joking way about him. Said he would crawl up in the crib and have a nap. Asked Lonnie if it was his baby crib. And when Lonnie said it had been his baby sister's and that she was dead, the yellow man was quiet a second, and then turned to him with moist gray eyes, and said, "That's a very sad story. Poor little baby girl." Jimmy Lee said it in such a way that the boy couldn't think of him just as a strange, gray-eyed colored man, but as someone who might be a friend.

"What your name?"

"Jimmy Lee Lee. Don't say it too fast because it sound funny. I wish I had a good soundin' name."

51

"Jimmy, Okay. Like Jimmy Olsen?"

"Who Jimmy Olsen? He play baseball?"

"Ball? No. He's Superman's friend."

"Oh, he a strong man."

"No, he's weak. Superman always have to rescue him." The boy was walking ahead, holding the doors. When they got outside, Jimmy Lee heaved the crib up onto his shoulder. It rattled and the boy thought the springs might drop out of it, but Jimmy Lee balanced it and carried it over to the truck, the same truck the boy and his mother had ridden in after the car wreck.

"Say Superman got a weak friend? What Superman want with a weak friend?"

The boy shrugged.

Having placed the crib in the truck bed, Jimmy Lee seemed to think a minute, then closed the bed gate. "Maybe that's what makes him strong. Having a weak friend he can save."

"He's strong because he's from another planet."

Jimmy Lee winked. "I reckon that's right." The wink and the little smile that followed it put a crinkle at the corner of his eye. The boy glimpsed the eye which was deep enough for him to believe that Jimmy Lee was from another planet.

After the truck pulled away, Aileen unfolded and examined the crisp five-dollar bill that Beah had paid her with. "Nice gal," she said, slowly turning to go into the house. "A little proud, that's all."

The next Saturday, Bertrand worked in the garden, forming soil into little pyramids with a shovel. The boy grabbed a paper sack with the seed and poked holes in the hills and pushed in the seeds—"two to a side," Bertrand told the boy. The garden soil had a clean damp smell and nothing was more fun, the boy thought, than to run his hands through the soft, clay clods, to pluck the worms and grubs to save for a fishing trip.

"Bertrand, I met a friend of yours," the boy said, searchingly.

"Who would that be?"

"Jimmy Lee Lee."

"What makes you think he is a friend of mine?"

"He colored, ain't he? Ain't you a friend to the colored man?"

"That is a manner of speaking."

"He's nice, ain't he?"

"Jimmy Lee is all right. A little foolish is all."

Bertrand was quiet for a long time and then the boy realized that Bertrand didn't like Jimmy Lee. Why would one colored man not like another? The boy stood and pictured Jimmy Lee, grinning and glowing golden in the evening sun on the day he had come for the crib. He wanted Jimmy Lee to be his friend, too, and he didn't know if he could be friends with Jimmy Lee if Bertrand didn't like him.

They had planted a dozen hills of squash, Bertrand moving quickly and the boy, deep in thought, following. Aileen brought a pitcher of water and Bertrand's glass, as she called it, the one she kept separate to serve him. Unusual for her, she lingered at the edge of the garden while the boy carried water from her to Bertrand. While Bertrand drank, Aileen asked where she could find tomato slips. Tomatoes were missing from her garden, and she couldn't find any volunteers on the property. Bertrand informed her that it was probably too late to buy the slips in the store, and any volunteers might be too big to transplant. After Bertrand had drunk and thanked her, and she had gotten the glass back, she said, "Miss Crookshank sent that Thompson girl by here to get my crib. Now, how is she kin to you?"

Bertrand explained the family connection, wiping his brow and leaning with one foot on the heel of the shovel.

"She put me in mind of you, a little."

Bertrand nodded. "All of us favor."

"It's good I could give that crib to her—look like she getting right along."

"I expect so." Bertrand lifted the shovel, indicating he was ready to begin work again, but Aileen continued.

"I reckon it was her husband that come with her, a light-skin' fellow?"

Bertrand shoved the shovel in the ground. "No ma'am. I know whom you talkin' about. But he ain't no more her husband than a man in the moon."

Aileen considered. "Then, they ain't married."

"No ma'am, *they* ain't married. But *he's* married. Now I ain't one to talk about folks, Mrs. Henson, and it ain't nothing we in the family are proud of, but that's just the way it is."

"Truth always best."

"Yeah, truth always best."

"She look like such a nice girl."

"Well, I ain't saying she ain't a nice girl—"

"Proud, though."

Bertrand straightened suddenly and then slowly pulled the shovel out of the soil. The boy looked at him, then his mother, and then back at Bertrand.

"I reckon she ain't no prouder than the next one."

Aileen flicked the remaining water out of the pitcher. It seemed to Lonnie that she hadn't paid attention to Bertrand's remark. She asked Lonnie to come to the house. On the way, she seemed distracted, her lips trembling. "Now, Aileen," she chided herself loud enough for the boy to hear, "it just a little, innocent baby. Baby can't help how it got here." Before she got through the door of the screened porch, she wobbled and was short of breath. She cried and sat down on the cinderblock steps. "That was Eliza's crib. Wayne bought it for me. I had no right to sell it for a measly five dollars." She looked at the boy. "It's like stomping on my baby's grave. I don't care that that colored baby is a bastard. That's *Eliza's* crib."

The boy put his hand on his mother's shoulder. "It's all right, Momma. That's fixin' to be a good little baby and Eliza won't mind it. Not a'tall." He tried to imagine how the baby might look, but couldn't.

"Goddamn Maribelle Crookshank. Always looking out for her niggers. Goddamn that bitch." It was a minute before she regained her composure. Then she took the boy by the shoulders. "Now, listen to me. Listen good, hear? You stay away from *him*. Don't go 'round him unless I'm out there with you. Understand me?"

"Him? Bertrand? Why?"

"Mind me. That' all."

"Why?"

She breathed deeply and wrung her hands.

"Bertrand and me are friends."

"You keep *that* to yourself," she whispered sharply and looked around. "*Come in.*"

Inside and calmer, she asked the boy to sit in the parlor with her. Never before had she asked him into the parlor, not even when his father had died. She asked if his pants were clean, and invited him to sit on the big chair, the one his father preferred. She sat on the sofa, perpendicular to him. Between them were a bible, a picture of Wayne in his army uniform and a baby's bonnet and booties folded and put in a fancy flat box just under the bible.

"Son, I want you to hear this from me first. Bertrand is a nice man, now. He intends nice. He is nicer than most of them. And I know your daddy liked him. But there is a way that things are done. Well . . . there's a natural way about things. The Bible tells about it. We don't hold nothing against colored. Colored, in their way, are just as good as white." She thought a moment, seeming to the boy to be reexamining her statement. "Lord knows, there's some good colored people. Bertrand's good. But, that doesn't mean we're supposed to mix too much. Of course, now, you got to have some contact. You can't help that. But . . . well, what I am trying to say is—" She shifted toward him. "—to keep a distance between you and Bertrand. Bertrand means well, and I appreciate him. But everybody around here don't see it that way."

The boy couldn't form whole thoughts for a minute. He watched his mother stand up and walk to the window and look out onto the front stoop.

"Momma, I ain't got no friends out here—" the boy started to say. He wanted to argue logically.

"You got friends at school."

"School's out."

"You'll find a friend. Even if you have to go to town. And Bertrand too old to be your friend anyway. He's a grown man."

"But since Daddy—"

"He *ain't* your daddy. No. He ain't your daddy," she said, turning in a sharp movement toward him. "Don't shame your daddy by saying a thing like that."

The boy's face was hot. He hadn't meant that Bertrand was his father. He knew that Bertrand was no substitute.

The woman softened. "Honey. I know it's hard, but life is hard. We're just barely making it and we don't need no trouble. Besides, Bertrand, he's proud."

"Proud? What do you mean, 'proud'?"

"Proud. *Proud.* I mean he's too smart for his own good. He don't hide it. Don't act humble. Bible says you should act humble. But it ain't so much The Bible. Around here, colored are supposed to be humble and he ain't."

"So?"

"So I don't want nobody to see you with him."

"Who fixin' to see us here?"

"People see things. People *watch.* People talk."

55

"Who watching?"

"I don't know—*people*."

"Why would somebody watch Bertrand for helping us?"

"They just do. That's all. Because he's colored. And he's too *proud*. A proud colored man gets watched."

The boy loved his mother. He knew that she bore many grievances, sometimes walking around with her right arm against her chest as if she were cradling them. It was not just Eliza and Wayne, but also the old woman for whom his mother's grief was akin to guilt. Aunty was old, yes, and crippled, yes. The boy knew also that his mother was relieved to see her pass. But without a husband, the house was a burden. An outsider, she had always kept to herself, and now the only one to offer help was a colored man, a colored man she deemed "too proud."

The boy was not satisfied with how his mother explained it and wanted to know what it meant to be "too proud." He imagined that it meant to be "kingly," to order people around, but he had never seen such behaviors in Bertrand. That night he wondered more about it and decided that he would spy on Bertrand. The decision delighted him. It would be an adventure, for he would find out all about Bertrand: What he did at home, the things he liked to eat, what his strange wife was like. In spite of his mother's admonishment, the next Sunday afternoon, while his mother napped, the boy set out to spy on Bertrand. He knew that Bertrand would be at church, and he knew the church sat on a bank, built up from the marshland of Geechee Creek, a large tributary of the river. He went through the woods to the river, and when he got there, he followed one of the many easy paths along the banks until he reached the creek. Following the creek was difficult, as the main path was on the side opposite him, but soon he came to a shallows and crossed. Then he followed the path, which went away from the forest and its floor of mayapple and wild ginger to run beside a marsh of cattail, cardinal flower, and jewelweed. He was careful not to slip into the mud, reticulated with rivulets and pools of quicksand. Before he emerged from the marsh, he heard music from River of Joy Church.

The church was typical of country churches, colored or white. It was a small, clapboard structure that could have been any farm building except for its vestibule and painted glass windows. Several cars were parked along the road in front of the church and in the churchyard were two wagons and two mules tied along a rail not far away. The music was pounding and rhythmic—piano—and what seemed at first like drums to the boy, but he soon discerned it as stomping and synchronized clapping. It was not like church music he was used to the few times he had gone with his father to the Methodist church. But colored people, he reminded himself, were mostly Baptists, and Baptists were louder, more unruly than the Methodists.

As he approached the side of the church, he saw through the opened windows people sitting inside, singing and fanning. A child, no older than five, looked out at him, and turned back, to report to an adult, Lonnie assumed. But he kept walking, and hoped that it would appear that he were merely passing by. At the front of the church, he saw that the vestibule doors were ajar, but there he saw the shadow of a man, an usher he assumed, so he kept around the church. But when he got to the next corner, he flattened himself against the side of the building. He could feel the building vibrating with the rhythm of the clapping and singing. It made his heart thump. A man's graveled voice was singing in a quick, heavy melody, "I been beated," and the people answered in rhythm, "Beated."

"Mistreated," the singer growled.

"Mistreated."

"Sho' nough, hmmmm, cheated."

"Cheated."

"Somebody always tryin' to put me down, but nobody going to keep me from my crown."

The singing continued as the boy slipped along the side of the church, hoping not to be seen from the windows by sliding under them. As he got near the back of the building, he saw an open door with steps leading down from it. He slid under the steps, and poked his head up to the level of the threshold of the door. From there he could see the inside of the church. In front of the altar stood Bertrand. He had been the one who was singing. Then there was a hum and a growl and shout from the rostrum as the preacher came forward and slapped the podium with his hand. Bertrand answered the slap with a stomp of his foot. The preacher slapped again, and Bertrand stomped with the other foot. There was clapping and shouting of "Hallelujah" and "Praise Be to God" from the congregation.

"*I don't know,*" the preacher sang out. "*I don't know.*"

Bertrand spun around in a circle, stomping the wooden floor so hard that dust sprang up around his feet. He wore oxfords, nicely polished, but now speckled with the dust. He had discarded his jacket, but still wore a tie tightly at the collar of his white shirt. The shirt was becoming stained with rings of sweat under the arms pits and around the collar.

"I don't know," the preacher said again.

Other people, men and women, old and young, joined Bertrand in the dance, but the boy only looked at Bertrand. At first it seemed a spectacle, something that embarrassed him. He thought that Bertrand would be embarrassed for him to know it. *Dancing in church—that's what niggers do. That's the way niggers pervert the worship of the Lord, by dancing around like a bunch of monkeys.* But as the boy watched, as the rhythm moved through the floorboards, through the clapboard, he began to feel an impulse to move with it. It was not quite the beat of his heart, not quite the pulse of his breath, but a rhythm that made his heart skip a beat and his breath catch.

Bertrand's face was swollen in the heat and sweaty, eyes closed and mouth set in the slightest, most pacific smile the boy had ever seen. He had seen pictures of Jesus in his mother's bible, and Jesus was supposed to have the holiest of all faces, but never had he seen a face that called to him with its openness, its serenity. Suddenly he saw that it was not just a face, but many faces. First it was his father's face—two men couldn't have looked more different, and yet, there was Wayne's face inside of Bertrand's. Then there was his mother's face, and the old woman's face. There were many familiar faces, people from around Talmaedge, colored and white, and then stranger faces—lean, hungry faces—faces with pained eyes, though Bertrand's eyes remained closed, and faces with laughing mouths, though Bertrand's mouth remained set in the smile. Then the face became the shapes of things he knew and loved from the forest—the face of the dogwood tree, the pignut hickory, the tulip poplar; the face of the yellow jacket, the damsel fly, the daddy long legs; the face the white-tailed deer, the spotted skunk, the woodland vole; the face of the whippoorwill, the barn owl, the turkey vulture.

"I don't know. I don't know."

Lonnie wanted to dance with Bertrand for he thought that Bertrand was no longer dancing on Earth, but that his soul had moved some place beyond, some place deep in the woods. He felt himself kick at the dirt beneath the steps, and he felt shivers run up through his body. He crawled from under of the stairs, still feeling the vibration from the church, only now it came through the ground. He found himself making a little stomp on the ground.

"I don't know. I don't know."

He stopped himself. This was wrong, he told himself. It was some-thing colored people did and white people didn't. He stomped again on the ground, but this time, he turned looking for a way to run. Bertrand was too proud, his mother had said. She had said to stay away. Now the boy felt like crying. His mother had said it was the way of nature. The Bible said so.

"I don't know what you come here for; I come to praise the Lord," the preacher said. "For only through the Lord can there be redemption. Only through death in this old life, and rebirth into a new life can you be saved. You must be born again through Jesus Christ, but to be born again, you must first die!" A rousing shout came from the congregation and once again, Lonnie moved close to the door and looked in. At first he didn't see Bertrand, and then he realized that Bertrand was nearly standing on top of him. He was no longer dancing, but swaying and rocking in place and rais-ing on toes. His body radiated heat and he smelled of hot cologne. Sweat dripped onto the dusty floor next to his feet.

"Too many people want to go to heaven," the preacher said, his voice settling into a speaking rhythm, "but they don't want to die. But it can't be that way."

"Hallelujah!" Bertrand shouted and clapped so loudly it startled Lonnie.

"If you want the reward," the preacher continued. "You got to pay the price."

"Hallelujah!"

"You can't go on doing the things of this world and say you saved. No."

"Hallelujah!" Bertrand's rocking increased in frequency.

"For there is a great day a'comin'!"

"Praise be to God!"

"A great day in the morning! A great day in the night! A great reck-oning day where all accounts will be settled with the only bill collector that matters—and if your balance isn't paid in full, then your immortal soul—said God Almighty—will be lost in the depths of eternal hell—and that is the one death from which there can be no rebirth! There is no redemption from hell!"

First Bertrand and then the entire congregation exploded into a fury of shouting, singing, and dancing. It was so sudden that Lonnie was star-tled once again and he tried to back away from the door. Then, he caught glimpse of a woman, who in all the crowded frenzy, sat quiet and straight in her flowered dress. She seemed to him to be in a different place than all the others, in a place that was as peaceful as sitting by the quiet waters of a lake. She turned and he saw that she saw him. She was not peaceful, but cut him with such a look of hatred that he felt a pain shoot through him.

"I don't know," the preacher shouted above the clapping and foot stomping.

The boy saw the way to the marsh and ran.

SEVEN

He said nothing of the visit to the church to Aileen, not only because she would have disapproved, but also because he felt she could not explain to him what it was he had seen. From the distance it was comedic, a kind of coon show like Amos and Andy from the radio, but up close it was something mysterious, and he had nothing to compare it to except vague memories of even vaguer dreams. Wonderful things happened in the dreams—travel to distant places, heroic adventures—things that excited him long after waking, but that he could not clearly recall. He wanted to go again and dance with Bertrand.

Later in the week, Maribelle Crookshank visited his mother again. This time she came into the house, sitting on the sofa as she had done when she first visited his father. She seemed nervous, fidgety as she positioned and repositioned herself on the sofa. "I've got something you should hear," she announced after the initial pleasantries. "But it is grown ups' business." She cast her eyes at Lonnie, standing in the doorway, and his mother asked him to go and finish his chores. He was slow to move, but went to the back of the house. He could hear Crookshank's nasally whine, but could not distinguish her words, and when she was gone, he returned to see what the matter was.

Aileen's face did not relay Crookshank's excitement, and when the boy asked, she said nothing was the matter. She seemed contemplative, so much so that she sat at the table in the common room and rested her face in her hands. "It's really nothing that needs to concern us." She reached out and took his hand. "Just you mind me and keep your distance from that Bertrand. That's all."

"Did something happen to Bertrand?"

"Oh, no. Far as I know he's not in it. But that light-skinned one, the one that took the crib—"

"Jimmy Lee?"

"Yes. He attacked Mr. Venable."

"He killed him?" The boy imagined the tall angular man who had stood in the road in front of the house with his father's shotgun.

"That devil? He's too wicked to be killed. No. Stabbed him, according to Maribelle Crookshank, but you can't believe a thing that gossip says. She's about the most irksome woman I know. And from a distance, I thought I would like her."

"He stabbed him?"

Aileen chuckled. "According to that old hen, he stabbed him in the buttocks. And that about suits him right. It's nothing for us to worry about, and Mrs. Crookshank just told me because of the crib, I reckon. Anyhow, let it be a lesson to us all, just to keep our distance."

The next day was Friday, and the boy expected Bertrand on Saturday. He decided to get ahead on the garden work. They were already late putting in the tomatoes, and he guessed that they just might not have any, since Bertrand hadn't been able to find any slips. It was too late to grow them from seed and his mother said she didn't have any money to buy seeds anyway. He thought he'd go over to the Feed and Seed by himself and ask Venable for some on credit. It was a long walk, close to eight miles, and he knew that his mother wouldn't allow them to be indebted to Venable. Then, he remembered that the summer before, Venable had had a tomato patch at the edge of a cornfield just up from the river. He thought that there would probably be a few volunteers growing around if he could find them. The place was not far—though farther than his mother would let him go—and he knew the path. It was the path that Wayne had taken many times when he worked for Venable, leading the mule with the boy astride.

The woods were becoming thick; the weather had turned hot, and the leaves had filled in the trees and undergrowth, but were still clean and bright. The path was plain. The first part of the path followed the nameless little creek to a marshy spot, where cardinal flowers and Joe-pye weed were growing, and cut up to the top of the ridge. On the ridge, the path was a little harder to follow, but he knew the way because it would take him toward the cut-off to Christmas Hill where the blackberries were. From there, the way to Venable's was in the opposite direction. He approached the field, not thinking about too much, just watching the way the woods looked, and smelling everything—the rich dampness of decaying leaves. It smelled better than any kind of tobacco or tea or coffee. Then he heard a little scream, and he froze in his tracks like a deer. He had the same feeling of danger as when he had dreamed about his dead sister. In the dreams he could never see her face, only the sprite form of a little girl.

He stepped off the path. The leaves crackled under his feet like cymbals. He tiptoed, pushing the leaves out of the way with his toes so that he touched only the soft, spongy leaf-mold. The scream came again, a high-pitched little yelp, he would have thought it was a dog, but it was a girl—and then a heavy voice that was a man. The voices sounded like they were coming from right over the ridge, and he had a feeling he was close. Suddenly, he moved aside a bush and he was right on top of them.

That the man and the girl were wrestling was his first thought, but he had never seen a man and a girl wrestle. She was down on all fours, her face was almost on the ground and the man was behind her, riding on her, with his pants below his buttocks and a ribbon of bandages untangling from his thighs. The boy knew they weren't wrestling, and even though he was innocent about all the configurations and complications of human lust, he figured they were fornicating. He had never before witnessed the act, but he had heard enough to know it when he saw it.

The man was Venable. But who the girl was would be a mystery to him for many years, and it would give him a little shock when he learned it was Jewel Mae Lee, Jimmy Lee's wife. By that time he would have lost any modicum of naïveté, but still the recognition would make him doubt that chance played a role in the tryst, or in his witnessing of it. It would occur to him that he existed in a realm of complete ignorance, an inferior level of human sophistication, one that was as malleable as tin to those who were his social betters. These betters, Venable being foremost, played games that dented and bent the pathetic lives of average people, and then left them to rust away.

All of this worry would come much later. At that moment, just the sight of the injured white ass humping the brown girl startled the boy so much that he took a step back and gave himself away.

Jewel Mae saw him first. She was faced away from him, but she turned her head back, her mouth opened and her eyes closed at first. Just at that time, the boy crunched the leaves, and she opened her eyes. She let out another little scream, not too different from the others, and Venable said, "Hold up, gal," and pulled her back into him. His voice was straining. "Hold up, gal." She was trying to pull away from him. And then, he saw the boy, too, and growled at him. Lonnie ran as fast as he could.

He had caught his breath by the time he got to the tomato patch, and then the excitement of the morning collapsed: The tomato patch had been newly plowed and planted with new slips. The boy couldn't find any volunteer slips. Venable probably had three or four hundred vines, which meant he was going to sell some to the cannery this year. The boy thought about how much Venable had, and how he and his mother had nothing—not even one tomato slip—and he was tempted to take a few of the plants. Venable wouldn't miss them. Even if he took a dozen, the boy thought, Venable wouldn't know they were missing and that would be plenty for him and his mother—enough to eat all summer, and to can, and to have green tomatoes for frying with eggs and making chow-chow.

But he had been told time after time, by his mother, by Wayne, by Bertrand, too, that a good man doesn't steal. Even if he's hungry, he doesn't steal. But to tell a hungry man not to steal, couldn't be right, the boy thought. That's what the rich folks who have plenty to eat would say to the poor man, but they didn't mind cheating and stealing from the poor. It didn't matter much whether the poor were colored or white, the rich stole from them if they wanted. Wayne had cropped a bit for Venable, and though Wayne had said little about it, the boy's mother had on many occasions called Venable a cheat. But they weren't supposed to mention that outside of the family, she said.

The blackberries may have been on Venable's property or they could have been on the lumber company's, the boy didn't know. Still, it wasn't stealing to pick wild fruit whether you were a human or a raccoon. So on the way back from getting no tomato slips, the boy took the cut-off up to Christmas Hill and looked to see if the blackberries were ripe. They were further along than he thought they would be. He stood looking at the great tangle of briars, taller than he, that ran down the slope of the hill. The breeze swayed the red tipped briars and cast sun and shadow about as if it were the surface of a lake. It was no wonder people said that Christmas Hill was haunted with the ghosts of Indians, pioneers, and slaves—restless, though they were, they all came here for the berries. Already most of the berries were plump and red, which is the way they turn just before they ripened, but many were already ripe, glistening black and beckoning. A blackberry goes through stages, the boy remembered in his father's voice, but he knew it too, from experience. First it's a pretty little, white bloom—looks like an apple blossom, except its growing on a briar. Then it becomes a little, hard, green berry. These are pretty rough to eat. Bitter as sin, and got a hair on them that scratches on your tongue. It seems forever for the next stage to come, but eventually they plump up and turn red and tart, and then before you can wink, they are purple and black and juicy and sweet. If you don't get them then, you risk letting them rot on the briar. You see one that looks so delicious, so black and fat, and when you try to pick it, it turns to mush between your fingers. If you were to taste it, it would taste like mud. It's going back to clay, Wayne had said, since the Bible says everything comes out of clay.

The boy figured that the next day he would come back with the pail and pick the first little crop of berries. Being the first, and being that the crop probably wasn't in heavy, he would probably just get a pint or two—enough for a small cobbler—or if he wished it, enough to eat with milk and sugar.

He was walking back down the path with the taste of berries in his mouth, not thinking about much and feeling pretty safe because he had sneaked by the place where the grownups had been humping, when suddenly there was Venable sitting beside the path with a mason jar full of what the boy thought was water.

Venable had seen the boy first and he spoke to him roughly. The boy jumped and froze.

"You see anything you like, boy?" Venable had a lean face with strong cheekbones and the kind of gaunt facial muscles that seemed to pull at the edge of his lips. His eyes fixed on the boy and the boy felt he wanted to crawl out of his skin. "I'm talking to you, you little spying bastard. You see anything you like this morning?"

"No, suh."

"No, you didn't." Venable drank from the jar and he cracked a smile. It was a funny, crooked smile that suggested that all the scare had been a joke and that he was a man who took nothing too seriously. "You must not have had any pussy before, then. Tell me," his eyes were nearly twinkling now, "have you ever seen a cock as pretty as mine?"

"No, suh."

"But you have seen plenty of cocks?"

The boy took a deep breath. "I reckon I have seen at least the one I got."

"You're trying to smart ass *me*, boy? Because you don't know what I would do to you. I would cut off your gonads and feed them to the crows." Venable was trying to look mean again, but he couldn't hold the face. "You know what gonads are, boy?"

"You would go to jail if you did."

Venable laughed. "Sit down here next to me. Come on. I'm just teasing you. I wouldn't hurt you anyway."

"You just said—"

"Haven't you ever been teased? Shit, boy, I've got kids your age."

"Yes, suh." The boy sat down across the path from Venable.

"Sit over here, a little closer."

"I feel close enough."

Venable held out the jar to the boy. "Care for a drink?"

"No, suh."

"Have you ever had a drink of water like this? It will make your pecker rise."

"No, suh. I had a drink of water before I left the house."

"What house did you leave? Whose boy are you anyway?"

"My daddy's dead."

"Who was your daddy?"

"Wayne Henson."

Venable grunted and looked down at his hands. Then he took a sip from the jar, offered it toward the boy again, and then took another sip. "He was a mighty fine man. I knew him all my life." Then his impishness returned. "Well, all of *his* life." He pinched the sweat from his narrow nose. "Wayne was almost too good. Never had too much fun. But then they say, the good die young. No offense, boy. But I am not planning on dying young. What about you? Are you going to live a long, happy life, or are you going to die young and sad like your daddy?"

It shocked the boy to hear the stranger call his daddy sad. "My daddy wasn't sad."

"I beg to differ. Your daddy was the saddest, poorest son of a bitch in this county. I'll tell you why. First, he was a good-looking man—not that

66

I take much stock in a man's looks—but he could have had just about any gal in this county including my own sister. But he let that one slip by. Of course, my momma would have killed them both, your daddy being white trash, but . . ." he sipped again, holding his finger in the air to hold the boy's attention, "but, the Hensons were never trash. Wayne was always good, well-spoken, and did what he was supposed to do. That's why he ended up with your momma and my sister with a rich Yankee up in Vermont—now, *that* just about killed Momma. But my philosophy is better a rich Yankee than a poor anything else."

"Yes, suh."

"Sister had a heavy crush on Wayne. I reckon I can see it. He was a tall, good-looking *hombre,* with that fair hair and—I guess you might call them—Aryan looks. That's a funny thing. He was the first one in Talmaedge to run off to fight the Germans. That broke Sister's heart—to see her old beau all decked up in a uniform, just as crisp as an autumn leaf, heading off to get his ass blown to shit by the Krauts."

"He didn't get killed by no Krauts."

"Any Krauts, son. Say 'any Krauts', not 'no Krauts.' 'No Krauts' is nigger talk."

"Bertrand don't talk that way."

"That's because Bertrand is a proper-talking nigger. Anyway, I didn't mean your daddy got killed in the war. I just meant that he *could* have been killed. Me, I got the farm exemption—being the only son and my daddy already dead from having been nagged to death by my momma. Besides, I was a little older than your daddy and a might bit smarter when it came to such foolishness as war. What's it to me if Germans take over Europe? That's over there, and it doesn't affect me one damn bit. They can take over Europe, England, China—even New York City—just as long as they keep their grubbing hands off Thousand Acres."

At the mention of Thousand Acres, the boy knew for sure he was talking to Vernon Venable, the man he had seen in the restaurant and who had killed Toby. It occurred to him that this realization should have awed him, but already he was beginning to feel the man not worthy of awe. "Bertrand said we had to fight for democracy."

"What the hell does that nigger know about democracy?"

"He said Hitler was a bad dictator and wanted to make slaves out of Americans—even the white."

67

"Shit, boy. Don't believe everything you hear from that blue-gummed nigger. Bertrand's problem is that he knows too much and doesn't know a damn thing. Let me tell you, a little knowledge is a dangerous thing."

"Bertrand says that, too."

"He does, does he? What the hell? Are you going to nigger school with him?"

"No, suh. He comes over and chops wood and stuff."

Venable sipped and let the jar rest on his lap and against his raised knee. "And what stuff?"

"Different stuff. Weeding and putting in squash and stuff for Momma."

Venable cocked his head and looked at the boy. He chuckled. "What else is he doing for your momma?"

The boy thought a second. "He plows, and he fixed the roof, sawed down a' old tree. Momma try to pay him, but he don't take no money. He say it's because of the war he and Daddy was in together."

"Were in together. Use correct agreement."

"Yes, suh." The boy fidgeted under Venable's stare, the eyes sparkling and a mischievous smile playing around the lips.

"Now, you say he doesn't take pay?"

"No, suh, he says—"

"What's he doing that he doesn't take any pay? He's uppity, but I don't suppose he thinks he's rich."

"He might be rich," Lonnie pondered. "He got a car."

"Car don't make you rich. Now, how many times did he go into the house?"

"Our house? He don't ever go into our house since Daddy died. He work on the outside."

"He don't take pay?"

"No, suh. Momma try to give it to him but he—"

"She comes out in the yard?" He rubbed his hands across his face.

"Yeah."

"When he is there, she comes into the yard?"

"Yeah." The boy felt uneasy. He remembered what his mother had admonished. "Of course, she do. It's her yard. She come out to tell him what to do. How's he going to know what to do if she don't come out and tell him?"

"That's all she's doing?"

"Yes, suh."

"She isn't talking to him?"

The boy's mind raced. "Of course she got to talk to tell him what to do, but she ain't . . . what you trying to say? She courting him? Momma ain't courting Bertrand. Momma *my* momma."

"You think your momma can't court? Your daddy's gone—"

Lonnie stood up. "Momma can court if she wants to court, but she don't want to court. She don't want to court Bertrand, that's for sure."

Venable's mouth formed a great, triangular smile. "How do you know she doesn't want some of Bertrand's big black dick?"

The boy fumbled for an answer, stood up, took a step away thinking he wouldn't answer, and then turned back, his fist balled and leaning toward Venable. "*If* she wanted it, she *would* get it. But she don't want it."

Venable chuckled and slapped his hand on his thigh. "Son, you know I'm just teasing you. I am a great tease, you know. I just wanted to get a jerk out of you. Now, don't be mad with me for my fun." He chuckled again and added, "Please."

"I got to be going on now, Mr. Venable. Momma will be worried about me."

"But forgive me first."

The boy considered. He had never talked to a grown-up this way, though he had been teased before. The man was asking forgiveness, and though he was angry still with him, he thought he ought to forgive. "OK. I forgive you. But I got to go on now."

"You go on then, but son—?"

"Suh?"

"Let's come to an agreement."

"Suh?"

"Don't say a peep about what you saw earlier. Do you understand me?"

"Yes, suh."

"I mean, don't tell your momma. And by God, I'll kill you if you tell Bertrand—have that nigger yapping my business around the whole county."

"I won't tell."

"Good. Because I don't *want* to tell what you told me."

The boy's stomach tightened. He couldn't remember what he had said. "What's that, suh?"

"About that nigger Bertrand and your momma."

"He just *helping* her."

69

"That's what you say." Venable sat up straight and took a sip. "You say he doesn't take money."

"No, suh."

"What does he take?"

"Suh?"

"Boy, nobody in this world does something for nothing." He softened. "We'll just keep it quiet. It's grown-up business and it can get a boy like you into a hell of a lot of trouble."

"But—?"

"But do you understand me?"

The boy's head swam. He didn't think he understood. "Yes, suh."

Venable pushed himself away from the tree like he was going to rise, but settled back. "Come here, son. Shake hands like a gentleman." He put out his hand and the boy took it.

"Goddamn, your hand is rough. What have you been doing with these hands, boy?" He held onto the boy's hand, feeling the palm with his fingertips. You've been stroking your log?"

"Yes, suh. I been helping Bertrand with the wood."

Venable let go of the boy's hand with mention of Bertrand's name. "You go on and be good. Help your momma. If your momma needs any help you can't give her, you let me know."

"Yes, suh." The boy walked a few steps and thought about the tomato slips, turned back. Venable had his hands in his lap. "Mr. Venable, we could use some tomato slips if you got a dozen or so you could spare."

"Tomato shoots?"

"Yes, suh."

"I'll see to you."

That was the last the boy heard of the tomato slips.

At first Lonnie thought the tall man who sat with his mother in the parlor was Vernon Venable. It startled him and he wondered if he were in trouble, then he thought that Venable had brought the tomato slips, answering his request in just a couple of hours. The man wore a khaki jacket; a brown fedora lay on the sofa beside him. He balanced a cup of coffee on his knee the way that Bertrand did. Aileen called him into the room to greet the man. It was Noland Jacks, the owner of Woodbine, the largest of the plantations in the county. He spoke politely to the man, and the man nodded at him.

Now, the boy could see clearly that the man having soft features and doe-like eyes was not Venable. His mouth was much fuller than Venable's, and his brown hair had only a bit of curl in it. His mother dismissed him. As he turned to go, his stomach knotted. *Why is a rich man in our house?* Jacks's reputation was that he bought poor people's property at unfair prices. If a farmer had had a low yield on tobacco or cotton, he might expect a visit from Jacks. His mother talked nervously, chattering away exactly the way she said she detested in Maribelle Crookshank. Lonnie thought there was even a bit of flirtation in her voice, and he turned back to look at her. She was not flirting, he saw; she was looking at her hands and he saw that they twisted one within the other. She asked him to go away again, but in a moment she called for him.

"My boy can tell you, Mr. Jacks," she was saying as Lonnie came back into the room. "Bertrand is a good, kind man and he does good work for me. Outdoor work. I have tried to pay him, but he doesn't take my money because my husband was a veteran."

"He's a patriotic man?"

"I reckon. Well, at least he is a helpful man. Look see, I am just a poor widow now. I am doing the best I can and I can use all the help I can get. Besides, my relations are in Savannah, and there is no one here to help me."

Jacks placed his cup on the table and sat quietly on the sofa. He seemed to have been in deep contemplation. Aileen kept talking, repeating herself, looking to Lonnie for confirmation that what she said was the truth: that she offered Bertrand money every time he worked for her, and he never took it. "Once he said that I should buy something for the boy, a soda or a Moon Pie, and Lord knows I would have liked to, but my money is tight, Mr. Jacks. Bertrand, he's a kind sort of man. A good Christian."

Jacks cleared his throat. "Pardon my interposition, Mrs. Henson. I do respect your situation, and I am satisfied that there has been no impropriety on your part. I am only concerned that Bertrand might have overreached, and especially with the incident concerning Mr. Venable—an attack by one of Bertrand's acquaintances—well, you can understand why I ask these difficult questions."

"I do. I do. And I regret to this minute that I sold my baby's crib to that nigger. Bertrand did ask me first, but it was Maribelle Crookshank that convinced me. Now if you want to talk about somebody that overreaches, you should talk to that Maribelle Crookshank."

Jacks chuckled and nodded knowingly. "But he, that is Bertrand, has never set foot in this house."

"Like I told you Mr. Jacks—I swear—only one time, in bad weather, my husband let him in. My boy and I went in the back room. They talked about that war, and Lord, we didn't want to hear any of it. I said to Wayne, that this just wasn't done. But Wayne—well, the war changed Wayne, Mr. Jacks. It's hard to explain, he was still my Wayne, but there was something changed about him, too." She cocked her head, started to explain, stopped. "I can't explain how he changed, just that he was not the same boy he was when he went off to that damn war. I think he saw too much death and so he wanted to be good to people, just as good as he could be—"

"And that included Bertrand—"

"If he had lived, he might have become a preacher."

They were silent for a minute.

"Sorry for your loss," Jacks said. "And as I said before, I apologize for the intrusion, but you do understand how important it is. We have a good life here—a good system between the races. Everybody is happy with it." Jacks smiled aloofly and picked his hat up from the sofa and put it on his knee.

"That's what I always told Wayne—"

"And what's your age, young man?"

The boy's throat had been closed up to that point. He had wanted to say something about Bertrand, but was afraid of saying the wrong thing. "Ten, suh."

"Ten." Jacks shook his head. "You are a large boy for ten." He turned to Aileen. "A handsome boy, ma'am. I'd always wanted a boy—children—but that's yet to come." With that, he rose from the sofa, pushing his tall frame from the seat. He tousled Lonnie's hair as he passed toward the front door.

"Bertrand," the boy blurted, "he's good."

"I'm sure he is."

Aileen opened the door for Jacks and he passed by her to the stoop.

"He help put in the garden."

Jacks nodded and said goodbye to Aileen.

"He split a cord of cooking wood."

Again, Jacks nodded, heading toward his car.

"He helped Daddy get a job."

Jacks turned to the boy, a quizzical look on his face. "He gave your father a job?"

"No," Aileen interjected. "It . . . It was just some veteran's papers or something. Something the Army sent here and Wayne asked him about it, Bertrand being a teacher and everything. Nothing ever came of it."

"Is that right?"

"You can see nothing ever came of it or we wouldn't still be here." Aileen laughed.

"Boy," Jacks asked, "what kind of job?"

Aileen placed her hand on Lonnie's shoulder and squeezed. Tension ran through his body. He looked at his mother, whose face had tightened around the mouth. "I don't know," he said, not sure that he was audible.

"You don't know—"

"No, he doesn't. He is just ten years old. He don't know and I don't know either, Mr. Jacks, because there was no job. It was a paper from the Army, that's all I know about it. Like I said, that war changed Wayne."

Jacks stared a second, then nodded, thanked Aileen for her time and drove away.

EIGHT

The morning after he witnessed the murders, Lonnie, dew-dampened after a night in the woods, stumbled into the house. The kitchen was quiet and cold, and he thought his mother would not yet be in her day clothes, but he found her dressed and sitting in the parlor. Stumbling forward through the gingham curtain that divided the parlor from the rest of the house, he managed one syllable of her name, but the other syllable was muted by what felt like a great bladder of tears that bulged behind his eyes and throat. After a moment, he caught his breath and called her, "Momma!" She did not move, not even to look up at him, but sat in the upholstered chair with her face turned toward her lap where her hands lay, one on top of the other. "Momma!" His tone softened and narrowed, whittled down by concern for her. *Is she dead?* He touched her on the arm, just below the shoulder, and she pulled her arm away. Still, not looking up, she said, keenly, "I told you to stay away from that nigger. I told you." She looked up and he saw, in the warm light that filtered through the cotton curtains at the window, that her eyes were swollen and red.

"What's the matter?" he asked. She turned her face away from him, and then he noticed her clothes, her apron, and he realized that she had not changed from the day before. "Have you been to bed?"

"No," she said, turning back to him now, her lips trembling. "And where have you been, Lonnie?" Now she extended her hand to him and pulled him in close to her, and pressed her wet cheek against his neck. "Where have you been! Where?"

He started to answer, but his throat shut off again and his mind spun with what he had seen and what he had feared when he first saw her. "Blackberries . . . ," he blurted.

She slapped his face.

"Blackberries? Goddamn *blackberries*. You've been picking blackberries all night? Who you been talking to? Did you tell anything to Mr. Jacks about Bertrand? I told you not to say a word. I told you to stay away from Bertrand. I told you he was trouble—"

"I didn't say nothin'—"

"Mr. Jacks told me you talked to Venable! He came again. Again! He and Maribelle Crookshank. Together! And what he told me you said—and what did you say?—*dirty, dirty, dirty*—" She began to slap him with both hands, striking about his head and shoulders and he bent over and put up his hands and leaned into the sofa to protect himself.

"He's dead!"

She continued to beat him.

"He's dead. He's dead."

"Who's dead?"

"Bertrand," he cried out. "Bertrand is dead."

She stopped beating him. "What do you mean, dead?"

"They killed him."

"Who?"

"They killed Bertrand."

"Who, goddamnit? Who?"

"Mr. Jacks and Venable and the others."

"Killed Bertrand?"

"Killed Bertrand," he said with a satisfactory wheeze. At last, he had been able to make her understand something.

"My God, no. No." She covered her face with one hand as if blindfolding herself.

They rested a minute, and he lifted his cheek from the sofa, noticing for the first time that it had a sweet, dusty odor. Finally, he began to relate what he had seen, beginning again with picking blackberries.

She interrupted him. "I don't care about that. We can't do nothing for Bertrand or any of them. We have to look out for ourselvess, Lonnie. You don't understand, boy. It's *you*. It's *you* that's done it. It's *you*—"

"Me? What did I—"

"You *talked!* I told you not to talk! It's what you *said* that killed Bertrand—"

"Momma!" He fell back onto the sofa, feeling faint.

"And it will kill me, too—"

PART TWO
IF I PERISH

NINE

The sunlight filtering through the canopy caught Bertrand's attention as he walked the path, hoe on shoulder, to the Henson place. It was the spring after Wayne Henson's death, and he was helping the widow and the boy to put in a garden. As he walked, he noticed that the leaves changed the color of the sunlight. Myrtle green in the shade, suddenly they were emerald, and radiant just like the jewel. He had seen this color in a movie in Atlanta. It was just before he was sent to Camp Claiborne. He and his cousin John Robert Thompson had paid their money in the front and followed the signs around to the side of the building and up a winding concrete staircase to the balcony. He had climbed slowly, he remembered, admiring the building's striped brickwork and the Arabesque design. John Robert had wanted to see this movie. He explained that he had wanted to see it for years. It was from a classic book. It was magical. Something he wanted his school children to see one day.

It was 1942, and Japan had attacked the country. Both men had decided to join the army. It was their duty, they felt. John Robert was the older at thirty-one. He had a teaching degree from Morris Brown College and had been teaching in Atlanta for nearly six years. At twenty-two, Bertrand had just graduated with a teaching degree from Fort Valley State. Teaching was a good profession for a black man, much less a teaching job in a big city, so Deacon, John Robert's father and Bertrand's older cousin, had argued with the younger men about the decision. "It a white man's war," Deacon had said. "All wars there's ever been were for the white man and the rich white man at that." Being young and game for adventure, he and John Robert saw it differently. Quietly, they said their goodbyes in Bethany and traveled by bus to Atlanta to get inducted. When he had been teaching,

John Robert had had a room not far from the university complex, but then, for a few days before the induction, they shared a room at the Butler Street YMCA.

Inside the movie house was decorated like an Arabesque fantasy, reminiscent of pictures he had seen in The Bible, Bertrand remembered. The ceiling was made to look like a starry night. He had marveled aloud at it. The movie was a children's movie full of witches and midgets and flying monkeys, but it had moved him. He still couldn't figure out exactly why. The singing was good, and he had always enjoyed good singing, but the story was too fanciful. Nobody could survive a tornado, and there wasn't any kind of magical land, unless it was heaven. Oz wasn't heaven, or else the girl wouldn't have wanted to come home.

He remembered how his nose had stuffed up and his eyes watered when the little girl got home. There is no place like home, she said. This was true, Bertrand thought, no place in the world like Georgia. No place in the world like the crow's nest of a Jim Crow movie house. Damn it. He had been going to be a soldier in the US army, but that didn't make a difference to the white man who took the ticket at the Fox Theatre and directed him to the crow's nest.

The emerald-colored city had glowed so green, and the light coming down through the trees had that same hallowed glow. The light fell in patches on the dried leaves and stands of fern. Lichen-mottled stones lay about as if arranged by angels. When the breeze came, everything danced: the branches, the light, the ferns. The light on the rocks made them seem to undulate, like a belly dancer. The leaves made the music. He took in a deep breath, so deep a pain shot across his sternum. This dancing, green and yellow of oak and elm and sassafras and sumac, was Talmaedge County. This music of breeze and bird song and the distant tinkling of the creek was home.

He took the hoe from his shoulder. He had intended to chop a few weeds for Mrs. Henson. He knew the boy would be there to so-call help him, and to talk him to death—but now, he thought, the garden wasn't so weedy as all that, a little dead nettle and chickweed, easy to pull—and just then, the breeze cooled the woods, and he wanted to enjoy it.

Ahhh. Bertrand, Bertrand.

He sat and leaned against a tree truck and let the breeze speak to him. *Bertrand.* He was a little ways up the side of a hill and could look down through a stand of trees and underbrush toward the dry branch at the bottom. There was something else about home, too: *Buchenwald.* It could never happen here. It could never happen in your own home. Yet, it was happening and it wasn't happening. What had those Jews been thinking when it happened to them? When the police came and said, come with us. Did they see it coming? Did they know it was about to happen and could do nothing about it? Or, was it like nightfall, like encroaching darkness, so gradual that you had to look hard to see the degrees of ever increasing dark, and then, before they realized it, the sun gone? Luellen said it had already happened. "What about the Japanese in California?" *But Luellen reads too much communist trash. She's going to get in trouble one day.* Still, he loved her. He loved the way she had layers of hardness and softness, and you had to be careful how you scratched her. He argued with her that the Japanese were the enemy. "They were as American as *you.*" She scoffed, meaning that neither were very American. "They had been here longer than most white people. Wake up, Bertrand, you have been sleeping too long."

"Then what's the difference?" he had challenged. "What make us want to go and round up a group of people unless they can be infiltrated by the enemy?"

She had rolled her eyes in a condescending way that he hated. "First of all, ain't no 'us' to it, unless you got a suit of white skin hanging in the wardrobe." She rubbed the back of her hand. "*Skin,* Bertrand, *skin.* Don't you ever forget about *skin.*"

"How can I with you around?"

She had been quiet a moment, thinking and twisting her lips. "You don't have to have me around. Somebody else will remind you."

But skin wasn't what killed those Jews. They were as white as the Germans. They *were* Germans, too. Some of them. Germans and Poles. But they were Jews. That was the difference. They lived apart from the other Germans. They had a different religion and different customs. Just like the Japanese in California had different language and different religion—well, maybe some of them spoke English and worshipped God, but at the core they were different. That was why they got picked out. You can't be too different from the majority, he thought.

Problem was that some people want you to be different. They keep on talking about how you are different and they won't let you prove you are just like them.

He picked up a twig, skinned it, and chewed it like a tooth pick. "That's just it," he said to himself aloud and chuckled. If the old wizard in that movie had any wisdom for him, it would have been just that. Not only did he have a brain and a heart, he has always been just like them. Only they couldn't see it. He had to prove it to them. Anything the whites did, he would do it, too. They had a Cub Scout troop, now he had a colored troop. They drove nice cars, now he drove a nice car. They would understand eventually. Wayne Henson had come to understand. It took being in the war, but Wayne eventually understood. How could he not? Suddenly Bertrand's heart stuttered and he threw his head back against the tree trunk. *Buchenwald.* His mouth filled with saliva. Every pore was trying to wash out the smell he imagined. The smell of the Jews of Buchenwald. It rode on the breeze. *Buchenwald.* The smell of rotting flesh.

He put his head between his knees and spat. The rush was over for now. He was in control once again. He wouldn't think about it for a while. He watched an ant investigate his spittle, a gloss on the dried leaves. "You don't want that spit, little ant, little soldier." It was a red ant. It reminded Bertrand of a dog. He chuckled. It reminded him of a man, too. He thought about how solitary the ant was, one ant—and as far as he knew, the only ant in the woods. What a big woods it was to the ant. What a big world. He had to pray, Bertrand thought. Thinking would drive him crazy or would drive him to drink. He had to pray. He pushed up from sitting and kneeled. What if someone saw him? Well, they would just think he was a man of God. What was wrong with that? He closed his eyes. "Oh mighty God . . . oh mighty God. . . ." There was nothing now but the image of the ant, and the sound of the breeze. Then there was a distant feeling, a memory he wouldn't allow for himself. *Oh yes—fear,* he thought.

After a while, he rose and walked, observing the light in the canopy. Again the light played elfishly with him, making flitting shapes in the canopy and bush. He was determined to pay it no mind. He didn't want people to think he was crazy. He didn't want to go crazy. But the light was like that of a rainbow, or a sunrise, full of subtle and mysterious colors. It made him feel that heaven was right on top of him, not some distant place talked about in *The New Testament,* but right here, all around him in the dome of the leaves. There was also the trickling of the river, the lovely sound of water flowing over the rocks, and echoing up the ravine. *Why is water so soothing? A gentle rain on the roof at night. Or even better, on a tin roof in a barn or shed.* As a boy, he loved just to sit in a barn and to listen to a summer shower. Storms were different—too violent. But showers came and went and came again like ocean waves. They gave life a clean rhythm, pleasant, predictable, soothing.

As he listened to the water, memories of the war swam up and the familiar emptiness he sought to fill swelled like a big bubble inside of him. *Falling light. Falling light. Fill it now with the falling light.*

At Weimar, the light had fallen just the same way, slicing the forest into planes of shattered glass; suddenly, he was again in the forest outside of Weimar, heading toward the camp. He didn't know what to expect there, though he had been told that it was a site of unbelievable horrors. He had seen horrors enough, the dead and the walking dead in a landscape gone to waste. He had helped lay waste to that landscape. Nothing, he knew, could be worse than what he knew war to be. Nothing could make him more afraid than the fear he had already felt. *Luftwaffe?* Planes—their whining falling out of the sky, a whine in the mind's ear and then, the rattle of the far away guns and the sizzle of bullets stitching through the mud. *Those sorry Jerrys.* You were talking to your buddy when a third eye blossomed in his forehead and his helmet cocked to one side.

The countryside around Weimar was not so different from Talmaedge County, forested hills and meadows—and on this day, full of the dampness that comes with early spring. He had gotten out of the jeep to urinate and walked a few yards off the road into a pine forest, large trees, with stands of understory hardwoods and shrubs, easy to walk through, the needles, damp and soft and full of aromatic rot. Scott and Bass were with him. They had been with him since Fort McCain, where the 183rd took basic training. Scott was from Atlanta, a prominent family. Bass, too, was from a good family, but a Philadelphia man. He was the country boy, but they all got along. They respected each other. They had gotten a command to go the camp, to render assistance to its inhabitants.

Then they came to a clearing under the pines, and suddenly he felt faint. Bass asked if he were all right. He said he was, but he had felt suddenly cold and empty as if he had been vacuumed out. Something haunted the place. He turned quickly, answering the sound of branches creaking in the wind. A voice. *Buchenwald.* Out of the corner of his eye, he thought he saw men, white faces in a group, in a line. When he turned, there were only the slim trunks of the trees, silvery birches. Now he couldn't urinate, though the other men did. Something was the matter here. In this spot, where he stood, the needles were blood-soaked; the trees, the birds, the insects had witnessed. He was still standing with his penis in his hands when he saw a man coming toward him through the shade and light. The man was dressed in a tattered coat that once had been stylish. His face was lean and pale. His eyes were sunken, but they had a sparkle about them that seemed to suggest a person of good humor. The man smiled and beckoned to him.

A little embarrassed, Bertrand put away his penis and started toward the man. He said for Scott and Bass to come with him, but he didn't look to see if they were following. He hadn't walked more than three steps, and suddenly he didn't see the man anymore. He shivered. He looked for Scott and Bass. They were heading toward the jeep. Bass yelled for him to come on. He looked again for the man, but saw nothing but the forest, the tree trunks, the underbrush. For a second, he thought he saw bodies crumbled on the ground under the bushes, dozens of bodies. A closer look, he saw only boulders. The breeze picked up. The trees creaked and there was a rustling sound. His skin crawled and he started back toward the jeep.

Falling light. Falling light, the breeze seemed to say.

"What?"

Fill it now with the falling light.

"Look like you just saw a ghost," Scott joked when Bertrand got back to the car. Bertrand said nothing and they rode to the camp.

It appeared before them as a large gated compound, familiar to Bertrand because the buildings reminded him of many of the barns and stables around Talmaedge County. They got out in front of the gatehouse, two long wooden buildings joined on the second story, by three tiers of smaller compartments, the top one being a stubby clock tower. The iron gates that had filled the space under the tiers had already been knocked aside. They went through.

At first there was nothing to see but a muddy yard and many rows of barracks and barbed wire fences along muddy lanes. Then, as if appearing out of thin air, as if his mind had not registered them on first sight, he saw a group of stick figures, human versions of the walking-stick insects. The sight of them drained him of all curiosity. His mind went blue. As they moved toward him he saw them more as one gangly creature than as individual people, a giant spider whose many legs wore the striped garb he associated with chain gangs. It moved as if it were stunned and crippled. Still, a tendril of fear sprouted in Bertrand's gut and climbed into his lungs. He made a slight motion toward his holstered pistol. Only when he made himself meet a man, eye to eye, did he know for sure that the thing was men. He focused on a young man, one nearly starved to death. The man's head was stubbed from a recent shave. His face was gaunt and eyes sunken. Scabs and scars covered his face, and his skeletal hands, webbed by scabs, reached out to Bertrand. The man spoke hoarsely, weakly, in a language that Bertrand did not understand. He did not know what to do, so he stood and stared at the man, who stopped and stared back.

The fear withered and slowly he emptied out. The emptiness had been coming for a long time.

"Johnson. Johnson!"

Bertrand slowly focused. Already Scott had turned him by the shoulders and was shaking him. "Johnson, are you all right?"

Bertrand thought he answered that he was, but he didn't know for sure if he had heard his own voice. Scott ordered him back to the jeep and gave him a rough shove in the direction of the gate. Outside the gate, his senses came back to him, prickling his face and hands. He realized he had urinated on himself and for a moment felt ashamed. But men in battle were always wetting themselves with sweat or piss or blood, so the shame of the stain soon faded, though soon came a greater shame. He had let down Scott and Bass. He had been afraid and that was all right. Men at war were always afraid. But he had gone somewhere and had become useless to them and to himself. Had he fainted? It was the emptiness. The emptiness that needed to be filled with something but it was something he couldn't manage. Was it anger? Was it hatred? The Bible teaches that we must love. We must turn the other cheek. We must love our enemy as we love ourselves. Must this emptiness be filled with love?

From time to time, even before he had left Talmaedge County, he had felt this emptiness. He felt it again and again during the basic training at Fort McCain in Mississippi. He had thought that Talmaedge County was the most prejudiced place on Earth, and spending time in Atlanta with John Robert and seeing the colored areas along West Hunter Street and in Sweet Auburn—where a colored man had a little better of a chance—had only reinforced his opinion about Talmaedge County. But then, the army sent him to the deeper South and he learned that the army, too, wasn't any better than Talmaedge County. Even the German POWs had privileges denied to the colored soldiers. The Nazis played volleyball while the colored soldiers washed their clothes and cleaned up after them. *This is how much you matter in America,* he had thought. *So little, so nothing, that a mortal enemy gets treated better than colored.* He wasn't stupid, he had decided. He had known all along things weren't equal, but somehow seeing the fascists being treated with dignities that he would never receive made knowing real, more real even than the daily humiliations of Jim Crow. After all, they were bearable, somehow. But if a fascist enemy had more right to decency than a native-born colored man, then he was nothing in the eyes of America, and yet he was fighting for America, risking his life for a nation that hated him. *No, I love my momma and I love my daddy. If the Nazis take over America, then they would put Momma and Daddy in camps and . . .* He thought like this for a while, and he felt a little better, though there was still a void in his stomach and his chest. Not even hunger filled it. Nothing filled it.

Recovered, he found Scott and Bass and they gave the prisoners what they had from the jeep: water, bread, rations, candy bars, and cigarettes. Eventually, a medical officer, who had arrived with another unit, ordered them to stop. Too much food too soon could make the men even sicker. Instead the three soldiers were ordered to reconnoiter. Scott put his hand on Bertrand's shoulder and told him he could wait in the jeep. Bertrand, looking at the many rows of barracks did not want to go farther, but he knew he had to. He would do it for Scott and Bass and for his mother and father.

Beyond the first barracks, he encountered more people—men and boys. A few, strong enough to talk, greeted them—*Guten Tag*—he knew, and the other sounds— *Drobyden—zdravstvuite—ahoj*—none of which he understood, but he nodded, tried to smile, but he wasn't at all sure that his lips moved.

He came to a pile of bodies. He smelled them first, and he knew what the smell was. In the war, he smelled rotting people often. Still, he didn't want to see them. He didn't think he could control his repulsion. He would have to become like the farmer burying the maggoty carcass of a cow, a doctor slicing a cadaver, or a child poking a dead rat with a stick. The decimated men laid body upon body, with mouths open, eyes opened or shut, bony arms and legs entangled, unnerved him. Later he would help to bury them, thinking at times in the funerary talk of the Baptist church—*ashes to ashes, dust to dust*—or sometimes, thinking about not breathing in or not touching the rotten flesh, and at other times his thoughts would be far away. At Martelange, the snipers picked them off one by one as they rebuilt the bridge that would allow 761st Tank Battalion, an all Negro battalion, to cross the river and help in the rescue of the 101st Airborne, an all-white battalion trapped by the Germans at Bastogne. He remembered that three men he knew floated in the river, pushed by the current against the decking or snagged on the pontoons. He had escaped by feigning death, lying limp on the wooden decking which rose and fell with the current in the blood-furled water while the stench of shit, loosened from his friends, wafted over him. He remembered how empty he was then. He remembered what the emptiness said: *You are shit. You are just shit to them. You are shit. You are just shit to them. You are. . . .*

He looked at the bodies for only a moment, then followed Scott and Bass into one of the bunkhouses. It was full of wooden bunks stacked five high, shelves more than bunks. On them lay the near dead and the newly dead. It stank and none of the soldiers could stay inside long. They found the medical labs with all manner of hooks and cutting instruments and jar after jar of body parts in formaldehyde—fingers, hands, toes and feet. Bertrand's head began to swim. It was too much to see, too much to believe—ears, eyes, noses and teeth. "They don't even do this shit to us at a lynching," Scott offered. Penises, testes, livers and hearts. Lampshades of tattooed skin. Flower pot craniums.

Outside the camp, the three soldiers sat in the jeep, neither speaking nor looking at one another. Finally, one of them said, "America, it ain't so bad, now." Bertrand looked up. Scott still looked dazed, but Bass was talking quietly. "First kraut I see is a dead kraut. Dead, I swear." Bertrand looked into the trees, the thick, dark pines at a little distance, and the slim, silver birches nearby. *There are plenty of fascists in America,* he thought. *Plenty who would do just this kind of thing. But America ain't this bad.*

Suddenly the light made the trees shine.

TEN

That afternoon, after working for the Hensons, Bertrand had returned to his little house where he lived with this wife, Luellen, and his mother, Milledge. They had remodeled the house after he had come home from the war, but it was still the same house he had grown up in, with his parents and a younger brother, W.B., now a school teacher in Atlanta. Milledge had taken the smaller bedroom downstairs, the one the boys had as children, and he and Luellen had the upstairs to themselves. There were also a kitchen, a parlor, and a front porch. Outside, they had four acres with a good stand of trees and enough open space for a large garden, a chicken coop, and a small pigpen.

He sat on the front porch, among the potted plants his mother kept, and rested. He had felt drained after hoeing a short while for Mrs. Henson, and with the help of the boy, he had managed to lay in a few hills of squash. Mrs. Henson had been asking about his cousin Beah Thompson, and her inquiry, full of suspicion, it seemed to him, had angered him. The anger, coming after the memory of the camp, had weakened him. He didn't like the woman. The boy, Lonnie, was an angel, much like his father. As a boy, he had wondered sometimes what it would be like to be white, to have good hair and light skin. He thought he might have looked a little like Lonnie had he been white. How easy the world would be. He could go anyplace, say anything, do anything. Now, he had come to realize that whites, especially poor whites, had their limitations too. Even Aileen Henson with her quiet distrust of him, or Maribelle Crookshank, the bossy know-it-all, had never been out of the state of Georgia. With his teacher's degree, he was better educated than they would ever hope to be. Yet, because of his dark skin, they would never accept him as their equal, much less as their superior. And it was skin that made the difference, he thought. He could talk to Aileen on the telephone, speaking just as properly as any white man in Talmaedge County, and she would "yes suh" him to death. He could tell her that he lived in a small house in the country with his wife and his mother, and that he was a deacon in a Baptist church, a school teacher, and that his name was Johnson, and she would still think he was a white man. But if he came to her front door, she would send him around to the back, and she would never, on her own, allow him into her precious parlor. But Wayne Henson had been different. The war had changed him. Both of them. Wayne saw beyond color and was brave, or silly, or crazy enough not to put credence in the prejudices of the old ways. That was why Bertrand wanted to help the Hensons, to help the boy, to help the wife.

His mother came in from her job as a housekeeper at Woodbine Plantation, having walked the three miles home. They spoke and Milledge went to her room, and after a few minutes came out onto the porch to join him. She had barely taken her seat, when they heard the groan of an engine coming down the long driveway, and they waited without speaking to see who it was. It was their cousin, Beah Thompson, driving her father's old truck. She was coming so fast that Milledge looked over at Bertrand with concern. For his part, Bertrand felt sleepy, and though he was aware of his mother's concern and the truck sliding in the soft dirt in front of the house, he was also calculating the length of the shadow of a huge tulip poplar as it stretched across the yard.

"What in the world, girl?" Milledge said out aloud and stood. When Beah didn't get out of the truck right away, Milledge thought out loud that the baby must have been coming. She stepped from the porch, and walked swiftly around to the driver's side of the truck. Then she called with alarm for Bertrand to come.

Peering into the truck, Bertrand saw Beah's face, eyes round and scared, and he knew it wasn't a baby.

"Jimmy Lee," she said, fighting to control her breath.

"What's the matter with Jimmy Lee?"

Beah opened the truck door. Her stomach seemed to balloon as she arched to slide out of the truck. Milledge held on to her while she made the jump down from the running board. "He is in trouble with the law."

Beah's hands felt cold and she shivered when they helped her to the porch. "Oh Lord, Lord God." She said, "Jesus, Jesus have mercy." Bertrand helped to seat Beah on a cane chair, and she rambled into the story of a stabbing, talking fast, incomprehensively. By this time, Luellen had come to the porch with a glass of water for Beah. She spoke calmly and authoritatively to Beah, drawing on what Bertrand recognized as her teacher's persona. Soon Beah began to talk more coherently.

She had driven over to Woodbine Plantation to pick up Jimmy Lee from work. Jimmy was still in the fields, she thought, so she parked the truck next to the fence just down from the barn and was leaning against the fence waiting for him, when she was startled by a voice behind her.

"You ever try a Piedmont?" It was a white man she didn't recognize at first, but she remembered she had seen him at her job, at Maribelle's Diner. It was Vernon Venable. She wondered what he was he doing at Woodbine, Jack's place.

"Sir?"

"You ever try a Piedmont cigarette?" Venable held the package out to her, shook it so three cigarettes telescoped out. "They not as good as Luckies, but they're not bad."

"No thank you, sir. I don't smoke."

Venable took one with his lips. Lit it from the butt he had finished. "You waiting for Jimmy Lee?"

"Yes, sir," she said. She couldn't keep her voice from rising, wondering why Mr. Venable would know anything about her and Jimmy Lee.

"He ran over to town for me and Mr. Jacks. He'll be back in a little bit."

"Thank you, sir. I'll go and come back in a little while, then."

Venable leaned his back against the fence, right next to her. She felt he was too close, stretching himself along the fence. "No need to run off. You can stay and talk to me a bit. He'll be back in no time." She scratched her head and looked at the truck and then her nails. "Now, now," Venable said. "What are you worried about? I just want to strike up a conversation with you. I was sitting over there by myself, and I see you over here by yourself, and I said to myself, 'I bet she'd like to try one of these new cigarettes.' That's the kind of person I am. It doesn't make a difference to me if you're white or colored, I can carry on a conversation with you."

"Yes, sir." She had tried to smile, had tried to seem pleasant, but she moved away from him, putting the hood of the truck between them.

He pushed himself away from the fence suddenly, crushing a stand of nightshade that had taken refuge from the mower by the fence post and moved down the fence so he was on her side of the truck. He pulled himself up and sat on the top rail. "Sure is hot today. I hate days like this. So hot and sticky." He let smoke out of his mouth without blowing and smiled. His smile was broad, triangular, and high-crested, and she thought he was clownish looking. Then he flicked his forelock to one side, and she had a sinking feeling in her stomach. "When it gets this hot, all I can think about is taking off my shirt to get comfortable. What do you do to get comfortable on a hot day like this?" The crushed weed emitted an acrid odor.

"There ain't much you can do. God made it hot, and God can cool it off."

"You mean to tell me, you just suffer in the heat and don't try to get any relief?"

"I don't always have the luxury of seeking relief." She realized her tone was getting sassy, but Venable did not seem offended; rather, he seemed to enjoy teasing her.

"You mean to tell me, you don't ever get relief?"

"Rarely."

"Ain't that a shame."

"That's just the way it is."

"But it doesn't have to be that a way."

"No, sir." She tried to look at him coldly. "It *doesn't* have to be that a way." She put her hand on the truck door handle, the passenger's side.

"Now, we aren't talking about the same thing, are we?"

"I think we are. We talking about the weather."

Venable stretched his hands above his head. "No. We aren't exactly talking about the weather."

"Then help me sir, what are we talking about?"

Venable gave her the smile. "We are talking about . . . a lot of things. Like . . . social equality." Now her stomach went into a tight ball. The baby in her stomach seemed to shrink.

"What's that?" She asked. She was trying to think of a reason to leave.

"That's when a good-looking gal like you and a handsome man like me don't have to worry about carrying on a nice conversation. We can talk like we are equals because people are equals. You are equal to me and I'm equal to you."

"I believe I'd better be going," she said and opened the truck door.

He jumped down from the fence and grabbed her arm. "Whoa. Hold up. You don't have to run."

"Mr. Venable," she said firmly, "I do believe I have to be going."

He didn't let go of her arm, just above the wrist. His hand was strong and when she tugged at it, she couldn't break the grip, in spite of the fact that they both were sweaty and the hand slid down to her wrist.

"We were talking just fine."

"Please let me go."

"How come you changed on me all of a sudden like that? What did I say to you?"

"Just let me go!"

She twisted her arm again, but he held it tightly.

"Tell you what? One little hug and I'll let you go. Just a little hug." He pulled her closer. She dug her toes into the ground, and he jerked. She stepped forward and dug in again, this time planting her heels right on top of his foot, but he pulled her closer, jerking her at will, first to the left and then to the right, as if to show her his strength. He pulled her forward again, against him, and her belly pushed against his thighs.

"*Pregnant!*" He let her go.

She stepped back and before she could think about it, she slapped him, her nails scratching his lips. He glared at her a moment, seemingly as astonished as anything. Then, he slapped her back. She fell against the truck. Her ears rang and the side of her face stung. When she could think clearly enough to look out for him, she saw that he was walking away, on the other side of the fence, across the pasture toward his place at Thousand Acres. Now, feeling her face for cuts, she turned and saw Jimmy Lee striding toward her. Quickly, she pulled her hair back around her ears, and ran her tongue over her lips. She hoped there was no mark on her. "Ahh, Jimmy Lee," she called, trying to make herself sound cheerful, but the ruse was in vain. Jimmy Lee glanced at her, checking, it seemed, to see that she was not hurt. He said nothing, but placed his hands on the top rail and vaulted the fence and went in a determined stride to catch Venable. "God, no, Jimmy," she called to him. "Jimmy, I'm okay. Stop! Come here now!" Jimmy paid no attention but continued after Venable. She climbed and saddled the plank fence, and slid down the other side and, as fast as her heavy belly allowed, ran after Jimmy, calling for him to stop. The pasture smelled of mold and wild onion and was spotted with dung. A short distance ahead, she saw Jimmy approaching Venable, and Venable stopping and turning. They seemed for a moment to be old friends, greeting and chatting.

Closer, she could see the stiffness in Jimmy Lee's body. Usually, his body was as loose as running water, but now it was a blade of ice, his shoulders flared and turned to Venable.

"Mr. Venable," she heard Jimmy Lee say. "I saw you hit my girl. Slapped her in the in the face."

Venable put his right hand in his pocket. "I'm sorry, Jimmy Lee. I had to."

"You ain't had to do nothing."

"She was acting fresh towards me."

Jimmy Lee's fists clenched. Beah was close enough to grab him by the elbow, but he shook her hand off. "You a liar." He drew back and raised the fists. "You a goddamn liar."

"Jimmy," Beah said, her breath heavy. "I'm all right. Now, Jimmy."

"Why don't you just cool off and we will talk about this later?" Venable said.

"She pregnant, Mr. Venable. She pregnant and she ain't no whore." Jimmy Lee gestured again with his fist.

"Jimmy Lee, I don't want to hurt you." Venable said. I like you, so I'm fixin' to give you a chance to cool off. Go on back to the barn and you won't get hurt."

Jimmy Lee remained stiff, breathing heavily, and clenching and unclenching his fists as if trying to make up his mind as to hit Venable or not. Beah took his arm again, working her hand down to his hand and holding it. He seemed to relax. He stepped backwards, shook his head as if to clear it. Then, as if to gag out frustration, he pulled his hand away from Beah and snatched at the air, opened his mouth wide and growled at Venable. He spun around to go, taking her hand again. Just as he did so, Venable said, "Now, that's a good boy."

Suddenly Jimmy Lee dropped Beah's hand, and before she figured it out, he was rushing Venable, throwing a flurry of fists in the white man's face. A hard one landed on Venable's cheek and he staggered, fell back. As he fell, he whipped his hand from his pocket, and released the blade of knife. The blade was narrow, worn and streaked, but its belly held a clean white edge. Venable swung the blade as he fell and Jimmy Lee dodged and pounced, landing so he sat on Venable's chest. The men tussled over the knife, Jimmy Lee bending Venable's wrist backwards. Venable tried to buck Jimmy Lee off, but the smaller man slid down onto Venable's stomach, riding him, and prying open his fingers. For a moment everything focused on the knife, and Venable's two fingers which held it. Suddenly it was gone. Venable twisted, rolling in dried dung, trying to come up on his knees, and patting the ground for the knife. Then Beah saw the blade by a clump of broomstraw. She wanted to reach for it, but Jimmy Lee was there first. Grasping the knife like a prod, palm up, he began to tease Venable with it. Then to her horror, Jimmy Lee poked at the white man, first in the fleshy part of the shoulder, then on the back of the arm; a long cut, more tearing the shirt than the flesh, from the rib cage down to the hip, and at last, as if insulting the white man, a punch in the buttocks.

By the time she finished her story, Bertrand was sitting next to Beah, but looking away into the woods that bordered the side of the yard. The shadows were now long and the woods dark, though the sunlight shone on the slick bark of a grove of beech trees. The trees had been there for as long as he could remember, and as a child he enjoyed climbing them. From the heights, he could see over the canopy and looked down on the patchwork of farm and manor house that was Woodbine Plantation. His life had been tied up with Woodbine Plantation and Mr. Jacks. Both of his parents had worked at Woodbine all their lives, his father in the fields and his mother in the house. The source of what little they had had been dependent on Woodbine, and it was with Mr. Jacks' tacit approval that he and his brother had been able to go to college. Jacks had given the parents a little raise when he learned that Bertrand had been accepted at the college in Fort Valley. He had joked to Bertrand's father, "Johnson, I reckon I don't need another hand as much as the colored school might need a teacher." Only his mother hadn't thought it funny. She declared, when her husband recounted the joke, that her boys would go to college regardless of what Jacks needed.

"Bertrand," Beah called to him, "what must we do?"

Bertrand turned to face his cousin. She had a pleasant, round face, typical of his family. She was a sturdy woman, shapely and pretty all together, and far too sensible, he thought, to get mixed up with the likes of Jimmy Lee. "Where's Jimmy Lee?" he asked, his voice hoarse.

"He's hiding. At first he didn't want to leave. He was saying a lot of foolishness about not caring what they did to him. That he would cut Sheriff Cook, too, if Cook laid a hand on him. But finally I got him in the truck and drove here. But I let him out just yonder in the woods." She pointed up the driveway toward the road. He's going to lay low and when night comes, I thought . . . I don't know what to think."

"Get him out!" Luellen shouted. She moved to stand in front of Bertrand. "Don't even wait until dark. Get a jump on Cook and go now. Give him the truck—Lord, Bertrand, he should have been half way to Atlanta by now."

"But that's what they might expect," Beah said. "They would have the roads blocked between here and Atlanta. I was thinking about maybe laying low for a day or so and then driving him to Macon or Savannah—"

"Macon is just as bad as it is here. No, go right now to Atlanta. I got some money. I'll give it to him. Tell him to go right now."

At the mention of Macon, Bertrand recalled a story he heard from his father about a lynching in Macon. What the colored man had done, he couldn't remember, but it seemed trivial in the scope of things. Perhaps he had insulted a white woman, perhaps even killed someone. The man had tried to escape by train, but the train was stopped in nearby Tifton, and the man was dragged off. In fact, all the colored men on the train were made to get off and some of them accused of loitering and thrown on the chain gang. The man was taken back to Macon and hanged downtown, just in front of the Bibb County Courthouse. He recalled so well his father's description of what happened after the hanging, for his father stood, and, as if pointing out directions to him, told how the lynch mob dragged the body behind a car, up Mulberry street, made a left on First Street, and then left on Cherry Street, over the brick paving and down to Third Street, and another left on Mulberry. When they arrived back at the courthouse, the body was merely tatters. He knew this could happen to Jimmy Lee. But another part of him wouldn't let him believe it. Things like this had happened in the past, but there had been a war, not just any war, but the biggest war there ever had been, and colored men had helped win the war. The war had changed things. Or had it? He wanted to believe it had.

Milledge stood noisily and went to the screen door. She opened it and turned back to the other women. "What this got to do with Bertrand?

What this got to do with us anyway? You, Beah, bringing this trashy mess up into my house. Jimmy Lee a grown man, let him do whatever he want, but leave Bertrand out of this mess."

"Cousin Milledge—"

Milledge raised her hand as if to swat Beah. "Your momma turning in her grave this minute. This minute, she turning in her grave."

"Cousin Milledge! What am I going to do?"

"You go with him for all I care. And what about your poor daddy? This'll kill him if you ain't already killed him with your whoring."

"Momma," Lullen said, "that doesn't help. Bertrand—?"

"But it's the truth!" Milledge slammed the door without going through it. "It's the truth!"

The women called his name again, and Bertrand considered them without answering. He looked at the trees again and then cleared his throat and turned to his cousin. "Run down and get Jimmy Lee and bring him to the house."

"Wouldn't it be better if he stay hidden?"

"He should run," Luellen said.

"He broke the law. He has to face the law."

Luellen gasped, was still a second, and threw up her hands in a quick motion. "You've gone crazy! What law? What law in Talmaedge County? They will *kill* him."

Bertrand answered slowly, rising from the chair. "That might be, but I don't think so. I think it's time we put some trust in the system."

Luellen stepped away from Bertrand when he stood, paced to the far railing of the porch, turned and threw up her hands again. "Trust the system! Like that Baker woman put her trust in the system?" Lena Baker, a colored woman, had been executed the year before for murdering her white lover.

Bertrand ignored Luellen and put his hand on Beah's shoulder. "I think what is best," he said, "is to face down this trouble. Now, Jimmy Lee works for Jacks, and I hear he's a good worker. Jacks depends on him. And Momma works for Jacks—"

"Leave me out of it." Milledge went inside and slammed the door again.

"Jacks has a lot of influence. He won't let anything happen to Jimmy Lee."

"You're crazy! You're gone completely crazy—"

"Luellen," Bertrand started calmly, and then he raised his voice. "If he runs, he'll be running for the rest of his life. And what if they catch him running, he's sure enough dead then. If he stays and fights this thing—after all, Venable *did* insult Beah—if he fights this thing, he might get off or maybe only spend a few months in jail. Then this baby," he pointed to Beah's stomach, "will at least have a father."

Luellen came to Bertrand, rushing across the porch and stopping just short of him with her hands before her, pleading. "What don't you understand, Bertrand? You think a mob is going to care that white man insulted a colored woman?" She pointed to Beah. "She is a *colored* woman. To them she is a black nigger woman. And she might as well be a whore too, being pregnant with a married man." She put her finger to her head, pointing with her index finger. "Think, Bertrand. Don't forget where you are, husband. You are not in Paris, France, or even New York City."

"I know where the hell we are."

"Then *what* are you?"

"I know what the hell I am."

"Then act like it, Bertrand. Act like it."

"Goddamn it, Luellen, I am acting like it. I am acting like a grown man in America. That's what I am and that's what I'll act like."

Luellen drew in a big breath. "You are a grown man, all right. But you are a nigger, a black, shitty nigger, to them. And you will be until the day your skin turns white."

"Please," Beah said. "This isn't about you, Bertrand. I came for you to help Jimmy Lee."

"It's about all of us," Bertrand said. An image of the camp swelled in his mind, the men looking like a giant insect. "But . . . but. . . ." He breathed deeply, focusing on Beah's round face. "You are right. You came to me for help. The truth is, I don't know any more than you what to do. If he runs, they'll catch him. If he hides, they'll find him. I say, he might as well face it and fight and trust that we can get justice."

"Justice!" Luellen screwed up her face mockingly. "What is that, Bertrand?"

"It's what I fought that goddamn war for."

"You fought for nothing, husband."

Bertrand turned to Beah. "Jacks might help us. But you and Jimmy Lee will have to decide what you want to do. I'll help where I can, but I don't know any more what to do than you."

"Run," Luellen said to Beah. "If you don't run, at least hide. Every minute you stay here listening to this foolishness, he one minute closer to dying."

They were quiet for a moment, watching Beah fidget and rock, her face contorting, but without tears. "Do you think Jacks might help?" she asked presently.

"No." It was Milledge, standing inside the screen door. "No. Let me tell you. I know more about Jacks than any of you. I worked for him since I was a girl. Long before nary one of you were born. And I tell you, you can't trust Jacks any more than you can any white man. Any of them. Jacks care just about one thing, and that's Jacks. Same with Venable, only Venable is as low and as trashy as a man can get. If a man could be a whore, it would be Venable. So your question got to be this, Bertrand. Is Jimmy Lee worth so much to Jacks that he can do without him? Worse than that, is Jimmy Lee worth so much to Jacks that Jacks will go up against his friend, Venable, and the God almighty Venable family, and Cook and every other white man, woman, and child in Talmaedge County to save him? You think about that, then you tell me something about Jacks." She walked away from the door before Bertrand could answer.

It seemed the moonless night came suddenly, without twilight. The sky was thick with stars. Milledge and Luellen and gone inside, and in spite of the anxiety had begun to cook. Beah went into the woods to find Jimmy Lee and he soon came to the porch, looking sheepishly at Bertrand. "Well, I guess you right, Bertand," he said. "Mr. Jacks, he ain't got nothing against me that I know of, and neither did Mr. Venable. That is, up until now. I take my chances."

Bertrand cleared his throat. As he looked at Jimmy Lee, he saw something in the man he hadn't seen before. In the dim yellow of the kerosene lamp, the man's lean, handsome face seemed gilded. He was about to admonish Jimmy Lee and remind him that he would have to pay for his crime with some jail time, at the least, but he also wanted to make clear that things could go very badly for him. Venable or Cook could stir up a lynch mob, or they might even go to court and he could get a long time on the work gang. But he saw, too, that Jimmy Lee carried himself straight, his broad lean shoulders held back in spite of an occasional dipping of his head in deference to his elders. At that point, Bertrand wanted to tell him to run, but Milledge brought out plates of food for the men, and offered one to Beah, who turned it down. Bertrand set his food aside, but Jimmy Lee sat on the porch step and ate the cold fried chicken and green beans. "Jimmy Lee," Bertrand said, solemnly, "you are a man."

"Yes, I reckon."

"You made a mistake, but you are not a coward. You are not a criminal. You are a good man."

"Yes, suh."

Bertrand swallowed hard. He felt as if he might cry. "I don't know what to say. I don't know what to tell you. I know that 'man can be a wolf to man.'" Suddenly, he remembered a phrase from his schooling, "*Homo homini lupus.* I have seen it. But, what good does it do a man to run? What kind of life is that?" His voice became a whisper. Jimmy Lee looked up at him and he tried to look Jimmy Lee in the eyes. "You know, they might kill you for what you have done."

Jimmy Lee's eyes widened and his mouth twitched, but he did not look away from Bertrand. "I know that," he said.

"Do you want to run? If you do, I will help you."

"I do want to run, and I don't."

"If you run," Beah said, "you might get away. Go up North, maybe to Chicago, and I will come and meet you there. Then we can have the baby. . . ."

"I could run, baby. But I don't know nothing about Chicago. And the way I figure it, I would have run all the way to the moon, anyway. Wherever I go, there's gonna be white people—"

"But they won't be Venable," Beah said.

"But they will still be white," said Luellen, standing at the screen door. She came through and held out a roll of bills to Jimmy Lee. "Here. Take this. It's about two hundred dollars. Take it and go as far as you can go. I say make your way to Atlanta, somehow, then get a train to Detroit and then sneak over to Canada. Don't listen to Bertrand. He's my husband, but he's a fool, too. If you sit here a minute longer, you are a dead man."

"Take it!" Beah screamed. They all looked up to see headlights coming down the driveway toward the house.

Bertrand's heart thumped rapidly and his breath went shallow. He sprung up from his chair. In his mind he saw the camp of Jews, the skeleton men coming toward him. "Okay then. Be calm. Go ahead, Jimmy Lee. Take the money. Run around through the woods. Get a car somehow, even if you have to steal one."

Jimmy looked back and forth between Bertrand and the woods. Then he took a deep breath. He took Beah's hand and squeezed it. Then he started walking down the drive, his hands raised above his head like a stickup in a Western movie.

ELEVEN

It was late when Bertrand went up to his bedroom. Luellen sat in the upholstered chair at the foot of the bed. She had her scrapbook unfolded on her lap. Bertrand sighed deeply, feeling a knot come into his stomach when he saw the book. "Oh, dear Luellen," he said, rubbing her shoulder with his palm. He felt her stiffen at his touch and withdrew without saying more. He sat on the bed, his back to her, and took off his shoes and socks, rolled the socks and placed them inside the shoes and pushed the shoes under the bed. Then he pulled off his pants and shirt and draped them over the back of the chair that stood on his side of the bed. Now in his underwear, he knelt beside the bed and quickly mumbled a prayer. This ritual of prayer, he had long thought, was useless. It was what children did and it did not carry favor with God for adults. "If I die before I wake, I pray the Lord my soul to take." It was all more complicated than that. For one thing, the Lord, for better or for worse, already had his soul. Still he knelt, asked for God's strength, and rose. Having had his knees against the wooden planks made him feel a bit more secure, but real prayer, he thought, was a continuous stream of meditation, coming out with each breath, coming in with breath, with sight, with sound. He propped his head on his pillow, put his feet up on top of the covers and looked across to Luellen, who sat in a pool of lamplight, slowly turning the pages of the large scrapbook that lay unfolded on her lap.

"Aren't you tired?" he asked, but she did not respond, and he knew there would be difficulty. As he watched her, his mind drifted. He thought about Jimmy Lee walking towards the police car, his silhouette, arms raised, black and ghostly in the headlights. Then he had to wrestle with Beah, trying not to hold onto her belly, lest he hurt her baby, as she struggled to get to Jimmy Lee when Cook and his deputies pushed Jimmy Lee against the sheriff's car, handcuffing him and beating him with their fists and clubs. When the deputies had gone, Beah threw herself on the ground and tore at the grass. When he tried to help her up, she screamed for him to go take care of his damn white woman. The comment stung him, not so much for what she said, but the contempt in her voice. He stood and looked at her, his hands by his side, as she kicked and clawed at the ground. After nearly twenty minutes, Milledge managed to get her up and back to the porch. Bertrand had driven her home and had tried to explain to Deacon, her elderly father, what had happened. When he left, he was still uncertain that Deacon understood fully.

Slowly Luellen turned a page of her scrapbook. The sound of the page turning indicated that the paper was heavy and soft. He had seen the book many times. She called it her *true* book of American history. She had been a history major when he met her, and she said she was collecting information for her own history of the United States. No happy slaves doing master's bidding would be in her book. No mammies wet-nursing the mistress' children. Enough of that. She said this would be a book of the naked nature of America, as beastly as it was foul.

"But Luellen," he occasionally argued, "all white people aren't bad. And even if they were, you can't think that way. For one thing, it is not Christian, and for another it will eat you up. Hating eats you up just as badly as being hated." She often dismissed him with a wave of her hand or countered that hate hadn't eaten up the whites. They seemed to be doing mighty well hating.

He glimpsed a page, a picture of men hanging from a tree branch. She was studying the picture, it seemed, rereading the caption for how many times, he couldn't imagine. The article was from the *The Chicago Defender* about a lynching in Southern Indiana, nearly twenty years before. Two boys, just teenagers, had been accused of raping a white woman, and murdering her boyfriend. Without trial, they were taken from their cells by a crowd, were beaten and hanged. Bertrand knew that reading the scrapbook just before bedtime, Luellen wouldn't sleep. The more she read, the more upset she would become, but he could do nothing about it.

"Luellen, honey. Come on to bed now. Let it go for now."

She looked more closely at the photograph, as if counting the details. Bertrand knew she was going inside of it, removing herself from the bedroom and drawing herself into the frame of the picture with all of its anxiety and tension. She would be one in the crowd, perhaps even the photographer, examining the bodies of the boys that swung from the tree like scarecrows, limp and tattered. In her mind she ran her hands over their bloodied heads, their necks cocked at odd angles. She looked into their dull eyes, oddly peaceful and already drying out. She was already becoming an unseen guest among the onlookers, a part of the crowd of whites—men, women, children. There was a couple holding lovingly to each other as if they were on a date at the fair. The people wore ordinary clothes, casual suits, open collared shirts, straw hats and calico dresses. She saw no hoods or sheets, no monstrous costumes with flaming crosses. These were the typical townspeople of a typical town. She might have seen some of them just last night at the county fair, or she might see them tomorrow strolling along Bethany's main street. They were townspeople in typical postures who could have been at any typical gathering of such people. They had not turned into monsters, neither had their veins emptied of blood and filled with gasoline. They could have been witnessing anything, a freak show, a wedding or a pig roast. That it was a lynching wasn't so uncommon, she would have thought. She had told him that the Romans flocked to see men chop each other to pieces with swords; in England, people jostled one another to watch beheadings and drawing-and-quarterings. Spectacles. To watch someone's intestines being drawn from his body and his body being sawn into quarters. What must go through people's minds who watch such things? She couldn't do it, she said. She could never do it. And yet, something in her said she could kill those whites in the picture if she had to. But that would be different. She could kill them but it would be no spectacle.

"Remember Mr. Wright," Bertrand said from the bed. Luellen looked up as if his voice annoyed her. She turned to another page in the scrapbook. The book was over a hundred pages and still she added to it. Nearly every time *The Defender* or *The Baltimore Afro-American* came, she found an article of a lynching or riot or rape to paste onto its pages.

Bertrand watched her thumb through the book, pausing momentarily over the pictures of grotesque corpses of black men, burned, chained to trees, mutilated. It seemed they fascinated more than horrified her. "It is a mystery," she had once blurted out to him. "What is it about the whites that makes them do this kind of thing?"

"It's not just white people," he had argued.

Oh, yes. She knew, she had told him. She knew in her heart that she couldn't say it was just the whites. She had heard about Indians scalping and mutilating whites, and somewhere she knew that black people probably had done similar things—and to each other. *Yes,* he remembered her saying: *Perhaps in some distant place and time, perhaps I would be one in the press of a crowd, a young woman in love, holding you, Bertrand, around the waist, while we watched a man flailing as a rope strangled him. Maybe in some distant place, Bertrand, but no. Not here. Here is Georgia. Here is America, beautiful and white. Here, whites are the monsters—yes, monsters,* she had said, *and we are the hunted.* She had caught herself. *Not Mr. Wright at Rosewood. He protected me. And your little friend, Henson, he might be all right though he has never been tested. You should never trust a white until he has been tested.* Bertrand sighed. "Won't you come to bed, now?" he asked.

She looked up from the book and sighed. "Who can sleep?"

"I know it will be hard, but you've got to. We've got to."

"Bertrand," she said distantly, "I wonder if they haven't killed Jimmy Lee by now."

His jaw clenched and his teeth throbbed. "To say such a thing, Luellen."

"Husband, don't fool yourself." She flipped the scrapbook shut and stroked her hand across the leather cover. She stood and went to her trunk where she put the book away, and then to a nightstand where she picked up another book, a slim volume by a colored author who had lived in Georgia.

Good, he thought. Perhaps now she will read herself to sleep. Perhaps the novel would take her mind away from stories of lynching. But then he worried that it might be a novel about lynching. "That isn't Richard Wright, is it? Oh, some other colored writer."

"Jean Toomer," she said, "A *Negro* writer."

He didn't know Toomer's story, and was afraid to ask. He hoped it was a love story, a happy story. But what *Negro* had a happy story to tell? He looked away from her, to the far window where a light breeze parted the sheer curtains. Outside the moonlight shone on the trees, and the tree frogs and crickets sang. He turned back to her, now the most beautiful creature of God's making. No wonder in nature matched her for strength and grace.

For several minutes he watched her as she read, seemingly with interest. She was a round woman, much like his people, but much darker in complexion. He loved the smooth darkness of her skin, so richly colored that sometimes it seemed to anchor sunlight, fluorescing it iridescent and purple. Now in lamplight, her color shone with highlights of yellow from the bridge of her broad nose and her round cheeks. Her face appeared calm, the surface of still water, but Bertrand knew that just below that surface she was perpetually on the verge of boil. This was a part of what attracted him to her, the feeling that she was miles deep. Though others saw her as doleful and sometimes spiteful, he forgave this in her, for he knew that when she opened, albeit sometimes a violent rupture, she opened to an inviting and seemingly unfathomable depth. He knew, too, from long conversations what lay in those regions.

When Luellen was six, she lived in Rosewood on the west coast of Florida. Rosewood wasn't much, but it was a colored town, and it was doing all right, a settlement of about thirty families, half of them related in one way or another. The men worked—every day except Sunday—either logging or tapping pines for oil. The turpentine gave the town a sweet, pungent smell. It was in her poppa's clothes. It was in the furniture. In the bed clothes. It was in the air when the wind blew just right. If it blew one way, it was the fresh, briny air of the Gulf of Mexico just five miles away; if it blew the other way—*Ahhhh!—Ahhhh!*, she would tell him. *Ahhhh! The pines!* The clean, cutting smell of the pine oil. When the trains passed through the town, loaded down with pines and cedar, there was that smell again, wafting through the windows; there was also the rumble and measured clanking of the train. It was so good to sleep by.

But then, they said, a man from Rosewood—never identified—raped a white woman in Sumner, just two miles away. *Who from Rosewood would rape a white woman from Sumner, when they got all them fine looking Negro women looking for husbands in Rosewood?* Luellen had asked him. *Women in all shapes and sizes. Tall and short. Bony, if you like bones, and plump, if you like a lot of woman to grab on to. They were light and dark, and all that goes in between. They had red hair, and brown. Black hair, or salty if you wanted an older woman. They had them with woolly hair, or long Indian braids. Round eyes that bugged out at you or narrow eyes you couldn't tell if they're sleeping or not. They were church women or juke house women. You could get them in just about any combination you wanted. So why would a man from Rosewood go over to Sumner for a piece of low class white ass?*

But they said somebody did.

The men from Rosewood and the men from Sumner all worked together down at Cedar Key, loading up the ships and trains. They knew each other, so over that long week the tension died down, especially since nobody could say who had done it, and everybody knew everybody. Mr. John Wright, the only white man that lived in Rosewood, had a store right there at the main crossroads, knew every black face, and he couldn't say who it was that had done it.

But they didn't know that in Gainesville. They didn't know that in Perry. In Tallahassee, they didn't know. In Ocala, and Jacksonville, and across the state line in Valdosta and as far away as Waycross and even over into Alabama in Dothan, they didn't know. They came, riding those same train tracks that took the logs out: Men carrying shotguns, pistols from the Great War, and sticks of dynamite. Some wore robes; some wore hoods. Some wore street clothes and fedoras.

They all came looking for that somebody that nobody could name. That nobody had seen, and the woman who claimed it, whoever she was, she couldn't say. *Just a black man. A big nigger. A big stooped over nigger with arms that stretched down past his knees. Hair on his back. And muscles. Big muscles, hard as chunks of tar, all bunched up around his neck. That's all she could describe. His big, black heaving chest, and how she beat her lily white hands against it. So the men came looking for the big nigger, but they didn't look hard.*

Bertrand turned to his side in the bed and pushed the pillow under his head. He drew his knees up toward his belly and took a deep breath, trying to distract his thoughts from Rosewood and the terrors his wife had suffered. Through the window on his side of the bed, he could see a bright half-moon riding like a boat above the woods. God is a good God, he thought. He will protect. In the morning he would go to Jacks and Jacks would help get Jimmy Lee a fair hearing. That was the best, after all. To follow the law. *Without laws, there would be chaos and chaos was what had happened in Europe—but no, there had been no chaos in Europe, only terror, and it was the law that had made the terror.* Again, he moved about in the bed trying to get comfortable, trying to induce sleep.

A candlefly rested on the ceiling in the circle of light cast by the lamp's chimney. Another flew past, throwing a soft, dark shadow across the ceiling. It looked for a moment like a bird had entered the room. But, he thought, this is not Europe. This is America, and we have fought the big war to make things right, so now things must get right. If you didn't trust that things would get right, then they never would. It was the lot of the colored man that we suffer, and yet to make things right we must risk suffering anew. But things would get right, he knew. He had faith that things would get right, even if Luellen didn't. God decrees that we must have faith and faith is evidence of things unseen. Of course, he didn't know what Jacks would say, but he had faith that Jacks was good. He turned again, this time glancing at Luellen. She sat still, her attention focused on her book, but he was not certain that she was actually reading it. Her lips seemed to move. "Luellen," he called softly, but she did not respond. Then she is not reading, he thought. She is dreaming and she would be dreaming about something from her hell book: The boys in Indiana hanged from a tulip poplar. The wood of that tree is soft, but apparently strong enough to hold two flailing boys. Or she dreamed of the man in Birmingham who was beaten and castrated just for the sport of white men. They left him on the side of the road to bleed to death, but he was found and saved. He disappeared from Birmingham, like so many others, to become a ghost in some Northern city. Most likely though, that flutter of her eyelids meant she dreamed of Rosewood. Dream on, my sweet, he thought. We'll get a cake out of it. The thought of a cake made him smile, for many such evenings, when this distraction set upon Luellen, she baked all night, something about the stirring of cake batter or the smell of baking soothed her. He closed his eyes, and the image of a hulking black ape came to him, and he knew that he was that ape.

Run. Run. Run.

Luellen's poppa had said it first. "Run, y'all, run! Don't stop 'til ya git to John Wright's." Then her momma had said it. Luellen had told him that her mother's voice was calmer than her poppa's, but repeated his instructions exactly. Momma handed Luellen her shoes and threw her jacket at her. Luellen sat down to put on her shoes, pulling at the knots in the laces, but Poppa grabbed her by the hand with such a jerk that she dropped the shoes. He pushed her out the back door. "We right behind you." Then Big Sis came out, her hair wild, her eyes wide, still crusted with sleep. Big Sis grabbed Luellen by the hand and dragged her, her bare feet tripping across the cold, sandy yard. They scattered the chickens, which had gathered in a hub around the front of the hen house. Her hand slipped from her sister's grip, and she fell face down, then sat up and puckered to cry, but then she saw, now that they were a little distance from the house, the columns of black smoke twisting above the houses, invisible except for the starlight.

Big Sis grabbed her by the waist and carried her a little ways. More white men than she had ever seen at one time in Rosewood rushed down the street. The men crouched like soldiers, in groups, each moving quickly from house to house, throwing bricks through windows, kicking in doors, or sometimes shooting into the house and tossing in a torch or a stick of dynamite.

She knew they couldn't run down the street to John Wright's. She turned with Big Sis, looking for another way. Then their house went up. *It just lifted up like a hand had picked it up and dropped it. Dust came out from under it, and then Momma screamed. Big Sis let out a sound. Who would have thought a girl, just fifteen, could make such a sound? If she had lived in normal times . . . if things had been . . . had been . . . she could have been Marian Anderson. Big Sister.* Even that scream, that terrified girl's screech was a sound like a giant songbird, a pure contralto note in the January chill, as clean as the smell of turpentine.

For what seemed a year, they stood and looked at the house. The scream had barely settled out of the air when Big Sis ran back, but before she got to the back door, the house became an angel. *Not an angel, but like an angel, folding and opening its wings. It glittered like the angels on Christmas cards, or the ones you saw in the windows of the white stores in Gainesville. It shimmered; it became wavy, papery. It fluttered. It turned as golden as a sunset. It sang, or rather it hummed, and whispered. It was doing all of that, and I was dancing. Dancing in that golden light trying to move close, then closer, and then closer into that light and heat. Trying to get right up next to Big Sis.*

Luellen had danced between the heat and the chill, hop-scotching across the thin line of singeing grass. Singing Poppa. Poppa. Poppa. Then, somebody grabbed her from behind. Scooped her up and put a big hand over her mouth. All she remembered then was the woods, being carried by the running man. The man occasionally said, "Hush, hush, child, hush." She saw the man's thumb as it moved in front of her eyes. He was a white man. She went limp.

When she came to, she saw a white woman leaning over her, and then a colored woman. Whispers, lanterns, and a dank smell. She wanted to scream, but then she recognized the woman: Mrs. John Wright, looking every bit like it was her last day on Earth. "Oooh, child," Mrs. Wright said, and pulled Luellen into her arms, "you gone be all right." Others were there. Cousin Tisha Mae, and Sister Velma Hawkins from down the street. Suzie Griffin from her class at school was sitting over in a corner clutching one of her precious dolls. They had all taken refuge in John Wright's cellar, the only building in the town that had a cellar.

They found Momma about an hour later. Luellen didn't recognize her. She sat in Sister Velma's lap, and Sister Velma said, "Daughter, yo' momma safe. We found yo' momma. Go now to yo' momma." But the woman they helped down the ladder into the lantern-lit cellar looked nothing like Momma. Her blistered face could have been her own, but the broken way she moved, and the dull stare and twisted countenance was not Momma.

They hid a day in the cellar, and sneaked out early on the second morning. Luellen remembered she alternately clutched her mother, and was clutched by her. At first she was the child, and then she was the parent. They went back and forth like that, not daring to speak, letting the others, Mrs. Wright, Cousin Tisha Mae, Sister Velma speak for them. They got into the back of a mule drawn wagon, and slowly, under the clearest, starriest sky she had ever seen, started down Highway 19 towards Gainesville. The air was sweet and charred, laced here and there with the acrid threads from still fuming homes. It was not until she was a little ways down the street that she suddenly shivered. The landscape had changed. Not a house stood, except occasionally a wall or a few beams of a flame-scarred frame. All that was left was John Wright's two-story house and store. No one resented it. How John Wright, a white man on his knees before white men, begged to save it while they hid under its floors. If someone on that wagon said anything, it was Mrs. Wright, but what she said didn't make sense to Luellen, then. " . . . He openeth the seventh seal, there was silence up in heaven . . . and when he openeth the seventh seal. . . ."

More tortured than these memories was what she imagined about things she never saw, the things she heard about, which replayed, amplified in her mind. She never found out how Poppa died—Momma simply couldn't remember. She asked around when she was older, and she got bits and pieces that didn't add up. He had died of a bullet, or from dynamite. She heard plenty of stories about how other men died. Mr. Jim Carrier was made to dig his own grave and then shot so that he fell over into it. Most folks were hanged, some with ropes, some with chains. Cousin Tisha Mae lost a son in the fires. Sister Velma's son had his brains blown out. *Lord God!* They said they found Big Sis in the house, a heap in a charred spot. She had been burned down to nothing, except her heart, because a human heart cannot burn. The form of her body lay in ashes. It was silken and powdered, black where her hair had been, white in the outline of her bones. But there in the middle of the powdery ribs, her heart. Red. A little singed and dried of all its blood. At the funeral Luellen wanted to open the casket, to see what was left of Big Sis. *Just her heart. That was God's doing. That was significant of something.*

For years, no one talked of Rosewood. Cousin Tisha Mae died, and then Momma, and then Sister Velma and soon there was no one in Gainesville left to talk about it. She went away to college at Fort Valley, and one day, sitting in Henry Hunt Library, she opened an old issue of *The Gainesville Sun* to find a picture of Rosewood. In the picture, a group of white men were standing around the smoldering remains of a house. She could never figure whose house it was. No other house was left standing to give her a reference. One of the men wore a brimmed hat, a stylish short coat, and riding boots. She couldn't see it, but she knew by the way he stood with his hands on his hips that he wore a holster and pistol. He was looking down at the remains of the house, which were no more than ashes and a few items that escaped the flames—a galvanized wash tub in the foreground, the frame of a metal bed still standing. Next to the photograph, an article, and every word of it a lie.

She tore out the picture from the paper, letting the sound of the ripping cut through the quiet library. She didn't care who saw her do it. That was the beginning of her scrapbook, her "America Book," her "Book of Little Terrors," her "Book of Remembrance" and her "Book of The Invisible History of the United States of Goddamn America."

TWELVE

Bertrand suddenly woke to find himself in the dark, Luellen apparently having blown out the lamp and gone downstairs. He couldn't decipher how long she had been gone but judged from the height of the moon outside the window that he hadn't been asleep for more than a few minutes. He could still smell smoke from the lamp, and from downstairs came the clank of the stove eye covers. He knew Luellen was starting a fire in the stove, preparing to bake cakes.

He lay for a few minutes longer, thinking that he needed his rest if he were to face Jacks first thing in the morning. He didn't want to be dull in front of the white man. He wanted to be able to answer him question for question and fact for fact. Jacks was an educated man, and so was he, and he wanted their meeting to be the meeting of two men of equal education, even if Jacks was richer. Experience, too, is a wealth, as is education, he thought, and Jacks' experiences could never compare to his. He had traveled to Europe, seen London, Paris and Berlin—though all through the lens of war. He had been to the deserts of North Africa, to the hills of Italy. Jacks, with all of his wealth and his University of Georgia education, had rarely traveled to Atlanta, much less out of the country. Bertrand had met all kinds of people in the army, people from all over the United States, North Africa, and Europe. Though not fluent in any foreign language, he had taken French in college, and knew enough of it and enough Italian to ask directions or to compliment a lady; he had a modicum of German and could order a ham sandwich and a beer. Jacks knew none of this. Jacks would see who he had become, no longer a potential farmhand, and never the colored school teacher that Jacks imagined him to be. He was his own man, molded by American experience. He was American.

Downstairs, he found Luellen striking a match across the stove top. The wood in the stove, doused with kerosene, exploded, and flames leapt above the stove top, until she covered the eye. She had already taken out her bowls, her flour and fresh eggs, gathered just that morning from the hens. As he came in, she smiled at him. It was a weary smile, one that signaled a resignation to her restlessness and the absurdity of baking a cake at midnight. "You might as well get your sleep," she said.

"I guess this thing got us both," he whispered, not wanting to disturb his mother, whose room was next to the kitchen, though he suspected that Milledge was already awake, having heard the clanking of the stove. He sat at the small table, facing her as she shifted flour into a mixing bowl. "What are you making this time?"

"Just a plain one, I think. Just a plain white cake."

"Maybe put on chocolate icing. Mrs. Crookshank asked for another chocolate one."

Luellen sneered. "I don't care what she wants. She'll take what I make." She measured in baking powder, salt, and sugar, cracked the eggs on the side of the bowl and poured them into the mixture. "Maybe this one will just be for us. I can't be worried about what the whites want just now."

"Maybe so," he said with a sigh. He didn't want to think about the whites either, but it seemed unavoidable. Colored people were always thinking about white people, from morning until night, worrying about what white people do or think. Maybe there had been a time, in childhood, before he had language, that he didn't think about white people, but for so long this world of Talmaedge County had been divided between white people and colored people, as if there were no other kind of people on Earth. There were the white churches and the colored churches, the white schools and the colored schools, the white waiting rooms and the colored waiting rooms. There was how you were supposed to act around white people and how you weren't, and what you could say and what you couldn't. This world of Talmaedge County was always sized up by what white people wanted and what they might do.

"For my birthday," he said, "I would like a special cake from you. With caramel icing, maybe, one like I saw in Paris with thin little layers with lots of creamy icing between the layers."

"They call it a torte."

"I don't know what they call it. But I would like to have one, just to taste something different. Maybe just before school starts up again, we can go on a picnic somewhere. Maybe down to those Indian mounds. We have never seen them."

"Do they let Negroes go there?"

"It's a federal park—"

"Doesn't mean they let Negroes in?"

"Well, then we'll just go down by the river somewhere. Find a nice shoal where we can spread out a blanket. We'll have Momma make a ham, or have Beah fry some of her chicken that the white folks so crazy about, and then for dessert we'll eat that—what do you call it—that French cake?"

"Torte. That would be nice." She buttered the cake pans, then opened the oven and held her hand inside to check its readiness. "One day, husband . . . one day." She sat at the table and folded her hands into her lap.

"And why not today?"

"I reckon you know that as much as I do."

"No. What I reckon is that if you don't try, nothing will ever happen."

"I'm all for trying." She clucked her tongue. "I just ain't for trusting."

"It seems to me that they go hand in hand."

"Not if one hand is white."

"You know that ain't the truth. What about your Mrs. Eleanor Roosevelt? You are always touting her goodness." Luellen had told him that Mrs. Roosevelt had started clubs for black women called "Eleanor Clubs." In these secret clubs, the women pooled their money and made plans for when they could take over the white households they worked for. Though she knew no one who belonged to such a club, Luellen had her own Eleanor Club box where she put away a few dollars every month from the sale of cakes and eggs.

"One in a million."

"What about Mr. Henry Wallace? You like him. If he runs for president he might even put a colored man on the ballot."

"It'll be the last colored man on a ballot, too."

"What about Mr. Upton Sinclair? You like him. You are always calling his name from *New Masses*. And one day the mailman is going to figure out what *New Masses* is then we will have to hightail it out of here." Luellen read *New Masses*, *Opportunity*, and *Crisis*, socialist leaning magazines.

She read pamphlets that promoted equality, one called the "Four Freedoms," and another "The Races of Mankind," and sometimes shared these with her school children.

"Yes," she said. "I admit it. And there was John Brown and Abraham Lincoln, too. But they aren't the regular whites. The regular whites will cut down a Negro as soon as look at you."

"Now that ain't exactly so—"

"It's true enough. You mark me. Oh, now, you hear them talk about being fair to 'our colored citizens' and treating somebody 'just like family.' But, husband, you know as well as I do—if a Negro stepped up into Bethany Baptist on Sunday morning, he'll be swinging from a tree by Sunday afternoon. And those same smiling church-going ofays will be talking about how The Bible tells us to separate the races—and if I'm not right, if the regular white isn't a prejudiced hypocrite then how do you account for these black-hearted politicians they elect? Negroes didn't elect them."

"I concede that point," Bertrand said, watching as his wife checked the oven again. "But there are many who would do right if given a chance, and I think the time has come. Take Wayne Henson. I had known of him most of my life. You might say we grew up together since he grew up just a mile or so through the woods from here, but of course, we grew up separately. And we went to the war separately. But, Luellen, something happened to make us come together. The war changed Wayne for the better—"

"And now he's dead, and I wonder which of these Ku Klux Klan bastards killed him. For all you know it could have been Venable *and* Jacks. In fact, husband, do you think anything goes on in Talmaedge County that those two county barons don't know of and approve of? Bertrand, I hate to say it, but you are wrong about Jacks, and you might as well have pronounced the death sentence on Jimmy Lee when you told him to trust the law. There is no law in Georgia that a Negro can trust."

"But things change."

"It hasn't changed, yet. And I wonder if you should go to Jacks tomorrow. It's too late for Jimmy Lee—that's a shame—but you needn't draw attention to yourself."

"It can't hurt to talk to him."

"You don't know that." She poured the batter into the buttered pans and put the pans in the oven. "This is such beautiful heat—" she said, "the wood stove—so rich and even. You can't get that from a gas oven."

Bertrand was thrown by her sudden change of topic and stared at her while she wiped her hands on her apron, stepped back from the stove, and looked admiringly at it. It seemed nothing special to him, a Kitchen Queen with a water reservoir, its top seasoned by many years of spattering grease. He was thinking it would be risky to talk to Jacks, and he would have to approach Jacks with just the right tact. Certainly Jacks would want to save a good farm hand, but he had to appeal to more than just what was practical. He would have to appeal to Jack's conscience, to his sense of what was right. "I wonder what Jacks thinks is right."

"What?" Luellen looked at him quizzically, then back to the stove. "Nothing. Jacks doesn't think in terms of right and wrong, just in terms of what he wants."

"He's had a mother and father, and no matter, he must have loved them. When you love someone, you would think it's wrong to hurt that person—"

"Of course he would think it's wrong to hurt someone *he* loved, whether it was a person or a cow. I see what you are trying to say, husband, but it won't work. Morality isn't how you treat yourself, it's how you treat others. These country ofays build glass houses around themselves so they don't feel what other people feel—that is what *Negroes* feel. We become things to them, slaves, animals—just things."

"I don't believe that. I mean. . . ." He scratched his head. "I mean, I see what you mean about the glass houses, but glass can be broken. I think about Wayne. Now maybe he was in a glass house, like you say, but then that glass got smashed open by the war, and he started to see people as just people."

"So it takes a war? Well, then, we need a war every day." She sat at the table across from him. "Don't think that I am saying things will never change, Bertrand. If I thought that, then why would I bother with the school children? But look, it took two hundred and forty-six years to abolish slavery and then we had a few years of the Reconstruction before the Jim Crow set in. . . ." She counted quickly on her fingers. "In three hundred and twenty-seven years, we have come just this far. I figure it will take another three hundred to get to back to the Reconstruction, when we can have more than one Negro in congress at a time."

"It's not that bad. Take Roosevelt, now, he had his 'Black Cabinet—'"

"Even that he called it such a thing as *black* shows you what he thought of us."

"But he had Ma Bethune to the White House and Ralph Bunche in the government."

"And when Walter White asked him to stop lynching, he wouldn't do it. Husband, they always have their favorite one or two of us. Their mammies and their uncles. But you cannot measure by that—you got to measure by the whole."

"You calling Ma Bethune, a woman like that, a mammy?"

"I am saying that it can't be right for just one or two of us. It's got to be right for everybody—even the whites. Yes, even these poor, scuffling whites like that Henson woman. So it doesn't matter if they make Ralph Bunche president of the United States—better yet, make Mary Bethune president." She waved her hand as if imagining a newspaper headline. "Ma Bethune wins presidency—first Negro woman is president! Now that would be progress." She turned sober. "But it wouldn't make a difference to a poor soul like Jimmy Lee." She opened the oven and breathed deeply. Bertrand could smell the sweet heat of the baking, full of vanilla. "Ahhh," she said, looking at him with what he measured to be glee in her face, "Baking is so wonderful, isn't it? It's the one thing that Momma kept doing . . . after everything changed. She made the most beautiful cakes, not to mention the taste. Oh, but if only I could make a cake like Momma."

"Luellen." He wanted to tell her to let it go. To try and get beyond Rosewood, to think about the future and let the ugliness of the past go away, but he said, "Do you think you can forgive them? I mean the white folks for what happened at Rosewood."

She turned to him and cocked her head to one side, seemingly considering the question. Then she turned back to the stove, shut the oven door. "I *have* forgiven, husband."

"News to me."

"I have forgiven, yes. You don't see me out trying to kill anybody, do you? I know I am hard on them. But I am not murdering them. If I had wanted to do harm. . . ." She chuckled. "I would put a drop of poison in every slice of cake that gets served at Maribelle's. Half of the whites in Bethany would be dead by now. Maybe Negroes forgive *too* easily. We don't have any IRAs or KKKs. We just get on along. But I haven't *forgotten*, now, and I never will. You don't expect me to forget my momma and poppa, do you? And Big Sis?" She sat again, subdued, as if sleep might at last be coming to her. "But they don't want to be forgiven, Bertrand. Have you thought about that? They don't even see what they have done wrong. Oh, they're good at whitewashing history. You can't erase history. It's in the people's bones and dreams. Everywhere you look, there's history."

"What y'all so loud about?" asked Milledge.

"Ahw, Ma, did we wake you up?" Bertrand asked, turning in his chair to look at her. She stood behind him in the doorway, tying the belt of her robe. Bobbie pins showed around the edges of the paisley scarf she had tied her hair up in.

"You would have, if I had slept a wink. What is it? Near to three o'clock? Lord, I ain't going to be no good tomorrow."

"Why don't you take the day off for a change?" Luellen said. "Let ole King Jacks fix his own breakfast."

"And he sure enough have a fit and fire me."

"Ahw, he ain't fixin' to fire you, not in a hundred years. He couldn't get along without you."

"That's the truth," Milledge said. She moved around to the front of the stove, opened the oven and looked in, and then moved over to a small table on the far side of the stove where there was a basin and a pail of spring water. She dipped water and poured it into the basin. "We'll just soak these dishes for tonight and wash them tomorrow, so we can go on back to bed."

"Momma, don't worry about the dishes," Luellen said, standing. "I'll clean up."

"That's what I'm saying, I don't want you to clean up. I want you to go on back to bed. Whether you sleep or not is up to you, but I just as soon have you upstairs."

"I'm sorry, Milledge," Luellen said. "With all that was going on, I got restless."

Milledge raised both palms to stop her. "I know, child. I ain't fussing. I'm just shushing y'all so I can get at least a wink of rest."

Bertrand and Luellen both apologized.

"As soon as the cakes are ready." Luellen gathered and started to put away the bowls and ingredients. Milledge still stood on the far side of the stove. She rubbed her palms against her cheeks as if she were trying to wake herself. Then she turned to Bertrand. "What this I heard you say about Jacks?"

"I've decided to go and talk to him about Jimmy Lee."

Milledge raised a finger as if to stop him. "Leave it. Leave it alone."

Bertrand sighed deeply. Long ago Milledge had lost maternal authority over him, so her admonishing finger no longer raised a sense of obedience in him. Yet, he respected her and did not want to be at odds with her. "Momma, I'm just fixin' to speak to him. That is all. I am just fixin' to ask him to intervene, if need be. Nothing more than that. Besides, how can I just sit here and do nothing to help Jimmy Lee? He's not family, but he is connected to us, now."

"He's a lowlife," Milledge said. "He ain't worth it."

"Every man, even a lowlife, is worth something. If not to you, then to God."

"Then you let God talk to Jacks. He do a better job at it than you."

"Momma, be reasonable."

"Be reasonable, *nothing*. Y'all figure you know everything because you went off to college and you're young and I ain't." She pointed to Bertrand, sharply. "Now, you listen to me. I know more about Jacks than you could know in a hundred years. I knew his daddy and I knew all about his momma, too. I knew about him when he was a boy and I know him as a man. I have cleaned every room in his house. I have cleaned his clothes, including his underpants. I have seen him when he was sleeping, and I have seen him when he was naked." She took a step closer to Bertrand as if to make sure he saw her. "I have seen him tell the truth and I have seen him lie. And I'm here to tell you, as God is my witness, Bertrand, you can trust Jacks no more than you can trust a rattlesnake!" She took a deep breath and looked like she wanted to cry. "Jacks is just out for Jacks! You think he helped you in college because he is a friend of the colored? He ain't friend to nobody. I don't know why he helped you and your brother, but I can tell you it wasn't because he is your friend." She turned to Luellen. "Child, it's going to be bad for me to say what I'm fixin' to say, but you have just got to let the law take its course. Jimmy Lee's been a rascal a long time, and things just caught up with him."

Luellen seemed to consider. "I told him to run. But he didn't. You can say what you want about him, but at least he didn't go down like some mumbling Step 'n' fetch it."

"Step 'n' fetch it?" Suddenly Milledge appeared angry, but she spoke softly. "You don't know the half of it. You are just a child. You ain't been nowhere. I ain't been nowhere either, but I sure know where I am."

"I know where I am, too. I know where I am better than you do." Luellen turned her back to Milledge and continued to put away the baking ingredients.

Milledge's lips pursed, unsure. Then she sighed. "Yes. I know you have had a hard life." She wrung her hands. "It's just that I don't like this talk. It scares me so."

Luellen turned again to Milledge. "I don't like it either. I'm with you, Momma. I'm against him talking to Jacks."

"If not Jacks, then who?" Bertrand nearly shouted. "We aren't just going to hang a man out to dry? Just forget about him are we? If Jacks can't help us, who do we get?"

"There must be a Negro lawyer in Atlanta," Luellen said. "We write to the NAACP or the ILD."

"Communists—Shit!—They'll lynch us all."

"They'll do that anyway."

"Not if Jacks is on our side."

"You and your almighty Jacks. He's got you blindsided."

"I ain't a mule for nobody."

"Not even for yourself." Luellen's voice seemed to drift away. "I told him to run. I am tired of all of this now. I want to leave. Go up North. Bertrand, I think it's time to leave this hell hole and go someplace where we can live. Canada or Haiti or back to Africa."

"Africa? You ain't African."

"I am not American, either. Not by the way I'm treated."

"Well, I didn't fight a war for Africa."

Luellen paused, cocked her head. "That's right. You fought for America, but that doesn't make you—"

"I am an American! What else am I?"

Luellen waved her hand in dismissal.

"Don't start talking about moving up North." Milledge spoke into the quiet. "Listen to me. You can have a good life here. You just got to know how to do it. You got to know where the lines are, what you can do and what you can't. You got to act right around white people, and when you around your own you can be yourself."

Bertrand had heard his mother and older relatives say this kind of thing before. Go along to get along, they sometimes called it. He understood well why they had acted that way, living a double life, a subservient one for the white people, and what passed for a normal one among the coloreds. "Momma, I love you, so I'm telling you. I am not fixin' to act 'right' just because some white man wants me to act a certain way. I'm fixin' to act just like a white man when I think that's what I want."

"Only one problem with that," Luellen said. "You ain't white."

"No, son," Milledge said. "You ain't white."

Bertrand rolled his eyes, "I ain't trying to be white, either. I'm trying to be a man."

"Your daddy was a man," Milledge said, "and he worked every day of his life for Jacks—"

"But times have changed now."

"And I might not be a man, but I am a person and I, too, have worked every day of my life for Jacks."

"But times have *changed*."

"I was there when his daddy died, and I was there during the boll weevil time, there in good times and in bad. He owes me, but that doesn't mean that I am less a human being because I step and fetch for a white man."

Luellen held out her hands to Milledge. "You don't step 'n' fetch— I didn't mean—"

"We all do. We do because we have to do it. Things ain't changed that much."

Milledge drew her arms tightly around her and started to squeeze between Luellen and the stove. "Don't burn your cakes."

"But Momma," Bertrand said, catching her elbow as she passed him. "Jacks does owe *you!*" She was his way to Jacks, it occurred to him. Of all the colored people in Talmaedge, his mother was the closest to Jacks. She spent most of her day in his house, caring for it, cooking for him, and she had done it for over twenty-five years. If anyone could appeal to Jacks, it would be she. "Momma, won't you say something to Jacks?"

"No!" She pulled her arm away. "About what?"

"You know what. Just ask him to keep an eye out for Jimmy Lee. To see that things go fairly. Tell him that Jimmy Lee is family."

"But he ain't, and I am not lying."

"Would you let a man go to jail, or worse, die, if you could prevent it?"

"What can I do?"

"Just talk to Jacks. Like you said, you know him better than anybody. He owes you."

"If he do, this is not how I want to get paid. Jimmy Lee will get what Jimmy Lee deserves."

"And what about Beah?"

"She won't be the first hussy without a husband."

"But she's family. What about cousin Deacon? It'll break his heart."

"His heart been broke, and his mind, too. I am not getting mixed up in this."

"What about me, Momma. Won't you do it for me?"

"You got no business in it."

"But I am going to be in it. I am going to talk to Jacks this morning."

"What for!" Milledge raised her hands above her head. "What for? I told you he don't care. He don't care about Jimmy Lee. My husband worked all his life for him and he didn't even come to his funeral. At least his ole daddy would have come and stood in the back of the church. But Jacks didn't even say he sorry to me. Not one mumbling word. I tell you, he don't care about nothing but Jacks."

"Please, Momma, all you have to do is walk in with me. You don't have to say a word to him. Just stand there when I talk to him."

"Let her be," Luellen said. She opened the oven and took out the cake layers, now risen and golden brown. The scent of them suddenly made Bertrand hungry.

"Please, Momma."

"No."

"Well, I'll do it anyway, with or without your help."

"That will be your last mistake," Milledge said, leaving the kitchen and slamming the door to her bedroom.

THIRTEEN

He slept only two hours, rose with the sun and shaved, washed himself in the basin, put on a fresh white shirt, gold colored cufflinks, a tie, a suit and his oxfords. He thought that he might wear his army uniform, but now that he had put on a little weight, the pants had become too snug. He hoped his church clothes would not overemphasize the point that Jacks should respect him. Jacks didn't have to like him, but he had to respect him. Bertrand gritted his teeth. Maybe it was pride, he thought. "Pride proceedeth the fall." But why shouldn't he be proud? He had done things to be proud of, damn it, and he was tired of being half a man just because white people wanted to treat him like one. He had been a corporal in the 761 Tank Battalion in General George Patton's Third Army. He had fought in the Ardennes and had helped to liberate a camp of Jews. He had done as much for his country, this United States, as any man, woman or child in Talmaedge. Half a man was half a life, and he wanted to live fully. Why shouldn't Jacks listen to him?

When he was dressed, he sat down on the bed next to Luellen. She appeared to be asleep, but he suspected her placid breathing a disguise to avoid him. He kissed her cheek. She seemed to stiffen, the breathing interrupted for a moment, but she did not open her eyes. Her last words to him before falling asleep had been that white men were bound to stick up for one another.

"I don't believe you give Mr. Jacks enough credit," Bertrand had said. "Mr. Jacks may be the best friend the colored have in Talmaedge County." He knew when he said it that he was overstating, but drowsiness was taking him, and he hadn't the focus to make good sense.

"Then the Lord help Talmaedge County," Luellen had said.

When he went downstairs, he found that his mother had already left on her two mile walk to Woodbine. She had rekindled the fire in the cooking stove and had made coffee, fried potatoes, and bacon. He poured a cup of coffee and sat on the porch. Looking into the woods, he watched the light play among the trees, light and shadow replacing one another as the foliage moved in the canopy, but always it seemed the same degree of light and shadow. By noon, it would be mostly light as the sun shone directly down on the woods, but at nightfall it would be all darkness. This, though, was nature, he thought, and it didn't always have to be this way with men. Men could let in as much light or darkness as they chose. They could live their lives in shadow, in ignorance, full of hatred and small mindedness, or they could embrace light. Wayne Henson embraced light. Who knows, even then, as he was sliding down the embankment with the buckshot riddled through his heart, he might have been reaching out to some great, bright spirit.

Bertrand put his cup beside the chair, rose, and took a deep breath. He would walk to Woodbine, even in his clean oxfords. If he drove the car, he might arrive before his mother, and he didn't want to get there before she had settled in and was feeding Jacks. He took his good fedora from the hat rack just inside the door. Besides, he thought, the walk would do him good.

The first view of Woodbine from the path was of the pastures. The path bled into a tractor road and led uphill between two fenced pastures, one for cows and the other for sheep. Cresting the hill, the view broadened and Bertrand could see the back of the manor house. Woodbine was a grand enough house by the standards of Talmaedge County, but it was square and white compared to the antebellum mansions with their fluted columns and brick porticos in the southward, cotton farming counties. It looked rather like an ordinary farm house, only larger and graced with a porch that curved from front to back. Its grandeur seemed to have come less from architecture and more from its position at the wooded hill's crest.

Bertrand stopped in the grove of old trees that populated the backyard. In front of him the path lead to the kitchen door, where through the screen he could see his mother moving about. Would it be too much, he thought, if he went around to the front door and knocked there? But the idea of his mother answering the door for him like a house servant was too much to bear. He wouldn't like it, and she would think him crazy. He took off his hat and rapped on the screen door. Immediately, his mother was there, her face full of expectancy. She smiled at him, queerly he thought, as if she were both happy and unhappy to see him, both resigned to his task and resistant to it. She did not greet him, but nodded toward a chair in the corner of the kitchen. He had been in this kitchen many times as a child, and it had changed over the years, the wood stove and icebox replaced by a gas stove and refrigerator. The sink now had running water. Still, the kitchen seemed antiquated, a holdover from the days of slavery, with its large fireplace and brick hearth. Woodbine, he knew, had not been a slave house, having been built after the Civil War. Still, its purple bricks and black wainscoting made the room seem as much a dungeon as a kitchen.

"He eating his breakfast," Milledge said. "You want me to tell him you here?"

"Ma—"

"I'll tell him. I don't want to, but I'll tell him."

When she came back, she nodded and held the door to the dining room where Jacks had started taking his meals after remodeling the kitchen.

Jacks let out a surprised chuckle. "Where are you going, Bertrand? Today isn't Sunday. Why look at you. Tie. New hat. Nice links. I hope you didn't put on all that finery just to see me. School teaching must be treating you well."

"Yes, sir. Well enough, but. . . ." Why should he have to defend wearing good clothes? "I got these in New York . . . with Army pay."

"Gold links and perforated oxfords? Army must pay mighty well, I'll say. Wish I had a pair like that."

Bertrand didn't know what to say, so he thanked Jacks. He felt his smile wriggle nervously.

"You cook another goat, Bertrand?" Jacks asked, referring to plate of barbecued goat that Milledge had brought to Jacks the summer before the war.

"No, sir. But I heard you liked my goat so much."

"Sure did enjoy it. You need to do that again, as I don't see barbecued goat around here much anymore. Times have gotten easy, and people only want to eat pork and beef. And chicken, of course." He smiled, indicated the fried drumstick on his plate, turned it over as if inspecting it and he lifted it

124

to his mouth. Chewing, he said, "Your momma fries the best chicken in the world. They say that girl at Maribelle's chicken is good, but I believe that Millie's got her beat."

Bertrand wanted to say that the girl was his cousin Beah, and it was Beah that he had come to talk about, but now Jacks was talking about eating fried chicken for breakfast. There was a coyness in his speech, and Bertrand thought that Jacks was toying with him.

Abruptly, Jacks sat back in his chair and asked, "Now, what can I do for you?"

Coming after the casual conversation, the question seemed overly formal, and Bertrand, in spite of having planned his speech, was thrown. Of course, he thought, Jacks knew why he had come, since it wouldn't have taken long for the news of the stabbing to have gotten around the county. Maribelle Crookshank would have known, since Sheriff Cook and his deputies ate in her restaurant and she supplied her leftover suppers to the prisoners at the jailhouse. If Crookshank knew, then every white person in Talmaedege knew within a few hours. They would already have met and talked it over. The talk would have been one-sided, of course, but not necessarily Venable's side. It would simply be the "white" side: *No colored man is going to do that to a white man and get away with it.* If Jimmy Lee had anything going in his favor, it was that no white woman had been involved—even so, Bertrand feared, gossip might invent one.

"You want something for your schoolchildren?" Jacks asked after a pause. "Something I can talk to the school board about?"

He was playing, Bertrand thought. The school board never consulted with him. He took what they gave him, old books, old maps, a bucket of nubs of chalk sticks. He observed Jacks, who appeared to be about forty-five, with fine crow's feet crinkling the corners of his eyes and a prominent bald spot on the top of this head. His face, though, still appeared ruggedly youthful, tanned, but red on the back of the neck. He was lean and held himself erect even as he ate. Bertrand straightened his own back and held out his chest. He breathed easier. "Well, yes sir. I do. But this is not about the school, sir. This is a very serious situation."

"You mean Jimmy Lee?"

"Yes, sir."

"What's serious about it?"

"I'm concerned, sir."

"Concerned? Since when has concern been serious?" Jacks stuffed his cheeks with biscuit sopped in the chicken grease and egg yolk.

Bertrand wiped sweat from his mouth with the back of his hand. Why was he letting Jacks get to him? Why didn't he just come to the point? "I don't have to tell you, sir, that not all our white citizens are as helpful to the colored as you have been. You have always given us plenty of work and paid us fairly."

"Get to the point."

Bertrand sucked in a breath. "I am concerned that Jimmy Lee gets fair treatment for what he did." Then he added carefully. "Allegedly—"

"Allegedly?" Are you saying he didn't do it? My friend, Mr. Venable, might object to that idea."

"I'm not saying he didn't do it, sir. I am saying that he isn't guilty of anything until he is proven guilty."

"Are you a lawyer, Bertrand? Did you study law down in Fort Valley?"

"No—"

"And what about the Army? They teach you anything about the law in the Army?"

"No."

"So don't you think you had just better leave the law to the lawyers?"

Bertrand felt sweat trickle from his armpits and down his ribcage. The suit coat was too hot and he wished he could take it off. "Well, see, Mr. Jacks, pardon me, now. We colored people, even we who got a little education, haven't had much experience with the law. They don't teach law at Fort Valley." He didn't want to seem ignorant. "They do teach a little history and a little civics, so we do get to learn a thing or two. But no, we can't say that we actually know the law. That's why I've come to you."

Jacks shook his head, amused. "Bertrand, you are a good talker, you. You would probably make a good preacher, too. But why come to me? I don't know anything about the law. There's a mighty fine law school at the University, but I never set foot in it."

"I was hoping, sir, that you could help to see that things went fairly for him." Bertrand hoped he didn't sound as if he were groveling. Why should he say "sir," with every sentence? Was Jacks so insecure that he needed every colored man to bend down to him? Bertrand reminded himself that he had fought in a war, and that Jacks hadn't set foot out of Talmaedge County. "You see, I saw a lot in the war, and I know how people can be—"

"So you've been around the world, Bertrand? You don't think I know that? Who sent you? Do you think you could have gone away to college, and joined the army, and come back here to teach school without my knowing it?"

Suddenly Bertrand's face felt afire and sweat rolled down his cheeks. He wanted to say "Go to hell." Jacks was a big man in the county, all right, but he didn't control everything, much less anything outside of the county. He, himself, had made the decision to join the army. He had discussed it with his cousin John Robert, and Deacon. Deacon had argued against it. He reminded himself that they had enlisted in Atlanta, far from the reach of anyone in Talmaedge County. He swallowed and concentrated on his purpose. "I didn't mean anything, sir, except that . . . I ain't saying what he done"—he realized his grammar had slipped, but didn't correct it—"was right or wrong, but it ain't right if he's not treated fairly . . . What, you might not know . . . sir"— He had said 'sir' again— "that you . . . you are tied up in this—"

"Me? How so?"

"Well, of course, Jimmy Lee is your worker—"

"And? . . ."

"And a good one, too."

"Yes?"

"And Beah, his woman . . . she is Deacon's daughter. Deacon worked for you all of his life right up until he fell sick. I believe he would come back today if he could."

"Deacon was a good man."

"And, of course, Beah, is my momma's kin—so Jimmy Lee is almost family to us, and we have worked for you, my momma and my daddy—"

"Yes," Jacks said, pushing away his plate. "I get the picture."

But does he really get the picture? Bertrand thought. He looked over his shoulder to see his mother standing in the kitchen, having left the door open. She appeared busy, but he could tell by her stiffness that she was attentive to every word he and Jacks spoke. She would critique him when he got home, but she would not help him now. "Mr. Jacks, begging your pardon, *sir*, I am not sure that you do get the picture." Jacks sat back in his chair. It made a loud squeak. "My *concern*—" Bertrand put his hands together, prayer-like, and pointed them at Jacks, underscoring his speech. "—is that things happen in this county . . . things that the law doesn't always control. And when you have a colored boy like Jimmy Lee attack a white man like Mr. Venable, well . . . that's a terribly big thing to happen. People talk about it, and that talk could get out of hand, and then . . . who knows what might happen, Mr. Jacks? In other words, Jimmy Lee is going to need some protection."

"What makes you think *I* can protect him? If the Klan wants to lynch him, how am *I* to stop them? You don't think I have any association with the Klan, do you?"

Milledge came to stand beside Bertrand. She wrung her hands in her apron. "Just that no harm would come to him if he was allowed to stay here at Woodbine. Just if you can go get him. Beah, she got the bail money. He can sleep in the barn. See, you are most rightly respected by everybody, and nobody would come—"

Jacks stopped her with a glance. "And I'm supposed to protect Jimmy Lee? I don't have a thing against Jimmy Lee. Hate to lose him. Best thing that could happen to him is that he gets sent over to Reidville and never come back. Bertrand, for Pete's sake, *tell me,* what do you reckon ought to happen to a colored man that stabs a white man?"

Bertrand fingered his hat brim round and round. "Well, if he did it, and I reckon he did, then he ought to be sent to jail. Leastways, he ought to go to the courthouse."

"You know, Mr. Venable is my friend and neighbor. How do you think he's going to feel if I harbor the man that stuck him with a knife?" Jacks clenched his teeth hard, but Bertrand wasn't sure that he wasn't fighting to keep from laughing. "Bertrand, do you believe in justice?"

"Justice?"

"Justice, Bertrand. You know what justice means?"

"Yes, sir. But it's a hard question—do I believe in it? I guess I believe in it—"

"Guess? Either you do or you don't."

"Well, I do. I went off and fought for it."

"Well, I'm glad you did. But tell me Bertrand. Tell me with all of your learning and all of your traveling, what is justice?"

Bertrand was unsure of whether the question was a trap. He studied Jack's boyish face with its quick bright eyes. Jacks seemed at that moment to be sincerely interested in knowing what he thought, but how many times had he heard of white men who have set up colored men just this way. "It's complicated."

"Hell, I know it's complicated, that's why I asked."

"It's doing right."

"But whose right? What I think is right might not be what the judge thinks is right. Isn't that why we just had that damn war because somebody's right wasn't the same as the other somebody's?"

"The Bible . . ." Milledge said.

"The Bible? More wars have been fought over religion than over land. Fact is, you don't know what justice is."

Bertrand wanted to say that justice was in the law, but he knew that too many laws in Georgia were unfair. They were made by people like Jacks for their own benefit. Perhaps, he thought, he should say that justice lay in God. It was beyond the law, even beyond The Bible. "The Constitution. That's where you will find justice, Mr. Jacks, at least the kind I'm talking about. 'We the people, in order to form a more perfect union, establish—'"

"You learn that in the army?"

"No, sir. I learned that over at the Normal School, right here in Talmaedge, many years ago."

Jacks sighed. "All right. Meet me here—this afternoon, after my dinner, with your bail money—and we'll take the car over and get him out."

"Thank you, Jesus, Mr. Jacks," Milledge exclaimed. Bertrand thanked him, too. When they got back into the kitchen, Milledge, in a near faint, leaned against the table. Bertrand helped her to the chair in the corner and watched over her until she declared, shaking her head, that she was okay. He felt dull, as if every sense had been dampened. Part of him said he had won a great victory, and another said he had fallen into a trap, and was only now in the moment between the release of the trigger and the clenching of the jaws.

FOURTEEN

Just four years earlier, in the town of Rome in Floyd County, on the western side of the state, the famous tenor Roland Hayes had been beaten. Hayes had been born in the area, educated at Fisk University in Nashville where he had sung with the famous Jubilee Singers. He had traveled all over the country and then to Europe on a tour with his own trio, singing classical songs in French and Italian, but also singing Negro spirituals. Luellen loved the recordings of his spirituals, and since the time she had been in college, she had played them on her old tabletop Victor Victrola. The phonograph was made of honey-varnished oak and had a tone arm and crank made of burnished and black-enameled steel. Luellen considered it a work of art. More than once she had said that the feel of the crank handle, smooth and oval, gave her nearly as much pleasure as the music.

Before Bertrand stepped onto the porch, having come back from Woodbine, he heard Hayes' articulate tenor coming from the front room. The lyrics gave him pause, and he stood by the screen door listening before opening:

I know my robe's gon' to fit me well
I'm goin' to lay down my heavy load
I tried it on at the gates of hell
I'm goin' to lay down my heavy load

For some reason the song seemed to encourage Luellen, but for him it seemed morose and ominous. Since he had learned of Hayes' beating, the song reminded him more sharply of his place, and the place of all Negroes in Georgia. Though Hayes had been born in poverty, the son of a slave woman, he had managed to become one of the wealthiest people in the country. He had become so wealthy that he had returned to Georgia and purchased the plantation, over six hundred acres, on which his mother had been enslaved. He had performed for the wealthy in New York and Chicago, and for royalty in Europe, and yet in Georgia, when his wife wanted to buy pair of shoes, she was insulted, and he was beaten and jailed for protesting her treatment.

Luellen was in the kitchen. Very much unlike her, she was still in her night clothes. She looked up as he came in, and gave him a smile, her eyes wide and questioning. "How did it go?" she asked.

He nodded his head, not sure what the answer was. "He said he would help."

"But?"

The question gave him a heavy feeling. "But . . . I don't know."

Hell is deep and dark despair
I'm goin' to lay down my heavy load

She sighed deeply, turned to the stove, and pulled at the sleeve of her nightgown. "You had breakfast?"

"No, not hungry." He sat while she ate, saying little, but listening to another spiritual sung by Hayes called "L'il Boy." The song was about Christ as a little boy. After listening to a few verses, he went upstairs, and took off his clothes, and lay on the bed, wanting to nap before he had to meet Jacks again. But he could not fall asleep. His mind went back and forth, replaying his conversation with Jacks and thinking about Hayes, who after his beating was accused by the Governor of having first attacked the white men who beat him. As drowsiness came, among the twitter of bird calls from the woods, he thought about Ester pleading for the lives of her people before the king of the Persians. When she thought she might be killed for making her plea, she replied, "If I perish, I perish." For some reason, he couldn't think of, that comforted him.

When he woke, Luellen stood over him. She was dressed in the flower-print dress she often saved for church. She told him it was almost time, and he was suddenly alarmed, worried he had overslept and kept Jacks waiting.

"No, husband, relax. I've taken care of everything."

She had already driven to Maribelle's Diner where she had picked up Beah, who was waiting downstairs. Quietly, they ate a lunch of ham sandwiches and buttermilk. Beah seemed cold to Bertrand while they ate, but as they got in the car to make the short journey to Woodbine, Beah touched him on the arm and he nodded back to her. It was both a nod of apology and one of forgiveness. Luellen drove. As they pulled off the main road onto the tree-lined drive that lead up to the manor house, Bertrand suddenly felt his stomach clench into a painful knot.

"Luellen. Beah," he said, trying to even out his breath. "Y'all don't come. Just let me go. Just let me do it."

"It's too late now, husband. Besides, we are here now."

"Y'all can wait with Momma, or you can take the path on back to the house. I'll go with Jacks."

"No," Luellen said calmly. "We all go together. It's better that women go along. Isn't that right, Beah?" Beah didn't answer. "With women along, there's less chance of anything happening."

They drove to the back of the house and parked. Jacks was waiting for them in the yard. He waved Bertrand over to his car. "Come Bertrand," he called, "you can ride with me."

"Don't you go with him," Luellen said. Bertrand opened the car door and swung his legs out. "Don't you go with him." This time Luellen hissed. Her jaws clenched.

"Mr. Jacks," Bertrand called. "How are you? I reckon we can just follow you down there. That way it'll be the least trouble to you."

"Don't waste my time, now," Jacks said. "Those girls can take your car home, and you come ride with me. So we can talk." Bertrand stood and shut the car door.

"We'll follow you," Luellen said.

By now, Jacks had walked over to them. He seemed impatient. "Y'all go on back home," he said to Luellen. Bertrand and I will take care of this."

"But this here," Bertrand said pointing to Beah in the back seat, "is my cousin Beah. She's the one who will pay the bail."

"She can give you the money."

"I wants to go," Beah said. She was looking at Bertrand, but he felt she was talking to Jacks.

Jacks kicked at the grass a bit. "Okay, then. Come on. What for I don't know. It's just another worrisome thing to deal with." When Beah didn't get out of the car, Jacks turned to her and said, "You are wasting my time."

"But," Bertrand said, "they will just follow behind us."

"The hell they will. I'm already stretching my neck out for you. I'm not about to go into town being followed by a bunch of women. Now you either want me to get Jimmy Lee out, or you don't. I just as soon see him rot in there. So either get in this damn car, or not."

"Come on then, Beah," Bertrand said softly. Beah got out of the car, and Luellen followed her.

"And where do you think you are going?" Jacks asked Luellen.

"I intend to accompany—"

Jacks threw up his hands. Then he chuckled. "All right. If this isn't some circus!" The women sat in the back seat, and Bertrand in front, next to Jacks. As he drove, Jacks questioned Beah about Maribelle's Diner. He wanted to know why she wasn't working at lunch time, and she said she had gone in early to prepare the food. He wanted to know if her recipes were her own, or Maribelle's. Beah said that some were hers and some were Maribelle's. Who owns the chicken recipe? he wanted to know. I guess that one belongs to me, Beah said. Bertrand saw her smile slightly. Well, Jacks, concluded, you should write it down.

The bail fine was only twenty dollars, which surprised Bertrand. Luellen peeled a twenty dollar bill off of her roll of nearly two hundred and handed it to Beah. On the way home, Jimmy Lee sat in the back, behind the driver, with Beah in the middle, next to him.

Bertrand's stomach bothered him less now. He watched the swells of fields and forests pass by, framed on the horizon by hazy ridges. A cooling breeze rushed through the car, and outside, the landscape was serene, so quite it seemed nothing moved. The leaves and needles of grand shumard oaks and loblolly pines, a hundred feet tall, did not stir. The hayfields, ripening in the sun, and the shrubby margin between forest and field, where so much of the drama of life and death plays out, were still as a Dutch master's painting. Suddenly, with all the worry he had had in the morning, he felt proud of Talmaedge County. I live in a beautiful place, he thought. Even after they turned off the main road and drove past the vast fields of Thousand Acres, the Venable plantation, he was calm. They entered the hilly woods that lead down to the bridge. From the crest he saw the glinting snake of the river, with its iron colored boulders and white stripes of riffles.

From the back seat, Luellen spoke into his ear, her urgent whisper bringing him from his daydream, and he saw several cars parked along the road flanking the bridge and a crowd of people standing.

"Mr. Jacks," he said. "What you reckon going on?"

Jacks said nothing, but began to slow the car.

Bertrand looked at him, now in profile, his eyes shaded by the brim of his fedora, his mouth set firm. "Don't slow down, Mr. Jacks. Just keep driving through."

"Let me handle this," Jacks said.

"Look," Luellen said into Bertrand's ear. "There's Cook's car. How did Cook beat us here?"

"Mr. Jacks, why is Sheriff Cook here? What's going on?" His stomach knotted, then relaxed. He knew what was going on. He looked at Jacks but could not read in his face whether he was a part of it or not. "You said you would help us, Mr. Jacks. That was your word."

"I did." Jacks' voice had an icy crack in it.

"And now you won't?"

"Let me handle it." He stopped the car halfway down the hill, a distance from where the crowd gathered. "Y'all sit still. Be calm, now. I'll see what this is about."

"Back up," Bertrand said. His vision had blackened around the edges. He was aware that Luellen was speaking, but he focused on the men in the crowd, then on Jacks, and back to the crowd. "Back up fast." He wanted to grab the gear handle, but Jacks hands clutched it already.

"Don't worry," Jacks said. "I will handle this."

"That's just empty sweet talk," Luellen said.

The crowd was coming toward them, about fifteen men. Two of them were Cook's deputies, but the others, though familiar, he did not recognize. They were beginning to leave the bridge bed and climb the hill toward the car. One of the deputies was signaling to Jacks to bring the car forward.

"Maybe they just want me," Jimmy Lee said. Beah sighed sharply and Jacks said again to let him handle it.

"There are women in the car," Bertrand said. "A pregnant woman."

"He don't care," Luellen said. "He's with them." Contempt was in her tone, and Bertrand felt it was meant for him as much as for Jacks. "They didn't stop for women and babies in Rosewood. They swarmed like rats. A little nigger meat on the ground and they swarmed all over it. They won't stop with just one of us. When they're finished with one, they'll go on to the next one." Her hands fanned in front of her, "and the next one, tearing everything to bits—"

"Stop!" Bertrand said, he turned and put his hand on Luellen's shoulder.

"Yes, shut up and let me think," Jacks said.

"About what?" Luellen said.

"They just want me. Just let them take me." Jimmy Lee started to open the car door, but Jacks ordered him to stop.

"Shut up. Sit still, and let me handle it." He let the car roll forward, slowly to meet the men in the crowd.

"Mr. Jacks," Luellen said, "why do you want to do this to us? What have we done to you that you've got to do this to us?"

"Luellen, he's trying to help us," Bertand said.

"What you think I'm trying to do, Luellen?"

"You know, Jacks." She emphasized his name. "*Mr.* Jacks, you're going to need a strong mind, because this won't be easy on you. You've known Bertrand and Milledge for all your life. I'm Bertrand's wife, Beah is Deacon's daughter, and Jimmy Lee has worked for you for a good many years. It doesn't matter that we are *Negroes*. You are going to need a strong mind—"

"Luellen!" Bertrand tried to cut her off.

She raised her voice. "If he's going to kill me, he's going to know he's killed a person!"

"Ain't nobody going to kill you!" Jacks shouted.

"Bertrand," Luellen said quietly, as the car approached the crowd. "The minute this car stops, you run. If you want to live. You *run*. All of you. *Run*. Run every which-a-way. Run and hide."

Run. Run. Run. Bertrand thought. Luellen had been running since Rosewood. But what good was running? Wouldn't they catch her eventually? Hadn't they caught her now?

"Bertrand, if you don't run, you won't have a chance."

Bertrand nodded. He could feel the car slowing.

"Cook *and* Venable," Luellen said, pointing to them. "Bertrand, you see this now?"

Yes, Bertrand thought. It was obvious, but what was he to do about it? He turned to Jacks, who was smiling for Cook and Venable. The car stopped and Jacks turned off the engine and pulled up the brakes. "Y'all just stay put. I'll handle this." He turned and stared at Luellen. His eyes were clear and he smiled a little, a little break around his mouth. "These are friends of mine. They do what I tell them to do. Now, you stay put."

"Mr. Jacks," Luellen said. "I see your soul. I know your soul. You are not a'tall as hard as you think you are. You will *feel* something. You will feel something for the rest of your life, and it will *hurt* you."

"Shut up!" Jacks said and got out of the car. He leaned back before slamming the door. "Bertrand, keep her put."

No sooner had Jacks slammed his door than Bertrand heard the pop of the lock on Luellen's. He turned in the seat and saw that already she had one foot out the door. Their eyes met, and he saw in hers the distant wildness of the Rosewood trance. He started to speak to her, and suddenly a swelling came in his throat. All was lost now. All the dreams of whatever God had created for them, lost. He wondered in that moment why it was that he had been born and survived the war, only to meet this fate, here, in his home country. Maybe he had never had a life, but was only a figurine played out on a master game board. Luellen would run. He grabbed her wrist, holding it tightly and trying to pull her back into the car. What had called them together? What had made them pull one into the other with gentle kisses on the lips and fiery passion? And, yet, they would have no children to follow them. What had given him a mother who had nurtured him, and now, would tear him away in her old age? Was this the will of God or was this the devil's world? Luellen pulled against his grip. "*Bertrand, you can see this now.*" He loosened his grip, and she snatched her hand free, swung open the door. *Run!* She pushed the door wide and slipped out of the Buick, got low against the fender, and ran along the side of the car and crossed the ditch. A car was pulling up behind them, but Luellen was already running up the hill. She moved slowly, scrambling on the embankment. Jimmy Lee had started to sneak out of his side of the car, and Beah, following him, tripped over the floor hump. Bertrand ached all over. His hand clenched the door handle, but he did not pull it. He saw that Luellen was on level ground and she was running hard. *Oh God, let her get away. Let her run! But where to? It was useless.* He heard yelling, and knew that the alarm had been sounded. Cook, pointing to Jimmy Lee, was rushing past Jacks. Bertrand looked up the embankment. He couldn't see Luellen, only a slant of light through the trees.

PART THREE
THE REDEMPTIONER

FIFTEEN

When he was a young man, Noland Jacks' grandfather had emigrated from Ireland with the great wave that came to America to escape the famine. He had come first into New York City Harbor, and immigrated through the Castle Garden Depot, where his name, Jackson, had been shortened by a distracted bureaucrat. It was well with the young Irishman, for he was full of the hope of remaking himself into a new American. Before his birth, his family had owned property in Donegal, but it had been taken by an Englishman, an absent landlord. Yet, he knew the property well. He had grown up next to it and had fantasized what he would do with it should ever the family own it again. Many a day, walking with his father, he stopped along the roadside and surveyed the rolling sweep of fields that once had held the Jackson name. He had seen the loss wear on his father, reducing and shaming him. Though the Jacksons were far better off than their neighbors, having a subsistence farm that produced even at the blight's apex, there was something stingy in that loss, as if God had played unfairly with them by making them Irish and Catholic so when the starvation was ravaging the country, he saw his chance in the great migration. In New York City he lived for three years in a tenement room with a half dozen other young men, working at whatever he could find, living on a meal a day, until he had saved enough money to travel. He took a train to Atlanta, where he learned of land for sale in Talmaedge. It was good land, and cheap. In the generation before, it had belonged to the Cherokees, but the government had taken it from them, relocated them, and given the land, rolling hills, and river bottom to a white man.

The young Irishman didn't care that he was considered an outsider in Talmaedge, and queer because he lived in an old slave cabin on his own property, the farm not having a manor house. In his mind, he at last had land, and land, he thought, made any man a master. He didn't care that some thought of him as an interloper. He laughed at the idea. They were all interlopers, he thought, all there for the same reason: for land, and for the value it had—mineral, fauna, flora—or just the pride a man feels when he stands on his own soil.

He had owned the property just two years when The War Between the States broke out. It was not his war and he declined to take a part in it. He owned no slaves, couldn't afford them. Besides, he felt in good company as many of the gentlemen slave owners, likewise, exempted themselves from service to the Confederacy. Conscription, though, forced him into service and he fought in Tennessee and Virginia before he could come home again. Secretly, he was glad the Southern states lost. He hadn't seen the value of the war, and it had cost him three years on his farm.

Returning, he was willing, unlike some of his neighbors, to hire the freed coloreds at good wages and to deal with the Union occupiers, and so he prospered during the Reconstruction. The farm expanded. He married a woman said to have had Cherokee blood and built the manor house. The house was named for the shrubbery, a member of the honeysuckle family, that his new wife planted. Spurgeon, his only child, was born soon after, and he took great delight, sitting on the side porch at Woodbine, surveying his fields, and telling his son the story of how he had earned their land. He was not a redemptioner, he emphasized. He owed nothing to any man. Everything he owned he had earned by the sweat of his back, and for that, no man would ever take it from him.

Like his father, Jacks had grown up an only child, the seventh and final of his mother's pregnancies. But he had not been doted upon. Mrs. Spurgeon Jacks, Violetta, though hard working, was often in poor health, a variety of female ailments the doctor said. She often said that she was not made for this world and would soon die. Spurgeon dismissed that idea. He proclaimed that there was nothing wrong with her but blue blood (she was a Talmaedge) and that a good regimen of work would thicken it. When she asked for help in the house, he refused her, saying that there was nothing a nigger could do in the house that she couldn't. Soon after Jacks turned sixteen, just as winter set in, a vulture came to rest on the front roof ridge at Woodbine. Spurgeon peppered it with buckshot, but it did not leave until it took Violetta with it.

Spurgeon was tall and inexplicably handsome given the looks of his parentage. He was serious, unsmiling. He bore the sadness of the Irish grandfather he had never met, grieving for the loss of land, and even more of the ambition of his father for acquiring land to assuage that grief. There is but one thing that can make you happy, he once told Jacks—that is land. Clothes, jewelry, cars—even love—cannot bring happiness, for they can easily spoil. But land is forever. It is a joy beyond wealth.

From Spurgeon, as Spurgeon had from his father, Jacks learned the farmer's trade. He managed livestock as well as he did cash crops. He understood breeding, disease prevention, and fattening stock for sale. He knew all about crop rotation, harvesting, and storage. It was rare, even in the time of the cotton boll weevil (when he grew corn), that his farm did not make a profit.

Though he had a vast knowledge of agronomy, he convinced his father to send him to the agricultural college at the University of Georgia. He had learned that Vernon Venable, his neighbor and friend, would be going there, and suddenly, a great desire to see the world struck him. He had never been far out of Talmaedge County, only to Atlanta and once to Macon. Though his father had passed along stories of Ireland and New York, and they had the means to travel easily to these and other places, Spurgeon felt no need to travel. In his last years, Spurgeon rarely left the boundaries of his plantation. But the young Jacks, spurred on by Venable, was in a rush to be a college man. Spurgeon relented, surprisingly easily, Jacks thought, but only on the point that a study of agronomy would improve their lot.

Jacks proved a good student. He never missed class, completed every lesson, even if he thought some subjects, like English literature, Latin, and physical education were useless to him. His social life was quiet. He attended home football games, fraternity socials, and Sadie Hawkins dances. But, in his sophomore year, when young men were expected to make commitments to one fraternal club or the other, Jacks did not, and soon found himself unwelcome at parties. He didn't mind.

On the other hand, his friend Venable committed early and enjoyed a vigorous social life. But his studies suffered and he was not allowed to return after the second quarter of his sophomore year. After that, Jacks redoubled his efforts in his studies, feeling that he had no true friends and only a few associations in Athens.

In the spring of his senior year, on the advice of Spurgeon, Jacks began looking for a woman he could marry. He found her in the rose garden of the horticulture school. Her name was Betty O'Cleary.

The summer after they were graduated from the University, Vernon Venable threw a dinner party at Thousand Acres for Jacks and Betty. They arrived in Jacks' new 1923 Chevrolet roadster, a sporty convertible that he had given himself as a graduation present. It had been two years since Jacks had seen Venable, and he wanted to impress his friend with the new car and the girlfriend. He wore an English driving cap and had grown a thin mustache. The long driveway up to the manor house ended in a roundabout dominated by a huge big-leaf magnolia. The tree was aglow, its hundreds of large paper-white blossoms reflecting the evening light. Jacks slammed the brakes, causing the roadster to spin in the roundabout and throw up a shower of river pebbles and dust.

Betty eyed him and they both laughed. She took off her scarf and tried to push her hair around her face. "Wait until Vernon sees us!" Jacks said. "He'll hoot." A thin, dark servant girl came onto the portico with its four ionic columns, and started to shoo them. Mrs. Venable didn't want them making a racket and throwing up dust all over the boxwoods and the front portico, the girl said. Jacks made a disparaging remark about Vernon's mother, then laughed and tooted the horn raucously until Venable showed himself at the door.

"Noland, you son of a bitch. Where the hell did you steal that god-damn car, boy?" Venable shouted, running past the girl and jumping down the portico steps. He ran up to the car, reached over Betty and knocked the hat of off Jacks' head.

Betty let out a soft cry, and turned to Jacks. Her red hair was still blown back from her face, her freckled ears were exposed, and her surprised, almost frightened look excited Jacks. They had spent many hours holding hands and kissing. Once he had even felt through her blouse and touched her breasts. Now, he felt they could become more intimate and the passion he felt for her, that sometimes gave him restless nights, could legitimately be satisfied.

"Sorry, Miss," Venable said to Betty, seeming to see her for the first time. He walked around to Jacks' side of the car. "God-a-mighty, but look at her. She's about the prettiest looking thing I done *ever* seen. He raked his fingers across the hood of the car as he walked, and looked at Betty. "Beau-ti-ful," he said and winked at Betty. Jacks thought that Betty looked curious for a fraction of a second, and then she opened her mouth wide in a silent laugh. "Mercy!" Venable exclaimed.

"Papa gave it to me for a graduation present," Jacks lied. "She cost nearly three thousand dollars, and I'd bet you there ain't nobody outside of Atlanta got one just like her. Not even those damn Talmaedge boys."

"Who cares what the damn Talmaedge boys got? You got the prize." Venable looked over at Betty again, and then at the ground, and kicked a little at the pebbles, before he looked at her again, right in the eye. "Noland," he said. "They teach you manners at the University?"

Venable snorted, a little embarrassed. "Manners is for niggers and fools." He cleared his throat, "Mr. Venable, may I present Miss O'Cleary, my intended."

"My gracious, Noland, you are one lucky son of a bitch."

Supper was served on the back lawn, in view of the fields sloping down to the river toward Woodbine. There were only Jacks and Betty and a local girl that Venable had been fooling around with. Old Man Jacks had been invited but characteristically declined. It was a young people's gathering so Mrs. Venable, too, kept to herself. She had her girls fry steaks and potatoes and boil sweet peas, fresh from the garden.

Venable kept up a pleasantly flirtatious chatter during the meal, but Jacks hardly said a word. The girl came to take the plates away, stacking the tray high with bones, fat, scraps of potatoes, beer bottles, and plates apparently to save herself a trip on her arthritic hip. When the cake was served, Venable poured a round of bourbon. Though it was prohibited, he had bought the bottle, for a goodly price he informed Jacks, from a source in Greene County. "Let's make a toast to the happy couple."

"A toast," his date said, "like in the movies? Ain't you suppose to have champagne?"

"You don't know what champagne is."

"Be quiet, Ven." The date took out her compact and started applying lipstick. "You want a touch-up, Betty?"

"Why Betty's lips are as ruby as a sunset," Venable said. He motioned to Jacks to drink.

"But we haven't said a toast yet," the date said.

"Oh. Well. To the happy couple!"

"That's nice," Betty said. She looked at Jacks and touched the hand he was resting on the table. "You have such nice friends."

"His only friend," Venable said. "Least his only friend in Talmaedge County."

"I've had better friends," Jacks said. He took a belt of the bourbon, winced, another, then set down the empty glass.

"Easy, Noland. You don't have my constitution."

"I don't want your constitution."

"Sure you do. Have another." Venable poured another stiff drink for Jacks.

"I always preferred a man who could show some moderation," the date said.

"Here's moderation for you." Venable poured himself a drink and belted it down. He leaned over and kissed the date on the lips.

"Ummm," she said, wiping smudges from her mouth. She feigned modesty and fanned a slap at his shoulder. "Why do you have to be so uncouth? Isn't he uncouth?"

Jacks took a belt. The bourbon felt hot in his throat.

Later they sat on the side porch, Jacks and the date on the wicker settee and Venable and Betty on the porch swing. "Why, there is nothing more to tell about," Betty was saying to Venable. "I studied to be a primary grade teacher, but my true love is horticulture. I just love the flowers. Don't you? Don't you just love all kinds of flowers? At my wedding I would love to have all kinds of roses. Not just white ones, but red ones and pink ones and yellow ones."

"Yellow?" the date asked.

"Oh, they are the most beautiful. At the gardens in Athens they have them. Noland's seen them. Haven't you, Noland?"

"What?" He had heard her speaking, a pleasant soft chatter as inconspicuous as cricket song.

"The rose garden in Athens? Anyway, they come in all shapes and sizes and colors. I just love them."

"You could be a rose, yourself," Venable said. "You look like your name ought to be Rose, or Petunia."

"Be quiet," the date said.

"But it's true, look at her. I'm surprised Noland hasn't nicknamed you 'Rose.' What is your pet name for her, Noland?"

"What?"

"Pet name?"

"The name she's got is good enough."

"That's what I say," the date said. "Some people call me sugar and some call me honey. But I just tell them that the name my momma gave me is the best."

"What about Cherokee Rose, since you come up from the hills?"

"Now don't go calling me a hillbilly."

"Oh, never," Venable patted Betty on her knee. Jacks thought he ought to object. He knew Venable had a rogue reputation. Yet he looked off to the fields, now grown dark. Stars were beginning to shimmer. The bourbon was making him sleepy.

"Just cause you come from the hills," Venable continued, "doesn't mean you got any billy in you." When Jacks looked back, Venable was pretending to examine Betty like a doctor or scientist, "No I don't see nary a spot of billy in you. Just pure Irish aristocrat."

Betty did her silent laugh again. "Oh, shut up. Noland, tell your friend to shut up."

"You better be quiet," the date said to Venable.

Venable leaned forward in the swing and poured a shot into Jacks' glass. "What you thinking about Noland? About married responsibilities? I just never in all my life imagined Noland Jacks with a wife. And such a pretty, rose petal of a wife, too."

"Noland, tell him," Betty implored.

Jacks rubbed his hands across his face. He stood a little awkwardly.

"Legs gone to sleep?" Venable asked.

"I need to walk."

Venable made a sweep of his arm toward the fields and the fringe of twilight on the horizon. "It's a goddamn free country."

"I'd like to walk, too," the date said. "I need to do something to liven things up around here."

"Why don't we all take a walk," Betty said. "I'd like to see the place."

"You won't see much in the dark." Venable said. "I just as soon sit here."

Jacks started down the stairs and the date got up and followed. She gave a glance at Venable. "Y'all coming?"

"In a minute," Venable said. "Let me finish my drink."

"Your drink!" the date said. "I prefer a man who knows his moderation."

"Who gives a damn what you prefer?" Venable said quietly.

Jacks stood at the bottom on the steps for a moment, his mind busied with the annoyance of the date. Then he remembered Betty and turned to her. She had the excited, frightened look again, and the look excited him. It was, to him, a look of extraordinary and unique beauty, like the exotica of some Shahrazad whose veil he would soon be slowly lifting: red curls, freckles on her neck, and full lips, nearly as full as a colored girl's. She was a rose, all right, just as Venable had said. She was a half-opened blossom and kissing her was like rubbing soft petals across his lips.

"Where we going?" the date asked. She slipped her arm into the crook of his elbow, and when he didn't hook it, she reached down and took his hand. "Alone, at last," she said and giggled. "Oh, don't be so stiff, I'm only teasing you." They began to walk down toward the barns. Faintly, the odors of both jasmine and rain were in the air. "Noland, you are a peculiar man. Don't get me wrong. You let Ven sit up there and flirt with your girl and don't say a thing."

The critique stung at first. "He's just teasing. We've been friends for a long time, now, and I trust him."

"I wouldn't trust him in church."

"But I'm his friend," Jacks said sharply. "Not his date."

The date dropped his hand. "Well, if that's the way you think of me. I'll just go on back to the porch."

Jacks tried to sound indifferent. "Suit yourself. Sugar."

"Well, I just might." The date stopped and put her hands on her hips. Jacks looked at her, but continued to walk. The way was illuminated by a filament bulb on a pole, around which insects swarmed. The peafowl rested in a cluster at the edge of the yard, barely visible. The cattle, too, had come to rest along the edge of the fence in several large groups, the white patches on their faces visible.

The date caught up to him. "Well, we can be friends, can't we? What did I do to you? I mean . . . well . . . you don't have to be so serious. So straight." She sighed. "I swear, you and Vernon look so much alike. You could be brothers. You're both tall and you've got that lanky look. I like a tall man. I am tall myself, as you can see. But, I swear, you are not a thing alike, otherwise. You could be brothers, but you're just not a thing alike." From the porch they heard Betty's laughter. Roughly, the date attempted to slip her hand into his again, but he pulled it away.

SIXTEEN

It was the bourbon that had made him do it, Noland Jacks thought. Bourbon was dangerous. Old Jake Beam, Old Grand Dad, Old Fitzgerald, Old Kentucky Gentlemen—all of them gentlemen, and he was not one. Venable was a Georgia gentleman, as much as they had gentlemen in Georgia, but he, himself, was an interloper. The gentry knew it and tolerated him; the crackers knew it and considered him uppity. The niggers knew, too, but to a nigger it was all the same, or it ought to have been. He had the fine house, and his mother had had Talmaedge blood. And he had the land. The land made it all possible. What he didn't have was the manners. Something in his bones and muscles prevented him from being gentry. He felt he had no easiness about him. He couldn't assume that the world was made for him because in his blood was the knowledge that land could be taken away. Those Cherokee chiefs knew it, and his Irish forefathers knew it, and so he knew it. It made him tense, but it kept him hard. Bourbon, on the other hand, clouded his mind, slackened his body.

The incident with the woman in the barn had been brief. All evening, she had flirted with him, winking, smiling, and touching him, and Venable had been doing the same to Betty. He had wanted to say something to Venable, to tell him to stay away from Betty and to tell him that Betty was not a whore like the other woman. That Betty was *his* girl, not Venable's. But the bourbon had shut his mouth. His jaws wouldn't work, and when he could open them, his tongue lay like a fat, slimy slug. Even if his tongue had been quick, his mind was no good. He seemed to have faded in and out of sleep. He followed the conversation all right—he had heard everything that Venable said, had seen every gesture, the way Venable bounced his knee, the way his thigh quivered like an eager stallion, and worse, the way Betty pretended to be upset, but with every gesture moved closer to Venable. "Oh, Noland, do something about your friend!" What could he do? He could have killed Venable. But it was he who acted like the gentlemen, then. It was he who had the degree, a Bachelor of Science from the University of Georgia. It was he who had the Roadster. It was his grandfather who had fought in The War Between the States. The Venables claimed colonels and the Talmaedges generals—but neither family had had a soldier in the war. And he knew it was he—*his* people—that had more money, more land. The Venables might call their farm "Thousand Acres," but he knew, altogether, if they counted every square inch, every fallow field, every sharecropper yard and weed patch, they couldn't muster eight hundred. But he and his old man, they had that much and that much again. But sitting there, that evening, bound by the bourbon, he felt like nothing. Like a nigger.

That was when he had decided to go for a walk and the whore had followed him. In the barn, she had said something to him about a kiss—after all, Vernon and Betty were getting along so well, she said, why shouldn't they? He didn't remember it all, but looking at her face, pasted with rouge and lipstick, and her cigarette-stained teeth, he couldn't bear the idea of kissing her. And still, he grabbed her by the shoulders and pushed her into the bales of hay. He pulled at her blouse and she started to fight him. "Not good enough for you! A hussy, like you! Not good enough!" He saw in her expression that she agreed, and he slapped her. She let out a surprised screech, and seeing that she was more surprised than hurt, he stepped back from her. "I'm sorry," he said.

"You will be! You will be when I tell Vernon."

Was he supposed to be afraid of Vernon Venable? He wasn't, and at that moment, he realized he wasn't. "I'd slap him, too. Give me a chance." But he wouldn't, and he wouldn't do anything else to the woman, either, he realized, because he was not a gentleman if Vernon Venable was one. He was not Vernon Venable. He was better than that.

It was a week later that he saw Betty again, and a week after that she was seeing Venable. That was all right with him. "Do as you please," he had told her, and he had said it coolly, and had looked at her and then turned to look at the line of trees along the river.

"If you put it that way . . . "

He hadn't answered her. He hadn't wanted to think about it, and then, suddenly, as if God had sent a balm to ease his pain, his father, Spurgeon, fell ill. Then Jacks had the farm to manage by himself, a house, and a sick father. He didn't receive an invitation to the wedding, and had he, he told himself over and over, he would have been too busy to attend.

A few weeks after the wedding, he told his father that he was hiring a housekeeper. The old man sat up in his bed, threw back the crocheted spread, coughed and pointed a finger at him. "There has never been a house-keeper in this house. You don't need one. You need a wife."

Jacks knew then that, whoever the housekeeper was, the old man would not be easy on her. He asked of his field helpers if one had a wife or daughter who could do house work, and Deacon Thompson, one of his favorite and hardest workers, said he would send his younger cousin. Her name was Milledge.

She had come early the next morning and was sitting on the steps of the back porch when he opened the door to go out to the fields.

"'Scuse me, sir," she said and averted her eyes.

The way she averted her eyes caught his imagination: there seemed a coyness, almost as if she were smiling at him before her eyes turned away. Then he realized that it was not shyness or flirtation, but respect. He was wearing only a strap undershirt, a threadbare one that he worked in, and her aversion had little to do with him, and everything to do with her sense of herself. She might be too proud, he thought.

"How old are you, girl?"

"Seventeen, sir."

"Have you done housework before?"

"Yes, sir. Around the house. I mean, I help my mother."

"Can you cook?"

"Yes, sir."

"What?"

"Just about anything you like, sir. Breakfast, lunch, and dinner."

"Cook and clean?"

"Yes, sir."

"Cook biscuits?"

"Yes, sir."

"My mother could cook good biscuits. Butter on the top. Soft inside and would cover them thick with honey or preserves.

"I ain't saying I can cook as good as your momma," she said. She looked up at him, turning her brown eyes for a flash, and then looking away again.

"So I hope you don't hold me to that high of expectation, sir. But I can cook good biscuits, and fry up bacon or ham, and fry eggs, and fix up some grits. Or if you want, I can stir up some griddlecakes or waffles. I even know how to make some scones or short bread and some yeast rolls, too."

The backyard was beginning to fill with green light, filtering through the canopy of the large trees. Jacks inhaled deeply. His stomach growled and he hoped the girl hadn't heard it. Then he laughed to himself. "I don't reckon I'll be needing all that. Just get on in there and start. Make two breakfasts. Make anything you can find. I'll have a big one, but the old man, well, see what you can get him to eat."

The girl came up the steps and passed him without looking at him. He went to the barns to give instructions to the workers, and when he returned, she was well underway making biscuits. By the time he had shaved and put on a shirt, the house was filled with the smell of baking bread, brewing coffee, and frying meat. She had laid the table for him and had placed the newspaper beside his plate. Somehow, though at first he didn't consider it, she had presented the meal at his usual seat. She didn't ask about the old man, but took a plate on a tray to him. Jacks waited to hear a ruckus, but there wasn't one. He bit into a hot biscuit without putting it on his plate, without butter or preserves. It was flaky and sweet, slightly different from his mother's, but every bit as good. He heard the old man talking, so he got up to go and see what it was he wanted. When he walked into the room, the girl was helping Spurgeon back into the bed, having helped him to the pot. Then, she wiped his face and hands with a wet cloth. Spurgeon looked up at Jacks and winked.

Jacks looked at the girl as she smoothed the covers around Spurgeon's thin legs, and put the bed tray on his lap. She was small, he thought, but she had full round hips and a pleasant air. Her motions were quick, efficient, and confident. When she finished, she left the room without a word.

"Where did you find her?" Spurgeon asked. He tasted a spoonful of the grits.

"You approve?" Jacks asked.

"What have I got to approve or disapprove? It's your farm now, Noland. It's no longer up to me." He chewed on the rind of a slice of bacon. "When the house started filling up with the smell of bread, I realized that I missed something. Your mother. Her cooking. Her singing and humming

around the house. I've got sense enough to know that my days are num-
bered, and I got sense enough to know that there's no sense in eating your
cooking for the last days of my life." Spurgeon didn't smile as he said this,
and though Jacks knew his father had not meant the comment as humor, he
smiled anyway.

"I'm happy to see that you have come around, Papa."

"I have not come around to any new position. You still need a wife, but
until you get one, this girl will do very well."

In the kitchen, the girl had kept his breakfast warm, and was already
gathering his dirty clothes for washing.

"I think you will work out just fine," he said to her. "What's your name
anyway?"

"Milledge, sir."

"What?"

"Milledge, sir. Like in Milledgeville."

"I'll just call you Millie," he said. He liked the sound of it.

Six weeks later, that ole turkey vulture that had come for his wife years
earlier, came to rest on the roof above Spurgeon Jacks' bedroom. Though
he could not see it, he knew it was there. He heard it hissing and flapping
its wings. He heard it claw the slate roof and the occasional splatter of its
guano against the rain gutter. He complained about it to Jacks and said he
wished Jacks would shoot it. Jacks shook his head, laughed, and patted his
father on the arm. The girl understood him, Spurgeon said, even if his own
son did not. Spurgeon couldn't eat the girl's cooking anymore, but Jacks
observed that the old man seemed to enjoy it when she attended him. It
was she who gave him his morphine, and so it was her brown face that
Jacks' father saw last before his glance drifted across the room and out of
the window. Jacks imagined that his father's mind was floating across the
fields, backwards and forward in time, riding the waves at the edge of a
great lake.

Did he regret his life? Jacks wondered of his father. Yes, but what person wouldn't? Was he terrified of death? He didn't appear to be, and with
each retreat of the waves back into the great body of the lake, his father
seemed less afraid. Not happy to die, but resigned. Had he done wrong?
Many things, Jacks knew. He remembered offenses against his mother and
himself. And there were many more good things he could have done that

he hadn't. Was he going to Hell? Jacks didn't know. He didn't feel that his father would. If there was a God, then he would be a forgiving God, a generous God; he would forgive his father for all the wrong he had done and for all of the good he had not done.

On his last day of life, Spurgeon seemed alert and anxious. He claimed that three other birds sat in the sill of his window. They had come long before the sun, he said, but in the new light, he saw them clearly: a robin, a jay, and a black-capped chickadee. They sang for him. The robin said, "chee-rup;" the jay said, "gaw-gaw;" and the chickadee said, "chick-a-dee-dee-dee-dee." The robin was his wife, the jay his father and chickadee, his beloved mother.

About noon, when Jacks was supervising his field workers, the girl approached him. She waited until she had his full attention, then said quietly, "I'm sorry, Mr. Jacks, but your daddy just passed."

The house was emptiest in the evening, after Milledge—Millie—had gone home. She prepared and served him his supper about five in the afternoon. It was a lighter meal than dinner, the midday meal, traditionally heavy in farm communities. Then she cleaned the kitchen while he sat on the side porch and smoked. By six o'clock, she was asking if there would be anything else. He never had anything else for her. She was thorough, and long ago, he had learned that it was unnecessary for him to inspect her work.

One day, the spring after his father died, as he looked out toward Thousand Acres, he saw a light shoot into the sky and explode. Milledge had just come out onto the porch to pardon herself, and had seen it, too. She gave a little start, and then a bit of a laugh and smoothed her hands across her apron.

"Well, God almighty, what do you think they shooting off fireworks for?" Jacks asked. "It ain't the fourth of July."

"No sir, I reckon it's the birth they are celebrating."

"Birth?"

"Yes, sir," Milledge answered. To him, her tone suggested his stupidity on the subject. "The new Mrs. Venable supposed to have her baby about now."

It hadn't occurred to him, but now it made sense. The quick wedding had been necessary. Perhaps it had nothing to do with love, but only sex, lust. He had had better control with Betty, apart from the long kisses, he had not been carnal with her, though he had wanted to. He was a man, after all, and not immune to desire. Many a night he walked around and around the grounds to wear it out of his thighs so he could sleep. "Birth?"

"Yeah, I saw her in town about three weeks ago, and she was as big as a house. Wouldn't surprise me if she delivered twins." Milledge said, and then seemed to catch herself talking too freely to him. To him, it seemed the first genuine thing she had said to him since he employed her, the first genuine display of interest or emotion, and he smiled.

"Tell me," he pressed tobacco into the bowl of his pipe, "you like children, don't you?"

"Why, yes, sir. I don't think I know of any person—any woman, anyhow—that wouldn't like to have a little baby. They are so soft when you hold them in your arms, and so. . . .

"Go on," he encouraged.

"Oh, I don't reckon you want to hear that foolishness, sir."

"Why wouldn't I? Why do people think I wouldn't want to hold a little baby in my arms?"

"Oh, excuse me, sir. I ain't meant to say—"

"You didn't. But plenty do. People think I'm hard."

"No, sir."

He could tell she was being disingenuous. "I know what they think."

"Well, maybe some folks do. But then, some people need to be hard or they won't get through. Doesn't mean you going to be hard for every minute of your life. You have your hard spells, and you have the times when you are not so hard."

"Is that so?" He studied her and he could tell that his regard made her nervous. He didn't want to make her nervous, only to talk to her. But what would be the use? She was a colored girl and she was smart, and a smart colored girl would never talk to him the way he wanted just then. It wasn't allowed, and he wouldn't allow it either.

A week later, a letter came from Thousand Acres. It was from Betty. It announced the birth of the child, a boy, and it expressed regrets, belatedly, for the death of his father. Then it invited him to supper. He stood for a long time in the middle of the kitchen floor, where he had opened the letter, having just come in from the mailbox. A reconciliation, he thought. What did he want to reconcile with the Venables for? He would always feel an outsider with them, the rejected boyfriend, the odd neighbor. Then he realized he was blocking Milledge's progress as she stood with a plate of food, unable to get around him to put it on the table.

"Scuse me, sir. Your dinner." He moved to the chair, the letter still held open in his hand, as if he were reading it. His hand shook a bit, and then he placed the letter on the table. "Is there anything I can do for you, sir?" Milledge asked, having laid the food on the table. Suddenly he realized what she meant. She was asking if he were all right.

"No. No," he said and picked up his utensils, bowed his head though he did not actually pray, and cut into his meat. It was a smothered fried pork chop. It was a meal his mother cooked, and when he looked up from the plate, he expected to see his mother sitting next to him, his father directly across from him.

"Is everything all right?" she asked, this time referring to the food.

"Yes. Yes. Delicious." He put the meat in his mouth. The gravy was savory and the meat tender, but he had no hunger, just then. "Millie," he said, "why don't you take a plate and join me?"

She was still for a minute and he looked up from the plate and saw that she seemed frozen by the stove, in the middle of spooning okra from a pot. "No, sir," she said hoarsely, "I'll take mine later."

It was his mistake. He wished he hadn't put her into the position. But she was smart, and she would figure a way out of it. And she did. She quickly finished spooning the food and excused herself, saying she needed to clean in the front room.

"Millie," he called, stopping her exit. "My letter is from my friend, Mrs. Venable. She's invited me to supper at her house on next Saturday." He wanted to ask, what shall I do? How can I go? And, then too, he realized he was already humiliating himself, acting like a spoiled child in front of his nigger house girl. Did he really expect an answer from her? "I think . . . I will not need you for supper on Saturday."

"Thank you, sir," she said. "I'll come for breakfast and dinner, as usual." And then, unexpectedly, she told him, "You'll probably enjoy yourself, to be with your friends." She had left the room even before she finished the sentence, and suddenly he felt the advice to be genuine. He turned back to the meal, but thoughts of his mother possessed him so strongly that he pushed from the table and went out to the side porch.

The air was dry and clear, and the temperature comfortable. Summer in Georgia was muggy and hot, but spring was full of clarity, color, and breezes. In the blue sky, there were, on occasion, migrating flocks of Sand-hill cranes or blackbirds. Azaleas, redbud, and dogwood bloomed. Here it is, he thought, all of Woodbine in her spring glory, like a jewel set in the ring of the horizon. It was all his, every square inch, all the way down to China. And yet, except for Millie, no person had set foot in the house, other than himself, since Spurgeon's funeral. The fields were generally active; he had twenty-five workers. He thought of some of them very highly. But other than a few business acquaintances and the colored workers, he saw no one. What shall it gain a man to possess the world and to lose his soul, he thought. "Now, Noland," he said aloud to himself, "Don't get sentimental on me."

Though usually punctual to a tee, Jacks found himself running late for the dinner with the Venables. First he couldn't decide what to wear. He had put on a jacket and tie, and then he thought of Venable, and took off the tie. Then he decided that he needed a smoke and he went out on the side porch, surveyed the field in the direction of Thousand Acres, and smoked. It calmed him for a while. But as he drove the Roadster up the driveway toward the manor house, old anxieties percolated in his stomach. He sat in the car for a moment, and a moment later he was face to face with Vernon Venable.

"Noland, you son of a bitch," Venable cried out. He extended his hand; Jacks reached through the car window and took it. Venable placed the other hand around his. Venable's hands felt warm as they gripped. "I've missed you, you bastard. Truly, I *have* missed you."

The elder Mrs. Venable came to the supper. She had been at the fu-neral, too, so, of the diners, Jacks had seen her last. Betty looked fresh, a little plumper than when she was in college, but happy. She insisted that he hold the baby, an unremarkable creature, as far as he cared. No one men-tioned the trouble that had been between them. This fact and the greasy food churned in his stomach. When supper was over, he and Venable with-drew to the yard, and he smoked his pipe while Venable drank brandy. It was here, sitting in the Adirondack benches under the glittering constella-tions that he tried to turn the talk away from the superficial. "The last time," he said, his stomach swelling with gas, "the last time, we sat out here—"

"Noland," Venable interrupted. "I am your friend, so let me give you some friendly advice. You are young and rich and you ain't all that bad looking. You go get yourself a wife. Betty has some nice looking cousins. And if you want to step out a bit—why, you can go to Atlanta, or Athens, or Rome. There are some nice looking girls there. If you are really adventurous, go on down to Augusta or Savannah—hell, even to Charleston. You'll find somebody who will tolerate you."

"I thought I had."

"But you hadn't, apparently. But that is no matter. You will, again."

Jacks puffed on the pipe. He wanted to argue, but he also wanted the pleasure of being with his friend—just being there with another human being that didn't work for him was enough for the moment. "I reckon that's right. Let the past stay past."

"That's the spirit."

"But . . ." He waited until Venable asked what. "But, you know I am no good with women."

Venable laughed. "Nobody really is, Noland. Just think about it. We're all just a bunch of horny dogs with manners. So nobody is really any good. It's just that you have to think you are good. Think that you are the last good-looking man on Earth. Noland, think about your land, your house. Now that's enough to make any man desirable. You don't even have to say a sweet, slick word to a gal, just tell her you own a thousand acres of land!"

"And then what?"

"And then," he lowered his voice, "fuck her hard."

He wanted to ask if that was what he had done with Betty, but he decided that they had made some awkward peace on the issue. "I . . . well, I—"

"Don't tell me that after four years at the University and you are still a virgin." Venable punched his shoulder to turn the comment into a joke.

"I didn't say that! I am just not as outgoing—as confident as you," Jacks confessed.

"I'll tell you what. Why don't we run up to Greene County, to Sals and Pals. I know a sure way to develop your confidence."

"A whore house?"

"It'll be fun."

"I wouldn't know what to do in a whore house. Besides, they are filthy, aren't they? Full of disease and no-class people."

"You sound like my mother, Noland. But really, it's fun. I'll tell you what to do. Just choose a gal, take out your flute and let her play it. You don't have to do a thing."

Jacks stood. He was embarrassed by the talk, but the sparkle that came through Venable's voice, even the smacking of his lips after a slurp of the brandy, intrigued him. He took a deep breath and looked at a peculiar star. It was slightly red in hue, and he had never noticed a color in the stars. He was a virgin, he thought. And besides, his father was dead. "All right then," he said. "Let's go."

Hillbilly music played on the phonograph when Jacks and Venable came into Sals and Pals. Lit with kerosene lamps, the place was no more than a large shack, with a downstairs bar and tables and upstairs bedrooms located along a loft. Men sat around at tables or at the bar, playing cards or checkers, taking sips of moonshine from jelly jars. Sals and Pals was sufficiently back from the main road, with a view of the valley, so any approach of revenuers would have been revealed long before they arrived. Though it appeared a relaxed atmosphere, the proprietors, one burly and the other a stickman, had guns in their belts and eyed newcomers with suspicion.

Venable was well-known, and warmly greeted by Sal and Pal and by several of the customers. "This is my *compadre,*" Venable announced, louder than was necessary for the proprietors to hear. "This is Noland Jacks."

"Ahh," Pal, the heavy-set one, said, "not the famous Mr. Jacks, but his son?" Jacks felt a little awkward. The man did not appear to be much older than he, if older at all, and yet he seemed to speak about him as if he were an adolescent. "Yes," Pal continued, "I know the reputation of the father." He did not extend his hand, and he only looked at Jacks to survey him, beginning at his waist where he might have carried a weapon, and then moving up and down. "Now, what would be the pleasure of you gentlemen?"

"What are you serving?" Venable asked, and almost before the question was completed, Sal handed him a jelly jar with a finger and a half of liquid in it. Venable shot it back, and winced.

"Sip, sip, sip," Pal admonished. "And for this gentleman?" He turned his head toward Jacks, but did not look at him.

"Nothing for me."

"Nothing?" Now, Pal looked at him. Then he smiled. "You have come for some other pleasure, no doubt. You have come for a little tillage? How appropriate for a gentleman farmer."

Jacks said nothing, but Venable laughed in a halting, high-pitched way.

"Sal," Pal called to the skinny man, "ask the ladies to present themselves, please."

Four women came from the back. Three of them were white and one was colored. Two of the whites were tall and slim, and one was heavy, with abnormally large breasts. The one that caught Jacks's attention was the colored one. She was small framed, but rounded and her skin was medium brown. Her hair was soft, like she had a little Indian or maybe even some white blood in her.

"What will be your pleasures, gentlemen?"

Venable sniggled again. "I guess . . . cause you see, I am a newly married man, so I will have to pass on the ladies—"

"No bims? Are you sure?" Pal turned to Sal. "Vernon Venable says, 'no cake.' You think he's sick? Bring him another hit of our lemonade." He turned back to Venable. "You see I got a fine, new colored girl there. Fine new coot."

Venable sipped the liquor. "My friend, Mr. Jacks . . ."

"How about it, Gentleman Jacks," Pal offered. "This here is Delilah. She cut Sampson's hair and turned him into an assman. He would walk a hundred miles for a taste of her cake. She's a sweet cook, too. You'll enjoy her. Step up here, baby," he called to Delilah. "Turn around. Show Mr. Jacks your assets." He patted her rump. "Smooth as a baby's. Would you like to feel it Mr. Jacks? Com'on, she ain't fixin' to bite. Are you, Delilah? She's tame as a wildcat."

The woman moved closer to Jacks, turning her body for him to see and using her hands to frame her breasts, and then her hips. Jacks didn't move. He breathed deeply and smelled her odor. It was floral. Lilacs or rosewater, he didn't know which. He noticed little glistening hairs on the nape of her neck. And when she turned again, he saw the shape of her shoulder through the gingham dress, and the way the dress fitted around her breasts. He felt his thigh quiver.

"Perhaps, she is not to your liking," Pal said. "Perhaps you would prefer one of our beautiful Saxon maids." He indicated one of the tall girls, who moved forward."

"No," Jacks said. "This one, here. She'll do."

Pal smiled and waved his hand, indicating to the girl to lead Jacks away. "Oh, yes," he said, as the woman led Jacks to the stairs, "she will do very well, Mr. Gentleman Jacks. You gentlemen prefer your colored coot, of that there is little doubt. But do not worry, Mr. Jacks. At our establishment, we take precaution against mongrelization. You are in fine hands. Please, do enjoy yourself."

The woman led Jacks into a room at the end of the loft. It was large enough for a bed, a chair and a washstand. As she shut the door behind them, there was an uproar of laughter from the men downstairs.

"What are they laughing at?" Jacks asked. He hesitated at the door, and reached for the knob. She stopped him with her hand on his. "Pal. He make some kinda joke. Don't worry. They ain't laughing at us. They wish they could come up here, too."

"That Pal, he's a Charlie Chaplin."

"I reckon." She was already unbuttoning her dress. The sight of her cleavage and the lovely brown color of her breasts excited him. As he watched her undress, he hardly breathed, then breathed heavily, and finally quit breathing altogether. He had an erection and though he knew it natural, he also felt embarrassed by it. What if she should see it? And then, once again, his attention went back to the woman, now disrobed. He had seen pictures, and she looked nothing like the pictures. She was not a marble statue of Aphrodite, or a plump, bestockinged French prostitute.

She began to unbutton his shirt and to push it back from his shoulders. She stroked down his back, and up and across his chest, and down his abdomen to his belt buckle. In a minute, his pants were down to his ankles, and his penis had found its way out of his undershorts. She asked him to step out of his pants, and he toed off his shoes and obliged. His nipples and penis burned. He was afraid to move again. She led him to a basin, and poured warm water from a pitcher over his penis and began to wash it with soap.

"What are you doing?" he protested tightly.

"Don't worry. I won't make you come. Not yet, baby."

He could feel himself coming and pushed her hand away. She handed him a towel and sat on the side of the bed and lay back.

"What do you want to do?" she asked.

"What . . . ?"

"Anything you want, honey."

"I . . ."

"Com'ere," she said gently. She sat forward, pulled his hips between her legs and parted her vulva with the head of his penis. An intoxicating smell arose. "Now, push it in, honey. Push it as hard as you want." He did and stopped. His whole body shook. "Now rock it, baby. In and out." She began to thrust and he followed her rhythm. On the fourth thrust, his muscles bunched up and his thighs convulsed. For a moment he was senseless, and then he realized that was it.

They dressed, and when he headed to open the door, she stopped him. "Let's wait a few minutes, sugar, so them downstairs won't start laughing."

After fifteen minutes of waiting, saying nothing, but looking at the woman, Jacks began to feel he was ready to do it again. This time, he thought he would do it better. But the woman opened the door and went down the back stair of the loft.

When Jacks returned to the bar room, he did not see Venable. Pal sat on a bar stool, far too small to accommodate his backside. "I can tell by your refreshed expression, Gentleman Jacks, that you enjoyed yourself. Would you like another ride on the merry-go-round, or perhaps you would prefer another merry-go-round? No? Well you will have to wait, nonetheless, for your friend Vernon is having a little taste of cake."

On the next morning, Sunday, Jacks watched as Milledge served breakfast. She was dressed for church, a simple dress, but better than the one she usually came to work in. He said nothing to her, feeling slightly awkward, slightly new, as if he were wearing new skin. He hoped the experience of the night before did not show on him, and yet it radiated through him, a sense memory that came in waves of pleasure. As she served him, he noticed the roundness of Milledge's shoulders, the color of her cheeks, and the tiny hairs like silk threads on her nape.

She excused herself to go to church. She would be back to serve dinner and to wash the dishes. When she had gone out of the door, he felt something missing, and went to the door to follow. He saw her head toward the barns, away from the direction she needed to go for River of Joy. But halfway down, she met one of his hands, Johnson, a young, but good worker. He could not hear what they said to one another, but the sound of high, bubbling laughter soon reached him. It was a familiar sound, one he had heard before, from Betty.

He went from room to room in the manor house, not an expansive house by any standard, but stately and spacious and furnished well with pieces from his mother's family. Milledge kept the wood polished and the upholstery clean. Hardly ever did anyone use the chairs in the parlor or the dining room, and because both he and Milledge entered and left through the back, the foyer, too, was not often used. The house seemed familiar and foreign at once, like the corpse of some beloved person. His mother. His father.

Looking through the lights that framed the front door, he saw Milledge and Johnson again, walking hand in hand, headed, he thought, to River of Joy. Ought he allow it? Courting on his premises?

The breakfast had gotten cold and he took it to the slop pail. He thought how foolish he must have looked, hiding his breakfast from a nigger wench. She wasn't his mother.

On the side porch, he took out his pipe and smoked. Maybe he ought to go down to River of Joy, too, he thought. After all, he had had a taste of color—he had had a whore—and she was good. Maybe he was a little bit colored now, too. Well, they all were—the colored were a little white and the white a little colored and they all had Indian in them, too. They ate the same foods, they spoke the same language, they prayed to the same God—when they prayed—*but they weren't the same.* The woman was a whore, paid for by Venable, saying he owed as much. But, again, he had *liked* it. He wanted more of it.

Why couldn't he have what he wanted? He was the owner of Wood-bine, the *master* of Woodbine. Virginia gentlemen always had their con-cubines; Carolina gentlemen had their mistresses; Georgia gentlemen had their gals. He could have a gal, if he wanted to. And he wouldn't have to pay a cent for her. Johnson could be taken care of. All he would do was to suggest that Johnson seek employment elsewhere, up North. Give him a train ticket and twenty dollars and tell him to seek his fortune in Chicago. And then he would put the girl in one of the cabins, maybe the very one his Irish grandfather started in. She would be comfortable and nearby and he could have her, her lovely arms, her round shoulders and hips, anytime he wanted. "Millie. . . ."

But that is what a *gentleman* would do—Venable, if he thought he could get away with it. "But I am *not* a gentleman. I am better than that." He thought about the prostitute and about Milledge. He shuddered. "I will never be a gentleman like that. Never. Never, if that is what it means." He gripped the porch railing and sucked in a breath. He could feel the hands of the prostitute on his back, his stomach. "Oh, Millie," he said. "Never."

SEVENTEEN

Betty sent one of the girls around to tell Jacks of the stabbing. Already, Milledge had gone home, so he had to walk through the house to the kitchen, yelling as he went to quell the urgent banging against the screen door. "Miz Betty, she say come here right quick," the girl said and scratched at her gray braids. "Mr. Vernon, he hurt."

"Hurt?"

"Yes, suh. Right smart hurt."

He couldn't get any other details out of the girl and soon threw up his hands, got his hat and car keys and drove to Thousand Acres. Even before he knocked, another girl opened the door, and he heard a commotion from the upstairs landing. One of the two daughters sounded like she was having a crying fit. He heard the youngest son laughing loudly. Swing music was playing. The oldest son, now a young man, greeted him at the bottom landing. Their eyes met, and then the young man rolled them toward the upstairs and shook his head. "It's all yours, Uncle Noland," he said, brushing by Jacks and leaving through the front door. Jacks started up the stairs, but stopped when he heard Betty. She was argumentative, her tone sharp, but her voice rhythmical, punctuated with soft sobs. "Take a gulp of this and lie still. Ain't nothing wrong with you that an aspirin couldn't cure," she said.

"There's no place on Earth that nigger can hide from me," Jacks heard Venable shout. "I'll kill him."

"I see you came mighty close to killing him just now," Betty said.

"He snuck up on me! Damn it! That nigger's dangerous."

"I reckon he's more dangerous than you think." She was mocking him. "Why don't you give Sheriff Cook a call?"

"Cook. Fuck. I'll take care of this myself."

"I'd prefer if you'd let Cook handle it."

"I don't give a damn what you prefer. That nigger is a dead nigger."

"Just shut up, please. All of y'all. Cora Mae," she addressed her daughter, "That means you, too." The crying continued until Cora Mae saw Jacks. She stopped herself with a snort, put her palms over her acne-covered face, and briskly retreated to a room at the end of the hall. Jacks knocked on the doorjamb, and Betty looked up.

"Oh, Noland," she said. "Thank God you are here."

"What's the trouble?" Jacks took off his hat and walked into the bedroom to find Venable lying across the bed on his stomach. His pants were strewn on the floor, and his buttocks were wrapped in a bloody strips torn from a sheet. Betty held a bottle of bourbon and a glass. "I was told you were hurt badly, Vernon."

"Nigger stabbed me."

"Some altercation of some kind," Betty said. "Noland, I am glad you are here to make sense of it. I've had my last with him. And I know, I just know it had to do with some gal."

"You don't know anything."

"I know you, Vernon. God, but I do."

"It's nothing, Noland. Nothing that concerns you."

"But you just said that the boy was one of Noland's. Noland," she said and walked toward him. "He said one of your boys stabbed him. Attacked him for no reason."

"Is it bad?"

Betty considered, looking at her husband's rump in the bloody sheets. "They don't seem very deep," she said. "I poured peroxide on them, and we are waiting for Dr. Talmaedge to come."

"Noland doesn't need to know all of that. Go away, Noland. Give me my privacy."

"If that's what you want."

"I called Noland here!" Betty said. She moved back to the bed and put the liquor bottle on the nightstand. "You said it was one of Noland's workers, so Noland will know what to do." She turned again to Jacks, and took a deep breath. Her red hair had grown less brilliant over the years, and now Jacks noticed a prominent gray streak in her forelocks. "It so aggravating, Noland. You wouldn't believe it."

"Be quiet," Venable said.

"You be quiet."

"Go home, Noland."

"No. You stay right here, Noland. One thing I can say about Noland is he thinks before he acts. He isn't ruled by impulse like you. I can't think what you must have been doing to that boy to make him want to attack you. He wouldn't have just attacked you. Some of that trash you socialize with over in Greene County would have, but a colored boy wouldn't have just attacked you. Besides, he's Noland's worker, you said." She looked at Jacks, her eyes seeming to plead. "So this involves Noland." She turned back to her husband on the bed and leaned forward and pointed. "Did you ever think about that? Did you ever think who else was involved when you did your deed? Did you think about me and the children? Did you think about our family? Did you even think about your own mother? Damn, Vernon. How can I depend on you? I can't. I have to go to Noland again and again and again. I don't know what I would do without Noland." She walked away from the bed to window, and pulled back the drapes. Her features lost against the bright backdrop, she appeared to be looking out at Woodbine. "He's a better husband to me than you."

"Goddamn Noland Jacks!" Venable said.

"If that's the way you feel," Jacks said. It gave him a mild sense of vindication to see the Venables in an uproar. Indeed, over the years, Betty had come to him many times, not quite a confidant, but with many complaints about Venable's lack of responsibility. He was happy that she realized that he would have been the better husband, but this tidbit did not fool him. Even now, as he looked at her, her broad hips silhouetted in the window, he knew that her affection lay with Venable and always would. "If he's not hurt, and Cook and the doctor are on their way, then there's nothing for me to do." Jacks turned to leave.

"I *am* hurt!" Venable's lean face showed a gray bristle over the lip and on the chin. He pulled his face into an expression of pleading. "Oh, come on, Noland. I didn't mean anything."

"You never mean anything," Betty said. "Noland, please talk to him." She left the room, stopping briefly to touch Jacks on the arm. After she was gone he smelled her perfume, faintly. Venable laughed, drawing Jacks' attention to Venable on the four-poster bed. He rolled onto a hip, and asked Jacks to pour him a shot of bourbon, which he finished in two swallows. "Don't you want to know what happened?" he asked Jacks. "It involves one of your niggers."

Jacks feigned disinterest, shrugged and sat in the chair at the foot of the bed, next to the window looking out toward Woodbine. From his position, Venable's lanky calves and his long feet lay prominently in sight. One foot pressed against a bedpost. The toenails needed clipping and the toes were hirsute and crooked. Jacks wondered how anyone could make love to a man with such poor hygiene.

Venable began his story. He had been sitting on the back steps of the porch of Woodbine sipping from a cold Pabst that Millie had given him, smoking a cigarette while he waited for Jacks to return from town. At first, he hadn't paid much attention to the colored gal standing by the truck at the fence near the barn, but a breeze caught her dress and blew it close to her body. My God! Would you look at that ass, he'd thought. She reminded him of some the colored gals he had had over at Sals and Pals, and a colored gal who was ripe for you was as good a coot as you could ever get, he told Jacks. He loved kissing their big, soft lips, and tangling his fingers in their scruffy hair. And the ass on this gal was so round he imagined how it must be to grab a handful of it, to knead it, to dig in deep into the firm, round rump and to shove his cock against it. Even now, thinking about it made his cock wiggle, he said.

"I am not interested in your proclivities," Jacks said. He uncrossed his legs, shifted in his chair and crossed his legs again. Outside, the evening was settling, but because he looked east towards Woodbine, he could only see the darkness creeping up from the river bottom with an occasional reflection to signal that the sunset was beginning to color the sky. If he were home, he would be sitting on his porch with his pipe, enjoying the spectacle. Venable chuckled, reached, and poured another shot of bourbon. "My proclivities! At least, I have proclivities." Suddenly, the swing music stopped and they heard Betty and her younger son arguing briefly.

Slowly, Venable continued his story: It was enough, just then, to run his tongue over the unfiltered tip of the cigarette and to look at all that butt and those nice plump tits filling out the girl's blouse. It slowed him down, so that he made longer drags and held the smoke down twice as long. He let it out slowly so that it filled the back of his mouth and lazily flowed out of his nose. How sweet to take in a mouthful of air and slow drag, all the time watching how that gal's brown calves flexed as she tiptoed against the fence, how her buttocks pushed against her skirt.

While Venable talked, Jacks wondered who the girl could have been. He had no girl on the property to match the description. Only Millie, and he no longer thought of Millie in such physical terms. Millie was a calming, pleasant, presence in his life, not the overripe corpus that Venable described. "Who was she?" Jacks asked, but Venable ignored him and continued his story. "Who was she?" he asked again.

"How the hell am I supposed to know? I never saw the gal before in my life. I came up to her and she looked over her shoulder. Pretty face. Nice full lips. Put me in mind of some lips on a gal over in Cartersville. It was like pushing your face into a mound of flesh. When they kiss, they can suck and lip your face until it is drooling wet. And what those lips can do to a cock! Make a tight little ring of muscle right around your head—"

"I am not interested." Jacks stood. He remembered the colored girl from Sals and Pals. She had been kind to him, he now realized. She had protected him from the other men. "Vernon, get serious, will you? So you tried to rape a colored girl on my property. Who was it?"

"That yellow nigger's gal."

Jacks racked his mind for a moment. "Which yellow nigger?" There were several who worked for him. "One of the new boys?"

"No that one who's worked for you a long time."

"Jimmy Lee?"

"I don't know what the hell the nigger is called. All I know is I didn't do anything to the gal but try to have a conversation with her. True, I looked at her. But looking doesn't hurt anyone."

"It must be Jimmy Lee," Jacks said. He had a feeling of relief. "Jimmy Lee is not a bad sort. He's a good worker. Good humored. A simple sort of fellow, but not a bad bone in his body."

Venable sat up in the bed and pointed a finger at Jacks. "Bad bone or not, your nigger tried to kill me! What do you say about that?"

Jacks leaned over the end of the bed. "Vernon, you tried to rape a girl on my property. In broad daylight. And don't tell me you were only looking. You don't 'just look,' and Jimmy Lee wouldn't have done a thing to you if you were just looking." Suddenly he felt nauseated and a little dizzy. "You're disgusting."

"You go to hell."

"You go to hell, too." Jacks said, put on his hat and started out of the room.

"Noland!" Venable called. The call was a command; Jacks hesitated, but decided to ignore it. A second call, quieter, was a plea, and Jacks turned back to Venable.

"Noland." Venable moved gingerly, leaning on an elbow. His mouth twitched, nervously. "Noland. I see the way you look at me. But I'm not like that. I'm not trash, you see. I play trash sometimes. I can't help it. I want to do right by Betty; you know, I love her so. You might not believe it, but I do. I do so much love her. But I just can't do right. I play trash, I do. It's expected of me, but at my core, you know me. I'm not trash."

Jacks breathed deeply and surveyed Venable who looked like a chastised child. He wanted to say something that comforted his friend, but seeing Venable, baring a vulnerability, the old hurt swelled in him and the impulse was to strike at him. "No one expects anything of you."

"That's not true. Even you do, Noland. Even you expect me to play trash. It makes you feel superior."

Jacks snatched his hat from his head, fanned it as if he would throw it at Venable. Then he took another deep breath. "Vernon, you are hardly playing. You are what you are." He walked out of the room, closing the door behind him.

The swing music had started again. Harmonizing voices sang, "Rum and Coca-Cola, Rum and Coca-Cola" to a Calypso tune. Betty yelled from downstairs for Beau, the younger son, to turn off the music. He yelled that he wasn't playing it, that it was his sister. Then Betty yelled for the sister. The noise gave Jacks a headache and he rushed down the stairs and out of the front door. He would have continued on to Woodbine, except that he met Dr. Talmaedge on the portico. The doctor, thin and patrician, was only slightly older than he, a cousin on his mother's side. They greeted one another politely, as they always did, but Jacks cared little for his cousin. The Talmaedges had always looked down on the Jackses. He had heard they referred to the one marital link, his parents, as an unfortunate liaison, but probably the best his mother could have accomplished given her lackluster beauty. They were quick to remind people that they were no relation to the Talmadges from the southern part of the state, their name having an extra "e," and their pedigree more distinguished, despite the fact that one of the Talmadges had been a governor. Before he got to his car, two police cars carrying Sheriff Cook and several deputies drove into the roundabout, their lights flashing.

"What's this about a murder?" Cook asked as he got out of the car.

"There's been no murder!" Jacks took off his hat and slapped it against his thigh.

They waited in the parlor until the doctor had finished with Venable. He most certainly would live, Dr. Talmaedge announced to the group. The wounds were largely superficial.

In the bedroom, Jacks again sat in the chair by the window. The sun had set, and out of the window he could only see the lighted path running toward the barn; the fields and river bottom beyond were dark. Sheriff Cook and a deputy stood by the bed. The deputy wrote on a notepad with a pencil. Venable talked loudly, dithering from outraged to pitiable. *Was it playing he is doing now?* Jacks thought. He studied Venable, looking for some sign of the contrite man of thirty minutes earlier. First, Venable extolled how dangerous Jimmy Lee was, how Jimmy Lee had attacked him from behind and for no good reason. Then he talked about how he had feared for his life, though gallantly he had fended off blows from his attacker. He admitted that the knife that had stabbed him was his own but that he had drawn it in self-defense. His attacker was not a big man, he noted. He was taller and heavier by fifty pounds, but Jimmy Lee was crazed, fierce, like a mad dog.

"And I wonder what set him off?" Jacks interjected.

"Does it matter?" Cook asked and looked back and forth between Jacks and Venable. "Niggers don't attack white men."

"But a nigger is a man, too. He's got pride and honor like a white man. Suppose someone had offended his honor."

Cook looked quizzically at Jacks. He snickered. "Oh, now, I see. Mr. Jacks, you are trying to protect your nigger. He must be a right good nigger. Jimmy Lee. I know him. He lives down with that Lee bunch that used to sharecrop for your daddy. One of the worst bunches of niggers in the county. The old man's a damn drunk. The brother is a drunk, too. The sister is a whore, and the so-called wife, she whores over at Colonel Rebel hotel. I ain't caught this one at anything, but it don't surprise me none that he'd do a thing like this. Bad breeding, you see."

"Bad breeding or not," Jacks said. "A man just doesn't attack another man without cause. What was the cause, Vernon? Tell them what the cause was."

Venable glowered at Jacks, then snorted and turned to Cook. "Mr. Jacks is forgetting that a nigger doesn't need a reason to attack a white man. If Mr. Jacks was even half a white man, he would know that. But he's neither much of a man nor a white man." His lips quivered, not quite a smile and he glanced up at Jacks.

The insult burned, and Jacks felt his tongue stiffen. He didn't know what to defend first, his manhood or his race. After all these years, after all he knew of the tawdriness, venality and disorder that was Venable, why would his tongue stiffen at an insult from the man? Jacks stood.

"Sit down, Noland," Venable waved him back to his seat. "I know you are a white man. Cook knows you are a white man and so does Bobby," he indicated the deputy, who looked at Jacks and nodded at the mention of his name. "But you also have to *act* like a white man. Play the role of white man that has been given to us since time immemorial. I play my roll, whatever you think of it. I do. Sheriff plays his role and so does Bobby. That's what people expect, Noland, white and niggers, too—especially from you who wants so badly to be respected."

Bobby nodded profoundly and Jacks glanced at him sharply.

"What I want to know," Venable continued, "is what you are going to do about your own nigger going around stabbing white men."

Jacks took his seat. Uncomfortably, he shifted. He felt Venable was playing a game with him, part teasing, part egging. Everything was a game to Venable. Uncle Rye. The girls at the university. Betty. There was no core in Venable, because everything Venable did was play. Jacks stiffened his back and sat straighter in the chair. *I can play, too*, he thought. *And better.* "What do you want me to do with him, Vernon?" he asked, forcing a grin. "You want me to noose him and dangle him from a tree? Maybe the big magnolia in your own front yard? Would that be a fitting place to do it?" Venable's jaw twitched and Cook looked back and forth between the two. The deputy looked at his pad. "But what I think I will do—" Jacks stood and came to the edge of the bed, mirroring Venable's glower "—is to give him one of my knives so he can finish the job."

"Shut up, you son of a bitch."

There is was. The real Vernon. Not playing. Trash. "Cook," Jacks said, facing the Sheriff and straightening his body authoritatively, "Arrest Jimmy Lee, take him to the jail house. Thirty days ought to be enough."

Venable cursed him again and sat up awkwardly on the side of the bed. Cook reached to help Venable, but Jacks swatted at Cook's hand with his hat. "You lie right where you are, Vernon. Talk about killing somebody! Best thing you can do is to lie still. If you can't take care of your family, at least let them take care of you." Again, he ordered Cook to find Jimmy Lee and make sure he got safely to the jailhouse, and left the room.

There was a light breeze in the night, and Jacks guessed that rain would come in a day or two. From the rocker on his porch, he looked out, and though he could not see in the dark, he knew rows of young corn ran from the end of the yard to where the river cut high banks in the field. There he saw the horizon of the forest against the starry sky. He lit his pipe. He liked to smoke. He enjoyed the smell of the tobacco even more than its taste. He had experimented with a number of flavors, but he preferred apple. It had a sweet smell, heavy in the air but light in his mouth. *Do you have Prince Albert in a can?* He chuckled, remembering a joke. *Do you have pigs' feet? Do you have oxtails?* His father had told him those. How Spurgeon had known them, Jacks couldn't imagine. But he did know that Spurgeon himself would never have played the prank, never would have asked a proprietor any of those questions: *Do you have Prince Albert in a can?* "Let him out, he's suffocating!" Jacks said aloud, laughing and shaking his head.

His corn was knee high and bright green when he could see it, the young leaves holding to their yellow color. Soon they would darken, become bluer. Corn was as American as apple pie, he thought, more so, since apples came from Europe and corn originated in America, first grown by the Indians. You never heard of Indian apples, but Indian corn was as common as anything. His was a yellow dent corn, and he already knew he would make a good yield off of it. It would be ground to make good yellow meal for corn bread and grits. He stretched his arms above his head, breathed in the apple-vanilla smoke that clouded around him. Then he thought of an old song Spurgeon had sung.

> Tobacco is a dirty weed. I like it.
> It satisfies no normal need. I like it.
> It makes you thin, it makes you lean,
> It takes the hair right off your bean.

It's the worst darn stuff I've ever seen.

I like it.

Again, he laughed to himself. A breeze danced through the trees. Even now he sat in his father's chair, the one from which Spurgeon used to survey the fields, looking for nothing, only enjoying what he saw. He had become his father, he thought, a man at last, a gentleman. He was a gentleman of the New South and one he thought Spurgeon would approve of. He remembered that it was on this very porch, more than thirty years earlier, when Spurgeon had turned to him, recognizing his maturity, saying, "I can't tell you what to do, but be a man and you will learn to be a man."

It had happened on the night of the lynching of Rye Johnson— "Uncle Rye," as he had been known to the white families until his lynching; after which, he was called "Nigger Rye" or "That Johnson Nigger," or "The Nigger Who Raped that Cuthbertson Woman." It was a Saturday evening, early August, 1916, Jacks remembered. He and Spurgeon were sitting on the porch. His mother was indoors, cleaning the kitchen. From a long ways off they heard a car, first on the road, and then sputtering up the drive.

"Model T," Spurgeon said. He did not take his eyes off the field, planted in tobacco that lay before him. "That'll be that ass Billy Venable." Few owned cars in Talmaedge County at that time. "Ask him what he wants."

Jacks had gone around the front, promptly obeying his father. It was indeed Billy Venable's Model T. Dented and muddy, it no longer looked new. Billy Venable was driving, and he blew on the horn, which sounded as much like a goose as it did a machine. Jacks counted six people in the car. Jake Cuthbertson was sitting in the front next to Billy Venable. In the back sat three men Jacks did not know, all of whom wore white. Later he learned they were officials in the Ku Klux Klan, visitors from Alabama. Vernon Venable stood on the running board next to his uncle, Billy.

"Where's your daddy, boy?" Billy Venable shouted.

"He's 'round on the porch, sir," Jacks answered, and as he turned to indicate, he saw his father come around the corner.

Spurgeon crossed his arms over his chest, holding his pipe in hand. "What can I do for you gentlemen this time of evening?"

"Oh, Spurgeon," blurted Billy. "Come out with us tonight. We got some coon hunting to do."

Spurgeon shifted on his feet and put the pipe in his mouth. "I don't reckon it's coon season, Billy."

The men in the car laughed. Venable laughed. All of them were drinking. "It's always coon season," Billy Venable said, and the other men in the car agreed. "Besides, we ain't fixin' to eat this coon. We might fry'im, but we ain't eating him." Again there was laughter.

Jacks wasn't sure what the men were talking about at first. He made eye contact with Venable, who beckoned to him with his head. There was a gleam of excitement in his eyes.

"Now, what this coon do to deserve getting fried?" Spurgeon asked.

Jake Cuthbertson volunteered. "Goddamn nigger took a shot at me. Near to hit me, too." The other men in the car laughed at his inflection.

"What nigger?" Spurgeon asked, his tone serious.

"That'll be Uncle Rye," Billy Venable said.

Spurgeon said nothing and sucked deeply on his pipe. Smoke coiled from his mouth slowly and formed a cloud around his head.

"Uncle Rye?" Jacks whispered, turning to his father. "Uncle Rye is a good ole boy. Uncle Rye wouldn't shoot at anybody." Rye was a farmer and a lay minister. Approaching sixty, he had taken on the snow-headed appearance of a good ole Uncle Remus from the picture books that the white children read in school. Jacks liked him. He often came into the Venable feed store to purchase pig feed or crop seed. He settled his bills in cash, and because he was one of the few coloreds in Talmaedge to own land rather than sharecrop, he rarely ran a tab at the store.

"What did you do to him to make him want to shoot you?" Spurgeon asked.

Cuthbertson looked around at the other men. "Let's just say that nigger and I had a discussion about a property line." Cuthbertson owned a small farm on the west side of the town of Bethany.

Spurgeon shook his head and smiled. "You got caught increasing your real estate, Jake?"

"Goddamnit, Jacks," Cuthbertson said. "Act like a white man."

Spurgeon cleared his throat. He stepped down to the top step of the porch. He spoke evenly. "Jake Cuthbertson, I don't reckon a piece of trash like you will ever tell me to act like a man, white or not. I know what I am. I know I would have shot a piece of trash like you, if you had come moving my property mark. Uncle Rye ought to have killed you, and I reckon he spared you just because you are a white man. Now, I am sorry for Uncle Rye. He's a man of pride and courage, as far as I can see. But if you think you got to go off now and lynch him up, then that's your business. It doesn't involve me any."

One of the men from the back seat interrupted. "It does too involve you. It involves every white man. A *nigger* has shot at a white man. Could have killed him. Could have violated his home, his wife, his children. Maybe *you* will be next."

Spurgeon did not look at the man, but continued to address Jake Cuthbertson. "I can take care of myself and my own. If I know of a nigger that needs lynching, I'll lynch him. And I'll do it sober, and I'll do it myself."

"Spurgeon," Billy Venable said and laughed, "That's mighty unsportin'."

"Well," Spurgeon said, "I guess I don't see the sport in it. Now, I advise you to go on home and leave Uncle Rye alone. I reckon, if he is as smart as I think, he's already half way to Atlanta—"

"No, he ain't. Got him, already," Cuthbertson said. "He over in the Bethany jail, waiting." Cuthberton grinned.

"Well," Spurgeon said, stepping back onto the porch. "Then, you don't need me." He walked back to the side porch.

Jacks admired his father's stature before the other men, the calmness of his voice when the other men's voices became jittery and feminine. Now he took the same stance as his father, on the top step, his arms folded. But then, Venable beckoned with his head again. He smiled and winked, and Jacks suddenly felt a rush of excitement. He shuttered to maintain control. He had never seen a lynching except on postcards, and now there would be one in Bethany.

"Com'on Noland," Venable said. "You fixin' to miss out on the biggest thing ever happen in Talmaedge."

"*This* year," one of the men in the back seat said, and all the men laughed.

Jacks went to the side porch and found his father standing in the dark, the glow of the pipe lighting his face as he smoked.

"Papa," he started, his tone slightly pleading.

Spurgeon didn't move to look at him. "I ain't the one to tell you to go or not to go. You the only one can do that. But I can tell you this. It ain't so easy as you might think to kill a man." He turned to face Jacks, his face cast in darkness. "If you go, even if you don't so much as throw a pebble, you are in it as much as the man who ties the noose. You might just be a bystander, but nobody is innocent, son. Even I, standing here, knowing it is Uncle Rye, am among the guilty. It is the guilt I bear for being who I am." The pipe glowed as he toked, let out a mouthful of smoke. "It's like standing in a great, muddy river. You can't help but to get wet."

The two were quiet for a moment. The car horn honked. "What must I do?" Jacks asked.

"Go," his father said and sighed. "But be a man about it."

"What does that mean, Papa?"

"You have to learn that for yourself."

Jacks rode on the other running board. He held on to the side mirror and braced himself against the back seat, so that his lanky body seemed to spread around Jake Cuthbertson. He turned his face over his shoulder to guard against the dust and flying gravel, but he also looked over the open car at Venable.

It seemed that Venable conversed with him, through his eyes, his smile, the nodding of his head and windblown hair. Jacks returned the smile, and felt genuinely part of the excitement Venable seemed to rouse. But there was a knot in his stomach, tied by his father. Why hadn't his father come? And what did he mean by being a man? He would watch someone die, he knew. He had never seen a dead man, but had read plenty about death in adventure novels and had seen pictures on postcards and in death portraits. Still he did not know what to expect, or how he would feel about it, especially since it was Uncle Rye, a man he knew. And his father had said it wouldn't be easy.

Again, he looked at Venable, who seemed to be on the verge of breaking into song. Venable's face was bright, lit by the newly risen moon. Behind him, the forest, with its tangles of vines, seemed to move. There was kudzu, he knew, but also Virginia creeper, with its elegant circlet of five leaves, trumpet flower, honey suckle, feral wisteria, poison ivy, fox grape—all tangling, twining, twisting like a roil of snakes in the canopy.

When the car slowed, as it approached the town square, Venable signaled Jacks and jumped from the running board. The square was full of people, the heaviest part of the crowd being in front of the small, brick jail, a wing of the tin domed courthouse. Mostly the crowd was men, but there were women and children, too. Many were drinking. Venable had beers in his pockets and offered one to Jacks. Jacks took the bottle, smelled it first, and when Venable laughed at him, took a sip. It was warm and tasted very bitter and he wanted to spit it out.

"You will like it better if you take a big mouthful," Venable said and demonstrated. He winced and laughed, his lips wet. The crowd jostled to and fro, expectant. Some asked when the lynching would start and noted the lateness of the hour, though it was only just after nine o' clock. "But these things can take all night," someone complained. Another said she objected to so much drinking, especially since the next day was Sunday. There were many strangers in the crowd, Jacks noted, and a few wore Klan robes of various colors. Some wore their hoods, resembling medieval priests, but none of them hid his face.

The crowd lurched and excited shouts and shooting emanated from the side of the square opposite the jail. The two young men went to investigate. When they got the story, Venable broke into high, choking laughter. A colored man had come unsuspecting upon the crowd and had wanted to know what was going on. When he was told, he began to run and some of the people chased him, throwing stones, sticks and bricks at him. Someone fired off some shots. "That nigger went lickety-split," a man said and laughed.

"Where's that Johnson nigger," someone else shouted. "We want that nigger Johnson." Two women talked about Mrs. Cuthbertson, wondering how badly she had been violated. "How filthy," one said, "to have that big, dirty, grimy baboon all over you. With all that hot nigger smell and sweat."

"I'd just like to *see* 'im," the other replied.

"We want Johnson!" a man shouted. "Nigger. Nigger. We want the nigger. Bring out the nigger now."

"Nigger. Nigger. Nigger," the crowd chanted back. "Great God, bring out the nigger," they seemed to chant. "Now is the time for the killing of the nigger; now is the time for the blood of the nigger. Hit's time. Hit's time. Hit's time for the killing of the nigger."

Again the crowd lurched and rushed toward the jail house door where the sheriff had appeared with Rye Johnson. Venable pushed through the crowd, Jacks following. Jacks did not recognize Rye Johnson and thought for a moment that another colored man had taken his place. But then he began to put together the man's features, the white hair, the round face, swollen and missing its spectacles. The body was bowed, wobbly as a rag-doll. It seemed to be leaning on the sheriff first and then the deputy. A great shout went up from the crowd, with hoots and hisses. Then it began to attack Rye Johnson with stones and sticks until the sheriff fired off his gun to calm them. "Here's your nigger," he shouted. "Eat him, if you can." He pushed Rye Johnson into the crowd. For a moment there was a scuffle and fistfights broke out among the men as they vied to get to Rye Johnson. For a while, no one had control of Rye Johnson as he was pushed one way and another, all the while pelted and beaten with objects as well as fists. When he was pushed near Venable, Venable struck a blow to the top of his head. He turned, grinning to Jacks. Jacks clenched his fist. He saw his chance to strike the man, who was now on his knees, his eyes round with fear. Jacks did not strike. When he saw Johnson's eyes, more like the eyes of a giant bird, or toad, nearly completely black, all pupil, he felt he *could* strike. It made him feel strong to see the man's fear, and he thought it would give him pleasure to strike him as Venable had done. The muscles in his arms quivered. He flexed his back and threw out his chest, but he did not raise his fist. His temples throbbed, pleasurably, with tension. For the moment, that was enough.

Rye Johnson fell and curled into a ball and the crowd showered him with spit, tobacco juice, and phlegm. Suddenly, he jumped up, bowling into the crowd, as if to escape. The crowd fell back in surprise, as did Jacks, when the man, sickened and gray in the face, ran toward him. Does he recognize me? Jacks thought. He remembered that the man had always been courteous, deferential, though not solicitous of him. "It's a fine day, Young Mister Jacks," he would have said with a nod. "A fine day, sir." When Rye Johnson turned away from him, Jacks realized that the man was crazed, no more than a baited opossum or a trapped coyote, desperate for a last resort. It was then that Jacks relaxed his chest. There was no longer a sense of danger.

Someone shot a gun, and the crowd quieted. Rye Johnson lay in the middle of Main Street. His leg was crooked under him, the shot having blasted open his knee. He let out a shriek, and seeing he was down, the crowd moved in with axe handles and tire irons. He turned over and over in the street, trying to escape the blows, but each way he turned, he was struck. Once again the crowd stopped, as a car backed into the street. The men in the car got out. Jacks recognized them. They were the men from

Alabama. It was Billy Venable's car and Billy Venable and Jake Cuthbertson were inside. Bending his broken leg back into place, the men tied one end of a rope around Rye Johnson's feet and held onto the other end like bronco busters, and got into the rear of the car as it drove away. They dragged Rye Johnson down Main Street, then turned just before reaching the Venable townhouse, and dragged him down Poplar Street. Then they went a short way down Dogwood Street, bouncing on the old cobblestones, to the delight of the oohing and ahhing crowd as it chased behind. "They are going to the old tree!" Someone shouted. Venable tapped Jacks on the shoulder, and they took a shortcut down an alleyway and across a fallow field to the very edge of town. It was in sight of Coon Bottom, where many of the blacks who worked as maids and lawn men for the townspeople lived.

At the edge of the field stood a large old beech tree. Its silvery bark shone in the moonlight and the wide spreading leafy branches cast down a puzzle of shadows on the ground. The bark of the beech was smooth and scarred with many initials and lovers' hearts. Already a noose hung from a thick, low branch.

There were a few moments of quiet, and then the young men heard the procession, headed by the honking car and followed by the shrill, nearly child-like screams from the crowd. Once the crowd had reconvened, one of the men from Alabama stood on the hood of the car. His white robe lifted in the breeze and shone in the moonlight. In a hoarse voice he spoke words that Jacks could barely understand. It seemed he spoke in English, but it resonated as ancient, more visceral and rhythmic. He gesticulated, throwing wide his arms as if to embrace the moonlight. The crowd encouraged him with hoots and shouts, and when he was done he cried out, "Thus always to niggers!" There was loud drumming as someone hit a stick against a large can. Then a group, perhaps five men, lifted Rye Johnson to his feet. The man had no fight in him. He was naked, bloody from head to foot. Large pieces of skin had been chafed from his face and chest. He could no longer stand and three of the men held him on his feet while the other two, fumbling, put the noose around his neck. They tied the end of the rope to the Model T's front suspension strut and Billy Venable reversed the car. Uncle Rye flew into the air, and much to the delight of the crowd, he twisted, pedaled and tried to pull the rope away from his neck. Before he settled, the drumming came again, and two men with cans of gasoline doused Rye Johnson and set him on fire.

In the morning the two young men sat in the backyard of the Venable's townhouse. After the murder, they had lost sight of Billy Venable, and though Jacks had wanted to walk back to Woodbine, Venable convinced him to stay. They had drunk more beer, and gradually, Jacks had come to like it, swallowing big, fizzy mouthfuls as his friend suggested. Venable still talked about the lynching. "That's one nigger that won't be troubling white women again."

"I reckon not," Jacks said. "But what woman was it? Was that the trouble?"

"Who knows?" Venable said. "The trouble is . . . the trouble is . . . well, who knows what the trouble is? Anyhow, it was awful silly of those idiots to burn him up with a rope on him. Any fool knows, you need to chain him if you fixin' to burn him. But anyhow it was *spectacular*. I never saw anything like it before—whoosh—and all that smoke and the nigger didn't even scream."

"No," said Jacks. The image was fresh in his mind, the orange flames and the charring body.

Venable sipped on his beer. He looked seriously at Jacks, eye to eye. Jacks could see Venable's eyes still bright with excitement. "Have you ever wondered," Venable said, "why it is that when you cook a chicken it smells so good and you want to eat it, but when you cook a man, it smells so foul?"

"No," said Jacks.

"Have you ever thought about eating a man, like those cannibals in Africa?"

Jacks didn't answer. He walked to the edge of the yard, where the periwinkle was beginning to warm in the sun, and vomited.

EIGHTEEN

In the week following "the incident," as Jacks referred to the murders of Bertand, his wife, Jimmy Lee and his girlfriend, he left Woodbine only once. On the first morning after, he went out to the fields to supervise the workers. The workers were quieter than usual, and he imagined that they were thinking about the murders. He hoped that they didn't associate him with them, and he looked for signs of fear or resentment in their faces. Their faces seemed empty of anything except servility. The servility he trusted, but the emptiness he did not. Once he made the mistake of asking the whereabouts of Jimmy Lee, and even then the workers' faces showed nothing he could perceive, not surprise at his mistake, not grief for Jimmy Lee. He asked, too, about finding a replacement for Jimmy Lee, but no one was forthcoming.

Returning to the house, he washed and dressed for breakfast, but coming into the dining room, he did not find hot biscuits and jam waiting, or hear Milledge's quick movements in the kitchen. After an hour of waiting for Milledge, he drove into town to eat at Maribelle's Diner. Assuming Milledge was busy with funeral arrangements, he asked Maribelle to send a girl to help him until Milledge returned. Maribelle, however, was indignant. She said that there had been no reason to kill her cook. The cook had been a good girl, and nobody fried chicken better than she. Now she, herself, was looking for a replacement. Jacks ate a sloppily cooked breakfast, made by Maribelle herself, and left. The next morning, he boiled his own eggs and ate them with light bread he had bought at the store. "Wonder Bread" it was called. It was a wonder any one could eat it, he thought.

For dinner, he made sandwiches of coldcuts and light bread, and that evening, Betty sent a girl around to ask him to come over to Thousand

Acres for supper. The thought of sitting with Venable sickened him, and he snapped at the girl, telling her that Hell hadn't frozen over. The next evening, the girl came with a plate of food in a basket. He ate the food, but he didn't want to see Betty, Venable, Cook, or anyone from town. The next days, he busied himself on the farm, walking around the pastures to take note of the size and readiness of his beef, supervising the sheep shearing, overseeing the castration of the shoats. In the evenings, after the workers left, he sat on the porch with his pipe and remembered his father and his mother.

Late on the fifth night, he walked through the house without turning on the lights, without turning on a radio, or reading a newspaper, and found his bed. Outside there was lightning. He stripped off his clothes down to his strap shirt and boxers and knelt beside the bed in prayer. His prayers had always been perfunctory, a brief acknowledgment of a greater power, but this night when he closed his eyes, images of the murders flashed in his mind. There was the brown, bloodied belly of Maribelle's girl, with its big cave of a navel and stretch marks. He had never seen a pregnant woman's belly before, and it now gave him a sharp sense of inadequacy never to have fathered a child. There was Bertrand's overly proud face, ballooning in his mind. Even cut and bruised, he looked proud, as proud as the morning he had come to ask for help, looking every bit as tar-black and liver-lipped as his father, Johnson. When someone, perhaps it was Cook's deputy, had said, "Nothing personal," Bertrand had replied, "It's personal to me." The crowd had gathered thickly around Bertrand, so Jacks had not seen when Bertrand was shot, but afterwards, he saw where the heels of the shiny oxfords had plowed a trough in the sand as the man died.

Since he did not want to think about these things, he stopped his prayers. He lay on top of his bed, his head elevated by pillows, and listened to the rain and mild thunder. The pillow cases smelled fresh from washing and reminded him of Milledge. He realized how integral to the house Milledge had become. Everything in the house smelled of her. She was in the washing, down to his underwear. She was the lemony smell of the furniture polish and its gloss upon the tables. How he moved around the house in the dark, a long learned routine, had been determined by her placement of furniture. His mother had originally placed the furniture, but slowly, Milledge had supplanted his mother's design, and after he remodeled the kitchen, there was nothing to be seen of his mother in that room. It was all Milledge's. *All Millie's.*

The next morning, sitting down to his boiled eggs, he came across a letter in the mail. The handwriting, strained and angular, was familiar; it was Milledge's. He hesitated before he opened the envelope, but tore off an edge and blew it open and pulled out a folded sheet, stenciled with a flower design. The letter read: "Dear Mr. Jacks, I am not coming back. Sincerely, Milledge Johnson." He stared a while at the letter, his mind blank, trying to comprehend what it really meant. She was not coming back, he pondered. But where had she gone? His heart suddenly throbbed and he stood up from the table, holding the page in front of him, reading it over and over again. Suddenly he had the feeling that he had hurt Milledge deeply, and the feeling surprised him. But of course, he thought, she had expected that he would have protected Bertrand. Perhaps this was her way of getting back at him for the murders. "But it is just as much Bertrand's fault as it is mine," he said to himself. He tore the letter, then crumpled it. Damn fool woman, he thought. Now she's gone off the deep end. He tried to eat, but couldn't. He walked around in the house. It had become disorderly in just five days. He had to get somebody in to clean it or he would have to do it himself. He went out to the fields again, surprising the workers with the break in routine. Later, he hotwired Bertrand's car and ordered one of his workers to drive it to Milledge's house. The sight of it disturbed him.

When Betty's girl brought around supper, he asked if she knew how Milledge was doing. "I heah right hard, suh," was all he got out of her. Later, smoking his pipe on the porch, he tried to imagine how Milledge might have felt. Bertrand was her eldest son, and it must have driven some sort of hole through her existence to have lost him. He recalled how he felt when his mother had died. It had been a sharply felt absence at first, but slowly it filled with memory. However, in the first days, he recalled how he seemed in a daze, how disordered existence had become, and how acutely physical the grief had been. He did not wish that on Milledge. He thought about what he might do to comfort her, perhaps send her a wreath of flowers. She liked flowers she had once told him.

That night passed restlessly, and he did not fall asleep until the sun was up. When he awoke, he realized he was late to instruct the workers, and rushing to the fields, found them earnestly engaged in the day's tasks. When he returned to the house, he saw that the screen door was ajar and he rushed in hoping to see Milledge. No one was in the kitchen and he concluded that he had left the door ajar on his rush out to the fields. He saw the crumpled letter on the table and spread it flat. The floral stencil reminded him of the dress that Bertrand's wife had worn.

That afternoon, he drove into Bethany, to Perkins' Funeral Home to buy flowers.

"When do you need the flowers?" the wife of the proprietor asked.

He said he wanted them right now. Today.

"But when is the funeral?"

He said he didn't know.

"Well, then," the woman said, "Who has the body?"

He told her he didn't know, that it was a colored funeral.

"Oh, a colored funeral. Probably Jefferson's over in Greene. That's where most of the colored around here go. I can call and find out."

Impatiently, he told her he didn't care who had the bodies, he would take the flowers himself.

"More than one? Do you mean the big funeral for them colored rascals? You don't want me to send flowers over for them, do you? Those murdering, raping rascals. A gang of them, too. Like Bonnie and Clyde. Now, you know, Mr. Jacks, that wouldn't look right," she said firmly. "Besides, those funerals were yesterday. All of them together. Four caskets up in that tiny River of Joy. I'd supposed every colored soul in Talmaedge County was there." She gave him a quizzical look. "Didn't you hear about it? They had to deputize some of the local men, Mr. Perkins included, to make sure there was no trouble of any kind."

He said that not only hadn't he heard, he didn't care. He only wanted the flowers. She went away and came back with a small wreath of lilies. It was for a funeral over in Madison, but she could make another one before it was needed.

With the delivery of the flowers as an excuse, Jacks went to visit Milledge.

They must have heard the car plowing through the slew of mud and whining and spinning long before he got to the yard of the little house because a man was standing on the porch waiting for him. He was a light-skinned man, favoring Bertrand, but Jacks didn't remember ever having seen him. Getting out of the car with the wreath held at his side, Jacks approached the man. The man didn't move away from the top of the stairs. This and the quick, alert way he talked made Jacks think that the man must have

182

been some of Milledge's people from the North. The man told Jacks that Milledge was very ill since the murders, and surely anyone would understand why she didn't want to be bothered.

"What's the matter with her?"

"She is distressed."

"Distressed?"

"Yes. Distressed. You know, upset."

"I know what 'distressed' means."

The man didn't say anything for a moment, only stared down at Jacks, meeting him at the eye.

"What's your name?"

"I'm W.B. Johnson."

"You a schoolteacher or something?"

"I am a *professor*. I teach mathematics."

A professor, Jacks thought. His mouth turned down at the corners. "Arithmetic? But you don't live around here, do you?"

"Not anymore."

"But you did once?" Then it occurred to Jacks that he was speaking to Milledge's younger son. "You must be Milledge's other boy."

"I'm her son, Mr. Jacks. I haven't been a boy in a long time."

Jacks thought how he would like to teach this man a lesson. Nothing drastic. Just slap him beside his head. "When do you think Millie is going to be well, son?"

The man shifted on his feet and crossed his arms. "I don't know."

"Well, what did the doctor say?"

"He didn't say anything. But I imagine that it will be quite a while, Mr. Jacks. It may be hard for you to understand since you have never had a family, but my mother just lost her child. True, he was a grown man, but he was her child—her first born. And it isn't the kind of thing that you say, 'Oh, he lived a good long life,' or 'God had mercy on him to take him.' It isn't a kind of thing like a car accident where you say, 'Nobody could have stopped it from happening.' This was a cold-blooded killing. Somebody planned it. Somebody put a gun to his head. Somebody pulled the trigger. The thing that hurts me is that my brother went over and fought the Nazis to keep—"

"I know all that. And don't you presume to know how I feel. I feel—I feel bad for Milledge, and for the family, too. It was a terrible thing what happened to Bertrand. Now, you might not believe me—I don't expect you or any colored person in Talmaedge to—I feel just terrible about this wretched thing. But I can't bring them back."

Jacks could see W. B.'s face flush. The young man shifted from foot to foot, like he might spring down the steps at any moment.

"You can find the ones who did it," W.B. said thickly.

This boy might not make it out of the county tonight. Jacks took a breath to control himself. "W. B., I know you are upset, so I'll just remind you once. It is talk like that that got Bertrand in trouble. Now, we've got a sheriff's department; we don't need any outside interference."

"Maybe you do."

There was quiet for a moment while Jacks looked the man over. He was a soft-looking man, tall, in his twenties, and already balding. He was well groomed and wore starched clothes and dress shoes. *A professor! What could he profess, teaching 'rithmetic to a bunch of colored monkeys?* Jacks took in a slow, deep breath and spoke heavily. "If I were you, I wouldn't go around saying things like that. You know as well as I know that the Klan killed Bertrand and they would have killed me, too, if I had gotten in their way. Now, I'd be careful, if I were you, because they aren't above killing a schoolteacher from up North."

"Is that a threat?"

This boy is stupid. He is asking for it. "I don't make threats, son. I don't have to. But if the Klan wants you, there isn't a place on Earth you can hide. Now, I'm not in the business of giving advice, but let me tell you this because you are Millie's boy. Get your black ass back to Detroit or Chicago, and keep your big mouth shut. Stick to teaching your A-B-Cs or whatever you teach."

Again, the young man flushed in the face. Even his neck turned pink, and Jacks saw his fists clench. He was about to speak again when the door opened and Milledge came out, supported by a woman who looked nearly white. Milledge looked old to Jacks, though he knew she was just over forty. Her face looked as if it had fallen—every feature sagged, the eyes, the lips, and the cheeks. Her hair was nearly all salt and pepper, hair he had never seen because she had always worn a scarf at his house.

"Millie!" His voice betrayed his shock at her appearance.

"Mr. Jacks!" she countered, a sharpness in her tone he hadn't heard before. "What can I do for you?"

"Well . . . I . . . was . . . *I'm sorry*, Millie. I'm sorry I disturbed you. I was just hoping you would be coming back to Woodbine in a couple of days."

"No sir," she nearly whispered. "I can't make it. Not right now."

She looked away from him and let out a deep breath. For a moment he thought she wouldn't breathe in again. "I ain't even trying to take it no more, Mr. Jacks. It done took me."

He raised the wreath, offering it to her, but no one reached to accept it. He nodded, recognizing that for the moment there was an unbridgeable breach between Milledge and himself. He laid the wreath at the bottom of the stairs, and, nodding again, went to the car. On the way back up that muddy drive, he knew he couldn't do another thing to Milledge. He would send her some money. A hundred dollars was good. She had been a good worker, and maybe in a month or two, her grief would quell. She might come back to him. But for now, he thought, he would have to find another girl.

He drove toward home, and slowed when he got to the driveway. At the other end of the shady drive, Woodbine looked more like a haunted house than his home. There were already too many ghosts there, he thought. His grandfather's, his mother's, and his father's, and now, he was afraid it would be haunted by Jimmy Lee and Bertrand and Millie, too. The workers would be expecting him to make his afternoon round of inspection, but he couldn't face any colored people just then, with their suspicious looks and whispers about him. Why did he worry about it so? Venable had far more to do with the incident than he, and Venable was probably somewhere fucking a colored girl. He continued past Woodbine, feeling a bit aimless. When he began to descend the slope going down toward the bridge, he gassed the car, letting the heavy vehicle speed toward the bottom. It felt for a moment that the car would take flight, zigzagging in the road. His stomach felt as if it were rising up in his chest, and when the car bounced and slammed into the bed of the bridge, he kept gassing it. Again it bounced when it left the bridge bed and started to climb out of the bottoms. All this time, he did not look below him at the river.

Maribelle gave him a cold look when he came into the diner. She was serving Cook and his two of his deputies. He nodded at Cook and took a booth in front of the window looking over Main Street, busy with people headed home from work.

"I'm still mad with you," Maribelle said. She took out an ordering pad and held her pencil poised above it. "What can I get for you, Noland?"

Jacks hadn't looked at the menu. "How about some fried chicken?"

Maribelle snorted. "That's what I'm mad about, Noland." She looked around the restaurant. There were only Cook, his deputies, and a couple. She slipped into the booth and sat across from him. "My new girl doesn't fry chicken. Not that that's all I'm mad about. I just don't see why y'all had to kill Beah. That girl was as innocent as the day is long. Just because she was tangled up with that rascal doesn't mean she did anything to deserve what happened to her—"

"I didn't kill anyone," Jacks whispered sharply. He looked across at Cook. "Don't say that I did. If I hear you say it again, there will be consequences for you."

Maribelle pursed her lips. "Well . . . it's what I heard."

"You *heard* wrong." He regarded the woman, who now would not look him in the eye. She was about his age, he knew, but her full, rosy cheeks and lively eyes gave her the appearance of a younger woman. His anger at her presumption faded quickly and he became aware of a feeling of emptiness and regret. He was hungry, too.

"I'm sorry," she said, looking out of the window. "You were there, though."

"Yes."

"All the colored folks say you had a part in it. That's all I know."

"Did you ask your friend Cook?" He glanced at the sheriff, whose mouth was stuffed with food.

"Well, I assumed—"

"You can't believe everything people say, much less anything a colored person says."

"I stand corrected." She paused, looking about. "Well, I can fry you a pork chop. Got some lima beans and tomatoes, and a right good piece of cornbread."

"That'll be fine."

She slipped to the edge of the seat, but didn't leave. "I suppose you'll miss your girl. She was with you such a long time."

"What do you mean?"

"Oh, she's leaving, if she ain't already left—"

He slipped forward in the seat. "What do you mean?"

"Just that my new girl said that your girl has people up North. Chicago, I think. And that today or tomorrow, she was leaving for up there. Couldn't take it here anymore, they say, since . . . you know, the—"

"Nonsense. I just left her." His body stiffened. He felt it acutely in the small of his back and his neck. He didn't believe that Milledge would leave him, much less that she could have stood in front of him, not thirty minutes earlier, and given him no hint that she was leaving.

"Oh. I'll have to have a talk with my new girl. I hope I didn't get a loose mouth. Beah, my old girl, was quiet. Couldn't get much out of her, but if she told you something, you could depend on it. But this girl I got now, I don't know her."

"It's that son of hers." He thought that he should go back and stop her.

"Pardon?" Maribelle cocked her head.

"She had a boy with her. Light-skinned boy. Said he was her son. The other son."

"Yes. That'll be the one, I hear. I never saw him to know him." Maribelle slipped back into the middle of the booth, placed her hands on the table, and leaned on her elbows. "They come and go. You hate to lose a good one and you do try to keep them. I've lost a-many to the factories over in Atlanta, when they started taking colored. Hurt business, here. This one has been with you many years, I know, even before I moved here, and I've been here twenty-some years. But you'll find another one, probably one just as good—don't look so glum—after all, it's not like you were married to her."

The comment stung him and he felt his face redden. "Like you say," he said after a pause, "I can find another one."

Cook and his deputies got up from their table and started toward the door. "See y'all for breakfast," Maribelle said cheerfully. When they were out of the door, she turned to Jacks. "It's a wonder I can stay in business with that bunch of free-loaders." She looked out of the window as Cook and the deputies got into their cars. "How he got into his position, I'll never know. Just low class. He doesn't think but one way. His way." Jacks watched the tip of her nose pull up and down as she talked. "You and I are different, you know. We have been places and seen things. We read about things. We have broader minds than people like Cook. We are more sensitive. I know he killed my girl as sure as I know anything. She was innocent and *pregnant*, too. He didn't have to kill the baby— and it was almost due. No room for mercy, or kindness. I don't know about the other woman, but I know my girl was sweet. She might have been tangled up with that rascal, but that wasn't entirely her fault. You and I understand these things, but someone like Cook, he never will. He doesn't see circumstances. For all he knew that rascal may have *raped* my girl, too. I don't blame him for the men. They got what was coming to them. We do have a right to protect ourselves, women, as well as, men. And there's just no justice in the law, anymore, with these smart aleck Northern lawyers twisting the law all about. A man has a right to protect himself and his women. Why, it's getting so a white woman can't walk down the street without attracting the leer of one of these *black* lunatics. Lunatics, they are, too—most everyone, revved up on liquor or cocaine or something. And they are born oversexed, especially these light-skinned ones. They got a little Caucasian blood in them and that emboldens them to think they are just like white people. It used to be that just the communists encouraged them, but now, the government encourages them, too. Not to mention their own churches. In a way, they can't help it, I suppose. You and I understand that." Suddenly, she turned to him, touching his hand. She had tears in her eyes. "I miss my girl so. I do. And not just because she worked for me. She was a sweet, sweet girl." Suddenly he, too, had a swell of emotion, but he couldn't say for what. He squeezed her hand lightly, and then, feeling ashamed put his hand on his lap. "I'm so silly," she said. "Let me cook you your pork chop."

When the pork chop came, it was a little raw around the bone. He ate what he could of it. She returned to the table and ate cake and drank coffee with him. It was the last of the cakes for a while, she said, until she found a new cake maker. The next evening he came again, and the next, until it was habit for him to take his supper with Maribelle. She talked a lot, most of which he could tune out. But he enjoyed when she talked of travel. She wanted to visit Paris and Rome. They could go together, she said. He imagined that they could, and so, one day after about six months of suppers, he proposed to her, and they married the next day.

PART FOUR
THE REDEEMER

NINETEEN

When he had driven beyond Atlanta's suburbs along US Route 29, he felt certain that he knew what he must do. He must kill Jacks, and the why of that was clear: It was his destiny. The idea had come to him gradually as he tried to explain to himself why he was driving to see Jacks. It was not what Jacks knew about the murders that mattered. It was what he, himself, knew. He had been running from it and yet had carried it in his head—the memory of the bloody thighs; Venable's smug face; Bertrand's dancing. And the snake-like look in Jacks's eyes. Having seen it all, it had called to him. It had clouded his mind, dragged him down all of his life. In the muddy alleyways of Cabbagetown. In the greasy galley of the USS Bennington. In smoke-filled cafes in Frisco—and dog collared to Aza X—*they exterminate little pups like you!* He had said many times that he ought to kill Jacks, but then the realization struck him, sharp, hard as a chunk of quartzite, that he *actually* was on his way to kill Jacks, and he laughed out loud. It was no longer a speculation, but an action underway. Suddenly, he became aware that he had placed the Colt M1911, his father's service revolver, beside him on the passenger seat.

But why kill? Daddy killed the German boy. He didn't like it. Bertrand saw the camp of Jews! There is no need to kill . . . except, Jacks has to die. He has to die because I want to live! Lonnie knew what to call it. *Redemption! That's what Momma meant!* He laughed short, hard chuckles. *On her dying bed, that's what Momma meant.* His stomach cramped. *I am a redeemer!* He barely held the car, a battered Volkswagen, in its lane. *Everybody wants to go to heaven, but nobody wants to die. But Jacks has to die.* To see evil, to be a witness to evil was a blessing for he knew now what evil was. To kill Jacks was not evil. It was redemptive. *Redemptive for Jacks? Goddamn Jacks. Jacks has to die so I can live! I have been dead. I am dead. I will be dead again. But will be alive when Jacks is dead.* He stopped laughing. His body slackened. He sweated profusely. Nothing made sense to him. The universe was all too big and too subtle, but yet he felt energized and directed by his new purpose. *I am a redeemer!* But what does it mean to redeem?

As he drove into the country, the hills, fields, and forests rolled up on either side of the road and moved from the windshield to the rear, and as he turned onto State Route 11 and then 15, then onto smaller and smaller roads, the sky became stormy and the landscape darkened, and the thickets—honeysuckle and kudzu—rose up like ogres along the road banks. Now he grew more and more uncertain of his purpose. He felt he was reverting to a boy, ignorant of everything and innocent of nothing.

In the week following the murders, Lonnie and his mother packed their belongings and moved to Atlanta. Neither wanted to go, and at the time, Lonnie didn't fully understand why they had to. He explained to Aileen that he hadn't been the only one to witness the murders. He counted on his fingers, naming the boys from his school whom he had seen on the bridge. They had even a better view than he, he supposed. Aileen responded angrily at first, then sullenly, spending most of their last day in Talmaedge County uttering no more than a few words to her son. When their fat cousin came, driving the Tudor Deluxe, they climbed in, Aileen in the front and Lonnie in his old place in the back. Though the car seemed familiar, its smell had become foreign, a mixture of stale smoke and sweat that even the breeze roiling through the windows could not dissipate. Behind them followed a pickup truck loaded with what furniture they could fit on it and driven by one of Jacks' workers. Their new home was on Short Street in Cabbagetown, a tenant's community for Appalachians who worked in Atlanta's declining textile mills. The brick smokestacks of the mills cast long shadows on the tiny bungalows and shotguns.

In the years that followed, Aileen worked hard at a mill, making feed bags and enough money to pay the rent and buy food for the two of them, but never enough for anything more than an occasional new dress. She was drawn into the congregation of a small church, where she became known as Mother Henson, just as Lonnie, like many boys in Cabbagetown, was drawn into experimentation with marijuana and petty crime. When he was old enough, he joined the service, but unlike most of the Cabbagetown boys who went into the Army or the Marines, Lonnie, remembering the sailors from Savannah, chose the Navy.

When he went to the base in Great Lakes, he imagined he would become an airman, a boatswain's mate, or even an ordnance man, positions that would take him far abroad. But before he could go into apprentice training, he fell into conversation with a cook who convinced him to become a commissary man. The cook was sitting on the concrete steps behind the mess hall smoking a cigarette. He was a fit-looking, brown-skinned man with a closely trimmed, balding head and a razor-thin mustache riding the sphincter of his lip. Lonnie thought the man winked at him as he passed, and wanting a cigarette, he told his fellow seamen to go ahead of him while he talked to the man. The cook was originally from Wilmington, North Carolina, he said, and had visited Georgia many times; so while they smoked, the cook asked about places in Atlanta, places unfamiliar to Lonnie. They were most likely in the Negro areas, the cook surmised, and there would have been no reason for Lonnie to have known them. Lonnie had heard of colored neighborhoods like Summerhill, Peoplestown, and Sweet Auburn, but had never been to them. In fact, he knew little of Atlanta outside of Cabbagetown, where the bright line of narrow Pearl Street separated the white neighborhood from colored Reynoldstown. The Reynoldstown people worked for the railroad and were said to have thought themselves better than those in Cabbagetown, so growing up Lonnie had learned to harbor resentment against them.

"Ahh, now," the cook disagreed. "They probably weren't any better off than you were." He smiled widely, flashing a gold incisor. "Think about it. If the work paid all that well, why was it work for Negroes?" The cook nodded with certainty and winked. Lonnie admitted the cook made sense and he felt a vague familiarity talking so frankly with the man. But the man was nothing like Bertrand. Even when he smiled, Bertrand carried a heavy sobriety, whereas the cook seemed light-hearted through and through. When they had finished their cigarettes, the cook advised him to scurry along lest he miss his supper. Inside, as he went through the mess line, he saw the cook, standing behind a pass-through that opened to the galley. The cook looked out and winked and whispered something to the line server, a colored boy about Lonnie's age. The server ladled heaping helpings of meat pie and fried potatoes on Lonnie's tray.

On subsequent evenings, Lonnie smoked and chatted again with the cook. They were careful that the drill instructor did not see them, and one evening they stepped inside the galley where Lonnie saw firsthand the food's preparation. It seemed an easy job to him, and the cook confirmed that not only was it easy, it was interesting—creative. He made up new recipes, and there was great satisfaction in seeing people enjoy the food he cooked. Further, the cook explained, he would never go hungry. Working as an airman or an ordnance man, you were always in danger and always hungry. But as a commissary man, you were down below deck, safe from bullets or crashing jet planes. You could still travel to all the ports, all over the world, but without the same level of risk. Further, you had access to all the food. The cook remembered growing up in Wilmington, always being hungry. He recalled that when the Americans started to airlift food to West Berlin, how he, nearly a grown man, wished the United States would airlift food to his neighborhood in Wilmington. "Times were rough," he said. He concluded by saying that once he left the Navy, he would have a skill. He would be able to get a cooking job in any city in the country.

"That's good advice," said Lonnie and nodded his head. "But let me ask you a question." He looked around and lowered his voice. "How come there ain't no white boys working in the kitchen? How come you are all colored?"

The cook grinned. "Colored boys think about their stomachs, first. We ain't so interested in taking over the world."

"But what about the Russians?"

"What about them? Russians ain't do nothing to the colored man."

"The Russians are trying to take over the United States, ain't they?"

The cook handed Lonnie a piece of ham from a pan that sat on the counter. "That's pure Virginia-cured ham. We just served it to the officers. All I can say is that the Russians never lynched a colored man." The comment struck Lonnie like a slap and he froze, holding the ham in one hand and a cigarette in the other. "What's the matter?" the cook said, and then cocked his head suspiciously. "I don't mean anything. I don't mean to cast any aspersions." Lonnie didn't know what "aspersions" meant, and the cook seemed to have read it on his face. "Blame. I ain't blaming you for nothing." He winked. "Well, I *guess* I got nothing to blame you for." He shifted back and forth uneasily and took a step back from Lonnie. "How's the ham?"

Lonnie tasted the ham. It tasted of salt. "Good." He felt his face flush and he thought that the cook would now consider him a lyncher. "I. . . ." He looked around at the young colored men, busy with cooking and cleaning pots. "I saw one once, that's all."

The cook nodded and put his hand on Lonnie's shoulder. "It's okay," he said quietly. "It's okay. Now, eat your ham and scoot on through here to the mess line before you get into trouble."

That night in his rack, Lonnie thought a long time about the cook patting him on the shoulder and saying, "It's okay." In the dim light, he could make out the bedsprings of the rack above him. Around him he heard the easy breathing and occasional snores of the other seamen. When he closed his eyes, he saw the face of the cook, with his gold tooth and winking eye. But rather than thinking of the cook as the cook, he thought of him as Bertrand. He thought of Bertrand sitting with him in the lamplight on the night that his parents went to the hospital. He thought about the small talk they had made that night and how, in spite of his father's apparent trust of Bertrand, he and his mother held onto their suspicions. How wrong he had been about Bertrand. He thought of Bertrand dancing in the church, how faraway his face looked and how his face had started to fill up with the faces of other people. It was more than his imagination, he thought. Bertrand was like an angel, and this kind man, the cook, was like Bertrand coming back to him. The thought should have comforted him, but then he saw the crumpled flower-print dress of Bertrand's wife, and her fat, bloodied thighs.

For several weeks he avoided the cook. He was coming to the end of his basic training, deciding on which apprentice school to attend. The apprentice schools were in places all over the country, and he thought he might try to go back to the South. After all, as autumn came to the Midwest, he realized that the winters might be far too cold for him.

One evening, as he went through the mess line, the server slipped a note onto his tray. It was from the cook, and it asked him to come to the back door of the mess hall just after the beginning of middle watch, at midnight. His stomach churned when he read the note. He couldn't imagine what the cook wanted. As he lay in his bunk waiting for the sound of the eight bells, his mind raced, one moment thinking that the cook would give him a going away present, or some helpful advice, and the next that he would chastise him for not coming around again. As he approached the back of the mess hall, the galley door opened, and he saw the cook wave eagerly to him.

"You came!" the cook whispered and pulled Lonnie by the arm into the dark galley. "Watch out for the pans." The cook led him through the galley into an office, where he shut the door and turned on a desk lamp. The office was small and cluttered, just big enough for a desk and chair. Papers were stacked on the desk and pinned to cork boards all around. "This is where I do my real work," the cook said with a wave of his hand. "You see, it ain't just the cooking; you've got to plan the meals and order the food, too."

"I see," Lonnie said, looking at the cook, who was not wearing his cook's jacket or apron. The men stood just a couple of feet apart in the office. Lonnie was taller than the cook and looked down on his head and the tight balls of hair around the top of his strap shirt. The cook's odor was sweet and spicy, and in the closed room, Lonnie could feel the heat of his body.

"You all right?" the cook asked.

"Yes."

"I was beginning to worry. I thought I might have upset you. Me, shooting off about lynching and all. I apologize if I upset you. I want you to know that I put a great deal of respect in our friendship. And I hope you feel the same way about me."

Lonnie thought a minute. He did like the man, but he was afraid of something about him that he couldn't name. "I do like you. But . . ."

"But what? Why did you stop coming to talk to me?"

"But . . . you remind me of somebody."

The cook laughed. His breath brushed against Lonnie's neck and Lonnie stepped back, his heels bumping the door. The cook laughed again. "Don't be afraid. If you fixin' to be a sailor, you have to get used to close quarters. Besides, I ain't fixin' to hurt you in any way. Now, who this I remind you of?"

Lonnie took a moment to say the name, but in his mind he shouted it several times.

"Who this Bertrand? Somebody you like?"

"Yeah. I liked him. Not at first. But I did like him."

"I hope you like me, too."

"Yeah."

"That's good." The cook touched his elbow, and ran his fingers down to Lonnie's hand and gripped it. His hands were strong and softer than Lonnie thought they should be. Lonnie squeezed the hand.

"He was like my daddy."

"A daddy?" the cook said.

"He was my daddy's friend. And he was colored and they killed him."

The cook let go of his hand. "They killed him?" A moment passed and the two stood, breathing quietly. "Was this the lynching you were so worried about?"

"Uh-huh." Lonnie swallowed and he felt his throat choke and his nose close up. "I didn't know it was him at first. I was out in the woods picking some blackberries, I saw them dragging something, and I followed. And I . . ."

"Now, now." The cook put a hand on the back of Lonnie's neck and stroked. "You needn't worry about all that now." Lonnie sobbed. The cook held his head against his bare shoulder. "Now, now."

The shoulder became slippery with Lonnie's tears. He couldn't remember the last time he had cried on someone's shoulder, and he thought it might have been Bertrand's. When he had tried to talk to Aileen about the murders, she had cut him off and walked away. He sometimes heard her weeping in the bedroom of the Cabbagetown house, but a closed door always stood between them.

"I should have done something," he said when he was able to manage his breath.

"You should have done something," the cook repeated sympathetically.

"I should have stopped them."

"You should have stopped them."

"I should have *told* somebody."

"You should have told somebody. But, who were you supposed to tell? You were just a boy."

"I was just a boy."

"You didn't do anything wrong."

"I didn't do anything wrong."

"You ain't to blame for nothing."

"I'm not to blame."

"No. It's not your fault. You are just as innocent as the day you were born." The cook took Lonnie's face in his hands. "So clean up those tears." The cook wiped tears from Lonnie's cheeks with his thumbs. "Now give me a smile." Lonnie smiled. He felt lightheaded and took a deep breath. "You want something to eat?"

"No."

"You sure? I got some ham."

"No. I'm not hungry."

"What about something sweet? Some dessert?"

"No."

"What do you want? What can daddy get for you?"

Lonnie hesitated. He didn't know what he wanted.

"You don't know what you want?" The cook's voice softened. "I bet I know what you want. You want what I want." The cook put his hands on Lonnie's shoulders and pressed down. He did not push hard, but Lonnie knelt so that his face was in front of the cook's groin. Quickly the cook unbuckled his pants and pushed his groin against Lonnie's face. Lonnie felt the bristle of the man's pubic hair on his cheeks. The groin smelled faintly of sweat and urine. I am not a faggot, Lonnie thought. Then he said it. "Oh, yes you are," the cook said. "You are *my* little cracker faggot." The cook brushed his fingers across Lonnie's hair. His penis was uncircumcised and seemed very black to Lonnie. Its veins were flush and it was beginning to fill. The cook pulled back the foreskin and the glans was blue and glassy. "Oh, you most certainly are," the cook said. He rubbed the glans along Lonnie's lips. "You most certainly are my little punk cracker. Now, open up." Lonnie opened his mouth.

For the ten years following, Lonnie roamed the seas as a commissary man aboard the USS Bennington, an anti-submarine aircraft carrier. The Big Benn, as the crewmen were apt to call her, was commissioned during World War II, and when Lonnie came aboard in Mayport, Florida, she was fresh from repairs after a boiler explosion. The explosion had killed over a hundred sailors and it had taken nearly a year to repair the damage. A part of the Pacific fleet, Lonnie found ports in San Diego, Pearl Harbor, Yoko-suka, Sydney, Subic Bay, back and forth across the ocean searching for the Russian submarines.

Though he spent more than his fair share of time in the brig for drink-ing and brawling, Lonnie proved to be a good seaman, and moved up in rate quickly. He was a favorite among the young officers for his easy accommo-dation of their cravings for home-cooked meals. For this, he was sometimes called, "Mom". Lithe and blond, he occasionally accommodated the officer's sexual urges. For this, he was sometimes called "Lonnie, honey," "honey," or "sweet tooth." He expected nothing for either service, and though, at first the rough trade embarrassed him, performing it also comforted him. There was no cuddling and little tenderness—he got that in port with women—but usually a teasing followed by a command, to which he bent like a willow, and the bending itself, the yielding to a greater, more certain power made him feel confident—transitorily—and gave his life direction. When a young officer's thighs seized and went slack, and he cried out his wife's name, Lonnie felt a flush of blood to his face and a shortness of breath. But in the hours following such an affair he berated himself. *A queer. A fucking queer. Oh, you most certainly are!* He thought of the cook and of Bertrand, and he felt helpless. "I was just a boy," he said over and over again. "I didn't do anything wrong." And yet, a feeling of complicity ached dully in every nerve. *But what did I do? What?* Drinking helped him forget the past, and so he got through.

He would have stayed on in the Navy, making it a career, except for an accident, in which a crate of canned foods slipped from its pallet on a forklift and crushed his foot. It was a miracle, the doctors told him that the foot could be saved but he would always limp. He was in Long Beach when it happened, and after spending some months in the Navy Hospital at Camp Pendleton, he was mustered out of the Navy, and made his way to San Francisco. There, he met a poet, who having rejected her slave name, called herself Aza X. He went to live with her in her apartment on the second floor of a walk-up, just off of Columbus Avenue in North Beach.

TWENTY

I am a redeemer! he kept telling himself. But what was a redeemer? He was driving on a narrow, asphalt road that curved up and down through the wooded hills. The road was unfamiliar to him and he wasn't sure any longer that he was on the way to Woodbine. Six months earlier, in the winter of 1973, his mother had sent a telegraph, asking him to come home from California, and against his will he drove back to the South, to Atlanta, to Cabbagetown. Aileen had contracted brown lung disease and had become bedridden. It had been coming on a long time, she admitted, starting with "Monday fevers," a reaction to the lint-filled air of the mill. She paid it no mind, suffering the tightness of chest, the coughs and the wheezing. She had to work, she said. But over the years the cotton dust scarred her lungs, irreparably.

One evening, as Lonnie tended her, spooning broth to her mouth as she lay propped up by pillows, he ventured to mention news he had read that day. Typically, they talked little because breathing was difficult for Aileen, and when she did speak it was about the church, the mill or the Bible, topics that did not interest him.

"Momma, do you remember Mr. Venable from Talmaedge?" Aileen's eyes widened; she coughed. He wiped spittle from her chin. "Well, he died."

Her face tightened and she tried to speak, coughed again before she found her voice. "Where you hear?"

"Read it in the newspaper." He was new to reading the newspaper. He bought it daily at the grocer on Carroll Street, and paging through it helped to pass the time. It reported heavily on the mayoral race, where a brash, young black man was challenging the sitting mayor, a white man. But what caught his attention that morning was an obituary. *Venable.* He overlooked the article at first, taking scant notice of the portraits of the dead that decorated the pages. Then, in sudden familiarity, he came back to the article. *Mr. Venable!* His heart thumped excitedly as he read. He hadn't known Venable's first name, but now to see it spelled out and to see the name of Talmaedge County brought a rush of recognition. He would have gone in to tell his mother right away, except that she had been sleeping.

Aileen adjusted the oxygen cannula, pushing it deeper into her nostrils. "What killed him?"

"Old age, I guess. Didn't say."

She grunted, closed her eyes for a moment. "How old?"

Lonnie left the room to find the article. When he returned, Aileen seemed asleep again and he studied her face. Venable had been seventy-four. Old enough. And his mother had not yet turned sixty, though the disease made her look a decade older. When he got up to go, the wicker chair squeaked and, she opened her eyes. "I remember," she said quietly. "He owes us a dog." At first the statement seemed amusing and Lonnie smiled. Then he remembered the tomato slips and a sick feeling came to his stomach. Often he thought about the murders, but for some years, living in the Haight-Ashbury, with its perpetual, psychedelic distractions, they had become more figments than real events. The memory of Venable made them real again, and he saw in his mind, as if it had only been a short time before, the man's crooked, yet threatening smile. "I forgive him though," Aileen said with a wheeze.

Lonnie sat again in the chair. He looked at Aileen's hands, still strong but with bony fingers that had reddened and clubbed from the disease. "For what? I don't." He felt a hot rush run from his chest to his face. "Neither Venable or Jacks. I hope they burn in hell."

Aileen looked at him a long moment. "Forgive and forget. 'For if ye forgive men their trespasses. . . .'" She paused for breath. "Our holy Father will forgive ye also.'"

"But Momma, after what they did. You wouldn't be . . . lying up here now."

"That was my journey," she said at length. She held out her hand to him, and he took it, feeling the bulbous fingers push gingerly into his. "It was my journey to salvation, Lonnie. God has his ways, we do not comprehend."

He wanted to crush her fingers, but held still. "They said things about you. Jacks and that Crookshank woman. And they took our house from us and chased us here."

"Yes. They wronged us." She patted his palm and took her hand away. "I was bitter many years, but I am grateful now that I found salvation. That He redeems us is truth, but redemption is just the journey. Salvation is what we all want, Lonnie." She coughed deeply and he waited and cleaned her mouth when the fit had passed. "They wronged us, but God is greater. I know this now, though I didn't then. I want salvation for you, too, son. It would make me so happy to see you give yourself to Him, before I pass. It would make me so glad to see you become an instrument of the Lord."

"They took Bertrand. I saw them. They took Bertrand and his wife and they shot them dead. How can I forgive them for that?" She was quiet for a while and he looked out of the window. Ragged children played hop-scotch on the sidewalk. Across the roofline of the houses, the brick chimneys of the mill towered.

"I don't know about all of that. Besides, that wasn't our business."

"Momma, it was."

Unable to speak, she shook her head vehemently.

"Bertrand was our friend. He helped us. He helped Daddy. He was in the war with Daddy. He was Daddy's friend."

She shook her head again, cleared her throat with a huff. "It was never, *never*, our business. Whatever happened, Bertrand brought it on himself. I pray for him. I do. But my soul is clean of all that, Lonnie. So is yours." She took a deep, cloudy breath. "No more talk of it. It will rot you. Now, what I am worried about is *your* eternal soul. Repent of your sins, Lonnie. There is room in His grace for you. You must forgive, repent, and accept our Savior's grace."

It was all hogwash to him and he wanted to tell her. Besides, what were his sins—what did he need to repent of? He was no thief, or a liar. He was no killer.

"Repent of your lusts," she said, as if she had heard his thoughts. "Lusts. Repent so that you may be redeemed. Repent and live a Christian life. Become His instrument. 'For all have sinned and come short of the glory of God.' All of us are caught up in 'the vain conversation'—yes, the life of sin, passed on generation after generation, but the blood of Jesus, redeems us and saves us."

He stood to leave. He wanted a cigarette, and would have to go outside of the house because of the oxygen tank. Quickly, she caught his hand, holding him while she rested.

"It is not easy, Lonnie, to find salvation. But the Bible gives us the way through redemption. He is our redeemer."

The Bible was nothing he could believe in. Yet, once he has seen Bertrand dancing. Dancing in the spirit.

> *I don't know.*
> *I don't know what you come here for;*
> > *I come to praise the Lord.*
> *I don't know.*

> *I don't know what you come here for;*
> > *I come to praise the Lord.*

He had seen Bertrand's feet stomp, stomp, stomp, then slide and stomp. *I don't know. I don't know.* And go back to stomp, stomp, stomp. Standing on the porch and looking out at the trash strewn street and dilapidated bungalows, Lonnie felt as if his own feet might dance. He lit a Lucky Strike and sucked in deep. The dancing was in his ankles and in his calves. *I don't know. I don't know.* His knees and hips were loose and his arms wanted to swing. Dancing, Bertrand had become more than human. An angel. An instrument. Yes! Bertrand was no longer part of this world. He recalled how Bertrand's face seemed to swell and transfigure into hundreds of faces. He was a trumpet. A redeemer! Couldn't every man be a redeemer? Couldn't he? Lonnie wanted badly to dance, to give in to the movement that quickened and transfigured, to be an instrument of something. No movement came. *I don't know.* Maybe it was just nigger dancing, after all.

Not wanting to go back into the house, he drove to Midtown, a shabby business district that seemed in a tug-of-war between dispirited hippies and crusading gentrifiers. The head shops and herbal stores were fast giving away to art studios and fern bars, but still the neighborhoods just off of the main street, between Tenth and Fourteenth Streets belonged to the bedraggled, the drugged, the witches, the homosexuals, and a few of the more experimental students from nearby Georgia Tech.

Twilight was settling in as Lonnie walked down Tenth Street. The shopkeepers pulled steel gates in front of their stores and prostitutes, women and boys, found their territory on The Strip. Lonnie walked briskly, madly swinging his crippled foot, sucking hard on his cigarette and jutting his chin forward as if he had a destination, a purpose. He crossed Peachtree Street without checking for traffic, knowing that the cruising Johns would see him and not hit him. He crossed Piedmont Avenue and cut through a grove at the edge of Piedmont Park, startling a couple of teenage boys who made a fumble of hiding their marijuana. From the street, the park's lawn sloped steeply and he let his legs swing in ungraceful strides as momentum took him downhill, and around by the stone boathouse and dock, and past the western edge of muddy Lake Clara Meer. At last, just past the playing fields, he stopped. There stood a statue of a green angel holding aloft an olive branch proclaiming peace between the North and the South. Below her a kneeling soldier held a rifle in his lap. The statue commemorated the reconciliation of the Confederate and Union states. "Cease fire," it commanded, and yet the soldier held tight to his gun, having seen the angel but not yet the olive branch.

The grove surrounding the statue offered a screen from the public and Lonnie took a joint from a stash he kept in a tin and lit it from the butt of his cigarette, tossed the butt at the base of the statue. *Cease fire.* The angel commanded cease fire and yet she looked dispassionately on the solider. Her arm raised the olive branch like a whip, he thought. *Whip the fucker. Whip him!* But then he thought the soldier looked like his father. His father didn't deserve to be whipped. His father was not a bigot. He knew real bigots, not just the petty redneck with his goose honking whine of "nigger this or that." He knew the kind who lived in fine houses and who had colored people that they treated "just like family" until they murdered them. He knew that he, white as he was, was a nigger, too. *What's a nigger, anyway? Being colored didn't make you one.* His mother was treated like a nigger all her life, as well as all the poor, dough-colored factory women at Fulton Mills and their sallow-colored men who worked as builders and mechanics and doormen. He knew because he had always known he was no better than a nigger—he was a nigger because being a nigger wasn't being a color. *Venable and Jacks!* In the dusk, the angel's wing resembled a vulture's. Her head, veiled, was the head of death. *Cease fire!* He began to shake.

It took him fifteen minutes to compose himself, and during that time, a young man settled down near him and drank from a quart bottle of beer. The man indicated he would share the beer for a hit of the joint, and came over to where Lonnie sat. The man wore a kinky afro, parted on the right, that seemed in the fading light to be as sculpted as topiary. The young man examined Lonnie and smiled. "I wish I had hair like that," Lonnie said. "You don't know how lucky you are. You don't have this tangling shit, constantly falling into your eyes and you can't do any styles with it. You just cut it or wear it long, but you can't. . . ." The young man continued to smile and smoke the joint while Lonnie talked.

"That's cool, dude," the man said.

Lonnie looked out at the athletic fields where vestigial sunlight streaked the ground. "I'm glad you think it's cool." He wanted to talk, to tell the stranger everything that had happened to him. "I have always thought colored people were cool. I know you hear this a lot, but I have a lot of colored friends. Or maybe I should say, I've have *had* a lot of colored friends over the years. I'm new to Atlanta, you see, or really, I just moved back after a while, so I haven't made many friends here." He paused, took a toke on the joint, and passed it to the man. The man toked, drawing in deeply and holding, and turning his angular, firelit face away from Lonnie as he exhaled. "I don't mean anything by it," Lonnie continued, realizing he had said "colored" rather than "black." "I'm just used to saying 'colored.' It never made a difference to me whether somebody was colored or white. One of my best friends growing up was a colored man. He was my father's friend to start with, but he became my friend too. . . ." His head ached in the temples, and he pulled up his knees and rested his forehead against them. The conversation seemed forced, as if something was pushing it out of him. *Just shut up,* he thought. He wanted just to listen to the crickets and the cars motoring along the street beyond the grove. He could drink this man's beer easily enough, and the man could share his pot, and they needn't say a word to each other. He had nothing to prove to the man and talk gained them nothing. "Friendship. I guess friendship is overrated."

He heard the man exhale and clear his throat. "What do you mean?" He asked sonorously.

"It hurts."

"Hurts?" The man sighed and spoke slowly, "Somebody fucked you up, brother."

The critique stung Lonnie, and he shifted his weight, turning to look more closely at the man.

"College Boy."

"What?" Lonnie asked.

"That's what they call me. 'College Boy.'"

"What college do you go to? Morehouse?" Lonnie named the only college for coloreds that he knew.

"Fuck no. Do I look like a punk-ass nigga?"

The ferocity of the reply startled Lonnie. "I didn't mean . . . I never been to college so . . . I thought it was a good college."

"It's good if you are a high-fallutin', high yellow nigga. I didn't go to college, either. I had the grades, but no bread."

Lonnie cleared his throat. "I guess you had more than me, then."

"You guess, but you wouldn't know."

Lonnie started slowly, and then said assertively, "I guess you wouldn't know, either. I mean about me being fucked up."

"Just you looked like somebody been messing with you. I can dig that. I know where you coming from with that. You ain't the only one somebody messing with. We cool?"

Lonnie considered. How could this man know anything about him? The man was half his age, and the thought of that gave Lonnie a chill. He was growing old. Thirty-seven. Decades had been lost in the curlicues of pot smoke. But more than that, he hadn't known what to do with himself. At least, the Navy had given him purpose, even if the purpose was a monotonous search for an elusive enemy. He hadn't dared think it in all the time he had been away from Georgia, but he had been running from Talmaedge. But why? His mother was right, what happened in Talmaedge had nothing to do with them. And yet, he felt he had been running from something he must do there. "Cool," Lonnie said. He sighed, looked toward College Boy in the darkness. "So yeah, I'm fucked up. Somebody fucked me up." College Boy said nothing. Lonnie wasn't even sure he was there, except the dark seem to deepen where he thought the man sat. "I was just a boy. Just a kid." Slowly, he told College Boy about the murders. He told of picking blackberries and seeing the men dragging Luellen's body through the woods. He had thought it was a bear, until he saw the flower print dress and the bloody thighs. Then the men were shooting the others on the shoal under the bridge and heel of Bertrand's shoe dug up the ground. When he finished his story, Lonnie looked up at the angel. College Boy said nothing, Lonnie called to him to make sure he hadn't left.

"You got some more smoke, man?"

Lonnie lit another joint and passed it to College Boy. The glow lit up the man's face, casting the shadow of his narrow nose onto his cheek.

"Why you tell me all of that shit?" College Boy's voice, though low, carried an edge. "Don't you think I know about all of that? Your friend wouldn't be the only one lynched by a bunch of crackers."

Lonnie felt a little scared. Was College Boy calling him a cracker? He started to say that he was innocent, only a witness, just a kid, but it sounded defensive and he stopped. He knew, too, that innocent though he was, he was white. After a moment, he offered, "What about Martin Luther King? He made things right."

"He's dead," College Boy said without inflection. "Crackers killed him, too. Probably FBI, who knows? Medgar Evers—dead. Malcolm X—dead. Seems to be a pattern." College Boy chuckled drily, then snorted. He handed the jay to Lonnie. "They say the next mayor is going to be black. One of them light-skinned Morehouse niggas. He be dead next."

The man's matter of fact tone caused Lonnie's stomach to ache. "But . . . but you're free, now, aren't you? Martin Luther King gave you your freedom. I mean, you're better off"—

"Than who? Than you?"

Lonnie felt he needed to think before he answered. He toked twice on the joint before passing it back to College Boy. He looked up at the angel, who was now just a vulture against the sky. *What does it mean to cease fire?* People were always having their wars, killing each other, and when they had had enough of killing, they declared 'cease fire.' But in a little while, they would be fighting again. People liked to fight. Why had Wayne gone to the war? Was it patriotism? All his father really wanted was to farm his own land, nothing fancy or big, just enough for himself, and to be at peace with his neighbors.

Suddenly, Lonnie saw a sharp, bright light and he fell back into the leaves from the force of a blow. He tried to sit up and scoot back from where he thought College Boy was standing, but another blow caught him in the front of the nose. For a moment there was blankness, and slowly he became aware of College Boy standing over him, his afro framed by the night sky. Then, there was shouting coming from the athletic field, and College Boy ran away. Someone was threatening to kill the nigger, and then someone else was squatting next to Lonnie, asking him if he were all right and pulling him into a sitting position.

"That nigger trying to rob you, man?" asked a woman.

Lonnie couldn't answer right away and the voices, coming to him from all sides kept asking questions about the nigger. Lonnie wanted to say that College Boy was not a nigger, unless they all were. College Boy was his friend. But all he managed to say was "friend."

"Some friend!" the woman said. "You know you can't have a nigger for a friend."

"Wait a minute," said a man. "Was there some faggot shit going on here? That's what I—*Goddamn it!* They're a bunch of queers. He's a goddamn queer. Serves him right."

The woman stood. "Nigger shouldn't have beat him."

"I'll beat the fucker," one of the men said. He kicked leaf litter at Lonnie. The group walked away, complaining.

Lonnie sat for a moment, awareness coming back. He patted the ground around him for his tin of marijuana and couldn't find it. Then, for a while, he thought of nothing. He was sure he hadn't slept; he hadn't been aware of thinking or dreaming. It was dark in the grove, but the streetlights shown in the lawn of the park. He felt a little cold and drew his stiff limbs together into a ball. Gradually he began to feel warm, and when he opened his eyes again, bright dabbles of light cascaded around him. He was in the forest he loved, in a rivulet of sparkles. Then he rose and saw the great forest from a thousand feet above, the various greens of all the trees and the fields, the jades and olives of the tangles of vines and branches mixing like the currents in a great green ocean. He saw the round tops and half domes of the Appalachians. Oddly, he even heard the clicking and screeching of the insects and squeaks and barks of the squirrels and voles. There were birdsongs and the music of all manner of creatures. He was floating on a river of air, tilting and ruddering in the current and he saw every beautiful and kind thing in the world he knew. Then, *Ahhhh,* he said to himself. *Ahhhh.* Just over that hill. *The blackberries.* Blackberries. Bursting with ripeness in the cool morning and the warm light.

TWENTY-ONE

He had met Aza X on Columbus Avenue in front of the Mona Lisa restaurant soon after his discharge from the Navy. He had been wandering, partly exploring, but mostly just walking. She was opening the door to the restaurant as he passed, and when a gust came from San Francisco bay and took her papers out of her hand. Limping, he had helped her chase the papers down, and when handing her a clutch of flapping sheets, he read the lines:

> Stars and moon are shining bright
> But the lynch man comes in dark of night.

The word "lynch" stopped him, and though he was not reading anymore, he stared at the page.

"Thank you," Aza said, a slight impatience in her lyrical voice.

"You wrote this?" he asked. He looked at her face, round with brown eyes and full lips. He wondered what a young woman—a girl, really—might know about lynching. She nodded aloofly and entered the restaurant. He stood at the entrance for a minute, and then followed her. At the counter, she ordered *insalata mista* with bean sprouts. He ordered spaghetti with meatballs, and as he stood waiting to pay, she beckoned him to sit with her. It was at their first meeting that he told her about the murders. She did not seem put off or surprised by his confession, and looking into her clear gray eyes, he could not help but to tell her more and more. With each revelation, she nodded, grunted encouragingly, or said, "I didn't realize that; I didn't know that." At the end of his spiel, she asked him if he wrote poetry. Not only had he never considered writing a poem, he had never seriously read one, and he told her so. "But you have so much to tell." She drew out the word "so" into an elongated note and he noticed the little "o" her lips made when she said it. "You should write a poem about it so people will know what happened. That's my purpose; that's why I am a poet. I am called to revolution, and poetry, my brother, can bring the man down."

"Bring the man down?" Lonnie chuckled, a little dismissively.

She sat back in her chair, her fork full of bean sprouts. "What's so funny?"

"Bring the man down? After what I just told you? It's amusing."

"Don't underestimate me." She hissed slightly. "Poetry has power, because it comes from the ancestral spirits. It can blow up this world." She leaned forward, a bit coyly. "But what would a white brother know about revolution? You are part of the power structure, my brother, part of the problem."

He wasn't sure she was offending him. "Am not."

"Are too," she said, drawing out the sound.

It sounded childish to say it, but he felt she was pulling it out of him. "Am not."

"Okay," she said with a nod of her head. "I'll take you for a righteous brother. Now, you got any weed? We can go and write a poem together."

"Oh?" he said.

Her apartment was a few blocks away, across busy Columbus Avenue on quiet, narrow Castle Street at the foot of Telegraph Hill. The apartment was an efficiency, with a galley kitchen to one side and a Murphy bed on the other side of the large bright room decorated with music and political posters. Not long out of the hospital, he had no marijuana, but she did, so they sat on pillows on the floor by the window and smoked several joints, drank cheap wine and wrote poems. Lonnie found that he liked writing poems, that he liked considering the meaning of words, their sounds. After a while they found themselves in a debate about lynching, Aza saying that a lynching always entailed a hanging. She asserted that was the way Judge Lynch, a real person she believed, dispatched of black people who dared challenge Jim Crow.

"But what would you call what I saw," Lonnie countered. "There was no hanging, just beating, and stabbing and shooting."

"Well . . ." Aza put her index finger to her chin. "I guess it was just a murder. Maybe you would call it a *mass* murder. Anyhow, at least in literature, you have to have a rope with a noose. The noose is the symbol of lynching and lynching is the symbol of three hundred years of the white man's oppression of his black brothers and sisters." She dragged on a marijuana joint the way she might have a cigarette, and turned her head and blew the smoke out in a stream. Then they wrote a poem about lynching. Aza started with the lines, reciting as she wrote. "Strange fruit swinging in the buck-eye tree/ Strange fruit swinging, beaten and gutted."

Lonnie leaned back on the floor. His head buzzed pleasantly, and Aza's voice soothed him. Closing his eyes, he imagined the site of the murders, now more than twenty years past. He recalled first the tangle of the black-berry bramble, and the plump shiny fruit that hung on them. And then the smell of the woods. It was late in the spring, and the woods were green and heavy with scents of the leaves and the smell of the leaf-mold where the litter had been dragged up. There was also the rusty smell of the river and the creosote from the timber of the old bridge. "Gutted? I don't think so. I don't think they gutted anybody."

But he remembered the story told to him a day or two after the murders that if you went to Venable's feed store, into the office, that sitting on a shelf behind Venable's big desk was a Mason jar full of nigger ears. Two of his school mates swore they had seen it. Four or five ears—a five-eared nigger, or one with three ears—two were black, two were nearly white and the leftover one was somewhere in between. Lonnie had been too distracted by the packing of the house and the sudden move to Atlanta to think about the trophies at the time, but now, with the talk of gutting, he wondered whose ears they might have been. He told Aza about the ears. She said nothing for a long time, and then she wrote, "I'm a killa. A natural born killa/ Gonna slice and dice, honkies beware/ this nigger is crazy and swinging razor in the air." She narrowed her eyes and bared her teeth as she chanted the lines and Lonnie thought that perhaps she could kill, and suddenly, in the marijuana-induced lethargy, he felt a pang of paranoia.

She noticed and touched his hand. "Not you, baby. I wouldn't hurt you."

"But could you? Could you actually kill somebody? I mean, kill white people?"

She sat back as if considering. "Intellectually, yes. Intellectually, it would be the only way to get their attention. If you don't blow something up or shoot somebody down, then they just assume that you like to be kicked around and they just keep on kicking. Who ever heard of reasoning with an oppressor? Nobody reasoned with Hitler or Hirohito. No, you just drop the A-bomb on their asses. But, could I really?" She leaned toward him, her face coming close to his. "Let me put it this way. I wouldn't *want* to." Her lips glistened and her breath smelled of the fortified wine, and he wanted to kiss her. He ran his tongue across his lips and she leaned in even closer. She put her hand on the back of his head and pulled his mouth close to hers but not touching. "I just wouldn't want to, but if I had to. I would. Like the brother said, 'by *every* means necessary.'"

He pushed his lips into hers and felt their soft fullness. They kept pressing together, hardly kissing, just pressing, and she pulled at his hair, pulling herself to her knees. Pulling on his hair hurt him, and he wanted to say 'ouch,' but the press of her lips sent tingles through his spine and he didn't want her to stop. She slipped her hand through the front of his collar, stretching the crew of his undershirt, and stroked his nipples, making circles around the areola with her finger. He moaned, his mouth still against hers. Then, without warning she pinched hard and twisted the nipple. He let out a yell, as much in surprise as in pain. He tried to move away, but she held onto the nipple, twisting harder and pinching. "I could kill you if I have to," she hissed, her voice both threatening and lyrical to him. "How many niggers have you killed?"

"None," he managed. "I ain't killed nobody."

"I don't believe you. Every whitey has killed somebody."

"No." He grabbed her wrist to pull her hand away. He knew he was stronger than she and could easily loosen her grip, and doing so would stop the pain. But it would also stop the pleasure and his penis was pushing tightly against his pants leg. "I was just a boy," he said.

"Yes," she said, letting go of both his hair and his nipple. "You were just a boy, you murdering bastard. Just a boy, but already a nigger-killer." She rubbed her lips against his cheeks and stood up. "You want to write another poem?" She shifted her weight on one hip and smiled coyly. "No? Then what do you want to do?"

His throat was tight and his voice shaky. "Fuck you."

She smiled, shifted her weight to the other hip. "That's always what the oppressor wants. And what do you get when you do it. You get pleasure, but you get pain, too. Right? That's the cost of being white. The guilt gets in the way of the pleasure."

"I'm not guilty." He wanted to laugh, but his libido surged and he only breathed hard.

"Your skin makes you guilty." She elongated the word "skin" and raked her nails across his arm, scratching but not drawing blood.

The accusation startled him and he pulled away from her, but she grabbed him by the collar and pulled his face against her breast. "Nigger-killers deserve to die. Do you want me to kill you?"

For a moment, he had no breath; his mind went blank and his body pulsated with pleasure. "Yes."

"Yes, *ma'am*," she instructed.

"Yes, ma'am."

She walked into the small bathroom next to the kitchen and shut the door. Before he could make sense of what had just happened, she came out dressed in a flowered moo-moo and carried a bamboo cane. In the light from the window, he could tell she wore no underclothes. She struck the cane cross her palm. "Now, come here."

He had been with many prostitutes in his travels, but he had always been straight forward with them. The image of Aza, feet astride and lashing the cane about, gave him a feeling of eagerness and danger and he thought he might come before she allowed coitus. He started to stand.

"Did I tell you to stand? I said to come here. On your *knees*. Crawl like a dog. *Crawl.*"

He crawled over to her, the wood floor hard against his knees. When he was in reach of her, she put her bare foot on his neck and pushed his face to the floor. Then she whacked him sharply with on the rump with the cane. When he protested, she told him to shut up.

"It hurts."

"Not as much as what you did to that woman, dragging her through the woods—"

"I didn't—"

"Shut up. If you want me to forgive you. Then shut up."

He complied. She struck him several times more, and then they made love.

In the morning, he awoke before she did, found eggs, vegetables and tofu in the refrigerator and prepared a breakfast for the two of them. As he cooked, he remembered that the lovemaking had been aggressive, rough. At the end of it, exhausted he had slept well and awoke energetic and happy, cleansed of some taint he didn't realize he had. He whistled while he cooked. When she arose, they pushed up the Murphy bed, moved the coffee table to the middle of the floor, sat on pillows and ate. She said she liked the breakfast and was impressed that he was a cook by training. She told him that he could easily find work in one of the city's better restaurants. She, herself, worked as a waitress in a diner near Korea Town. He told her he didn't need a job, that the Navy paid him for his disability. He sent a little home to his mother in Atlanta. Then she invited him to stay and help her with the rent and with her poetry, but only on the condition that he remembered who was boss.

"You mean, I'll pay half the rent, but you'll run the show."

"I mean, you will pay *all* the rent, and I'll run the show."

He considered. The rent was not expensive and he had enjoyed the sex, not just the coitus, but the fantasy, the roughness of her. When she had put her foot on his neck and pushed his face against the gritty floorboards, he imagined Bertrand's wife's face dragged through the leaf-rot. Something connected. His mind raced to name what he had felt: Pleasure, yes. Pain, yes. But also he felt malleable, reshaped by her, as if her shouting and whacking, pinching and twisting, squeezed impurities out of him. "You are still fixin' to beat me all the time?"

"When I want to. *If* I want to. Any way I want to."

He laughed to himself, scrambled eggs in mouth and nodded. "Okay. I'll stay."

After he settled in, they wrote "Give me my money," a poem about reparations. Again, they were sitting on the floor in front of the big window, drinking wine and smoking marijuana. She was telling him about the Black Panther Party which had recently formed across the bay in Oakland. She was considering joining it, but looking at the news flyer, she was beginning to think it would require too much of her time, taking away time from her poetry. "My calling," she reminded him, "is to revolutionize through the word. People need the word as much as they need bread and houses."

She sounded grand and poetic to him, like the portrayal of a poet in a movie.

"I told you," she said, "don't you laugh at me. I will hurt you. I will kill you if I have to." By now, Lonnie saw little threat in her declarations, but he apologized. "Now, now, sweetie, can you forgive me?"

"Why should I? You white people always want to be forgiven, but you don't want to do anything for it. I forgive you today, tomorrow you'll be backstabbing me. You promised us African people forty acres and a mule and we got Jim Crow. White men are devils, just like the brother said. There is only one thing you understand and that is power."

"I ain't got no power."

"You got more than you think. Your power is in your skin, my brother."

He looked at his forearm, pale with red splotches from grease burns and the scratches she had given him. "Power? Aza, I grew up poor. Poorer than you. My daddy did his best to get along with colored people—I mean, *black* people." To say 'black' seemed strange to him, but he knew it was what she preferred. "We never had any forty acres and a mule neither."

"Neither were you a slave."

"Neither were you."

"But I come from *en*slaved people."

He was quiet for a moment, having no answer. He drank a bit from the strawberry-flavored wine. He had tasted good wine in the officer's mess and decided then, that he would buy a bottle of good wine for them. "My people were just farmers—"

"They farmed the Indians' land."

"Yes. I guess."

"Stolen land."

"We didn't steal it. It was stolen from us, in the end. He thought about Wayne, and struggled to hold back tears. "Goddamn it." His nose closed up. "My daddy was a hardworking man. A smart man, too. He was a good man, Aza. He never hurt anybody—except a boy—a soldier he killed in the war, and that tore him up." Lonnie wondered if he had been to a war like his father if he would be a stronger man than he was, then he would go back to Talmaedge County and face Venable and Jacks.

Aza stroked the back of his hand and then fitted her hand inside of his. "Ok, pet, I believe you. You didn't do anything. You are not to blame for anything."

"And my daddy neither."

"And your daddy neither."

"And my momma. She ain't done a thing. She's working herself to death in a factory in Atlanta."

Aza took her hand away. "Then who? Who's to blame? If every white son of a bitch says 'I am innocent; I never did a thing.' Then who do you blame?"

He looked at her round face, tense at the jaws. She was not a beautiful woman, he decided, but not plain either. She reminded him of some of the village girls in Okinawa. No one was to blame, he wanted to say. No one and everyone, too. There were no innocents among them; they were all

215

complicit in each other's grief. "I can't say. Certain people, I guess. The same people who do everything in the world."

"Whoever. We have to kill them."

He thought for a flash about killing Venable and Jacks. He was a good shot and he would shoot them. Killing them would make him feel like he had done something. Something for Bertrand. Something for his mother and for himself. "I would like to. But that wouldn't be right. That would just be revenge. There's got to be more to it than revenge."

She seemed taken aback. "Oh shit, Lonnie. Nobody's *really* going to kill anybody. A poem can't kill anybody. It's all a metaphor for what we want."

He used his cigarette lighter to relight the joint. "What do you want? I don't know what I want—I want to do the right thing."

"And what is the right thing?"

"I don't know."

"And that's why you will never do it." She turned away from him, took up the pad and pen, began to chant and write:

> I want my money, I want my land, I want my mule
> I want it now.
> To buy me some herb, a big ass Caddy,
> A ticket to Mother Africa.
> "I want my money, and I want it now."

She stopped chanting while she scribbled down the new verse. Then she took deep breath and let out a shout.

I want my money, and I want it now.

She glanced at Lonnie, her eyes squinted and a smile at the corner of her mouth. He moved restlessly, clenching his buttocks against the wood floor.

"What about me? Don't I get my money, too?"

"You are pathetic." Aza shook her head. "A pathetic poor-ass cracker."

She rolled her eyes. "Lord, if I have to have a white man, why couldn't he be one of those rich motherfuckers. Some kind of banking tycoon?"

"'Cause you ain't with me for my money." He winked and placed his palm on his thigh next to his groin.

She pursed her lips and leaned toward him. "Then for what, whitey? You ain't got nothing else I'm interested in."

"Are you sure?" He let his voice drop.

She picked up her pad and composed two more verses while he watched. She chanted out the poems, her eyes focused on the ceiling or out of the window looking across the street at the opposite building. Though they were only a short ways from the Coit Tower, a landmark, the narrow street blocked their view. After a chant, she wrote on the pad. He liked the way her breasts bounced when she shook the pen to get the ink to flow. He liked the intensity on her brow, and the faraway look her face took on when she was concentrating. Looking at her, he would not imagine that she was writing about killing white people, but about fields of daffodils and rainbows. Why was it, he wondered, that she was so angry or seemed to be. She had had advantages that he hadn't, as far as he could tell. She was better educated, had come from a richer family. Perhaps, she sensed in him his long, nagging feeling that he had done something to cause the murders in Talmaedge County. He remembered how angry his mother had been with him in the days after the murder, as if he had insulted her. She often said that she didn't care that Jacks stole her house from her, having paid her half its value, but that no amount of money could restore her reputation. When she talked about this, she often mentioned Maribelle Crookshank, cursing her or stamping her foot instead of cursing. At first, not understanding, Lonnie asked, but when his questions were met with his mother's retreat to her bedroom or to church, he learned not to say anything or even to speculate.

"Can you ever forgive white people?" he asked Aza. He mumbled the question and she, looking annoyed that he had interrupted her, asked him to repeat it.

"For what?" she asked, impatiently.

"For . . ." he couldn't think for what exactly. "For all we have done to colored—I mean black—people."

"Can I? Can I personally?" She put the pad and pen on the floor and looked past him out of the window. After a moment, she said, "Yes. Yes, I think I can. I mean, it would be hard—to forgive *all* white people. But if you mean to forgive *certain* white people, like you, for instance, well then, I think I could. But *all* white people? It's just too many different circumstances."

He swallowed hard. There seemed to be an enormity in the moment. "Then, can you forgive me?"

She cocked her head and snorted. "For what? You haven't done anything. Not to me." She scooted on her knees closer to him. "Loverboy, you are as innocent as the day is long, as far as I'm concerned. I can easily forgive you, baby, if there is anything to forgive. But white people in general? I mean white people as a race? That's a different question. "

"But I *am* white."

"Yeah right. My po-assed white nigger. I forgive you, baby. I forgive you because you want to be forgiven. But white people as a race?" Suddenly, she grabbed him, her palm against the back of his neck. "I shouldn't trust your ass, though. You probably will find a way to backstab me, mother-fucker." She pulled his head toward her breasts. "But if you backstab me, if you hurt me, if you even dare to disappoint me . . . I *will* kill you." She stretched out the sound of "you."

He breathed in the smell of her breasts, perfumed with talc but slightly sweaty. Then, his mouth pressed against her and his tongue licked in her cleavage. Just then she slapped the back of his head.

"What did you do that for?" he asked.

"Because you didn't have permission. Remember, I'm boss here."

"I'm sorry."

"Not as sorry as you're going to be." She stood and pushed him with her foot. "You want to be forgiven? You want me to forgive you?"

"Yes, ma'am."

"Then you will have to do more than ask. You'll have to show it."

"How?"

"If you don't know, how the hell can I explain it to you?"

"I don't know what you want me to do."

"Beg."

"What?"

"Beg for it. Like a little yellow cur that wants a bone. Beg. Roll over. Play dead."

He had worn the dog collar she had strapped on him that night for nearly two weeks, until just an hour before he had come into the club in the cellar of the Mona Lisa to hear her performance. It had been a token of their relationship, like a wedding band, and she had often introduced him to their acquaintances as her love slave. But, that night, as he watched her perform many of the poems they had written together, the slave was contemplating his escape. While she worked at the diner he had visited the Haight district, invaded by hippies. Twice he had dropped LSD with a colony that had taken residence under the trees at the end of Waller Street in Buena Vista Park. Two teenage girls, Klara and Katrina, cousins they said, were a part of the colony. He had enjoyed making love to them when he was high. They became like a four breasted Aphrodite, each breast covered with an aureole half its size, and with nipples that sparkled the colors of prisms in sunlight. From head to toe, his body had felt like one gigantic glans, responding with excruciating pleasure no matter where they kissed or stroked him. When he came, he seemed to have blanked out, first growing so tight he thought his head would explode, and then falling into a deep, soft blackness. Was he dead? He didn't care. When he opened his eyes, he was looking up at a leafy canopy, and he had thought at once of the woods in Talmaedege County, but it occurred to him that Talmaedge County was a part of another world, one that overlaid the one he had now entered but could never touch him. In the early hours of the morning, as the influence of the acid wore off, he decided that he had enough of being Aza's slave and would join Klara and Katrina in a union of free love. He enjoyed sex with Aza, but the relationship was arduous. Always there was some friction, some strain about skin or murder. With the cousins, everything was easy. They giggled at everything he said or did. And they were white.

The club was windowless and smoky, lit by a row of ornate sconces loosely attached to its plaster walls. It seated no more than twenty people at its five café tables, so the patronage squeezed around a small stage, balancing their drinks and cigarettes as if they were walking on see-saws. Lonnie had arrived early and settled at a table just in front of the stage, a low platform hardly bigger than a milk crate. He had a bottle of grappa and had sipped away for an hour, when finally Aza, having been upstairs preparing for her performance, pushed her way through the crowd. There was a spattering of applause from some of the patrons who recognized her. The goateed, bereted proprietor stood on top of the platform and yelled for quiet. He welcomed the audience, and then shifting into an intonation, recited a poem about universal love. When he was finished, he acknowledged the clapping and finger snapping. "Aza" he announced, without intonation, "means 'power' in the African language. Our next poet is a powerful sister, a powerful poet, a powerful and beautiful black spirit of universal force."

Aza stepped up onto the stage, seeming to ignore the hoots and clapping around her. She raised her arms above her head and looked up at the low ceiling. She called this portion of her performance inviting the ancestors. Slowly she brought her hands down on the top of her hair, cropped in a short natural style after the singer Odetta. Then she moved her hands down in front of her face, eyes closed. She began to hum, and brought her hands across her breasts, and down by her side. She wore a blue oxford shirt, Lonnie's in fact, tucked inside a pair of black pedal pushers. Her hips swayed back and forth now, and she began to chant. "I'm a killa; I'm a killa." She opened her eyes, and it seemed to Lonnie, that she stared straight at him. Though she seemed entranced by the rhythm of her chant, Lonnie thought he saw a trace of an amused smile pass her lips. He placed his hand on his neck, where the wide, leather dog collar had been. She didn't seem to notice the absence of the collar.

"I got my gun, my A-K 47, got my shot gun, double-barrel,
Gone ride through Alabama, side-saddled like a belle,
Gone give them crackers a piece of my homegrown hell
I'm a killa, a killa, a natural born killa."

The audience hooted and clapped. Lonnie didn't hoot, but sipped his grappa, rolling the burning liquor across his tongue. He always enjoyed Aza's performance of this poem, the way she swayed her big hips, and mimicked shooting pistols with her fingers.

At the end of her set, Aza reprised "I'm a Killa," raised her arms to thank the ancestral spirits, and ignoring the mostly white audience, exited the stage to many hoots, and claps, and finger snapping. In a few minutes, she joined Lonnie at the table. His stomach churned. He wondered how he might broach the subject of their splitting up. She drank down a glass of grappa that he had poured for himself. Then suddenly, she grabbed onto his ear and twisted. "Motherfucker," she said. "I told you I would kill you if you backstabbed me." For a moment it seemed she would twist the ear right off of his head. Tears came to his eyes. Then she let go, stood and smiled. "I see you have freed yourself at last."

"I—"

"I don't need to hear your explanation. Did you leave the rent money?" He had. "Well, that's all I ever needed from you. Now you are free to go. Watch out for the dog catcher, though. Remember they exterminate little pups like you." Then she leaned on the table, her face in his, and spoke slowly, "And if I ever see your po' honkey ass around here again, I *will* kill you."

TWENTY-TWO

Coming home after the night in the park, Lonnie found that Aileen had taken a turn for the worse. She refused to eat, waving away the spoonful of broth he held to her lips. "Just let me rest," she said with difficulty. Periodically, her breath seemed to fall into the well of her stomach. The stomach sometimes rose and fell, but Lonnie could not discern any movement in her chest. Often, he called softly to her, and after a few moments, she would open her eyes. Once or twice, she even smiled. Then, as if vultures, the church women appeared, one at a time, letting themselves in and with few words to Lonnie, taking the chair near the foot of the bed, their bibles in their laps. The vigil continued all the day and into the night. In the morning, when he tried again to feed his mother, a woman, older and gaunter than the rest, admonished him. "Give her rest." The woman was prune-like but she emanated the beatific aura of a long suffering saint.

"Momma," Lonnie said quietly, his face near Aileen's mouth. "Won't you talk to me?"

Aileen turned away from him. He could see her jaw quiver. Turning back to him after a minute, she whispered slowly between her labored breaths, "In Him . . ."

"What's that, Momma?" Lonnie and the woman both leaned in close to Aileen's mouth. "In Him . . . we have . . . redemption. . . ."

The woman finished the phrase. "Through His blood, the forgiveness of sins, according to the riches of his Grace. *Ephesians,* chapter one, verse seven."

Lonnie was quiet for a moment. His mother was dying and he didn't know what to feel. He didn't think he would miss her. He knelt by the bed and squeezed her hand. Lightly, she squeezed back. Her eyelids fluttered and closed. Her pale face, moist and cool to Lonnie's touch, occasionally twitched. Her shallow breathing rattled and paused for long times. A quarter of an hour passed while he held her hand and he began to sob. He sucked in great chest-fulls of air, and bellowed. When he had gotten control of himself, still holding his mother's hand, the beatific woman, as if making a benediction, said, "For the wages of sin is death; but the gift of God is eternal life through our redeemer, Christ Jesus." The next morning, with yet another church woman by her bedside, Aileen died.

Lonnie had been sleeping, and was awoken, he rushed into the death room. Three women were attending Aileen, sponging down her corpse in preparation for the undertaker. He stood at the threshold and watched, and then feeling acutely useless, he went back to his room.

He thought he should cry, but could not, even though he felt he was filling with grief and fright. "Why? Why? Why?" It didn't make sense, this life. Why live at all, if so little good would come of it? The only answer he got from the whitewashed plaster walls of his room was that his question was incomplete. It was not a question of why his mother was dead. It was instead, indeed, a question of why any of it happened. From the beginning. From the day Venable ran over Toby. From the day Bertrand gave them the grouse. Why had Eliza died even before she was born? And his father? His years of wandering, he realized had also been years of hiding. Hiding from Venable and Jacks, but also from himself, from life, and from what he knew he had to do. He had hidden in the narrow, weedy lanes of Cabbagetown; he had hidden in the swells of ocean and in the Navy galleys and brigs; he had hidden behind a persona with a van dyke and dog collar, and then behind an unkempt beard and long hair and nakedness. He had hidden in the paisley haze of marijuana smoke and the stinking slosh of cheap beer. He had hidden under the blare of loud music and wild dancing. "Cease fire," the statue commanded, and yet who among them listened? Not Venable, not Jacks—not even Mr. Jacks who was supposed to have been better than the others. He was supposed to have been the reasonable one, the calm one, the one who would not let things get out of hand. And yet things had gotten out of hand, and everything had been ruined. Bertrand had been killed and Bertrand's wife and the yellow man who was so friendly to him and the man's girlfriend and the baby, too. And his mother, Aileen, had done nothing. Only once had she even come outside the screen door when Bertrand was around, and yet her name had been dragged through a toilet and she had been run out like a whore, his mother and himself, too. A whore and a whore's son. Nigger-lovers! And yet, he *had* loved Bertrand—nigger or not—he had loved the man.

Once Bertrand had shown him how to dance, and he had become frightened and ran. It was the dancing, he thought at last, the dancing that led to something. *I don't know.* The dancing had led him to see something he hadn't wanted to see. Why had *he* been allowed to *see* it? *I don't know. I don't know. I don't know what you come here for—*

His eyes teared up and his hand shook as he lit a cigarette and sucked in smoke. His face and chest felt hot as he exhaled and watched a column of smoke rise toward the joists in the unpaneled ceiling. He realized, then, something he had felt a long time. He hated. He hated Venable. He hated Jacks. He hated. He hated. He hated.

He had driven into the country, the hills and forests closing in on either side of the road and swallowing his view from the windshield to the rear. He turned onto State Route 11 and then 15, then onto smaller and smaller roads; the sky became stormy and the landscape darkened, and the thickets—Virginia creeper and kudzu—rose like ogres along the road banks. He felt he was reverting to the boy he once was, ignorant of everything and innocent of nothing, and he grew more and more uncertain of his purpose. *Everyman is his own redeemer.* He reminded himself. *Is that what the Bible said? What did the Bible matter? I am my own redeemer.* He recalled that his mother would have disagreed and relied on the Lord, but where had that gotten her? She had been worked to death and now lay on a cooling board at Patterson's. It wasn't her hard life or even her death that angered him most. It was how they had sullied her—Jacks and Crookshank—and then, with saccharine sanctimony, robbed her of the little house and sent her packing. And all because Bertrand was kind to her. Bertrand, his father's friend.

At first he didn't recognized the town of Bethany. It seemed a faint impression of itself, practically empty of people except for a bench-full of elderly black men, sitting with legs crossed, fanning at gnats, taking squint-eyed notice of his passing. Though unsure, he drove steadily toward Woodbine. His stomach seemed to float up into his chest, as one in freefall. He did not even slow when he passed over the river where the old iron bridge once stood, now replaced by a concrete span. Not when he passed the old homestead, now a fallow field—in fact, he didn't even recognize it. He

223

would have passed by the entrance to Woodbine, too, had not the tree-lined entrance and the somewhat worn manor house seemed familiar. Then, as if he were as much an observer of his actions as he was the progenitor of them, he applied brakes hard and skidded along the road. The pistol, his father's service revolver, fell out of the passenger seat onto the floor. For a moment he didn't know what it was there for, and then it scared him. *Jesus was scared. Yes, Jesus was scared and Bertrand was scared, too.*

The cornfields at Woodbine glowed yellow in the stormy light, and the clouds above them were colossal black and purple blooms. Now and again, tongues of lightning jagged the clouds. He parked, climbed the porch stairs, noting the chipped and peeling paint of the stair railing. Responding to a call to come around to the side porch, Lonnie stepped slowly. His weight, slight as it was, dangerously depressed the squeaking planks. With the pistol in his waistband covered by the hem of his tee shirt, he walked stiffly, aware that the gun pointed at his groin. The man called again, adding a curse word, and a woman shouted for the man to be quiet. Taking a deep breath, Lonnie presented himself.

The side porch was long and narrow. It was set with a rocking chair, an ottoman and a small wicker table, and it looked out on an expanse of fields that seemed to stretch to the horizon. A gaunt man sat in a wheelchair that faced him.

"Well?" The man said, squinting through heavy rimmed glasses that sat crooked on his face. Before Lonnie could answer, the man admonished him. "If you are selling any goddamn bibles or encyclopedias, you are wasting your time. In fact, if you are selling anything at all—"

"He might have something *I* want," the woman called from just inside the door.

"He's got nothing *you* want," the man said to the woman, and then to Lonnie. "Well?"

"Mr. Jacks?" Lonnie swallowed the words and was not sure he had said them above a mumble. His jaw was sore from the beating in the park, and he felt it when he opened his mouth.

"What do you want? You one of Betty's boys?"

Lonnie shifted his weight to his bad foot and back again. This was not the Jacks he expected. No longer a tall, square-shouldered man, the man before him was boney, wrinkled—if anything, a curmudgeon. Jacks wiped drool from the corner of his mouth, blush with a rash.

Not Betty's boy. Who am I? What do I want? Be scared of me, old man. I am your redeemer.

"Well?" Jacks said again, shifting forward in the wheelchair. Though gaunt, he looked solid. His chest was ruddy where it showed at his collar, and his once pleasant features had become hard, cut deep with lines on his cheeks and his temple knotted with veins. He adjusted the glasses with the hand that held the handkerchief. The right hand, Lonnie realized, was paralyzed, its fingers curled against the palm. A newspaper and a pipe lay on the table next to the chair, but these looked untouched. A television played just inside the door. "Maribelle!" Jacks called anxiously. The tremble in Jack's voice encouraged Lonnie and he stepped toward the old man. For a few seconds the sunlight pierced a cloud and Lonnie held his breath. The light made him feel powerful and recommitted to his cause.

"I am Lonnie Henson. Remember me?" The sound of his name echoed in his head. *I am Lonnie Henson! I have been around the world and have come back!*

Jacks stared blankly and called again for his wife.

"My father was Wayne Henson. My granddaddy Big George Henson. You remember?"

"Henson?" Jacks continued to stare, seeming to study him.

"Aileen was my mother." Lonnie's fingers brushed against the handle of the pistol. *Quick. Quick. Now.* He imagined he pulled up the hem of the shirt, drew the gun out, aimed, all in a smooth motion. He hesitated only long enough for Jacks to see what was happening. Then his fingers squeezed the trigger and *Cease fire. Cease fire. Vengeance is mine!* But at that moment, the woman, whom Lonnie immediately recognized, came out of the house and let the screen door slam behind her. He dropped his hand to his side. The woman, also, gaunt, was erect, intent. She looked him over from head to foot.

"Oh, yes," said Maribelle Crookshank. "I can see the resemblance. Well, how are you, sweetie? You've been in an accident? Have a seat." She waved him toward the ottoman. "Did Mr. Jacks offer you a seat? Did Mr. Jacks even offer you a drink of anything? We have some good, sweet tea. I bet you don't get good, sweet tea over there in Atlanta."

"Who is he?" Jacks hit the arm of his chair with his good hand. "Who the hell is he?"

"Noland, you be quiet. You don't need to use that bad language." She turned to Lonnie, smoothing her apron. "Mr. Jacks, as you can see, isn't as you remember him." She circled her finger next to her temple and mouthed, "A little mixed up." Then in a normal voice, "Out of his head half the time. Comes and goes." Jacks cast a look at her. "Yes, he has had his trials and tribulations, as have we all. So, do forgive his manners."

"Goddamn manners! Who is he? What does he want?"

"I don't care what his business is. Decent people offer people a seat and a drink. It's basic hospitality, Noland."

"I don't care for anything," Lonnie said.

"Are you sure? I've got a nice cake. A seven-layer torte, it's called. Oh, it is good—and rich. Almost too rich for my blood."

With Crookshank on the porch, Lonnie felt the moment of action pass. He couldn't just shoot the old man; now, there was a protocol. "No ma'am," he said, refusing the cake.

"Don't know what you are missing." Crookshank seemed to sing the words. She gestured again for Lonnie to sit on the ottoman, and took a seat in the wicker rocker beside the wheelchair. "Now, tell me, how is your momma?"

Lonnie had started toward the ottoman, but the question about his mother stopped him. *What does Maribelle Crookshank care about Momma?* He almost said it, but straightened his body instead and spread his legs apart. "She's dead."

"Oh no!" Crookshank said. "Gone? Passed away? How long? Oh, how I know you miss your momma! I often thought about her after she went up to Atlanta. What a hard time she had, especially after your daddy—" She put her hand against her cheek, a nervous gesture, then looking out at the fields, continued to talk rapidly. "And all that other foolishness that happened around here. So sad." Snapping open an opera fan, she rocked in the chair. "Looks like that storm is going around, but we needed the rain."

"My daddy—"

"Such a shame," Crookshank said. "A loss to everybody. But then, he went through rough times—the war and all—but wasn't that such a long time ago? It chills me to think how long I have been on this earth—you're still young—you think nothing of time—but I am constantly aware, at my age, that time is passing, and fast." In a quick, sharp motion, she swatted the fan against the side of the chair. "And look at me now, just sitting here looking at the clouds pass—rocking and looking at the clouds—like an old lady. But I am not that old! Sitting around, that never was me. Tell me, ahh—Johnnie—do I look old to you?"

Lonnie started to correct her, but her question made him trip over his words.

"I don't expect you to answer. It's not a question that a gentleman would answer. It's just to say that—I am *not* old. Mr. Jacks is old. He's retired in the worst kind of way. He has conquered his kingdom and now settled in it. Like Augustus Caesar. He thinks this, this little bitty Woodbine, is the whole of the world."

"Shut up," Jacks said, not looking at her.

"It's not even a decent plantation. It's more like a jail house." She looked at Lonnie, rolling her eyes at Jacks. The gesture felt both intrusive and intimate to Lonnie. Involuntarily, he stepped back, and then forward.

Oh, Johnnie, you have a *bad* leg. Please, take a seat. You just standing there is likely to make me nervous. How come you got a bad leg, sugar?" She bared here teeth, a smile. "I am not going to ask you to sit again. I have asked three times now, so my duty is finished. Anyway, how did you hurt your leg, sweetie."

"In the Navy." Hesitantly, he took the seat. *Wait. The moment will come. Soon.* From where he sat he could see Jacks's paralyzed hand, fingers swollen, the nails long.

"The Navy! You hear that Noland? Johnnie was in the Navy. I want to hear about all the places you have been. I'm going to travel, too. When we were married, Mr. Jacks promised me travel. But all he did was to take my restaurant from me—you remember my restaurant, don't you? Maribelle's. I recall that you and your family visited often. And we had the *best* food in that little place. Did you come through Bethany? Did you see it, now? All boarded up. He *took* my restaurant—and boarded it up. We didn't need it, he said. A wife's place is in the home. What does he know about a wife?"

"Shut up." Jacks voice pitched high.

"Shut up, yourself. You might own Woodbine, but you will never own me." They were quiet for a moment, both seeming to catch their breaths, both looking over the railing at the fields. Lonnie, too, breathed heavily. He felt things were wrong. He had come to confront Jacks, but Maribelle Crookshank was in the way. *Kill her, too.*

Crookshank smiled unevenly. "Anyway, tell me about your travels. Where have you been? Did you go to Europe? Ohhh, Europe! I've got my *Fodor's,* my *Fielding's and* my *Frommer's.* I am ready for my grand tour."

She looked at Jacks. "And it *will* come to pass. It's not a waste of money if it makes you happy."

"We—in the Navy—we didn't go to Europe. We were assigned to the South Pacific."

Crookshank looked disappointed. "You went to Hawai'i, then?"

"Yes."

"And Tahiti?"

"Once."

"And Fiji."

"Yes, ma'am."

She seemed to brighten and leaned forward in the rocker. "And I bet, Formosa."

"No, ma'am. But we went to Japan."

"Oh, yes. Tokyo. I bet that was interesting."

"And Australia."

"Now that's another place I'd love to go. You hear so much about it. And they are white there and they speak good English."

"Yes, ma'am."

"I don't think the boy came to give you a world tour. She fancies herself a jet setter, a goddamn Hollywood movie star. She's just a country woman, rooted right here."

Crookshank scowled at Jacks' interruption. "But can't I just have nice conversation?" She flicked the fan, "Or maybe he came to rescue me from this . . . this *penitentiary*. Look out there," she pointed toward the fields. "Nothing. Nothing but dirt, and mud and flies. Good Lord, I want to move back to town so bad . . . it . . . it upsets me." She looked at Lonnie, pleadingly, as if he had indeed come to take her to town. He met her eyes and then, looked down at his feet.

The moment was coming again. He felt it swelling up in him. His biceps and forearms twitched.

Crookshank broke the silence. "Now, sugar, what brings you here? Just passing through? You heard about Mr. Venable? Such a good man, too."

Again, Lonnie met her eye. *Liar.* He remembered her asking, "May I say, 'You betcha?'" *You betcha, my ass.* He looked at the old man whose attention had drifted. *What brings me here?* He snorted, smiled, said quietly, "To kill you."

Crookshank leaned forward as if to hear better, then she sat back forcibly in the rocking chair. "Me? What have I done?" She looked nervously toward Jacks, but he seemed unaware. She shifted forward in her chair. "What did you say?"

Her discomfiture made Lonnie smile. "I said I am going to kill you." He emphasized "kill," reminding himself of Aza X.

Crookshank glanced left and right as if looking for a weapon or a route of escape. She sat deep in the chair and rocked it forward hard to get her feet under her, but fell back. Then, eyes on Lonnie, she shook the shoulder of Jack's paralyzed arm. After a bit of fumbling that made Lonnie chuckle, she got the old man's attention. "Tell him what you said," she said to Lonnie.

"I said I am going to kill you."

"Kill me?" Jacks looked at his wife, quizzically.

"That's what he said."

"Are you one of Betty's boys?"

"He's that Henson boy." Crookshank shouted at him. "That Henson woman's boy." Jacks continued to look perplexed. "The one that went off to Atlanta back in—Lord, Johnnie, that was so long ago. Whatever happened then has been long put to rest. You can't have bad feelings about something that happened that long ago."

Feelings? Why would I have bad feelings? First of all there was only one feeling and it was neither good nor bad, broken now and again by what he thought might have been moments of happiness. In the galley of the USS Bennington. With Aza X. With the cousins, Klara and Katrina. But in those moments, he was only a buffoon— *Lonny, honey. A pathetic little cracker. A yellow cur that wants a bone. A white nigger*—And like clockwork, he fell back into the dronish sleep-walk of his life. Once, though, he had breathed and was alive. When he hunted with his father; when he picked blackberries on Christmas Hill; or, planted the garden with Bertrand. He had danced! *The old bitch is right. That happened long ago.*

The pistol pushed into his waist. He imagined that Crookshank could see it impressed through his tee shirt. But he didn't touch the gun. Jacks seemed not to know who he was, and there could be no redemption in killing him. "Listen," he said to Crookshank. "Maybe I won't kill you. You aren't worth it to me. But he should at least know who I am. Make him know who I am." He stood up and Crookshank recoiled in the rocker.

"He won't remember you. I told you he's mixed up. What you have to remember is that he *helped* you. He was the only one to do it. He and I. We got your momma away from here and in one piece, too. And this is your gratitude?" She leaned forward in the chair and flicked the fan. "What would your momma say about that!"

Crookshank's sudden vehemence threw Lonnie off balance, his weight landed on this bad foot. *What would Momma say?* He knew but his mind was blank. He saw his mother on her death bed. *Salvation.* "She said she wanted salvation."

"Salvation? What does that mean? Only Jesus Christ can give you salvation."

"Has He given it to you?" Lonnie sneered.

"He doesn't have to. I have been good to people. When my time comes, He will know that."

"Who is he?" Jacks asked again.

"He's Bertrand's little white boy."

Bertrand's little white boy! Bertrand's boy! "Bertrand was my friend," Lonnie corrected.

"Bertrand!" Jack's sat up straight; his face glowed with recognition. "That proud nigger?" He studied Lonnie. "He did have a little tyke that followed him around day and night. So, that's you? All grown up." He dapped his mouth his handkerchief. "And wanting to kill somebody, too!

"He's not going to kill anybody. He just came to talk," Crookshank said. "Take your seat, Johnnie."

"*Lonnie.* My name is Lonnie."

"Lonnie." She fanned. "Take your seat, Lonnie." He sat. For a moment the three of them looked out into the yard, the shadow's lengthening. "You're a good boy," she said, turning to him. "I see you are. Mr. Jacks and I are good people, too. Lord knows, we've tried."

"You have a funny way of being good. The way you killed Bertrand."

"Bertrand." Jacks said. "That proud nigger came to me, asking me . . . and I helped him."

"We both did."

Lonnie shifted on the ottoman. The gun slipped in his waist band and he drew it out of his pants.

"Take my advice, sugar," Crookshank said, eyeing the gun. "Let it lay. It's history. It doesn't matter now. It was a terrible thing that happened, no doubt, and it upset a lot of people—me, included. But things have adjusted around it. It's a wonderful thing about people. We can adjust and keep on. We don't worry about old things like that."

A pain fired in Lonnie's temples and he slapped his hands on his sweaty face. "Oh, God," he said, looking at Jacks. "Is that what you think? Is it that easy for you?"

"Easy? Nothing is easy."

"*You* killed them. I *saw* you—"

Jacks breathed hard, looked at Crookshank, then to the fields beyond the porch, and back to Lonnie. "You don't know what you saw." He leaned forward in the wheelchair, both feet flat on the floor as if he were preparing to catapult himself toward Lonnie.

Lonnie leaned to meet him. "I saw *you*."

"Saw what? See me shoot somebody?"

Lonnie shook his head. His neck was stiff. He hadn't seen Jacks kill anyone. He had only seen him in the crowd and then driving past after the murders. "But you were there."

Jacks sighed and sat back in the chair. "Many people were there, as I recall. Memory isn't perfect, mind you, but as I recall, *you* were there, too. Yes. You were there, and as I recall it, I was there because of *you*. But of course, you were just a boy. Ten, twelve? You raised a complaint with Mr. Venable, remember? You said that the nigger Bertrand was bothering your mother, coming every day to your house under the pretense of chopping the garden." The old man grimaced, stained teeth showing roots.

First Lonnie remembered Venable and Toby. Toby lay on the roadbed and Auntie was coming with the shotgun. Lonnie's sight began to blur. Jacks and the expanse of fields beyond became watery. "Wait!" he said. But he could not think why he wanted Jacks to wait. "I wanted tomato slips . . . that's what I wanted. I saw Mr. Venable with . . . a woman . . . a colored woman and . . . but I never told him anything about Bertrand."

"You told Mr. Venable that Bertrand was bothering your momma. That he was coming to your house, uninvited."

"Yes, doing chores for her like he was her husband and refusing her money," Crookshank said. "If it wasn't true, you shouldn't have said it. You knew the ways of folks around here. You knew folks wouldn't stand for something like that around here. Why would you tell something like that, if it weren't true?"

The planks creaked under Jacks's chair. "If I am mistaken about Vernon, I am not mistaken about this: You told *me* the same!"

Lonnie turned away from Jacks and looked toward the front of the house. He couldn't see where he had parked the Volkswagen in the roundabout. His head throbbed lightly and he took a deep breath. *They are lying. Trying to confuse me.* He had come for something. He squeezed the stock of the pistol.

"Yes," said Jacks. "I recall it like it was yesterday—and the look on your mother's face."

Lonnie spun around, both hands on the gun's stock. "Liar!"

"She had the look of . . . well, a wounded kind of look. Unsure of what to do, and, I'd say, she looked grateful that the awful truth had been revealed. She knew, if you didn't, what would happen to that nigger. She wanted it to happen, no doubt. Yes, I'd say it was a look of relief. She was—"

"It's a goddamn lie. Nothing happened between my momma and Bertrand. Bertrand just helped us was all. And you turned it into something filthy. Now you are trying to twist it about again. . . ."

"He lies about a lot of things." Crookshank pulled herself by the arm of the chair and stood. "He is a pathological liar, if you ask me, but he isn't lying about that. It wasn't your mother's fault, not at'all. She was just a poor war widow, and he came along, a big, educated, *important* sounding man. A school teacher—army man—he played on that bit, being an army man. I knew him well because he brought in the cakes that his woman baked up for me. How could your mother resist him, big as he was? Who knows, he could have used some kind of voodoo spell on her. They do that, you know, with chicken bones and such. And those educated ones, they bedevil white women! They want so badly to show themselves decent, they must have a white woman. You did right—you did the right thing by complaining to Mr. Venable. It's unfortunate that things turned out the way they did, but that was the way they had to. You didn't ask that man to bother your mother. You didn't invite him to step into your daddy's shoes. He brought that on himself and all the consequences that followed."

All the consequences that followed! Lonnie's mind replayed the meeting with Venable. He remembered Venable's hindquarters flexing in the mottled light—and the grunting sounds—and running—and then being startled by Venable sitting by a tree—and asking for tomato slips—and, yes, he recalled, there was some talk of Bertrand. "But I never said—"

"I just regret they had to kill my girl. She was a sweet girl. The best cook I ever had."

"I didn't kill anybody," Jacks said.

"Did I say *you* killed anybody?" Crookshank made a loud, mocking "tsk" and walked into the dark of the house.

"Well, now," Jacks said after a pause, and then turning back to Lonnie, "Son? You look like you are about to burst out crying." Lonnie wiped at his face. Just then, lightning forked brightly across the sky, and they both looked. It took several seconds for the grumble of the thunder to reach them. The storm had moved to the north and the sunset once again turned the west into a fire-colored landscape. Lonnie looked past Jacks into the yard beyond the end of the porch at the old trees and their graceful shadows. He cleared his throat. "Okay, Mr. Jacks. Why, if you didn't do it, did they . . . the others . . . have to kill him? I mean, why didn't they just run him out of the county or something?"

Jacks wiped his mouth. "There were a lot of fellows down by the river that day. Vernon, Cook, maybe that deputy of his, some of the Greene County Klan boys. I'll venture you that each man had his own reason for being there, and I couldn't tell you half of them. Some maybe for sport, and some for revenge, and some for spite, and some for curiosity, and some for religion, and some just because they were too afraid not to be there. But none of those were my reasons. There is no one, easy answer—you think it's like your A-B-Cs—the quick of it is Bertrand *needed* to be killed. Some people just *need* to be killed."

Lonnie shook his head, throbbing less now.

"Now, listen. Listen and you will better understand me. Just listen."

They both listened. Lonnie heard a breeze rustling in the oaks on the backside of the house. Two crossed limbs yawned as they rubbed one another. A whippoorwill sang in the distant woods and the insects—crickets—made a chorus. Suddenly it seemed the world was full of insects' songs—clicking, buzzing and screeching. Jacks took in a deep breath. He seemed to be breathing in all the sounds, every sound the land made.

"I hear it all right, Mr. Jacks, but I don't hear it the same way you do."

"No. You don't. You are not me."

Lonnie looked at his hands, gripping the pistol. He remembered when he first saw the M1911, a 45 caliber, laying atop his father's shirts in the duffel bag. "Bertrand was my friend."

"Are you so sure? You are a white man. You are a part of what white men do."

"I am not like that!"

Jacks turned to face the fields and said quietly, "We are all guilty and innocent alike."

Lonnie raised the gun. His arms had tensed so tightly they were locked at the elbow. By degrees he moved his finger to the trigger. Then he loosened his shoulders and biceps and his elbows unlocked. Jacks didn't seem to notice at first, perhaps because of the darkness seeping into the twilight, but when he did, he said calmly, nearly bemused, "You don't know shit about guns, do you, boy?"

"I know enough to pull the trigger."

"But do you know enough to aim?"

"Mr. Jacks, do you believe in salvation?"

Jacks looked out at his fields, again. The sun was behind the horizon and the storm clouds exploded with light.

"I am the redeemer who will bring you salvation."

Jacks snorted. "You won't kill me, son, but one day I will be dead. Sooner than later. I will die in the grand bedroom, here, at Woodbine. There will be fresh linen on the bed and soft pillows. I will not be thinking about Bertrand, or you, or your mother. I will be thinking about my own mother and my father. I will be thinking about Woodbine. When my last breath leaves my body, do you know what it will say?"

"It will say, 'I'm a murderer.'"

Jacks turned back to Lonnie. "It will say, 'I am satisfied.'"

His shoulders and elbows tightened and he squeezed the trigger, lightly at first, feeling the blade of metal in the crook of his finger, then harder. The trigger slid, and his arms sprang up with the recoil of the pistol. He didn't realize that the sharp snap and blast he heard was the gun's report.

The chair pivoted backwards on its wheels and crashed to the floor. Jacks remained in the chair. His left foot kicked weakly, then stopped. Crookshank came to screen door and opened it. She looked at Jacks and then at Lonnie, her face blank and white. She started to shut the door and then stopped. "I . . . I already called the sheriff."

Gradually Lonnie took notice of her, dropped the gun. "You ain't worth it," he said.

"Okay," she said.

He felt his pulse pounding in his neck; his face felt flushed, and his body rushed pleasurably with each breath. He was strong. Clean. Yes, cleansed and strong. Baptized! He remembered the way Jack's foot had twitched and the wheel on the chair turned round and round. "That son of bitch said that he would die in bed. Satisfied! But who is satisfied now?" He was crossing the concrete bridge again when it hit him where he was. He was at the river. The river, where once the iron bridge crossed. The water below was the color of muck and cut across with frosty rivulets. The car's fender scraped along the bridge's railing, and Lonnie jerked the steering wheel, over correcting, and braked the car half in the ditch at the end of the bridge. He got out and walked down to the bank. The river seemed much closer than what he remembered, and the smell was different, the smell of wet concrete. But the little shoal was still there, the place where Cook had dragged Bertrand's wife, and where Bertrand and the others had lain when they were shot. He stood on the bank for a long time, breathing deeply and slowly, each breath filling his body from head to toe. Vaguely he remembered; vaguely he felt. The place was both outside and inside of him. Around him he felt the crowd, the three women from the town, the men with the beer, the boys swinging from the girders. They flitted on the periphery of his vision, shadows in the twilight. He walked down to the shoal, the sand crunching under his shoe. It was musical. The sound of the water, making the rivulets, splashing against the rocks. Musical. It was all music and dappled light and the smell of damp earth. He sat in sand, sat just where he imagined Bertrand's heel had dug. Then he leaned his head back and looked into the sky. He had killed Jacks! He had redeemed himself. *Yes! I am a redeemer!* But the moment he thought it, he realized he did not feel redeemed. He didn't know what redemption felt like. He had never felt it, or seen it. Besides, it was not redemption he wanted. He wanted salvation and salvation, if there was such a thing, had eluded him. What he was, was a murderer. Like Jacks. Suddenly, the music of the river stopped. Breath drained out of him. He felt cold, worn out, and useless. He fell back on the sand; the back of his head punched into the damp ground.

In his dream, he became the vulture. From the height of a thousand feet, the swells of fields and forests, framed on the horizon by blue ridges and transfixed by a glinting, snaking river, impressed his eye with such a sense of serenity that the landscape seemed newly dead, as it might be just after the Rapture. Nothing moved below. No mouse scurried along the edge of the fields. No mole poked its head through the broken loam. No squirrel scuttled up a tree trunk. Not even a branch stirred in the trees—shumards, loblollies, elms. At this height the wind buffeted his ears with such a constant and even whir that it washed out all other sounds. The updraft of the thermals caressed his feathers and warmed his body. He lay on the air, tensing and stretching his broad wings to better steady himself as he coasted the rising air in a half-mile wide circle. He felt powerful. Full of purpose, as he surveyed the hayfields, ripening in the sun, the margin between forest and field. *I am the redeemer come to bring salvation!* But all was motionless below. No buzzing blow fly, or ticking death watch beetle. No cackle from sister crow. No caw from brother jay. Suddenly, he smelled old death stinking up from a sandy strand along the river just down from the iron bridge. There were old bones, human bones—all sizes—there. Fragments abandoned, blood and marrow, long digested by bacteria.

But an animal moved in the landscape. It was a boy picking through bramble. The bramble snagged him, engulfed him like a wave, and weighed down on him. Still the boy picked through, struggled through. It would be impossible for him to escape, and yet, Lonnie knew, as he lay, looking into the blue-black, still sky, if he tried hard enough, there was hope.

AFTERWORD

You are a white man, play your role, America's sotto voce chorus, is not a murmur but a roar in *The Vain Conversation*.

In this gripping story, the character Noland Jacks is explicitly reminded of his duty as a white man on several occasions, and, as the descendant of Irish immigrants, he requires not only a reminder but also a demonstration. In Anthony Grooms' fine novel he receives both. Jacks learns to what roles a white man is *entitled* in Jim Crow's America.

You are a white man, play your role, the character of young Lonnie Henson is told indirectly. After his father returns from the war with a new eyes on race relations, young Lonnie will learn to what roles a white man is *limited* in Jim Crow's America.

You are a white man, play your role. Of the three charged words in that admonishment—white, man, and role—which word most earns our attention? Which word most warrants our caution? Which word most deserves our fear? It is popular in the academy to describe social roles as "performances." We "perform" gender. We "perform" race. We "perform" class. How do we perform those roles for which we are not cast, but conscripted? Roles we did not seek, but found ourselves playing unawares?

In the case of Noland and Lonnie, two characters a generation apart, this question haunts them throughout their days. In the Jim Crow South, what is the spiritual and moral configuration of the hierarchy of identity? Is Noland first *white* or a *man*, and are his actions indeed only a *role*, no more his true self than an actor donning puff breeches and a ruff to strut about for four hours is truly Iago, only a *role*, a veneer thinner than the bootblack Richard Burton wore to play Othello? And if Noland, who finds himself party to a murder not of his design, plays the vilest of roles for only a brief moment, can he ever truly leave the stage, or has the scripted hate seared his soul?

Inspiration for the answer might be found in science because No-land's and Lonnie's predicaments raise questions about possibility, change, transmogrification. At stake is not one man or one boy, but the entire United States of America, as well as the larger world—in long—anywhere people have been infected by colonialism, oppression, and racial or sexual or cultural terror. In other words, *one* of us is *all* of us, and if even one of us is truly *incapable*—not resistant, but fundamentally *incapable*—of transformation we are all damned—both citizen and state. This concern is especially relevant in the current moment, a time of turmoil and un-certainty, a time when populist surges are swelling into cataracts of sharp, stark fear.

But miracles abound—*For what else does it mean to be alive?*—and a metaphor for impossible possibilities becoming real can be found in sci-ence, namely in the form of a transmutation that has held metaphorical sway over the human imagination for thousands of years. The Japanese poet, Moritake writes:

> A fallen leaf
> Flew back to its branch!
> No, it was a *butterfly*.

This popular haiku is distinguished by a clear image that excites the mind's eye and imaginative faculties as well as speaking to a deeply felt human sense of telos and greater purpose. The haiku also echoes a scene in a play by Masaoka Shiki in which a character mourning a dead friend asks whether the soul of his dearly loved acquaintance is like a butterfly, and will return to the branch of life, or is like a leaf, and is forever banished to the afterlife, the land where men cast no shadows?

Certainly the complexities of religion would inform one's answer when faced with an enquiry regarding the ultimate disposition of the soul, but within the bounds of a single life or the across the historical arc of a single country, is it possible to speak with surety and to say that, *Yes*, this man's friend will return?

As we know, the butterfly is not returning per se, but is born of death. The caterpillar, the chrysalis and the flying flowers we so admire share little in common structurally. Caterpillars are born with imaginal discs that hold the blueprints for the butterfly and when those blueprints begin to unfold the caterpillar's immune system perceives them as assailants, and attacks them ferociously struggling to maintain its terrestrial "caterpillar-ness" until, at last, fatigued, it succumbs to the dream within the imaginal cells and blossoms into the butterfly.

Humans, unfortunately, perhaps, have more say in their transformation. We often resist because that transformation, that symbolic death, is not bodily, but of the ego, which has deep, deep claws. The body may go gentle, but the ego rages always. *Is that not its very reason for being?* Can the imaginal cells, the seeds of love and possibility planted in all of our hearts, transform a boy conscripted into the role of "white man" in the Jim Crow South? Can the imaginal cells, the seeds of the hope for equality planted in this country's chartering documents transform a country with a legacy of inequity into a vision of human unity?

While reading *The Vain Conversation*, which, like the best fiction, resists dispensing easy answers, you ask yourself many questions, the first of which is: At what price race? It is popular to say that "No man is free until all are free" or that "All are oppressed if even one is oppressed." While these pithy sayings give hope to many, functionally are those adages but mere platitudes meant to console the suffering and encourage the just? Does racism cripple those who wield the whip as well as those whom are whipped? Will four lynching victims live on in the hearts of the murderers, corrosive and stinging; and live on in the hearts of grieving loved ones, calm and soothing? In other words, is Kendrick Lamar right to say that "The one in front of the gun lives forever"?

You will have to answer those questions for yourself. All I will tell you is the conversation in this novel is anything but vain. The question you will most likely ask yourself, reader, having finished this novel is: Am I attacking my own imaginal cells, or am I willing to be changed. Again, a question you can only answer. But as is the case with all good novels, the experience of reading this one illuminates all the right questions.

T. Geronimo Johnson